Also by Alice James

Grave Secrets

Grave
Danger

Published 2023 by Solaris
an imprint of Rebellion Publishing Ltd,
Riverside House, Osney Mead,
Oxford, OX2 0ES, UK

www.solarisbooks.com

ISBN: 978-1-78618-840-3

10 9 8 7 6 5 4 3 2 1

A CIP catalogue record for this book is available
from the British Library.

Designed & typeset by Rebellion Publishing
Cover and internal artwork by Gemma Sheldrake

Printed in Denmark

THE
LAVINGTON WINDSOR
MYSTERIES

Grave
Danger

AN ADVENTURE WITH ZOMBIES.
AND VAMPIRES. AND SNOGGING.

Alice James

SOLARIS

To Larry, Kate, Mark and Brendon;
your lights burned so very brightly.

"I don't ask for a lot in this life—just perfect shoes, enough money to pay the bills and a super-hot boyfriend who isn't on the run from the police or dating my best friend on the side. And I hardly think I'm being picky—I don't even need them to be warm and breathing; a sexy undead guy would suit me nicely."

SINCE VAMPIRES CAME OUT of their coffins just a few short years ago, nothing in our world has been quite the same...

Lavington "Toni" Windsor is a Staffordshire estate agent by day but at night she raises the dead. She often finds herself summoned to the local morgue by her brother William, a police detective, so that she can interrogate recent murder victims about their deaths. She does the hard work and... he can take the credit.

Siblings. Seriously, who'd have one?

In Book One, *Grave Secrets*, she meets the charming vampire Oscar, who hires her to find him a luxurious undead-friendly dwelling. The two fall in love and before long are making plans for happily ever after, even though their relationship is complicated because vampires have no interest in monogamy and Oscar already has a boyfriend. The adorable young doctor Peter has followed him to England from their Assemblage in Germany, but he is miserable and misses his home. Toni helps Oscar to buy a beautiful but tumbledown home, Lichley Manor, and they plan for her to leave her tiny cottage, where she and her brother grew up as children, and move in with him.

But nothing is simple. Vampires are legal in Europe, thanks to the good work of the philanthropist and healer Dr Lenz Lange who has been healing children since becoming a vampire centuries ago. But they are illegal in America, where the terrible actions of the undead mafia family, the Gambarinis, have turned the nation against the fanged brigade. Oscar's Assemblage is at war with members of the Gambarini clan who have fled from Chicago to Staffordshire and are causing chaos and a great deal of death; indeed Oscar is only in Staffordshire at all because the local vampire lord, Benedict, has summoned him back from Dr Lenz's Assemblage in Heidelberg to help bring order to the county.

The Gambarinis cut a swathe through Staffordshire, and kill two of Toni's friends, lovely old Amelia Scott Martin who baked Toni cakes and the kindly vampire farmer Hugh Bonner, who she has known all of her life. However, the Gambarinis then ask Benedict for peace and he agrees. Toni is furious that they will go unpunished and hatches a plan whereby she lures them to the church by her house and raises the entire graveyard to take them down with the help of Bredon Havers, a zombie who has become one of her best friends. He is three hundred years a corpse but as charming as ever—and a master swordsman. With his aid, she defeats the vampires, but only just.

She goes to Benedict's Assemblage to crow over him, but the conversation doesn't go as expected. He is impressed by her actions but it's clear he knows she is a necromancer. Toni has kept her skills a secret from everyone except her family; the vampire farmer Hugh once told her that vampires fear necromancers and have tried hard to wipe them all out. She doesn't know any other necromancers and, now that her grandfather is dead, she has sometimes wondered if she is the only one left. Benedict also tries to persuade her to leave Oscar, though he won't tell her why. She laughs at the very idea and tells him that love is the only thing that matters in life. Still, she can't help wondering why he asked...

Chapter One

I KNELT ON the cold tiles of the morgue floor and threw up for Britain. And then, because I'm no nationalist, I threw up for Europe. I brought up my dinner and then my lunch, followed by breakfast. I think I puked up everything I'd eaten in the past week or so, maybe the past year. Had there been a global shortage of diced carrots, I had it nailed in about two minutes flat.

"I told you it wasn't pretty," my brother Wills said, kindly holding my hair out of my face while I moved on to some solid dry heaving. "Are you done?"

"Yup, so done," I croaked. "If I throw anything more up it's going to be an internal organ because nothing else is left."

Wills helped me to sit up and lean against the wall. I closed my eyes and waited for the room to stop spinning unhelpfully around me. It took its time.

"Thank heavens for small mercies, because I only had the one bucket ready," I heard him say. "I did warn you."

He had. More to the point, my brother was known for his strong stomach, so if he was unsettled by what he'd seen, I should have kept my eyes shut. He'd been a policeman for more than a decade and you see the darker side of life that way. I, on the other hand, was an estate agent, and the worst my day job usually exposed me to was bad interior decorating. It was usually largely free of crime and corpses. But at night? A somewhat different story...

At night, I raised the dead.

I would have preferred a quiet graveyard—the morgue gave me the creeps—but my brother didn't have the option of checking the residents out for an hour or so at my convenience. So, I was back again, surrounded by the recently deceased, salt cellar at the ready, putting a suitably macabre end to my Saturday night.

It used to be that Wills was the only person who knew about my power. Or so I thought. In recent months, a few more people had worked out my secret. And I'd realised that a few others had known it all along. Still, most of them were dead, or at least undead, so it was still fairly privileged information. Certainly, Scotland Yard didn't know yet. I hoped to keep it that way.

It was a chilly January night. Wills had rung that afternoon to ask if I would raise a corpse. The morgue was usually deserted from about two in the morning, so we could sneak in and interrogate the victim. He had sounded upset, which was unlike him. I get upset easily, so I wasn't expecting our rendezvous to be a barrel of laughs. Still, I'd agreed—Wills didn't ask often, and I figured God gave me my gifts for a reason. Justice was as good a reason as any.

Of course, sprawled against the chilly morgue wall, trying to calm my churning stomach and checking my hair for vomit, I was starting to regret my earlier virtuous impulse, but it was all a bit late for that. Wills patted my shoulder as I tried to swallow down the acid in my throat.

"Sorry, Toni. I forget you don't see this kind of thing every week. If it's any consolation, Agnes puked her guts up when she was at the scene this morning."

"It's not, but thanks. Can you find me some water or a can of something to take the taste away?"

"There's a drinks machine in the hallway. I won't be long."

I took deep breaths as he headed off into the half-lit building, fumbling for change. I spent far too much time hanging around dead people, though I ideally preferred them to have been dead for some time. The man I was currently dating, for example, had been a corpse for centuries. I bit my lip. The passage of time, I was starting to realise, hadn't taught Oscar much about being a great boyfriend. Ruminating on my poor dating record at least calmed my nausea, though, and by the time I heard Wills' footsteps returning, I had hauled myself to my feet and was leaning on the empty trolley where I had dumped my handbag.

"I got you a ginger beer," he said, opening the can and putting it into my still shaky grasp. "Get some sugar inside you before you try anything else."

I knew he was right. After a few minutes I had drunk the whole thing and was feeling vaguely human again. I straightened up without reeling and gestured at the sheet-shrouded trolley that had set me off.

"OK," I said. "Let's start over."

"Sure?"

"A bit. What did you say her name was again?"

"Annabel Hornby," he said. "Bella to her friends. She was just a kid."

And he pulled back the sheet.

I looked down at her again and grimaced, but this time I was prepared. It wasn't the congealed blood in her hair that had set me off, or the flattened patch of her head where her attacker had stove in her skull. It wasn't her face, swollen and reddening, with eyes that bulged and a tongue protruding slightly from her lips. It wasn't even the green and purple bruises around her throat, all too clearly showing where strong fingers had clenched her life away. No, it wasn't any of those.

The problem was it was like looking in a mirror. The girl on the trolley? She could have been me.

Ginger hair? Check. Green eyes? Check that, too. Full on freckle infestation? Definitely. The resemblance was uncanny.

We weren't perfect doppelgängers. Her red hair was a touch darker and not quite as curly as mine. And close up, there were other differences: she was bigger built, and her face, rounder than the one I saw in the mirror each morning, sported dimples I would have killed for. But there was another thing that made her feel like my dead twin.

She went to my school.

She was a Havers Grammar School girl. Just like me, just like my father and just like my grandfather before us. She was wearing the same school uniform that I had spent seven years loathing. I don't know how many hundreds of times Wills must have watched me stomp out of the house in an identical getup. I had passed the fearsome eleven-plus exams that he hadn't even deigned to sit and, a term later, I was walking through the hallowed gates.

I felt a morbid affinity with my dead companion; like me, she must have slogged her way through a pile of exams to earn her place. And like me, every weekday morning she had been forced to don a hideous bright blue uniform, possibly designed for the sole purpose of clashing with red hair. There the similarities ended—I was alive, she was dead. Sometimes I felt my life sucked, but at least I had one.

"Poor little thing," I said, stupidly, the words coming out without bothering to pass through my brain. "She's so young."

"When I saw her at the scene, for a moment... it's not that I thought it was you, Toni. I just knew how I would feel if it was."

I hugged him. My brother wasn't usually such a softie. There were four years between us, and when you're young that seems a lot. Your older brother stops being keen on things just as you start to get into them—he's always telling you how lame your interests are, just when you hoped he'd be impressed by you being super cool... But the older we got, the less the gap seemed to matter.

A while back, I'd begun to worry that he viewed my necromancy as a useful booster for his career. These days I knew it was more that his need for justice had grown with each injustice he'd had to watch go by. My brother was alright. Not that night, though; that night, he was nearly as shaken up as I was.

"Now I understand why you were upset earlier," I said, picking up my handbag from where it had tumbled behind the trolley when I'd decided to explore all the many variations that antiperistalsis had to offer as an extreme sport. "You hardly said a word on the way here."

He shook his head jerkily, as though he was shaking off a fly.

"It's... Toni, she's just a little girl. She's twelve, for Christ's sake. She's wearing friendship bracelets. What kind of monster kills children?"

There was no answering that. I hadn't raised many dead children. There's often nothing there, and that's dangerous (unless you *want* a demon from one of the inner circles of hell slipping into a nice empty body and eviscerating your entire village, which personally I'm not in favour of). But Annabel had been dead for just a day so we would be safe. Even in children, the soul hangs around for a while, though you can tell it's restless and has places to go; when I'd raised 'Jellybean' Jane Doe not so long ago, she had been just a revenant's breath away from quitting this realm for good.

"So, how did she die? Was she strangled?" I asked, ferreting around in my handbag for perfume, but Wills didn't seem to hear. "Bro? Come on: tell me what happened. What do I need to ask her?"

"Sorry, Toni," he said. "Sort of. Whatever freak did this, we think they clubbed her unconscious and then throttled her."

He visibly pulled himself together.

"She was killed in the school. She started there in September. The caretaker found her this morning. Agnes thinks she was killed early last night, knocked out with something damn heavy and then strangled. Her mother has had serious 'flu which turned into something more serious at some point yesterday—galloping pleurisy, I think. The poor woman fell asleep in the afternoon and was still nearly unconscious when we rang her doorbell this morning. She didn't know what day it was, let alone that her daughter hadn't come home. She's in hospital now being treated for shock and pneumonia. Not that it would have helped—we'd have started looking for Bella earlier, but she was dead long before she would have been reported missing."

I looked at Bella. Two of her front teeth had been knocked out by whoever had attacked her. I would have hazarded a guess that her jaw was broken. It was hard to imagine the rage that her attacker must have felt to do this to someone who couldn't have fought back, who was just a child...

"Right," I said, dumping my handbag onto the floor. "Let's get this cadaver up and chatting. No time to waste. What do—"

There was the sound of a door slamming, and I clapped both hands over my mouth.

"Holy ginger bollocks," my brother muttered. "Quick, hide!" He slid open an empty steel drawer. "Get in."

I looked in horror at the shiny, coffin-sized space he was gesturing at. It smelt slightly of bleach and possibly formaldehyde.

"I'm not getting into that," I hissed. "I'd rather go to jail."

Wills gave me a shove.

"Well, I'm not going to jail," he said. "You don't want to think about what happens to coppers when they end up behind bars. In!"

I cast him an unloving look, but he was busy scooping up my handbag. As I reluctantly wiggled into the drawer and lay back, he thrust it into my arms.

"Be quiet," he said.

And then, to my horror, he shoved the drawer all the way closed. I lay, paralysed, in the chemical scented darkness. I was thankful I'd already puked up a lifetime's supply of vomit; my prison definitely wasn't the venue for a second round of projectile chunks.

But we were only just in time. Mere moments later I heard a woman's voice.

"Hello, who's there? William, what the hell! You shouldn't be here. We've talked about this."

I recognised the voice and breathed a sigh of relief; it was Agnes, the detective who had been assigned as my brother's partner just a few months before. It wasn't good that she had found Wills skulking around in the morgue in the dead of night —really, he and I needed to be more careful—but at least she was unlikely to dob him in. Or at least I hoped so. Maybe as his sister I was biased. Maybe he was so annoying to work with that she'd love him to be banged up in a cell with Kevin the Kitten Killer and Paulo the Puppy Purée-er.

"Agnes." Wills' voice was filled with relief. "Look, I know I shouldn't be here, but I couldn't sleep for thinking about Bella. I thought someone should be with her. What if it's a serial killer? We can't let this happen again."

I blinked in surprise even in the darkness. Who knew that my brother could be such a remarkably good liar? It was really quite unfair, as I couldn't tell a whopper to save my life—believe me, I've tried many times.

"Oh, William, bless you, you soft touch." Yup, she'd fallen for it. "But you still shouldn't be here, OK? Not on your own, anyway. What if the evidence got contaminated? Do you want me to stay with you and help take notes?"

"No, no," I heard Wills blurt hastily. "Um, look, you're quite right. Totally. I'll shut everything down and head home."

"Well, make sure you do. I'll swing round again in half an hour, and if I see any lights still on, I'll be dragging your arse home, partner."

I heard footsteps and then the sound of a door. Moments later, my prison began to slide open, and I found myself blinded by the overhead lights. I sat up too soon and whacked my head on the top of the cabinet.

"Arse," I said. "You know, you provide the worst evenings out on record. At least when I raise a corpse in the graveyard, I pack a picnic. And some wine."

But Wills wasn't listening.

"Hurry," he said. "We have twenty minutes, tops, to raise and cross-examine Bella. We'll just have to wing it on the questions."

I shrugged and looked at the poor dead girl's mauled face. I felt my nausea evolving into a torrent of fury on her behalf as Wills hurriedly related to me the results of a frantic day of painful interviews and crawling around the school grounds on his hands and knees.

Bella had been in her second term at the grammar. She cycled to and from the school with brothers from the same street, Keith and Barry Pakeman, and on a lot of weekday evenings she played netball either at the school or in the park with her girlfriends. On Friday night, though, she had been playing football instead, mucking around in the floodlit area of the park with Keith and Barry and another girl from her netball team who also lived close by. The four had—inevitably—lost track of time, something they had only realised when torrential rain had driven them off the pitch. They headed home at top speed to avoid incurring curfew penalties from their respective parents.

Their route took them past the school where, to their surprise, the gates were open and some lights still on. Bella had announced her intention of picking up the geography homework she had forgotten to take with her earlier in the day. But her friends had disagreed. They didn't want to leave her on her own, but they were all late already and soaking wet. A short quarrel had ensued, which ended with Bella storming into the school while the rest went on their merry way home.

Within hours, she was dead. I wondered how her friends felt now. Scratch that—I didn't want to know. My not-boyfriend Peter had nearly died the previous autumn when I'd left him alone for just a few minutes to make a phone call. I knew in my mind that had I been there with him, we would probably both have died. That knowledge hadn't stopped me blaming myself for leaving him. But Peter had lived, and Bella was dead—her friends would probably never forgive themselves. Guilt is a dangerous game.

"School visits used to be my favourite," Will said miserably. "You know, turn up, give a rousing talk about safeguarding, tell them all not to take drugs and see who looks guiltiest... I don't think it'll ever feel the same again after today."

I looked at his pinched face and vowed to myself that I would find Bella's killer. I'd bring them to justice or—so help me—I'd take them down myself.

"I'll summon her," I said. "Let's see if she can tell us what happened. We'll do our best, Wills, but we don't have much time."

I finished the rough circle of salt around the trolley, joining the ends neatly together. For Christmas, Peter had given me a tiny antique German salt cellar. Made of brass and shaped like a little castle, it was one of the tackiest and most cringe-worthy trinkets imaginable. But it poured out a lovely even narrow line and held just enough salt to easily draw an eight-foot circle. It was typical of Peter's sense of humour and practicality that he had brought me something so whimsical—and so useful. Anyway, it had lived in my handbag ever since and made my nightly summonings that much easier.

Then I took out an atomiser of expensive eau de toilette. I'd bought it on a whim, and inevitably got home to discover I no longer liked the smell. Impulse decisions will be the death of me... I moistened the whole length of the circle, misting it with perfume until it glistened. Good to go.

"OK, bro," I said. "Zombie time. Get ready for the un-deady."

For my next trick, I would raise Bella Hornby. As a comedian, I was pants. As a necromancer? I was the best you got.

"Annabel Hornby, I summon you. Come to me."

And she did. She sat up and opened her eyes. One was red and bloodshot where blood vessels had burst. The other was nearly as green as mine. She looked round vaguely. Every now and then, you find a revenant who still has an interest in the world of the living. This wasn't going to be one of those times. Bella was already bored.

I handed her a full-size Melton Mowbray pork pie. I'd picked up three in the clearance aisle at the supermarket. Looking at Bella in action, I didn't think they would hit their use-by date. She ate the whole thing in about four seconds, and she didn't bother with a lot of chewing.

"Annabel Hornby," I said. "Tell me about your death."

She looked at me.

"I heard a noise," she said. "I heard a noise, and something hit me."

"What kind of noise? Was it a voice? Did anyone say anything?" I asked.

She shrugged.

"I just heard a noise," she said. "And then something hit me."

I almost growled in frustration.

"Do you know what hit you?"

This time the shrug was joined by an apathetic eye roll.

"I heard a noise," she repeated dully. "I heard a noise…"

"Yeah, yeah," I interrupted. "Let me guess: something hit you?"

She nodded.

"That's right. Can I have another pie?"

And that was where our luck ended. No matter what I asked her, she hadn't seen, smelt, tasted or felt a single thing to give us a clue as to the identity of her murderer. Did she have a boyfriend? Nope. Anyone who might have wished her harm? Goodness, no. Did she see anyone else in the school? Not a soul. We questioned her until my brother was out of ideas, I was out of pies, and we were out of time. But it wasn't helping. Bella couldn't tell us who'd killed her because she didn't have the faintest idea.

The only thing we'd found out for sure was that she had indeed been clubbed unconscious before being strangled—whoever had murdered her hadn't done anything by halves—but that was hardly helpful as we didn't have the murder weapon. Even Wills knew we had to throw in the towel when Bella mumbled for the twenty-somethingth time that she'd heard a noise and something had hit her.

"I don't want to come in on the side of the murderer, but if she wasn't already dead I might strangle her myself at this point," I said to Will. "We should probably throw in the towel now before Agnes decides to sneak back and come to some seriously wrong conclusions or—worse than that—the right one."

"Toni, if this was a normal interrogation, I might wonder what she was hiding or lying about. But she's told us everything she can. Either she doesn't have anything to help us, or we don't know what questions to ask her."

He looked at his watch and then dragged a hand through his hair; he'd been doing it for a while and it was in a fine state of disarray.

"Either way, sis, we're out of time. We've been at this for twenty minutes, and I don't plan on letting Agnes drag me off to headquarters for a psych assessment. We know for certain that whoever strangled her, they knocked her out cold first—but the doctor presumed that already from the amount of blood and the swelling. I hate to say it, but I think I dragged you out here for nothing. You might as well let her go."

"Fair enough. Annabel Hornby, I release you. Return to the earth from which I called you."

She closed her eyes and lay down. I felt the power draw her back into the next realm even as it sucked the salt straight through the tiles of the morgue floor into the bowels of the earth. And that was it. No fanfares and no music. Bella's spirit was gone as completely as though William and I had never disturbed her rest.

I was glum as my brother manhandled Bella back into her drawer. I washed my hands free of pork pie and waited impatiently while he erased all signs of our secret visit. That done, we scurried rather dejectedly back to his car.

"Well, she was annoying, but she didn't deserve to die that way," I said. "Is there no clue as to who killed her?"

"There are plenty of clues and a couple of prime suspects, but it's rather odd and quite frustrating," he said. "And I wanted to make sure we didn't miss anything. She shouldn't have been able to get into the school at all, but the caretaker had left the gate unlocked."

"We had a crazy bad-tempered handyman when I was a pupil, Spikey Mikey? Is he still there? The tall guy with the buck teeth and a stupid pointy beard... He was creepy, always pushing around this stupid cleaning trolley with the squeaky wheel. He was really mean, too—he would whack us with the handle of the floor polisher if we got the tiles muddy. Could he have killed her?"

"Yes, I mean, it could have been him, but I can't think why. And if you watch the tapes, I don't see how he would have known she was there."

"Go back... what tapes? There were never any cameras in my day."

"They were put in two years ago after someone vandalised the science block. But the headmistress didn't want cameras recording the children's day-to-day lives. She said that was out of order. So, they just record the gates—who goes in and out."

"But…" I was confused. "Doesn't that mean you know who was in the school? I've heard that people other than me have a social life and everything; there can't be that many people who want to spend their Friday nights back at school."

"There shouldn't have been any! Michael Spectre is the guy you've been calling Spikey Mikey, right? Well, he cleans the floors at the weekend. He cleans the downstairs floors on a Friday night, which is what he did, and the upstairs floors on a Saturday morning, which is when he found Bella's body."

"How could he miss her when she came in?"

"I've watched the tapes—I watched them for hours. After school closed at five, Mikey went home and ate tea. He locked the gates, because the school was empty—or at least it should have been—and no one else had any business to be there. He came back at half past six. He unlocked the gates to let himself in, but then he locked them behind him. He began to clean downstairs with that big machine with the rotating brushes. At eight, he got peckish, and went to his car for his thermos and sandwiches. That's when Bella came in… she was so unlucky. At the precise time she and her friends were arguing about whether to wait for her, the gates were unlocked, and Mikey was munching on egg and cress in the car park. She went in, her friends rode off, and minutes later Mikey finished snacking and came back in, too. He locked the gates again behind him. Two hours later, he left. He came back this morning and dialled 999 after about an hour. He said today he was cleaning the upstairs floors and he found her. Her homework was lying on the floor next to her body, so I suspect she was killed very soon after she entered the building. Her classroom is upstairs—I think she just had time to go up, find her books, and get most of the way back to the staircase before… wham. One dead schoolgirl."

"So, Mikey killed her, surely? No one else went into the school."

"Well, there's more," Wills said. "This morning, as us bobbies and our sniffer dogs searched the school for evidence, we found another student in the grounds reading a comic and he's managed to ruin everything."

The miscreant's name was Paul Mycroft and, under duress, he had shown them how he got in. The school bordered Rugeley Moor Wood, and an eight-foot-high wire fence separated the two. But two weeks before, where the playground behind the netball courts petered out into a dense shrubby area, Paul had made himself a secret entrance. Using wire cutters, he had clipped a neat aperture, some four-foot square, leading through from the wood to the school grounds. He came and went as he pleased, making the out-of-hours expanse of the grammar school into his own personal fiefdom. And that was the problem. Absolutely anyone could have got into the school any time they liked. The cameras only recorded those who had chosen the legitimate mode of entry.

"Could Paul have killed Bella, then?" I asked. "He knew the way in. He used it all the time."

"Well, sis, he could and looking at his family it wouldn't surprise me; my guess is he's the local dealer. But, if it was him, why the bloody hell was he sitting in the boiler room reading *The New Adventures of Spider-Man* three hundred yards away from where he'd left the body the night before? And why wasn't he looking out for policemen? Hell, why didn't he scarper long before we found him? The other thing is—I don't see why Paul would ever have spoken to Bella. He's upper sixth. This is his last year. He's eighteen. What interest would he even have in a twelve-year-old girl? And he's a geek as well as possibly the local weed provider— she played sports every day. I mean, I'll check him out, but to the casual eye, they don't have the slightest connection."

I could see my brother's reasoning. The man who could have killed Bella most easily had no reason to. The person who had made it impossible to tell had probably never met her. And anybody else in the county could have nipped in and done the deed.

"Were there any tracks?" I asked. "Footprints, maybe? I seem to remember it's muddy around the woods by the courts."

My brother heaved a put-upon sigh.

"Well, there might have been before the caretaker got in there with the floor cleaner and four litres of bleach. Now you could safely eat your dinner off it. And an entire army could have sneaked in through Paul's little entrance without leaving a trace—we had two inches of rain last night. Quick, duck down. That's Agnes' car."

I slumped down. I was starting to see the problem: no suspect, no motive—and no evidence thanks to Spikey Mikey and the clean machine.

"I CAN'T HELP you, Wills," I told him as he drove me back home. "It doesn't look like Bella can reveal anything you need to know. If you like, I can call her back another night and ask her if she knew Paul or Mikey better than she should have done. Or if any of them ever threatened her. Or if, I don't know, she'd found out Paul was a drug dealer and was blackmailing him. We would probably have thought of that if we'd had more time."

"You couldn't do that tonight if we went back? If maybe someone faked some 999 calls at Junction Fourteen and got Agnes nice and busy? You know, just asking for a friend..."

I snorted with laughter.

"You wonderfully law-abiding public servant! No, not twice in one night. I've tried. The dead can rise just once on any night—no idea why."

"Oh. Sorry, I didn't know that."

There was no reason he should have done. Did anyone know except for me? I was the only necromancer I had ever met apart from my dead grandfather, so there was no one I could ask. Much of what I knew was self-taught.

"Tonight would be pushing it anyway," my brother carried on. "Ten to one Agnes will be waiting there with a taser to drag me off even if I manage to convince the emergency services that aliens have landed at Eccleshall Common and are marauding round the village with their probes. Bah. Anyway, we haven't talked about you all evening. How are you? I haven't seen you for a couple of weeks. How's your incredibly complicated love life?"

Oh, that.

He paused, and then said carefully, "You've lost weight, you know; you don't look great. Are you and Peter still OK? I mean, I really like him, sis. He seems like a keeper."

Oh, everyone liked Peter, from the postman to the cat; it was like a new national sport. But a keeper? Well, unfortunately, that was none of my business. I shrugged.

"What can I say, bro? It's incredibly complicated. Let's talk about something else."

So we did, but it didn't make any difference. We could have talked about raindrops on roses and whiskers on kittens. We could have singlehandedly thrashed out a solution to climate change and world peace. Seriously, we could have come up with a unified theory of physics, but absolutely none of it was going to help me sort out the monumental mess I was busy making of my life.

Chapter Two

IT WAS ABOUT six in the morning when Wills dropped me home at the little cottage where he and I had grown up together. On the way, we'd stopped at the all-night petrol station to eat cheese toasties and chocolate together. He'd bought me a coffee to go when we left. I let myself in and took it through to the kitchen, where I sat at the table drinking out of the paper cup.

My brother had touched on a sensitive subject. It wasn't that I didn't want to confide in him—I just didn't know what to say or where to start.

I'd met Oscar in the bar of the Old Mitre five months ago. He'd looked at me, brushing his straight blond hair out of his amazing blue eyes, and in that moment, my life had changed. He was beautiful, charismatic, impulsive and adorable. And he was a vampire.

I'm not biased against the undead. I mingle with them all the time. Some of my best friends are corpses. But dating Oscar wasn't easy. Was it my fault? I thought it was. I loved him. I loved the old-fashioned and slightly formal way he spoke, the elegant way he moved and the way he made love to me. Scratch that—the many, many ways he made love to me. I even found his foibles adorable; he was hopelessly disorganised, massively optimistic and got through cars like most people get through a bottle of gin.

I would have done anything to make him happy. But I couldn't let him drink my blood.

Don't get me wrong; I didn't have some huge philosophical objection to a vampire drinking my blood. I just found the whole idea physically repulsive. I'd given blood twice in hospital and passed out both times. The thought of letting my lover sink his teeth into a vein and suck the stuff out? No, thank you very much indeed. There was no way I could see it as a recreational activity.

I kept trying. Every time we made love, I resolved to let Oscar feed, but I just couldn't go through with it. A couple of weeks ago, we'd agreed to try, even though I was utterly terrified by the idea. I meant to; I really did. But at the last minute, my whole body had independently revolted against the concept. I'd had to fling myself out of the bed and throw up over the rug. Sexy touch, Toni. Nothing says throw me down and shag me like a woman ejecting internal fluids like Old Faithful. We hadn't tried since, but I knew just how angry and frustrated my long-toothed lover was becoming. I just didn't know what to do about it.

Of course, I could have asked my brother to take me to Oscar's house, the beautiful home I had made for us. For five months, in between my day job, I had bossed around builders, rowed with roofers and got into palavers with plumbers. I had learned the difference between hardwood, softwood and hardboard—the key is in the price—and chosen light fittings, skirting boards and curtains. In Lichley Manor, I had created one of the most beautiful little dwellings in the county for my vampire boyfriend. I wasn't sure he'd noticed, mind, but I'd done it anyway. I'd made a truly elegant space for us to sit around being discontented in, and if things didn't improve it was never going to feel like home.

So yes, even though I could have asked Wills to drop me off at Oscar's house for the rest of this long January night, I hadn't done so. I'd come home to my safe, fang-free little cottage to sit at my own kitchen table, fretting about how to change things I couldn't change and how to mend a relationship that I just kept breaking.

I finished my coffee, crushing the paper cup into a soggy little ball and hurling it into the bin as though it was responsible for all my ills. It wasn't, but it hadn't been enough to wake me up, so I put the machine on to make another. I was tired, but after the evening I had gone through with poor dead Bella, I knew sleep wasn't an option. I sat with my back to the door, watching Winchester, my elderly orange cat, napping against the warmth of the Aga. The pallid, January sun had inched its way over the horizon and was making a half-hearted attempt to melt the frost on the lawn when I heard the front door go.

"Toni, you here?" a voice called. "I have breakfast."

It was Peter. Peter, the man who was not my boyfriend. He had told me quite openly that he fancied me and would like our relationship to leave the friend zone. However, he was also Oscar's other lover, and I was pretty old-fashioned in my outlook on love and relationships. I was still seeking a version of happy-ever-after that didn't need an instruction manual. So, I hadn't succumbed. There were times I wished I'd met Peter first, but life doesn't come with a time machine.

He dumped a pastry-scented paper bag onto the kitchen table and his coat onto a chair.

"Hey, you," he said cheerfully. "Was it as bad as you thought?"

I stood up and poured myself into his arms.

"It was vile," I said, the words somewhat muffled as I spoke them into his chest. "It was completely vile. And I didn't do any good either. The poor thing had no idea who killed her."

"I'm sorry, liebling," he said. "Have breakfast and tell me about it."

I flung myself back into my chair and tipped the contents of his bag onto the table. Two croissants, two lardy cakes, and a tuna puff that I knew was destined for Winchester's bowl. I picked up one of the croissants and dipped it into my cooling coffee.

"She was just a schoolgirl, Peter. And she went to my school. She even looked like me. It was awful."

I told him about the doomed cycle ride, the caretaker and his sandwich break, the secret school entrance, and the sad end of Annabel Hornby.

"Why did Paul want to get into the school out of hours?" he asked when I had finished. "He went to a lot of trouble to make sure that he could come and go as he pleased."

It was a question worth asking. He'd made a doorway that he could easily use time and time again, and it wouldn't have been an easy task. It wasn't something he'd done on a whim.

"No idea," I confessed. "But Wills thinks he was the school's supplier of happy pills and recreational herbs, so maybe he dealt drugs from there. His family isn't the nicest."

Peter shrugged.

"It might not matter. As your brother said, it's not as though he had anything in common with Bella. They may never have spoken to one another. But it might be relevant."

I finished my croissant and moved on to the lardy cake. Annabel was preying on my mind and Peter could tell.

"Are you working today?" I asked, as much to change the subject as anything else.

"I am," he said. "But not until the afternoon. I need to talk to you about that. Oh, and there was another thing. Let me take a shower first and shave."

I put more water in the coffee pot. Frustrated by inactivity, having already steam-cleaned my entire house and ironed everything bar the lawn, Peter had begun volunteering at the local children's hospice. In theory, he read to the children, supervised playtime, and provided an escort on excursions. In practice, having a Heidelberg-trained oncologist on site was something the hospice could only have dreamed of, and I knew he had quickly become indispensable.

A few minutes later, he re-emerged, barefoot and bare-chested, wearing black jeans. He was carrying the contents of my washing basket, which he casually sorted into the machine as I poured coffee. He took two plates out of the cupboard and sat down opposite me.

"So," he said, confiscating the sugar bowl after I had put three or four spoons into my mug, "I had two things to talk to you about. The first is that Benedict has a job for you."

"Oh, God no; please, not that."

Benedict was the arrogant and bloodthirsty vampire in charge of the undead in the little county of Staffordshire. I didn't like him, and I rather thought the feeling was mutual. The antipathy didn't stop him trying to get his hands up my knickers every time we met. It did mean that I tried very hard to only visit the Assemblage stronghold in the daylight.

"It's not as bad as you think," Peter continued blithely, sliding one of the plates underneath my half-consumed lardy cake and putting his croissant on the other. "Is this my coffee? Thanks. He doesn't want to see you; he wants you to talk to someone."

"Thank the Lord rejoicing. Who?"

"Did you watch that program about the vampire itinerant healer?" he asked. "Hildred Rutherford."

Ah, the mysterious Hildred. She'd travelled up and down the country for centuries, healing sick children and taking her payment in the blood of grateful family members. Always alone, she had no coterie and no friends. She was a powerful healer, too, and these days—now that she didn't have to stay so undercover—her services were always in demand. She still moved from family to family, staying a couple of weeks and then moving on, but fame had enabled her to become very picky about who she gave succour to. And, boy, was she picky.

"The crazy woman who wore a lot of cheesecloth and had very bad hair?"

Munching a mouthful of buttery French dough, Peter nodded.

"Her, yes. It turns out that she's in Staffordshire right now. Benedict's pissed off because she didn't ask his permission and hasn't paid him a courtesy call, but he's also worried that she will get staked because she infuriated so many people with that documentary."

Oh that. Yes. *Hildred: A Good Witch for Our Times* hadn't so much been reality TV as a reality check on just how much racism, intolerance and prejudice you could fit inside the body of a single undead bigot. (For the record, the answer was a metric fucktonne.)

The passage of time hadn't given Hildred Rutherford any

kindness towards the world, but it had crystallised the things she disliked in it. The list was unending. She disliked cats, dogs and men. She wasn't keen on gay people, people with dark skin or people with excessively light skin. She had an aversion to North and South Americans and to Europeans from both East and West; her feelings towards people from Asia and Australia were decidedly cool. She didn't like religious people. Or atheists. Or Satanists. She disliked vegetarians, skinny people and fat people. I'd heard her diatribe on the shortcomings of those who played darts, practised yoga, read novels or enjoyed cycling. No minority groups escaped her repugnance, and most majority groupings got short shrift, too. Oh, yes, and for the final clincher? She thoroughly loathed other vampires. The woman was an equal-opportunities hater.

"Why me? She could probably find several reasons to detest me. I have red hair and I'm short. I don't remember them on her list, but the programme was only ninety minutes long."

"Benedict said that she also hates him and everyone in his Assemblage," Peter said. "And here is where it gets technical. It turns out that Benedict and my dear mentor Doktor Lenz have been arguing about something for months. I have no idea what but—take it from me—Lenz is as argumentative as Benedict, so it could be about who left the lid off the toothpaste at the outbreak of World War One. Which means that Lenz hasn't fully released Oscar back to Benedict's service yet. I didn't know this until last night, by the way. But the end result is that officially you and I— and Oscar—are a coterie that's still affiliated to Heidelberg."

"I am an honorary German?"

"Ja, darling. Certainly as far as the vampire community is concerned. And Lenz is the one person in the world who Hildred definitely likes, so she should be well disposed towards you."

It didn't sound like the world's best assignment, but it was a lot better than having to go up to the Stone House and be in the same room as Benedict Akil. If he was in a good mood, I might get my thigh fondled. A bad one might see my throat ripped out.

"What does he want me to do?"

"I think he just wants to know what's going on. He's in two minds about staking her himself, in my opinion, for entering his territory without his leave. I don't suppose he would mind if someone else did it for him. I think he would mostly prefer it not to happen on his turf. I have an address for you."

That sounded like the Benedict I knew and hated. I couldn't complain, though; in all the months that had passed, he hadn't asked me to do anything for him. I had got off lightly. I rolled my eyes.

"Fine, I'll do it. What was the other thing?"

Peter toyed with his croissant. Then he carefully broke off a corner and chewed it.

"Yes..." he said after a while. "Toni, the hospice would really like me tonight. I have finally sorted out all the paperwork to volunteer as a doctor rather than a teaching assistant, and one of their medics is sick."

"You mean I would be on my own when Oscar wakes?" I asked. I was trying to restrain the panic in my voice but I could hear it rising to a squeak.

"Yes, but I've checked—he's due at the Stone House all night. He can find someone to feed off when he gets there. He does it all the time."

Ah, the perils of dating a vampire. We'd got around the problem of my blood phobia by ensuring Peter was always around when the sun went down and Oscar awoke. Older vampires don't need to feed every night anyway, and at nearly three hundred years of age, Oscar certainly counted as older. He could definitely sustain himself snacking once or twice a week. But I knew him too well... as the sun went down, he would awake, horny as hell and full of a thirst for blood. Who would want to sustain themselves on alfalfa sprouts in a world full of chocolate? Not my Oscar. Peter wanted the world to be one way, and I couldn't blame him. I wanted it to be that way, too... But it wasn't.

"Fine," I said, even though we both knew I was lying. "No problem. Go ahead."

He cheered up visibly. No, I realised. I was being unfair. Peter didn't know I was lying. Peter, dearest Peter... he had given up everything for love; everything that gave meaning to his life he had thrown aside to follow Oscar here to England. And now that the little haven of domestic bliss I thought we'd created for the three of us was tumbling down around us... could I blame him for not wanting to see? I really couldn't.

"Besten dank," he said, casually breaking the tuna puff into little pieces. He scattered them on my empty plate and put it down for the cat. "What do you have planned for today?"

"I didn't have anything planned," I said. "But now that you've given me a mission, I might go over and scout out Hildred's address while it's light. I'll be back at Lichley before it gets dark, I promise."

Before it got dark, and my love awoke to find me there. And only me. No Peter to give him blood, just the girl who kept refusing, and couldn't come up with even the slightest reason why. At first, we had just assumed it would come naturally. Tomorrow, I would be fine, we had assured one another. But tomorrows had come. And gone. And come and gone again.

And in truth I wasn't getting any closer to overcoming my revulsion—no, my terror—of letting him drink my blood, and I could tell that his patience was wearing very, very thin. Vampires aren't cut out for patience. They weren't really cut out for domestic bliss either, and I worried that he was bored, that even if everything else had been hunky-dory, Oscar was just plain ennui-ed out of domesticity. Life with Peter and me was full of daily chatter and simple peril-free occupations. Oscar, I had fast realised, had no time for domestic chatter. Oscar liked passion. He positively enjoyed peril—the shedding of blood, a fight to the death, a fearsome night-time chase, a breathless shag... Oscar didn't want a peaceful life. He didn't want a single peaceful night.

"Peter," I blurted out miserably, "what are we doing wrong? How is this supposed to work? You and I have been hideously sleep-deprived for months. Most days that I am working, I fall asleep at my desk. How did it work in Germany? How does Benedict make it work?"

"We're doing pretty much everything wrong," he said, a touch forlornly. "Lenz runs the clinic like a military operation. Everyone lives on site, there's a timetable for everything. For someone like me, it's perfect. Oscar was so busy keeping on top of the crazy Czech and Polish vampires who are always drifting across the border that I never saw that much of him until we came here. We snatched the precious hours that we could."

I raised my eyebrows.

"I take it that 'keeping on top of them' didn't involve checking their paperwork."

Peter looked a touch embarrassed.

"You know Oscar."

Oh boy, did I. Nobody loved a little recreational fight to the death like my main man Oscar. I topped up my serotonin levels with retail therapy. Oscar, if his scrumptious undead body of buffness contained anything as mundane as serotonin, kept it at a healthy psychopathic level by admiring the gloss of his expiring enemies' blood on his hands.

I shook my head.

"What about feeding?"

"Ah, you're forgetting what we do at the clinic. There are always hordes of grateful parents clustering round trying to donate. I've seen one cry when she didn't get on the blood roster."

"And here?"

Peter shook his head.

"I don't know how I ever expected it to work out," he said. "As well as his vampire cohorts, Benedict employs an impressive network of security and admin staff. A lot of them aren't strictly members of any one vampire's coterie, but they are all expected to be available to feed. And Toni—it's only you who doesn't want to! I'm not blaming you, I promise, but when a vampire feeds on you, it's like the best sex you have ever had. No one minds. So, when we lived there, Oscar was never short of someone to feed off.

Now there are just the two of us… one of whom—if you will forgive the phrasing—won't put out."

"But he's over there almost every night now that he's Benedict's head of security again. Why does he need to make such a fuss about it?"

"Toni—and, again, I'm not trying to blame you—he's frustrated. For a vampire, making love is just foreplay. Taking blood is the real deal. Oscar feels you're holding out on him—and he doesn't understand why. And I'll be honest: I don't understand why either."

"I think it's because I am a necromancer." The words just slipped out; I'd been thinking them for weeks, but had been reluctant to voice them. "I don't think it's just a phobia. I think it's something about me. Oscar thinks I'm the world's biggest tease, Peter, but I can't help it."

He was silent for a while. Then he wandered over to the stove and picked up the round, orange cat. He lolled in his arms like a furry glove, purring and rhythmically flexing his fat little paws.

"I never thought of that," he said eventually. "You could well be right. Look, Toni, I'll go back now. There is a library of stuff on this kind of thing in the vaults at the Stone House. It never occurred to me to look there for an answer. You go and see where this crazy cheesecloth-wearing vampire is staying, and tomorrow morning when I get back from the clinic, I'll tell you what I found."

I got up from the table and stood at the sink, looking out of the little cottage window onto the square of my lawn. It was a view I had looked at since I was a tiny girl. Usually it calmed me, but how could I be calm when the man I'd thought I would spend the rest of my life, my charming, witty, sexy undead beloved, seemed to be slipping away from me, and when I wasn't even sure I wanted to stop him escaping any more.

"Thank you," I said quietly. "Because, Peter, this isn't working. Oscar is angry with me all the time. If we can't find a solution to this…" I broke off. "Peter, he is kind of a jerk."

There was a very long pause.

"You've never said this before," Peter said, his voice clipped. "What are you telling me?"

"I am not telling you anything," I said. Could I really be thinking of dumping the person I was in love with? Ruining this fragile domestic bliss that was so fleeting and so damn complicated...? If so, I wasn't ready to admit it yet. Not by a mile. "It was a mistake. Forget it. I'm going to find this stupid vampire. I'll see you tomorrow."

And I left him there. I put on my coat and walked out of the house.

Chapter Three

GRAND GESTURES ARE all very well, but in Staffordshire in January on an icy Sunday morning, gloves are better. My emotional storming out of the house had left me sitting in the rust-mobile, wishing either for an early spring or heating that worked. I was going to get neither, so I just started up the engine and sat waiting for the windscreen to clear. In the Morris, that would take about fifteen minutes.

I had nearly a clear view of the road ahead when a banging on the window broke me out of my reverie. I wound down the glass. It was Peter, still bare-chested with wet hair, but he had put on footwear of some kind. He handed me a scarf, woolly hat, gloves and my phone through the window.

"We'll talk about this tomorrow," he said, very gently. "There's nothing you can't tell me."

I nodded, a little overwhelmed. I watched him walk back to the porch in the frost and let himself into the cottage. I put on the hat—a cheerful knitted beanie he had given me at New Year. Then I shook my head in confusion, put the car into gear, and drove down the hill through the village.

I drove past what I assumed to be Oscar's latest car. It looked like a credit card on wheels. The bonnet was slightly domed, presumably to make the point to idle admirers that the engine was twice the size of theirs. The custom paint job was the exact shade of red of a yuppie's leather sofa. It was about eleven hundred horsepower of machismo on wheels. I wondered how long it would last before he wrapped it round a tree. The roads looked set to stay icy for a while, so about a week was my guess.

The address Peter had given me for Hildred was in Etching Hill, not a million miles away from the grammar school. On a whim, I drove past the school gates first.

I saw my brother standing on the pavement, along with Agnes. There must have been another eight or nine police cars in the little parking area that the teachers usually used for their cars. I pulled up next to Wills and Agnes and wound down a window.

"I could do a doughnut run if you like," I said. "I could get a tray of coffee in for the officers of the law?"

"Forget coffee, you're exactly who I need," Wills said. "The headmistress broke down in tears every forty-five seconds until I sent her home. We need to get a sense of how this place works. We haven't had a callout here since someone broke into the science block a couple of years ago and redecorated it with eleven litres of fluorescent pink paint and a lack of artistic integrity. Until Friday night, it was the most crime-free school in the county. We need someone to show us round and I'm afraid you're it."

I looked around—he had a point. Not much had changed in the eight or so years since I had left. The trees were a little taller and the paint a little more faded, but even the graffiti looked familiar. At the top of the wall by the netball courts, someone had stencilled the legend: 'Let Roger's todger be your lodger!' Even in my day, no one had a clue who Roger was, but the paint was too high for anyone to have the energy to scrub it off.

I walked Wills around the school. The locations represented a litany of all the things I'd been crap at as a teenager: being popular, getting a boyfriend, getting in on time, finishing homework, passing exams... But there were good times to remember, too. I'd had my first snog in the science lab. I'd learned to put on nail varnish with Helen, hiding in the loos with little bottles of lacquer that quickly filled the cubicle with the heady scent of pear drops. My school days hadn't been an unalloyed joy, but I felt at home in an odd way.

"Well, she was a first year, so she would never have gone over to the Convent," I said. "Unless she was up to no good, she should have stayed in the main school block, so we can concentrate there."

My brother looked confused.

"What's the Convent and main school thing? I haven't heard anything about it."

"The grammar was set up a couple of hundred years ago when the Dominican Catholic order that was here founded a girls' school, so the nuns lived in one building, the convent, and the classrooms and the pupils were next door," I explained. "The nuns have all gone now, though, so the convent has become part of the school. It's where the sixth form classrooms and the staffroom are, so only the older kids get to go there."

We walked the route Bella would have taken, where she would have parked her bike before heading into the assembly to sing a tuneless hymn or two and filed out to the chorus of the school song, a long dull aria that enunciated the names and virtues of the school's founders. I named the various classrooms as we passed them and tried to give my brother useful gossip. Agnes was writing down everything I said, which was disconcerting.

"That's the main school," I said, pointing. "You've probably been all over it. Inside it's basically a ring with rooms coming off on both sides. The upper storey is humanities—History, English, Geography—so I am guessing that's why Annabel went up there on Friday night. A lot of the teachers put marked homework on a table outside the room when they're finished."

The main school, about a hundred and fifty years old and built of dark clay bricks, had spawned a mess of cheap little single-storey units, thrown up over the past fifty years as the school expanded. They were joined to the main building by awkward corridors that rejoiced in being swelteringly hot in the summer and bitterly cold in the winter. Inside, the whole school appeared to have been painted in a fetching shade of phlegm. The colour had faded in patches to a subtle tone somewhat akin to vomit. As an estate agent, I would probably have called it ecru. Or taupe.

"This is the Gillaham Block," I said, as we passed an ugly glass and pebbledash pre-fab. "It's named after the first headmistress, Sister Mary Gillaham, and it houses the first and second year form rooms. Next door is the Fountain Block, and that's the Cemetery Block."

"Why are they called that?"

"Oh, gosh, ancient history, bro. The grounds were turned into allotments in the war, and afterwards, no one could remember what had been there. Later all the modern classrooms were built, and it was only in the eighties that the original plans were unearthed. The Gillaham Block is built where there was a statue of Sister Mary Gillaham, the Cemetery Block is where the nuns who founded the school were buried, and the Fountain Block is where there was a commemorative fountain dedicated to Saint Francis of Assisi."

"Well, sis, you learned something while you were here. Are the graves still there?"

"Goodness no, they were all moved to Baswich."

We walked to the main doors, panelled with scratched old-fashioned security glass, a misty grey in colour and set through with wire mesh. Wills swung one open for me.

"There are plenty of entrances and exits," he said, "but they are all wired into the fire alarm system. So we can be sure that none of them were used the night Bella died."

"You mean that whoever killed her, came in and left through these doors?"

"That's exactly it. And they must have gone up using the main stairs here, because there is no other way to the upper storey."

I thought about that, and then shook my head.

"There's another way. I'll show you."

I took him through the hallway and down a dark passage that ran the length of the school. Along it, paintings of the pious ladies of the cloth who had run the school eventually gave way to photographs, each with the name beneath in handwritten gothic script. It led finally to a cloakroom. Behind rows of coat racks, a dirt-coloured curtain hung from an old pole. I pulled it back.

"See?"

The inner and outer lift doors were made up of a lattice of black metal bars. I knew from experience that they slid open to reveal a tiny, stuffy space with insufficient lighting and ventilation. Wills didn't touch anything, and I imagined he was planning to dust for prints and traces.

"Does it still work?" he asked.

"It does, but it's not licensed to take people because the doors are dangerous—you could catch your hair or a hand. It's used to take heavy things up and down between the floors. Though I confess, we did use it when I was here if no one was watching. It's the only way up on this side of the block. You can summon it if it's on the wrong floor, but it won't come unless both sets of doors have been shut on both floors. So, you could leave them ajar and be sure you wouldn't be disturbed."

"Let me not think about why my virginal teenage sister would be hunkering down in a dark lift not wanting to be disturbed! Would Michael Spectre have used it? Should his prints be on it?"

"Mikey? Definitely. He used it to take the cleaning machines up to the second floor and down again. You couldn't get them up the stairs on your own."

It took rather more than two hours before Wills was happy to let me go. I was torn between nostalgia at being back and discomfort at the knowledge that we were only there because of Bella's demise. I watched as two PCs took fingerprints from her desk and later as Agnes broke open her locker. They didn't look like they'd found the answer to any burning questions. Later still, we walked back to the main entrance. Spikey Mikey's paraphernalia had been lined up by the stairs. There was the trolley with its squeaky wheel, just as I remembered. There was the rotary brush floor cleaner, a little more battered, but otherwise unchanged. The floor polisher was new, a shiny solid metal beastie that must have set the school maintenance budget back a fair bit. Mikey was still the God of Bleach.

Times change but not so very much.

We headed outside and walked back through the gates to my car. I saw a tall, good-looking boy of eighteen or so, bracketed by police officers, being escorted to a squad car. He was wearing black jeans and a rock t-shirt—a Peter in training. In fact, with his buzz-cut hair and glasses, he had more than fashion sense in common with Peter, and my heart went out to him. He was trying very hard to look cool, but none of us were fooled. He looked terrified and tired.

"Who's that?" I asked Wills, though I thought I had guessed.

"Paul Mycroft," he said shortly, confirming my suspicions. "He's been showing us his routes in and out of the school."

"Has he told you why he wanted to come and go?"

"Nope."

"Does he have an alibi for the night Bella died?"

"Nope."

I looked at Paul. He didn't look like a killer to me. He looked like a nerd.

"None at all?" I asked Wills.

He heaved a sigh.

"He doesn't come from a nice family, Toni. Christ knows how he got into the grammar. He has two elder brothers, neither of whom can read from what I can work out. One of them is in jail for dealing. The other is on probation for GBH, as is the dad, who by the way lives four doors along with his new girlfriend. Paul says he was home all Friday night, but his mother—when we woke her from her chemically-induced trance—struggled to remember his name, let alone whether she had seen him that evening. We might not have discovered a motive yet, but he certainly had the opportunity and he even more certainly doesn't have an alibi."

Oh. I looked at Paul. He'd passed enough exams to get into this place. He'd hung on for nearly seven years despite coming from a family where the phrase homework meant going round to someone's home and working it over. He took his final exams in the summer. I no longer needed to ask him why he wanted to come

here at all hours to hide out in a boiler room in a deserted school…
The wonder was that he'd gone home at all.

Paul was looking at me, another civilian flanked by police.
Perhaps he thought that, like him, I was desperately trying to prove
my innocence. I gave him a supportive finger wave. He responded
with a sudden grin, reminding me more than ever of Peter.

"He doesn't look like a murderer, Wills," I said.

"Sis, they never do," he said. "They never, ever do."

After bidding Wills and Agnes goodbye, I drove to the address
Peter had given to me: Melody Whitman, 167 Ashbrow Lane,
Etching Hill. It was set well back from the road at the foot of the
hill, where the cul-de-sacs gave way to the forest of Cannock Chase.
It was a nasty, thirties single brick cube in a nasty thirties estate
where all the houses had been wedged in too close together. The
garden had been slabbed to minimise maintenance. The guttering
was grey plastic. The windows were unpainted aluminium. It had
the look of an unloved rental. I wouldn't have taken it onto my
books.

To my surprise, a sports car was sitting in the drive. Peter could
have told me the make, model and exhaust circumference. I could
see that it was pale blue and expensive.

The driveway being occupied, I parked on the road and walked
up to the front door. I pressed the doorbell and heard it ringing
somewhere in the house. No one came. I pressed it a few more
times before realising that I could hear low voices inside. If I'd been
calling for work or for myself, I'd have turned tail, but I was here
for Benedict. 'They weren't feeling sociable' wasn't going to wash
as an excuse.

I wondered where Hildred could possibly be, though. The house
was far too new to have been constructed with a cellar. Vampires
like small, secure spaces to rest in, and Oscar had told me they
prefer to be far underground. The nasty house I was looking at had
a lot of low points, but they were all in the aesthetics not the depth
of the basement.

I walked around the back and let myself quietly into the kitchen.

I'd have described it in a brochure as in need of modernisation. I personally thought it was in need of six litres of petrol and a match, but Bernie had assured me that phrases like that don't make sales. Nasty yellow surfaces had been paired with cheap units. The unit doors had been badly painted in a colour that paint cards call avocado and everyone else calls turd. Yup, definitely a rental property.

A girl of about twelve years old was sitting at the table, quietly reading a book. She was perilously thin, and all her hair had fallen out. The book was *Northanger Abbey*, which endeared her to me immediately. When she looked up and saw me, I put a finger to my lips. If whoever was living here didn't want visitors, I would get my information where I could.

"Hi, I'm Toni," I said, sitting opposite her. "Toni Windsor."

She smiled. She didn't look ill—now that I looked closely, apart from the hair and the thinness, she looked like someone who was getting better from a long illness. Her colour was good, and her eyes were bright.

"I'm Kathy," she said. "I like your hat. My head gets cold all the time."

I took it off and handed it to her.

"You can keep it if you like," I said. "My boyfriend gave it to me for New Year, but he would want you to have it."

She put it on. She looked adorable. At the back of my mind, I realised I had just introduced Peter to someone as my boyfriend. For the past five months, I had just given up correcting them. Now, it appeared I had thrown in the towel and started doing it myself.

"Thank you," she said. "Please tell your boyfriend how much I like it. Will you take a picture with my phone, please?"

I took a few with her phone. And then with mine. I suggested a few books she might enjoy if she liked Jane Austen, and she gave me a friendship bracelet.

"How are you getting on with Hildred?" I asked as she tied it on to my wrist.

Kathy looked conflicted.

"She's super creepy," she said, "really, with her weird hair and her weird way of talking. And she hates just about everyone. And she makes me taste her blood, which is just freaky. And I'm not allowed outdoors, because we're here secretly, you know. But I'm getting better. I can walk up and down stairs now, and I don't throw up anymore."

"That's brilliant news, Kathy," I said. "And some vampires can be really creepy. Don't worry about it. I've met a couple who would give you bad dreams."

"Thank you," she said. "I would like to go home though. Mel is cross all the time, and Uncle Jasper is nearly as creepy as Hildred."

At that moment, our illicit tête-à-tête was interrupted. Two people wandered into the kitchen, and I could tell neither of them was happy to find me there. The woman was an unlikely blonde who would have carried off the illusion better had she dyed her eyebrows or even her moustache to match. She was wearing a dressing gown, pompom slippers and a cross expression. The man annoyed me more, somehow. He had a sleek, smug look to him, with slicked-back thick white hair. His nails were polished, and he wore an ugly chunky watch that you needed bigger shoulders to carry off. He looked like the sort of man who'd inherited money but bragged about how he made it. I had a gut feeling he also bragged about how fast his sports car went but had never taken it over eighty.

"Who the bloody hell are you?" he snapped.

I'd learned a few tricks from Benedict, so I didn't reply. I just looked at him in silence for a few moments.

"I'm here to check up on Hildred," I said quietly when he had started to fidget. "Please take me to her."

He looked disconcerted, reinforcing my feeling that people usually did what he told them.

"It's daylight; she's out cold," he replied shortly.

"Well, she'll be at her most agreeable," I said. "I've seen her in action. The last thing I want to do is meet her when she's feeling chatty."

"Who are you anyway?" he asked again. "Why should I take you to her?"

I picked my words with care; I'm naturally an honest person. More to the point, the more lies you tell, the more you have to remember.

"My coterie is from Heidelberg," I said, "and I am here at the behest of Benedict Akil. If you can't oblige me, I am sure he will be more than happy to pay you a call in person after dark."

If they had the slightest idea what I was talking about, I thought that should do the trick. The woman hadn't a clue. The man recoiled—he knew, alright.

"Fine," he said angrily. "Fine, I'll show you where she rests."

He took a bunch of keys out of a drawer and led me back out of the kitchen and into the garden. A stone shed that looked a lot older than the house was partly concealed by trees at the end of the garden. The door was secured with a fat chain and padlock—they wouldn't have presented much of an obstacle to the undead, but they could give a mortal attacker a few minutes' pause.

My reluctant host unlocked the door and led me into a small square room without windows. Storage racks were set into the walls, and an access hatch, locked in the same manner as the door, was set into the floor.

"She's down there," he said.

I turned on the torch of my phone and closed the shed door. We were pitched into an awkward half-light. The man sighed and began to work a second key into the mechanism. When he was done, he flung back the hatch. Stone steps led into the darkness. He made a helpful gesture.

"After you," he said nastily.

I thought the building was an old icehouse; it had probably belonged to whatever long-gone mansion they had knocked down to build the ugly housing estate. I looked down into the aperture of the trapdoor. It was as dark as a very dark place. There were spiders the size of very large spiders. I was fairly sure there was an ill-natured super-powerful vampire napping down there, too. And Mr I've-got-a-sports-car-but-no-idea-how-to-drive-it didn't look well disposed towards me.

"After you, actually," I said as blandly as I could manage, "if that's OK."

It probably wasn't, but he headed down the stairs. I walked after him slowly, letting my eyes accustom themselves to the near total darkness. My phone cast a thin anaemic beam of illumination on the chunky wooden coffin that was the sole item in the cellar apart from a lot of coal dust and the burgeoning population of arachnids.

"You're joking," I said. "An actual coffin... What century is this stupid woman from?"

"The seventeenth," said the man grumpily, "and it took me two hours to get the bloody thing down the stairs."

The coffin looked brand new to me. It was made of dark wood with heavy brass fittings on the side. Mr Sports-car-loser was checking the illuminated dial on his watch, so I scoured the coffin until I found an undertaker's mark. Culham and Warbeck, Penkridge Lane. I didn't think the man had noticed what I was doing.

"I'm Toni Windsor, by the way," I said, brushing dusty spider web off my jeans. "I'm only here to check up on her, you know."

There was a pause.

"David Masters," he said carefully.

Of course he was—I could see a hundred and one ways of getting Uncle Jasper out of that. I decided not to call him out on his lie and instead fiddled with the coffin lid. It didn't open.

"She had me fit a lock on the inside," he said hastily.

I gave the coffin a shove. It certainly had something in it. Maybe a sleeping vampire, maybe the long-lost remains of Lord Lucan... I couldn't tell. I gave up. I'd poked around and asked some questions. Seeing as he was now blatantly lying to me, asking more seemed a waste of time. And Benedict hadn't been very specific about what he wanted—to find out anything else, I needed to come back at night.

"I'm done," I said, stepping back from the coffin. "If I were you, I..."

My voice faded away. David Masters was staring at the coffin with a look of loathing so intense that I forgot what I was even saying. I hadn't seen hatred that strong before. He'd forgotten my very presence, so I made my way round him and headed back up the stairs without waiting for him. Maybe he could light his way with the dial of his stupid watch. I didn't care.

I wanted to say goodbye to Kathy, but the kitchen door had been locked while I was covering my clothes with coal dust. Melody clearly didn't want me to have any more girly bonding time. If Melody was even her name, which I doubted; no one in Staffordshire was called Melody.

Chapter Four

STARTING UP THE car, I realised that I was exhausted and running out of Sunday. I had also managed to forget about lunch, so I drove to Lichley Manor and frisked the fridge. My cunning plan almost failed entirely, alas, because with Peter in residence, it was full of healthy green things. I shoved them to one side and pulled out a packet of sliced cheese, some cooked ham and a half-eaten jar of olives. Because I had picked up some good habits from him in the past few months, I did at least put them on a plate before wandering upstairs.

The house was blindingly hot. On a cold January afternoon, it was probably one of the few places in the entire county that didn't require two jumpers. Vampires love the warmth and Oscar kept the heating running twenty-four-seven with a healthy disregard for utility bills or the passing of the seasons. In the summer, I had a feeling casual visitors would have to wander round the house in their underwear. Well, at least dinner parties wouldn't be boring. I stripped off my coat, gloves and scarf and dumped them on the bed.

Our room was blessed with a bank of arched window seats that looked over the lawn. I'd copied the original furnishings: soft rugs on an oak floor and green silk curtains. I'd had the elegant daybed that the previous owners had left re-upholstered. I'd created a space that was pretty in the day; at night it was beautiful and slightly exotic. It was the culmination of every romantic gothic dream. It was the room that Oscar and I were meant to love one another in, to lounge around and laugh together in... That night, I couldn't face it, so I made my way to Peter's room.

Ah. A subtle difference. A bright white box with pale wooden floors. Apart from the bed, there was a wardrobe that blended invisibly into the wall, a desk and bookshelves. The bookshelves contained books. There was nothing else.

I sat on the bed and plaited my hair to stop it tangling too much. A discarded t-shirt lay on the eiderdown. I picked it up and buried my face in it. It smelt of hospital disinfectant, sweat and aftershave. It was not a particularly romantic aroma, but it was uniquely Peter. It was not Oscar. I stripped off down to my underwear and climbed into his bed. I hugged the t-shirt to me. Before I drifted off, I had time to wonder what the hell I was playing at with my life. I had been telling myself for a gazillion years that I had the most appalling taste in boyfriends. Why didn't I ever listen to myself, and was I about to be right all over again? Sleep came before I found the gifts of logic, wisdom or twenty-twenty hindsight, just as it did every night.

I woke to find Oscar's cool hands on my body and his lips in my hair. After some months of assiduous practice, he knew just how to press every one of my buttons, and I dissolved at his touch. Who was I kidding? He hadn't needed any practice; he'd known from day one. I wound my arms around his neck and held him to me.

"My lovely Toni," he said. "Waiting here for me like journey's end. Have you seen the weather?"

The weather? It was the last thing on my mind. The storms and tumults his hands had put me in mind of could all happen right there on the mattress.

"It was cold and wet, Oscar," I said, peeling off his shirt. "It was just horrid."

"You must see it now."

He stripped the eiderdown off me and, ignoring my squeak of

protest, swung me into his arms. He carried me through to my bedroom where the windows showed me a glittering, white scene, as sparkly as a Christmas card and just as pretty. While I had slept, it had been snowing with a vengeance.

The lawn, the trees and the hedges had all vanished under a thick blanket; concerningly, so had my car, but the view was too lovely for me to care. The moon was nearly full, and—having deposited their load—the clouds had withdrawn a little, leaving a vista so bright that I could see the individual tracks where birds had hopped across the grass. The room was suffused with moonlight.

"It's lovely," I said. "I haven't seen snow like this in ages. It must have begun right after I fell asleep. We should make a snowman. Oh, look, it's started up again."

But the moonlight shining on my skin had diverted Oscar's attention to a different and more immediate landscape. He deposited me on one of the wide, cushioned window seats and knelt before me. He began to run his hands through my hair, teasing out the remains of my braid and tangling his fingers in the mass of ringlets released. God gave me hair the colour of a tangerine left out in the sun; in the light of the moon shining off the snow, it looked almost white.

"I know exactly what we should do," he said, "and it has nothing to do with snowmen."

He put his hands on the skin of my waist and then slid them upwards, cupping the outer curves of my breasts with his fingers through the thin silk of my bra and bringing his thumbs up to stroke the bare skin where it spilled out at my cleavage. I leaned into his touch.

"After, then?" I said, in what I hoped were persuasive tones. "Come out with me into the snow."

He threw back his head and laughed. His sharp teeth caught in the light. The first time I'd ever seen Oscar, I'd thought how beautiful he was. The passage of time had only reinforced my first impressions. Anyone better looking would have to be banned under the Geneva Convention.

"You want to play in the snow, do you? Right."

Oscar swung me to my feet. He put his hands to the casements of the window and pushed them open. The left side swung free, but the right, where the hinge stuck slightly, twisted and shattered under his impetuous touch. Glass showered down into the snow. He strode over to the bed, stripped off the eiderdown and covers, and then flung them out of the window.

"Oscar," I protested, "what are you doing?"

"It was your idea," he said, picking me back up and stepping through the window. He sprang lightly down the fifteen feet or so into the white drifts covering the lawn. "You wanted to play in the snow."

He dropped me onto the soft, cold expanse of the bedding. The snow was falling heavily again, the flakes clustering together like tiny puffs of foam. In the freezing January air, his hands felt warm on me. He shredded my lingerie with vampiric expediency and—as I mentally allocated the next day's lunch break to phoning a glazier and buying new underwear—stripped off his own clothes.

"The flakes melt so quickly on your hot skin," he whispered, laying himself on top of me. "Must it be a snowman, lovely Toni, or will I do?"

"Um," I managed, "you will do."

He was carefully kissing the snowflakes off my torso, his lips brushing the little crescent moon-shaped birthmark just over my heart. But then one landed just a hair's breadth from a nipple, and I could tell he had forgotten the weather entirely. I'd forgotten things, too—like every single time he'd ever annoyed me or hurt my feelings. It's amazing how hormones turn off all the logical parts of your brain. Carnal lust is a great leveller.

Oscar wasn't the most gentle of lovers, but he was always generous. Nothing pleased him more than watching me fall into paroxysms of delight. I never had to worry that he would take his pleasure without giving me mine and that evening was no exception. I lay there in the aftermath, wondering if I'd misjudged him, gazing at the stars as his body sheltered mine from the falling snow. I had a feeling that round two was in the offing, but lying on a cooling eiderdown with my less-than-room temperature lover stole my warmth, and melted ice crystals were pooling in crevasses I usually earmarked for other uses... Nope. No amount of passion was going to get me hot enough for second helpings.

"You've done it this time," I murmured into his neck, when I had recovered enough energy to speak. "I'm actually going to freeze to death."

"That's very unfortunate. Are you sure?"

"Yup. Definitely. The goose pimples have taken over my body and they are now a deadly and unstoppable army."

"Well, if you are quite sure, my love," he said, with mock sadness. "I suppose we should do it properly."

And he lifted me into his arms and tipped me, naked, into a snowdrift. I shrieked and scrabbled, and he tussled with me in the snow. Thankfully, he let me win before hypothermia took hold, and I pinned him to the ground, straddling him so that only the skin from my knees down was pressed into the snow. He was still laughing, his hair by then wet and his hands icy on my waist.

"You complete arse," I protested, laughing too hard myself to do more than lob snow at his face. "I'm so bloody cold. Take me inside."

"Right now?" He slid his freezing, wet hands upwards.

"Yes! Right now, crazy man. No, stop that!"

"Very well. If I must."

He put his hands to the ground and levered himself into a sitting position and then swore suddenly. He lifted his hand and I saw that a shard of glass from the window had speared the heel of his wrist. Blood was running down his skin in a shining black line.

I felt his whole body change, surging with passion, and the bottom dropped out of my stomach. Me, I saw a wound, torn flesh and pain; my mind jumped to tetanus injections and hospital visits. Oscar? To him it was foreplay personified. He turned to me and held out his wrist with mute entreaty. His face was alight with desire. I felt mine fill with fear. And revulsion. I was already gagging.

"I can't. I just can't," I whispered. "Oscar, please don't."

He shook his head in confusion. I could see he wasn't taking in my words. He looked at his wrist and idly yanked out the chunk of glass. As I watched, he pushed it back in, an inch or so from the first gash, and a second creeping track of blood began to run down his arm. He brought the bleeding wounds to my mouth, and I turned my face away.

"Drink, beautiful Toni," he said. "Let me in."

"I can't!"

I shrank back and tried to push myself off him, but he tossed aside the piece of glass he was holding in his other hand and grasped me roughly by my upper arm. His fingers crushed me so hard that I thought my bones would shatter. I winced and cried out in agony, but he didn't even appear to notice.

"Just drink it," he said, his voice turning from arousal to frustration. "Why do you do this? Why must you always do this?"

He brought his wrist back up to my lips, and I thought he would force it into my mouth. I screamed in panic, and then I was fighting him off for real. He ended up on top of me, holding me down by my wrists. He had them pinned above my head in an agonising grip.

"Please, Oscar, stop," I whispered. "You are really hurting me."

I didn't think he had registered what I said. He continued to hold me down. The cold of the snow was biting, and as the adrenaline of earlier excitement drained away, I began to shake.

He looked down at me for a few moments. His blood had smeared over me in patches as we fought. I could feel it drying on my face.

"What's the point?" he said. "What's the bloody point if you don't want it?"

He stood up and flicked his wrist in disgust. The blood sprayed across me in an arc and left a Milky Way of black stars across the snow. He stormed back into the house.

"Why the sodding hell," I asked no one in particular, "does my sodding boyfriend have to pick a row when I am naked in the sodding snow?"

I scrambled to my feet and pulled the mostly dry coverlet off the entirely wet eiderdown. I wrapped it around myself and made my way to the front door, careful to avoid the caltrop trail of glass shards that Oscar had left when he broke the window. My feet were numb in seconds.

"Why can't we fall out over the kitchen table like normal couples?" I continued through chattering teeth, using a corner of the coverlet to wipe blood off my face. "Is that not dramatic enough for you, Oscar? Do I need to take up sky diving so we can squabble at an acceleration of nine point eight metres per second squared?"

Oscar had left the door open. He had also left it in one piece, which given his mood left me grateful for small mercies. I pulled it to behind me and followed his wet footprints to the drawing room. He was sitting on the spine of a sofa staring out of the window, his back to me.

The room was warm but by then I was shivering uncontrollably, so I lit the fire anyway. Peter must have laid it earlier, and it caught without the need for a second match, the carefully packed newspaper spreading flames to the kindling and then to the dry, oak logs. I curled up on the hearthrug and let the radiant heat begin its work.

Squabbles left are bound to fester, and procrastination wasn't one of my many faults. I waited until I had warmed through enough to speak, and then tied the green silk of the bed cover firmly around my modesty. I took a deep breath and approached my sulking boyfriend.

He was still gazing at the view through the window. I didn't see anything through it that put me in a good mood. There was the sodden, blood-stained wreck of my eiderdown. There was a veneer of glass fragments, reminding me that had I even wanted to sleep in my now bedding-free bed, there was probably a fine gale swirling around the room courtesy of the broken window. I concentrated instead on the fine view of a naked Oscar that my line of sight afforded me. That pretty much always put me in a good mood.

"Oscar, my darling, please don't be so angry," I said, with as much composure as I could scrape together.

Not a lot, as it happened. Oscar didn't do maintenance. Repairing the debris of the night's debauchery would as always fall to Peter and to me. I'd never minded before. Oscar was so prone to shredding my clothes in moments of passion that I had finally accustomed myself to letting him pay for them. He could also be hard on furniture that got in the way. The décor in the house had distilled down to solid, vintage wood as a result. And he and Peter shared blood. With tremendous abandon from what I could gauge from the aftermath. You wouldn't believe the things blood won't wash out of. There was a reason the house had no fitted carpets. And we had bought an industrial steam cleaner.

These domestic tasks rarely bothered me. They seemed a modest price to pay for the pleasures I got in return. But if they were to stem from a night of Oscar behaving like an arse... well, then I could imagine some resentment building.

And while I loved him madly, I wasn't stupid. He'd been less than gentle with me on more than one occasion when I wouldn't let him feed or give me blood, but never remotely like this. I could already see dark handprints forming where he had crushed my wrists. I didn't like to imagine what my upper arm would look like in the morning. If this was a trend, I wasn't going to stay around and follow it through.

"I'm not angry," he said suddenly. "But we can't go on like this."

Oh, great. Absolutely bloody fantastic. On top of everything else, I was about to get dumped. I only knew one way to stop a man dumping me, and after everything that had just happened... I just couldn't be bothered.

"I suppose not," I said, suddenly filled with exhaustion.

I looked at him, the lovely line of his body in the moonlight. I'd never fallen this hard for anyone. Oscar was fun, adoring and whimsical. But he was also arrogant and thoughtless, and over the months that had passed, he'd worn me down. I couldn't imagine not loving him. But I realised with a sudden rush that I really could imagine living without him. After tonight, it was almost going to be a relief.

"So, I've made some decisions for us," he continued, as though I hadn't spoken. "There's no time to sort this out tonight. I am due at the Stone House shortly. It must wait until tomorrow."

Right, OK. I hadn't got a clue what he was talking about but I clearly wasn't getting dumped—just as I was starting to wonder if that wouldn't be the easiest option… I moved to sit next to him, wrapping the coverlet around both of us and leaning against his shoulder.

"Stop being cryptic, please, sweetie," I said. "What has to wait?"

He looked down at me. There was something grim in his expression that made me wary, something I hadn't seen before. I drew back a little.

"Tomorrow we will share blood, Toni, and we will set a date for your ascension."

Huh? I inched back a little more, annoyed that I had shared the coverlet with him and couldn't now get further away.

"OK, now you're not just being cryptic, darling, you're being incomprehensible," I said, as reasonably as I could manage. "No, we won't, and what does that even mean?"

"Your immortal transition," he said. "I've made up my mind. You will become one of the vampire kind."

What was it about my life since I met Oscar that I spent so much of it with my mouth hanging open, paralysed with disbelief at whatever the hell was going on around me? I'd never actually swallowed a fly, but then it was mid-winter. Eventually, I shook my head, and sought for the power of speech.

"OK, and we won't be doing that either," I said. "Have you gone completely insane, Oscar?"

"I won't risk losing you the way I lost Peter's mother," he said, ignoring me again. "If she hadn't delayed, she would be one of us now."

Yup, completely insane. I stole back the entirety of the cover from him and edged towards the fire.

"Oscar, you can't go around giving me ultimatums like this," I said. "That's not how a relationship works."

He shook his head.

"I'm not giving you an ultimatum, my love," he said. "I'm not asking you to make a decision. I've made the decision for you. It's easier that way."

"You don't get to do that! I decide what's best for me. You don't get to make my decisions, Oscar."

He seemed unbothered by my protests. He wandered over to me, and taking my face very gently in his hands, he kissed my forehead.

"I have to, my love. How else can I be sure you will make the right ones?"

And without a backward glance he headed up the stairs. I moved to sit once again by the fire. A few minutes later I heard the door slam behind him as he headed out for the night.

I had postponed the inevitable realisation for months, but there was no more escaping it: it was once again official. I had really, really terrible taste in men.

Chapter Five

NECROMANCERS TAKE THE living power of the day and force it into the dead. At any rate, that's what Peter had told me. He'd read in the scripts at Heidelberg that mortals accrue the energy in the hours of daylight, and it's that which nourishes a vampire when they feed. It's what keeps them immortal. The blood? That's just a medium for the stuff.

Me? I don't just accrue the energy; I absorb far, far too much and I need to use it up. I need to burn it off or go crazy. I'd raised poor Bella the previous night, so I would be OK for an evening. Even so, I thought of heading up to one of the cemeteries and flexing my necromantic muscles. It always put me in a good mood, and the night was still young.

But I'd only managed a couple of hours of sleep before Oscar woke me, so I decided to focus on rest and recuperation for a change. I had a bath and soaked off the detritus that you accumulate during a shag on the lawn, snow or no snow. Small twigs, grass stains and gravel if you are interested. Oh, and in my case, smears of unwanted vampire blood. Oscar could damn well keep the nasty stuff.

Then I dressed in clean clothes, spent twenty minutes scraping snow off my crappy old car and drove back to my own home. It wasn't the gracious dwelling that Oscar lived in, but it was my own space. I had planned to sell it or at least rent it out when I moved in with Oscar and Peter. I'd never done so; no matter how much I adored him, dating Oscar had never felt like bedrock that I could build my life upon. Stress dropped off my shoulders as I parked my rusty old Morris at the familiar kerb and let myself in.

Winchester greeted me with a soft mew. I'd had him for six months now, and his fragile, wistful ways always gave the impression that another one might be too much to hope for. I'd installed a cat flap without much hope that he would use it, being so doddery and on his last legs as he was. And indeed, I rarely saw him step outside. Still, the constant influx of dead moles, dead voles, dead rabbits and on one occasion the still-damp corpse of a full-sized moorhen provided hefty evidence that he wasn't as infirm on his fat little paws as I'd assumed. Also, Miss Heliotrope next door had started walking her repulsive little pug Waffle while Winchester was having his nap. The cat might only have one of his two fangs left, but he kept that remaining one sharp.

I took the cat up to bed with me in lieu of a hot water bottle and slept straight through until the sound of Peter cleaning his teeth in the bathroom dragged me back to consciousness.

"Can I assume a good time was had by all?" he asked, moving the cat to the foot of the bed and climbing in behind me. "I found half your knickers in the hydrangea and Oscar's jeans in the pond."

He slid sub-zero temperature hands around me and pressed his cold form to my back.

"Bloody hell, you're freezing," I protested sleepily. "Get off me until you warm up."

"Nein," he said, burying his cold face luxuriously in my neck. "The second law of thermodynamics says this is the best way. Entropy will be preserved. Soon we will both be warm. You have to take one for science."

"Bugger science," I muttered, too sleepy to protest.

In truth, I didn't plan to protest too hard. He was appealingly hot blooded. In a couple of minutes, he would be giving off a damn sight more heat than the cat. He was also a peaceful bed mate. I relaxed back into the twin arms of Peter and Morpheus.

I was woken what felt like moments later by the unwelcome shriek of the alarm clock. I ignored it until it was superseded by the equally unwelcome sound of Winchester batting the wretched thing onto the floor. It landed with a dull thud followed by an expensive sounding silence. It wasn't the first time. Winchester and I were cutting a swathe through the timepieces of Staffordshire.

"Cat one: Toni nil," Peter said sleepily. "Do you mind if I sleep in? I'll come and take you out to lunch at one?"

"I'd like that," I said through an enormous yawn.

I splashed water round randomly in the bathroom and then looked around for some clothes that weren't too crumpled to wear. The presence of a neat pile of ironing reminded me once again that Peter's many virtues stretched a lot further than radiation and conduction. I pulled on enough layers to keep out some of the January cold, starting with thick black tights and a knitted dress in the same colour and adding jumpers until I thought I was giving the season a run for its money. Finally, I made an unimpressive and largely unsuccessful attempt to drag a brush through my hair. I'd clearly made enough noise crashing around to thoroughly wake Peter, who sat up with an air of resignation.

"I'll do it," he said. "Bitte gib mir das."

I handed him the brush and he teased out the tangles with gentle, competent strokes.

"You're done," he said after a couple of minutes. "Go forth and bring quality rural real estate to the masses."

And he clapped me casually on the upper arm in exactly the wrong place, just exactly the spot that Oscar had clenched the previous night. I cried out in pain and any remaining somnolence left Peter.

"What the hell happened?" he demanded. "You were fine when you left me."

I thought about what to say. If I told Peter now, he would get no more sleep and I would never make it to work. I'd been too upset to think much about what had transpired the previous night, but I had a feeling it was pretty relationship-destroying. It wasn't a quick chat we could have over a piece of toast before I went off to perform my day job.

"I need to talk to you about that too," I said. "But I'll take the afternoon off because it's going to be a long chat."

He frowned but didn't argue, and when I put out the light again, I heard him lie back and pull up the eiderdown. I didn't stay to watch Winchester moving into the warm spot I had vacated, but I didn't need to. Like death and taxes—and my ability to make stupid choices with my love life—some things are inevitable.

It was still snowing so I pulled on my lovely cream, fur-lined winter boots, guaranteed to improve your attitude to winter mornings, grabbed a coat and drove to work. I expected an easy day—January is always quiet. People have this desperation to be in their new homes for Christmas, so December is crazy—but come the New Year, those planning to move are done. And people get up on a frosty morning, think about the effort of de-icing the car... and either cancel their viewings or just don't turn up at all.

The only note in my diary for the day was to hire someone to house-sit for Eleanor Johnson, an elderly client who had decided on a whim to visit her nephew in Sydney for six months. I struggled to put up with her for six minutes, so the nephew had all my sympathy. I'd been feeding her fish for a week now, and the thought of walking past her ugly, ceramic gnomes in order to let myself in and be oppressed by her ugly, simpering, ceramic ballerinas was depressing.

The roads were thick with snow which appeared to be sitting on a slick layer of ice; they were bad enough that it was the best part of an hour before I finally pushed open the glass office door and was able to start removing layers. Bethany, our teenage receptionist, was taking advantage of a quiet morning to paint her nails. Bernie, my lecherous boss, was sprawled in a chair crumpling up sheets of the *Staffordshire Agricultural Bulletin* and tossing them in the general direction of the bin. As I watched, he tore out a page entitled 'Your Massey Ferguson and you!'

"There you are," he said, missing the bin for what appeared

to be the fiftieth time, judging from the number of paper balls accumulating around it. "Don't take any more clothes off: I'd love to see you naked, but Bethany booked you a viewing in Lichfield at nine-thirty, and in this weather you'll be pushing it."

"If I get there at all," I grumbled, pulling my coat back on. "Have you seen how it's sticking to the roads? All I had planned for this morning was finding someone to house-sit Eleanor Johnson's place in Rugeley. Which house am I showing?"

He looked faintly embarrassed, ripping off a sheet bearing the legend: 'Winter tractor maintenance: twelve dos and don'ts'.

"Actually, it's Cathedral Wharf."

I swore.

"Bernie, that's been on our books for two years and it's going to stay there. No one will ever take that site. You're wasting my time and your money sending me over there."

He tossed another ball at the bin. It bounced off the wall and rolled under a desk.

"I'm paying you anyway, and there's nothing else for you to do," he said. "And as it happens, the client asked for you by name."

He handed me a piece of paper on which Bethany had scribbled 'Jeremy Emerson' in biro. Our office had heard of technology in the same way that I had heard of existential philosophy: the allure hadn't been there.

"Fair enough," I said, shouldering my bag. "If I don't go now, I'll definitely be late. I can't remember who Jeremy is, but he might be that guy from the Birmingham Green Shoots project who rang last week."

Cathedral Wharf was the worst prospect on our books, and we were never, ever going to get rid of it. We didn't do a lot of commercial sites, and we'd taken this on reluctantly. It was the wrong property in the wrong place.

Anyone who knows the pretty town of Lichfield will be confused even by the name. The river doesn't go through the centre of the town at all, and the cathedral isn't there either; it's partly up the hill, even further from the water. But in the craze for marinas that took over the whole of Britain in the eighteen hundreds, a plan was launched to build a section of canal that would link the river to the town centre and the cathedral.

It was doomed. The bedrock was too hard, the distance too far, the gradient too steep and the pockets of the developers too shallow. The only part of the plan that was successfully completed was Cathedral Wharf, a bijou arcade with a glass roof, built to house a couple of dozen outlets—perhaps a gentleman's tailor, a milliner, a tobacconist and suchlike. It had been designed to sit at the edge of the marina and had instead ended up slap bang in the middle of nowhere. It had never opened. A century on, the glass roof had fallen in, and the two storeys of shops would have been a deathtrap even without eight inches of snow concealing all the holes in the floors. I'd shown the place to a hundred or more out-of-town developers. They all came expecting a view of water and the cathedral. They all left disappointed.

I was lucky enough to follow a snowplough into the town, enabling me to get to the arcade a little before nine-thirty. It was an ornate building built in a horseshoe shape, with a crescent of boutiques looking onto a central courtyard. The floors of the upper storey had fallen through in dozens of spots. I'd brought two hard hats and a waiver for Mr Emerson to sign in case he broke his neck in the snow.

I parked on the road and unlocked the ugly double gates that now closed off the courtyard from potential footfall. I'd had them fitted when we took on the property. The site had zero commercial potential, but it had much to offer those looking for somewhere to shoot up or doss down. I couldn't stop the local feral cats and foxes from making themselves at home in the ruins of Cathedral Wharf, but I drew the line at the local feral youth.

My last viewing here had been at Christmas, before the onset of the New Year had driven potential customers into hibernation and my commission below subsistence levels. Since then, the lock appeared to have survived several attempts to force it. The key would no longer come out while the gate was open, but I didn't fear that anyone would wander in and take it while I was showing the mysterious Mr Emerson around. Had the footfall in the area been higher, I would have found a buyer a long time ago.

I left the key in the gate and walked across the courtyard holding the hard hats and my handbag. The walls were high enough that the sun had barely made it over, and the whole area was chilly and uninviting. Without the preservation order that made it unsaleable, the whole structure would have been bulldozed decades ago.

It still had a certain architectural charm if you liked ruined buildings. Broken-off iron spurs that had once supported the glass roof poked into the sky. If you had a death wish and made your way up to the second storey, you could look through tall arched windows that must once have gazed down on the elegant sprawl of old Lichfield. A century later, you could admire the wall of a disused tannery and a supermarket car park.

A noise at the gates caught my attention. There was a man standing just inside them with his back to me, Mr Emerson, I presumed. Burdened with hard hats, I approached him.

"Good morning," I said. "You must be Mr Emerson. My name—"

I broke off in shock as he turned around. I realised in a flash both who he was and what he had been doing. It was Uncle Jasper, the man who had introduced himself to me as David Masters. And he had just locked us both in and pocketed the key.

"What the bloody hell do you think you're doing?" I said.

My mind was spinning. How had he found me? What did he want? I couldn't begin to guess. I began to inch backwards nonetheless, because one thing was perfectly clear: I was in trouble.

"Yeah, I'm sorry," he said, though he didn't sound it. He ran a hand restlessly through his sleek hair. "You were just in the wrong place at the wrong time."

I edged further away.

"I don't even know who you are!" I protested, my voice rising. "There's no need for this."

He shook his head and took a step forward.

"You'd work it out," he said, confusing me even further.

"I would have done this yesterday, but I couldn't risk Kathy seeing. She doesn't deserve that."

"Neither do I," I snapped, preparing to run for it.

But before I could much more than turn on my heels, he lunged forward and shoved me hard between the shoulder blades and I went flying across the courtyard face down in the snow. The hard hats and my handbag spun off into the middle distance.

I slid along for a couple of yards. The snow had cushioned my fall, though, and I was winded rather than hurt. I scrambled to my feet, surprised that I was getting the chance to do so. Glancing behind me, I saw why. My attacker was crushing my phone and my rape alarm to smithereens under his smart, shiny shoes.

What did he think I'd seen? And how could I get out of this? I've never been given to panic, but my strengths come out at night. Right then, all I could think of was that I was wearing better footwear than him for fighting to the death in the snow. And I probably knew the layout of the arcade better than anyone else. They weren't going to give me much of an edge, but they were all I had.

I took advantage of his preoccupation to flee across to the left side of the courtyard and into the thoroughfare that led through the derelict shops. With the snow recording my every footstep, any game of hide and seek was going to be of short duration, but if I could just buy myself some time, I might come up with a better idea.

There were holes in the roof, letting light in from the row above. I scurried to the first of the stairways that led to the upper level. I went up it at a run and headed into one of the shops at random. A massive hole had swallowed up most of the floor, and while some flimsy and now rotten sheets of chipboard had been leant against the wall, the space behind them was too small for me to conceal myself. I flattened myself against the near wall so that I couldn't be seen from the passage.

The snow muffled my pursuer's footsteps. I didn't hear him until he strode past the doorway of my hiding place. But stride past it he did. I hoped he would get to the end of the crescent before turning round. I had bought myself maybe thirty seconds. More in hope than confidence, I pushed over one of the damp, rotten boards. It slammed onto the floor with what sounded like a massive boom in the snowy silence. I inched round the wall to the far side so that the board lay between me and the doorway. Moments later, not nearly thirty seconds, I heard footsteps returning. My attacker appeared at the entrance. I shrank back against the wall, trying to look small and scared. It wasn't hard, which was good because I've never been much of an actress. He looked across at me. There wasn't a lot of expression in his eyes.

"I'll make it quick," he said.

From a pocket he took out a pair of leather gloves and a length of what looked like washing line cable. He put on the gloves and wrapped some of the cord around his hands. I didn't think he planned to dry his budgie smugglers on it, and I shook my head in disbelief. How had I made such an enemy without even trying?

"What the hell did I even do?" I asked.

He shrugged.

"As I said: wrong place, wrong time. I can't have this fall back on Mel and Kathy."

And he took a step towards me and fell straight through the chipboard and onto the rubble of the floor below.

Any slim hopes that he would break his wretched neck were slain by the stream of curses that followed. And they weren't pain-filled enough to suggest that the speaker needed to spend the next few weeks in traction. I looked down to see him glaring up through the hole. His face was cut and bleeding freely, and I rather thought his nose was broken. The knuckles of one hand had split open and were oozing blood. The smug look that had been winding me up had finally been wiped off his face, but he still looked healthy enough to hunt me down and garrotte me.

"How about we call it a tie and go home?" I called down, more in hope than expectation. "We can think of this as a phase we grew out of as we matured and learned important lessons about life?"

He spat out something; I thought it might be a tooth.

"I won't feel so bad about killing you now," he said.

That would be a no then. I'd tried.

I fled back into the main upper passageway and scurried along its length, glancing into the shops as I passed. Most were empty or full of rubble. Almost the last one I came to was slightly different. The ceiling above had fallen through entirely, allowing a thick white carpet of snow to cover the floor. I could see why: a huge great length of one of the steel girders that once held up the glass roof of the arcade had crashed through. Chunks of it still littered the room. Some more sheets of chipboard leant against the far wall at an angle, making a tiny triangle that I could just have crept into.

I didn't. Instead, I took off my coat and balled it up. I took several careful steps towards the chipboard and stuffed the coat behind it so that just an inch or so poked out. It was a nice bright green, hard to miss against the snow. Then I walked backwards, treading carefully in my own footprints so that just a single track led to my coat. En route, I picked up one of the lumps of broken roof spar, a chunk of metal about eleven inches long that weighed as much as a suitcase. It was icy to the touch even through my gloves. I took a final step sideways, pressing myself once again against the entrance wall so that I wouldn't easily be seen by someone glancing into the room. As a final lure, I lobbed a single glove into the centre of the floor.

It seemed just moments later that I heard his tread in the corridor. I assumed he was looking into the rooms as he passed them. He stopped at the one I was concealed in, presumably catching sight of my glove, and then laughed.

"Nice try," I heard him say. "But not good enough."

He stepped past me into the room. I swung the chunk of metal at the back of his head with all my strength. I must have made a noise, though, because at the last minute he spun round to face me. Instead of clubbing him on the back of the head, my weapon crashed awkwardly into the side of his face.

The result was horrible. There was a fleshy crunching sound and blood sprayed everywhere. He dropped to his knees, clutching his face. I stood there paralysed just for a moment with indecision, but it was too long. He reached out a hand, seized my ankle and wrenched. I went down, losing my balance completely and dropping my weapon.

If luck had been on my side, it would have landed on his stupid, bloody head. It turned out I wasn't feeling lucky, because the wretched thing missed him entirely and rolled away across the floor out of my reach.

"Arse. Arse. Arse," I muttered. "Why does this always happen to me?"

My attacker didn't answer, possibly because he understood the question to be rhetorical but more likely because I had just broken his jaw. He hung on to my ankle and began to drag me towards him. I grabbed onto the side of the doorway, but he yanked hard, and my fingers slipped free. I scrabbled and kicked out at him with my free foot, but he managed to seize it in his other hand. I found myself on my back sliding across the snow-covered floor.

He let go of both my feet and lunged over me, pressing me into the ground with the weight of his torso. He was on his knees, trying to catch both of my wrists in his hands. I knew if he managed that, it would be game over, so I twisted and turned like an eel, trying to keep them out of his grip and wriggle free. He managed to grab one, but when he pulled back to aim for the other, I drove my upper body towards the sky and head-butted him as hard as I could in his raw, bleeding mouth.

He howled in pain and lurched back from me, and while he didn't loosen his grip on my wrist, he was flailing, and I pulled his arm into my face and sank my teeth into his hand until I tasted blood. He wrenched it free, finally letting go of my wrist. He briefly cradled one bleeding hand in the other, leaving his head undefended for a moment, and I punched him as hard as I could in his injured jaw. He brought both his hands up to defend himself, and I reached back behind me to get both of mine on the edge of the door again. With a jerk, I pulled myself free of his weight, dragged myself back to my feet and took off like a whippet down the corridor.

I had only got a few yards when I had to brake so hard that I tumbled in the snow and fell to my knees, skidding in the ice. Ahead of me, the floor of the corridor had fallen in entirely. It explained why my attacker had turned round so quickly the first time. Below me, there was a dark space filled with rubble. I had come to the end of the road.

I looked behind me. There he was, emerging from the room we'd been fighting in, and blocking me from the stairs back down. He was limping. Blood was dripping from his face. He was swaying slightly and walking very slowly. But he was still quite capable of killing me and clearly determined to try. I pressed my fingers to my temples and tried to think but nothing was coming to me. He was twenty feet away from me, then eighteen, then...

"Quick!" A sharp whisper came from my right. "This way— hurry."

Through the high, glassless arch of the window aperture, I could look across the ten- or eleven-foot gap between the arcade and the red brick walls of the tannery next door. There, crouched in the aperture of a similarly broken window, was Paul Mycroft, of all people, the sixth former I'd last seen in police custody. I didn't have time to wonder what the hell he was doing there, because he had levered an old wooden ladder across the void between us, making a terrifying and fragile escape route for me. Forty feet below I could see the road and the pavement. A familiar blue sports car was parked there, a long, long way down...

I looked back down the corridor. Six feet away from me stood the man who wanted me to die that day, blood patinating the snow at his feet and murder in his eyes. I flew across the ladder like a cat and into Paul's arms. He kicked it free, and it tumbled into the alleyway, turning over and over before landing with a satisfying thud on the roof of the car. I heard glass break, and the ladder flew off into the snow in two pieces.

I sat down on the dusty ground of the tannery floor. I didn't say anything, I just breathed. Relief flooded into my body in warm waves. After a couple of minutes, a limping figure crossed the road below us. He clambered awkwardly in through the damaged door of the blue car. It shot off down the alleyway and screeched away around the corner at the end, mounting the curb for the last nine yards. Yup, he drove just as badly as I'd expected.

"Are you OK?" Paul asked cautiously.

I looked down at my feet. My luscious, cream, fur-lined boots were splattered with blood. But none of it was mine. All I'd come out with was two grazed knees and three chipped nails. I looked up at Paul and grinned.

"You should have seen the other guy," I said.

"I did," he said with respect. "And I'm never getting on your bad side."

Chapter Six

AFTER A WHILE, the cold of the tannery floor began to seep into my derriere, and I realised that my coat was still stuffed behind some rotting boards in the arcade. I turned to find Paul watching me with a certain wary esteem.

"I'm Paul," he said. "I saw you at the school yesterday."

We shook hands.

"Toni," I said. "You didn't look like you were having a good day."

"Better than you have been having today?"

I nodded and bounded to my feet. Escaping certain death had left me full of energy.

"Right," I said. "Let's go."

"Are you going to call the police?"

I looked up at Paul. Like most people, he was taller than me. I thought he was probably as tall as Oscar, maybe five eleven. He was wearing a t-shirt I was sure that Peter owned. It was black, and on the front a burning skull had been impaled on what looked like a mammoth tusk. If anyone tried to kill him, and he subsequently smashed their face in and totalled their car, I wanted him to know that calling the police would be a good response. It just wasn't going to be mine. Calling police over vampire business generally just led to dead police. I didn't want that on my conscience.

"Paul, I'd love to be setting a better example for you," I said, "but no, I'm not going to call the police. For a start, that jerk smashed my phone and for the rest... They couldn't help. I have to sort this out for myself. Do you mind?"

"God, no. After this weekend, I don't want their attention either. I would have called them myself when I saw you were in trouble, though, but they impounded my phone as evidence yesterday. And there wasn't time to find a call box."

We walked down through the dirty shell of the tannery. In the eighties, it had been partially converted for storage and bays of empty steel shelving now stood gathering dust.

I asked Paul the question that had been preying on my mind.

"Why were you here? I mean, thank you for saving my life and everything, and forgive me for being paranoid, but how come you were in the right place at the right time? Were you following me?"

He shook his head, pushing open a fire door. It disgorged us into the narrow passage between the two buildings and I led us back to the arcade gates. They were swinging open, the key still wedged in. My attacker had clearly had the same trouble with them as I had, and hadn't waited around to lock up.

"It's *almost* a total coincidence," Paul said as I led us in. "Though, in a way, I was following you. Why are we coming back here?"

"To dig my car keys out of the snow, I hope," I said. "Go on."

"Oh, yeah. Well, I came here to the tannery a few months ago, back in the summer. It's not so far, and I have a moped. I was looking for somewhere to doss, to do my studies. And I saw you. You were showing some businessmen round the arcade. I didn't know who you were or anything. But yesterday I recognised you at the school—it's your hair. Now my den at the school's off limits, I need somewhere to work and, when I saw you, I remembered this place."

My bag lay where it had fallen. I didn't have to dig for my keys—they lay in a scattered crescent of belongings. I crouched down in the snow and gathered up bits of my paraphernalia—lipstick, hairbrush, another lipstick, lockpicks, a torch, a packet of mints. I opened the latter and passed one over to Paul.

"Could you study here?"

He shook his head.

"In the summer, maybe. It's too cold right now."

I stood up and looked at my rescuer. He was just eighteen years old, and he'd overcome tremendous odds to get to the grammar school. His family probably didn't know or care that he faced a raft of exams this summer that would determine the path of his life. I didn't approve of the fact that he might be funding his textbooks by dealing dope to schoolkids with more money than sense, but judging other people was exhausting, and I tried to avoid it.

"I need to retrieve my coat and then I need coffee," I said to him. "Come with me. I'll buy you a new phone and some cake."

THE WHOLE SEQUENCE of events, fleeing for my life around the building with Mr Lying Tosser No Name, had taken a stupidly short amount of time. I reclaimed my coat and then drove us into the centre of town. I bought Paul a rather nicer phone than I could afford and a new one for me, ignoring the rather incredulous looks the saleswoman threw at my bloodstained boots and skinned knees. Next to the phone shop was a café. I told Paul to order whatever he liked. Being a teenage boy, he ordered a full English with extra sausages and a slab of cake the size of my head.

He ate the breakfast at a pace that one of my zombies would have struggled to match. Halfway through the cake, he looked up at me; close up for the first time I noticed that he was sporting a black eye.

"Why are you doing this?" he asked.

I shrugged.

"You saved my life, Paul. I wasn't joking. I had my back against the wall, and I was out of ideas and places to run to."

"I didn't kill her, you know."

I looked at his hands, clutching a half-eaten slice of Battenberg. They didn't look like a killer's hands, but what did I know? I was the girl who'd decided a murderous vampire's henchman was an undercover cop just a few short months before. Peter and I had nearly died because of my assumptions... And while Paul looked perfectly sweet to me, he had no alibi for the night someone had clubbed a little red-headed schoolgirl to death and left her bloodied corpse cooling in a school corridor. I drained my coffee and waved for a refill. Was I just being naïve?

"I never thought you did," I said carefully. "Did you even know her?"

"Bella? I didn't even know her name until yesterday. I did speak to her once; early in her first term she asked the way to the chemistry lab. She's a ginger like you, and I remembered her hair. But that's it. She wasn't in chess club, which is the only club I'm in that takes first years. Why were you with the police yesterday? Are you a suspect, too?"

I wasn't sure what made a good reply. I didn't fancy lying to Paul. On the other hand, telling him that I raised the dead to cross-examine them didn't seem like a good idea either.

"I'm just helping them with their enquiries," I said with a sigh.

"Apparently I'm doing that, too," he said bitterly, "which is why I have no phone and no moped anymore."

"How did you get into Lichfield today then?" I asked, draining my second coffee far too fast.

"I took the bus, but there aren't many running in the snow. Why?"

I got to my feet and walked over to the till to settle up. Paul followed me.

"I'll drive you home, then," I told him. "If you can risk being seen in a car as uncool as mine, of course."

He thought about it.

"It's got to be cooler than my bike," he said, "though that should have a bit more street cred now it's been impounded by the cops."

I drove home slowly through the snowy landscape. Staffordshire has soft, rolling hills. There aren't the impressive peaks of Derbyshire, and unlike the Lake District—where the ranges look like giants hacked them out just the week before—the countryside has a finished, rounded look. I'm biased. I've always thought it the prettiest of the English counties. In the snow, it can't be bettered.

A thought occurred to me halfway back to Rugeley.

"Paul, are you in a hurry?" I asked him. "Do you have to be somewhere?"

He'd been quiet on our drive back, fiddling with his new phone in the passenger seat next to me. He was an eighteen-year-old male. He was probably working out how to download porn onto it.

"Nah. School's shut until tomorrow so the cops can finish gathering evidence," he said. "Why?"

"Just an idea," I said. "Bear with me."

I pulled up outside Eleanor Johnson's mumsy little two-up two-down redbrick house. It had occurred to me when driving Paul back how close it was to his school. From their snowy blanket, a battalion of gnomes stared up at us. Some held gardening tools or fishing rods. One held a placard reading 'A gift from Merthyr Tydfil'. My fingers itched for a hammer.

"Why are we here?" asked Paul as I led him up the icy garden path.

"Eleanor is paying us for a house-sitter," I said. "She wants someone to feed her fish, leave food for the cat and turn the lights on and off. I thought you could study here, and I think it would be fine to stay over if things got too much at your place. The money isn't much, but I'll make Bernie pay you in cash. Just don't for goodness' sake tell my brother where you're staying or he'll absolutely kill me and we've had quite enough murders already."

He looked around the small front room, which had apparently been upholstered in doilies to provide a suitable backdrop for the vile, ceramic ballerinas.

"It's perfect," he said.

"Is that sarcasm?"

He shook his head decisively.

"You're forgetting. My normal study venue is the boiler room behind the tennis court. This place has central heating, and I can't see a single used condom or syringe. It's terrific. Will the cat be OK if I miss a day?"

"Yup, don't worry about it. The cat moved next door about a year ago. It only comes back for the extra food. I think its tolerance for the simpering ballerinas is lower than yours. But if your brothers find out about this place, I'm confiscating the key."

"They won't," he assured me. "I'll make sure."

"And no drugs."

He gave me an odd look, and just for a moment I questioned if I was being wise.

"I don't even smoke," he said.

Something in his voice sounded different. Was he angry? I wasn't sure.

"Fine," I said. "Just needed to say it."

He gave me that odd look again but then a car backfired on the road and distracted me and when I looked back at him, the expression had vanished.

"No problem," he said, and I let it drop.

It struck me only after I'd bid him goodbye that I'd forgotten to ask him how he'd acquired his black eye.

I DROVE BACK to the office in a thoughtful mood. The snow wasn't melting, and I had a feeling the sky had more in store for us. I'd thought the weather might make Peter late, but he was waiting for me at the modest offices of Bean and Heron when I returned. Bethany was fluttering her eyelashes at him. Bernie was glaring. Peter was reading a newspaper, but he jumped to his feet when I came in.

"You're freezing," he said, pulling me very casually into his arms and kissing the top of my head. "You also have shredded knees and only one glove. And I think maybe you have gravel in your hair… Not the best viewing ever?"

I shrugged.

"He wasn't a serious buyer," I said lightly, conscious of Bernie listening to us. "And I was bored of those gloves anyway. Where are we going?"

"I thought the café next to St Mary's?"

We wandered out into the white street. The snow had begun to fall again, and I pulled my green coat around me. "Do you mind if we go back home? I have a feeling this isn't a restaurant conversation."

He hugged me to him.

"I did wonder. I took the bus, so we can both go in your car. Why do you have blood all over your boots?"

"Oh, that," I sighed. "None of it's mine." Peter looked anxious and I could tell an interrogation was coming my way but I didn't feel it was the time so I just shook my head. "I'm all right, I swear, but it must have something to do with Hildred Rutherford. Which means someone needs to tell Benedict about it, and it's not going to be me."

"Nice try—he terrifies the life out of me."

"Maybe Oscar will speak to him. If he's even speaking to me by the end of this evening, that is…"

"Can it be that bad?"

"Peter, it might be."

He drove us to Lichley. He'd shovelled a path clear to the door at some point that morning, and when I went up to my room to remove a few layers of clothing, I also saw that he'd nailed boards over the broken window. In the heat of the house, I changed into jeans and a long-sleeved top, mulling on the strange bunch of contradictions that made up Peter. Stubborn but passionate, talkative but private… I often felt his fevered domesticity was a reaction to inactivity; it wasn't one I minded, and when I made my way back to the kitchen, I found he had made us both sandwiches and tea. I sat down at the kitchen table with him and toyed with my sandwich.

"So," he said, sitting opposite me, "how shall we do this?"

"I'll tell you about last night," I said. "Then it's done, and you can tell me whether anything you found out today can help. Then we will worry about Hildred."

"In Ordnung, fire away."

I told him hesitatingly about the previous night. I looked at my tea while I did so. I didn't have to see Peter's face to feel him getting angrier and I tried to make it as short as possible.

"So, basically," I wrapped up, "he expects us to share blood tonight and he wants a diary date for me to join him in the lovely world of crazy vampire craziness. Neither of which is going to happen so…" I trailed off. "So, tonight is pre-ordained to be a complete buggering disaster."

Peter didn't say anything for a while. Then he looked up at me.

"Take off your top," he said quietly.

I stripped it off and sat there in my jeans and bra. The outline of Oscar's hands was written in green and black on my wrists. My upper arm was worse, swollen into red and purple whorls. Peter put his head into his hands and said nothing for a while.

"I could kill him," he said into them eventually. "And you know what makes it even worse? Oscar's not much of a healer, but he could have taken the edge off this. And he didn't even try. He just left you like this all day. I could stake him."

"Hey," I said, patting his arm. "They're just bruises."

He shook his head.

"But he could have eased them," he protested. "And Toni, I'd be less bothered about him bugging you for an ascension date, because he's always on at me about that. But blood sharing—this is what I've been reading about today, the records I went through in the Stone House vaults. And I don't think you *can* give him your blood, even if you wanted to."

"What?"

"I know a lot of things I didn't know yesterday. When a vampire feeds, they crash through any resistance you have to their powers, and instead of the pain of having a hole gnawed in your neck, you experience all the bliss they feel when they feed. It's quite unconscious and uncontrolled, but it's also very powerful. So even a weak vampire will be able to overwhelm a strong human and make the taking of blood extremely pleasurable."

"Ugh."

"You always say that. And here's the thing—it's an extension of their compelling powers that allows them to break through."

"Compelling powers that I am immune to."

"Ja. The very same."

"So it doesn't work on me because I am a necromancer?"

"Ganz recht. Exactly. Oscar could certainly feed on you—but I doubt he could make it anything other than an extremely painful and unpleasant pastime."

"No vampire boyfriends for Toni, then."

"It's not that clear cut, as it happens," he said hesitantly. "There may be a way. I told you before that vampire law mandates the extinction of necromancers; well, I was wrong. It turns out there is one exception. There is a single place in the world where the Assemblage master made necromancers both legal and protected."

"Really? Now I am interested. Where?"

"Staffordshire, Toni. Right here. Sometime rather more than a century ago, Benedict Akil changed the laws of his Assemblage."

I was flabbergasted.

"Why the bloody hell would he do that?"

"It's no secret; his consort for forty years was a necromancer."

"What's a vampire consort when it's at home?"

"It's a formal union between a mortal and a vampire. They are quite unusual."

"I'll tell you what's unusual: Benedict found someone who could put up with him for forty years."

Peter laughed, but my mind was whirling. Benedict had known what I was from day one. Did I give off some sign he could pick up on? He'd known more than one necromancer before me, it now seemed. Maybe he could feel my presence in the same way I could feel the presence of the vampire kind.

"But here's the thing," Peter continued. "He is hardly the restrained type—they must have found a way to share blood for it to work. Maybe he's able to use his powers of attraction. Camilla tells me they are legendary. Or maybe there genuinely is some technique that you and Oscar could learn."

"If I can be bothered to even try."

Peter looked at me across the table. He was suddenly very solemn.

"If, indeed… if you can begin to forgive Oscar for his appalling behaviour of last night. If you can be bothered to try to talk some sense into him about your ascension. If he will ask Benedict how to share blood with you. A lot of ifs, Toni, but right now the first one is the only one that matters."

Peter was a doctor. He healed the sick. Violence sickened him, and I knew he wouldn't blame me whatever I decided. What would be left of our friendship if I left Oscar, I didn't know… But as I reached across the table and took Peter's hand, I realised with a sudden shock which one of them I would mind losing most. And it wasn't Oscar.

"Yes, I could forgive him," I said carefully. "I could, if I felt he really regretted what he had done."

I remembered my brother Wills telling me that Henry's brother had confessed to once hitting his wife. She had forgiven him, but he had never forgiven himself. He said that every time he looked at himself in the mirror, he hated the man he saw there—just a little— for what he had done. I'd done stupid things in my life and regretted them. A lot. I would forgive a repentant Oscar.

Peter squeezed my hand.

"Thank you," he said. "Thank you for giving this a second chance."

"Let's not dwell on it," I said, pouring more tea. "I still need to tell you about Hildred, and time is passing. The sun will set around four and I'm hoping you will put your jugular on the line to put Oscar in a good mood."

"Unlike you, liebling, I look forward to it," he said. "Now tell me what happened today that meant I had to put your new boots into soak."

Peter was a thoughtful listener, and he didn't interrupt. I gave him an abbreviated version of the day's events. I thought it was sufficient for him to know that my assailant had been serious about trying to kill me, not necessarily how very nearly he had managed to pull it off.

"You know what I think, Toni?"

"You think we need to tell Benedict."

"Ja."

"Fine, we'll tackle that afterwards. If necessary, we can draw lots. Now, let me have a bath and some sleep, and I'll come downstairs an hour after sunset?"

"It's a deal."

WHEN YOU DATE a vampire, you catch your sleep when you can. Before I met Oscar, I struggled to sleep in the day. No longer. The sight of a pillow was all it took. Sometimes I would be snoring before my head actually touched the thing, and that evening was no exception. I woke to find the sun had set, the boards Peter had nailed up on my window were not working very well, and that the heavens had deposited another few inches of snow over the county and over a fair proportion of my bedroom.

I pulled on jeans and—on impulse—a tiny strappy top that showed off every inch of bruising on my arms. I failed to brush my hair and stuffed it back into a ponytail. If Oscar wanted to shag someone who knew more about coiffuring than how to spell it, he could date a hairdresser. If the next hour didn't go well, he would be free to do so.

I wandered down the stairs in my bare feet. No one was in evidence, but the door to the cellars was ajar, so I headed into the echoing lower chambers. I hadn't done a lot yet to the basement levels of the house apart from having them cleaned and damp-proofed. So far, I'd installed some massive heaters and a safe area for Oscar to spend the day. But the cellars had stood the test of time and didn't need a lot doing to them.

In the main chamber I heard male laughter, and when I walked in, I saw Oscar was sparring with one of the other vampires from the Assemblage. I rather thought his name was Aidan, and he'd seemed down to earth and even quite shy on the one occasion I'd spoken to him. I got the impression he'd taken over as head of security in the years that Oscar had been in Germany and was very glad to step down again. At any rate, I'd quite liked him, which was more than I could say about most of the other members of the undead brigade that I had met, though that wasn't actually saying a lot.

What had occasioned the laughter, I wasn't sure. Aidan was completely outclassed and Peter, leaning casually against the far wall, was calling unhelpful advice.

"That's it, Aidan, bite his kneecaps off," he said cheerfully as an easy blow from Oscar bowled Aidan right over and onto his back. "Go for the toes."

Oscar threw his head back and laughed and I stood in the doorway watching him. He was still the most beautiful man I'd ever met, and standing there laughing, with no shirt on and sweat sheening his torso, he took my breath away. His gold hair caught the light and his blue eyes, the shocking blue that vampire eyes always are, were sparkling with laughter. He saw me standing watching him and stopped. He held out a hand to Aidan and helped him to his feet.

"And I fear we must stop there," he said good-naturedly. "We can have a rematch tomorrow should you wish."

Aidan shook his head.

"Well, we can," he said, "but I doubt the outcome would be any different."

"Peter," I said hastily, "can you speak with Aidan before he goes? Tell him about Hildred?"

"Of course," said Peter. "Aidan, I'll walk with you to the gate."

I watched them head up the stairs together. When they were out of sight, I turned back to Oscar. I wasn't holding out a lot of hope for our evening. He hadn't seemed pleased to see me.

"Well," I said a little sadly, "let's get this over with, sweetie."

I headed up the stairs and wandered into the drawing room. The fire was burning merrily and through the windows I could see the snow falling thickly and heavily again. If Oscar hadn't been such an enormous pain in the arse, I would just have opened a bottle of wine and we could have had excellent make-up sex on the rug. That was what any couple with a grain of sense between them would have done. But no, not us; I'd had to fall in love with the crazy, blood-obsessed vampire, so instead we were going to have a lovely row about who had rights of access to my jugular.

I sat on the rug by the fire and looked up at Oscar. I held out my wrists; in the firelight the black bruises looked hideous. My upper arm looked worse.

"Are you going to heal me?" I asked gently. "Will you do that?"

He looked at me rather sternly.

"When we've talked," he said. "Not before."

And that's when my heart broke. I almost heard it shatter. I certainly felt it. Oscar wasn't the slightest bit sorry about what he'd done. He still thought it was my fault he'd covered my arms in bruises. As far as he was concerned, I hadn't done what he wanted, so I'd got what I deserved.

"I don't know you," I said. "I'm so stupid."

Oscar sat opposite me on the far edge of the rug. If he'd heard what I said, it meant nothing to him.

"My love," he said. "Are you ready?"

Ready? I just wanted to get up and leave. I was about to break up with the man I'd hoped to spend the rest of my life with. I was going to lose my happily ever after, and Peter with it. I was about to throw it away with both hands and I couldn't see another way. I'd fallen in love with a monumental jerk. Again.

"No," I said. "No, I'm not ready, and Oscar, I doubt I will ever be. I know you don't have the slightest interest in my hobbies, but I like beach holidays and croquet. I even like gardening. And—for what it's worth—I enjoy my job, too, and you are still the only client I have ever had who wanted to view their house at night."

He shook his head dismissively.

"Peter is a doctor," he said, "and I accept that he will struggle to practice after his transition. So, I am prepared to wait. But Toni, you are an estate agent. The world hardly needs more estate agents. I won't wait for that."

I bridled at the dismissive tone in his voice. Had I really been so in love that I never noticed the lack of respect? I'd saved Oscar's life when he was chained up in silver manacles about to make the world's first undead snuff movie. Had he forgotten?

"You're an arrogant arse," I said. "I would have given you the rest of my life, but I'm buggered if I'm going to give up my mortality for your convenience."

He reeled in shock.

"Are you mad?" His voice was full of confusion and anger. "I have given you everything. You could have no more considerate lovers than Peter and me. And you are affiliated with the two most powerful Assemblages in Europe."

"You're hopeless," I said. "I only ever wanted you. And I always loved you in spite of you being a vampire, not because of it. Are you going to heal me?"

"No!"

"I didn't think so. Oscar Wolsey, I love you more than I thought it was possible to love someone. But you're the worst boyfriend ever and I never want to see you again. I'm leaving now, even if I have to walk home in the snow. Sod you and your bloodsucking Assemblages."

I made as if to stand up again, but he caught me, this time by my ponytail, which I hate.

"No," he said, almost thoughtfully. "You're maddening. Each time I think I have you, you slip away. But you're mine. And if I can't have you no one will."

He pulled back on my hair, exposing my neck.

"Let me go, you undead creep. I hate you and I never want to see you again!"

I didn't see his fist coming. I only knew it was his right one because it hit the right side of my head. Vampires can punch through brick. My fragile little mortal cranium didn't stand a chance.

There was the sound of a million eggshells breaking. Or perhaps all the china plates ever fired in the Five Towns. And then blackness. More blackness than I realised had ever existed or ever would. It swallowed me up.

Chapter Seven

My GREAT-GREAT-GRANDFATHER Ignatius Windsor was renowned as the most powerful necromancer in our family. Since he was the only one of my predecessors to keep any kind of written record of his hobby, it was hard for me to make much of a comparison. But he thought enough of his abilities to summon more than the dead from their graves. He was happy to summon the denizens of Lucifer from their circles of Hades and bargain with them. He summoned demons.

Mostly he summoned the same one. Azazel claimed to be a fallen angel, cast into Hell for giving gifts to mortals. I'd heard him swear blind that he only wanted to do enough good deeds in the world to merit entry back into Heaven. But demons lie all the time—they only have to tell the truth in a contract written in blood—so it was anyone's guess if he meant a word he said. I didn't like him, and I didn't trust him. I'd never tried to cut a deal with him either—I'd never wanted anything badly enough to risk the consequences.

There are so many bases to cover… Just suppose you bargain for money. The next day, your best friend in the world dies and leaves you everything they possessed. How do you feel? Fancy a shopping spree? Didn't think so…

Or suppose, like those foolish ancient Greeks, you bargain for love that's been stubbornly unrequited, only to find that your beloved, once enamoured of you, has a jealous streak a mile wide and kills your family, your dog, your cat and your hamster so that nothing can get in the way of your grand passion. How's true love working out for you now? Not quite what you wanted?

That's why contracts with demons have to be so long and convoluted. They are full of more disclaimers than a double-glazing guarantee.

For the first time in my life, I was tempted to draw one up myself. I wasn't sure what painstaking sub-clauses it would need to make it watertight, but the main thrust would be simple enough: if I made it through this, I never, ever wanted to see another vampire again as long as I lived.

"Haven't you given her enough?"

The words drifted into my ears from a long way away. I thought it was a woman speaking. I couldn't work out if I knew her. I couldn't work out a lot. I was somewhere warm and soft, but my limbs had turned to lead, and my eyes didn't work, let alone my power of speech.

The second was a deep voice, a man's, vexed and impatient: "How the bloody hell should I know? There isn't a textbook for this, Grace."

"I've never seen you so angry."

"Christ all bloody mighty, don't tell me. I waited a century for her, and then Oscar sodding Wolsey not only steals her out from under my nose, he almost kills her. I nearly had him staked out in the rising sun. I may yet do so."

I thought I recognised the second voice, but I couldn't be sure, and then the blackness came back and took everything away again.

Later I re-emerged in the warm, soft place, but I still couldn't remember how to wake up or open my eyes. There was a taste in my mouth like salted caramel and hot cognac, the most exquisite thing I had ever tasted. I wanted to ask for more, but my lips still hadn't worked out how to form words.

"Nein. Please don't send me away. Let me stay with her."

A different voice, a man's gentle tones, a soft, slight European accent... This voice I surely knew? This was the voice of someone I loved, someone dear and special. I couldn't remember their name, but they sounded sad and lost and I wanted to reach out and hold their hand.

"I'm not sending you away," the deep voice replied. "I'm sending Oscar away because if I have to hear him explain one more time why none of this is his fault, I really will kill him. And I'm sending you with him in the faint hope that you'll keep him out of trouble. Could you try to do that for me?"

The blackness came again, but less dense and overwhelming than before. I was sick of it by then, and began to shred my way through, pulling free of curtains of dark stickiness, heavy and smothering. When I finally emerged, I felt trails of it fall away behind me into the empty depths. The last cloying coils slipped free... and I woke.

I was in a bed that made the term king-sized sound modest. It was piled with deliciously soft pillows. An eiderdown of awesome fluffiness had been topped with a diaphanous panel of brushed silk, forest green and embroidered with dragons and other, stranger mythical creatures.

The room's owner liked mirrors. A lot. The stone walls were covered with them, broken up by curtains in the same pleasing green. There was even a mirror on the ceiling above the bed. Hang on, I'd lain here once before... I realised in shock where I was. I was in Benedict Akil's bedroom. Worse than that, I was in Benedict Akil's bed. And I was naked.

I sat up in a rush. Stripping the cover off the bed I wrapped it under my arms like a beach sarong. I stood up and walked towards the main room, trailing acres of green silk. And at that exact moment, Benedict himself came out of the bathroom.

He was clearly halfway through getting dressed. He'd got as far as a pair of black jeans and low leather boots, but he was bare-chested and casually squeezing water out of his hair with a towel. I was taken aback not just by his sudden appearance but also by his sheer physical appeal: I'd never seen a man so nicely put together.

His skin wasn't as dark as Henry Lake's, but it was oak coloured and disconcertingly perfect. And there was a lot of it. It's easy to miss how well built a man is when they are wearing a shirt. Benedict was extremely well built. As I stared, a drop of water escaped from a tendril of his wet, black hair and crept down his sculpted chest. I watched quite involuntarily as it made its way across his six pack and finally dissipated in a thin line of dark hair that began a little below his belly button and disappeared into the waistband of his jeans.

I realised in horror where my eyes were dwelling and hastily brought them up to Benedict's face, but it was much too late. He was watching me intently. Far from his usual inscrutable demeanour, he looked quite delighted to find me ogling his crotch.

"How unexpected," he said gently. "And how flattering. Did you want me to take anything else off?"

"Christ, no," I said. "In fact, you should put a shirt on."

He laughed.

"I didn't expect you to wake today," he said, wandering past me to the main room, towelling water out of his hair.

"How long have I been here?" I asked, following him through by dint of dragging about four yards of embroidered dragons behind me.

Benedict tossed the towel onto a sofa. There was a shirt lying on the back of it, immaculately ironed linen in a dark wine colour. He pulled it on and began to button it up unselfconsciously.

"Six days," he said. "And if Peter had been less competent as a doctor or a driver, you wouldn't be here at all. And just in case you're worried about running into him around the Assemblage, I've sent your precious Oscar away to stew at an Assemblage in Wales for a few weeks while I decide what to do with him... I'm still favouring a nice sharp stake."

I looked up at him and bit my lip. He'd warned me about Oscar, and I hadn't listened. He'd even tried to bribe me to leave the man and I'd told him love would make everything work out. So far, he hadn't uttered the words 'I told you so'—for which I was grateful—

but he must have been thinking them.

"I need some clothes," I said.

"There are some by the bed," he said. "Camilla put them there."

There was indeed a neat pile that I had missed. There was also a generous plate of sandwiches. I grabbed both and locked myself in the bathroom. I stuffed my face, splashed water around and pulled on jeans and my cream winter boots, miraculously bloodstain free. There was a fitted black camisole top that I didn't recognise and a low-necked cashmere jumper, also black. They still had tags on, which I tugged off.

When I emerged, Benedict was sprawled on the sofa by the fire, gazing into the flames.

"Come here," he said, in his usual autocratic way, without turning to look at me.

There didn't seem to be a lot of point in arguing so I sat next to him at the farthest end of the sofa. He gazed into the fire for a while. Then he turned and eyed me thoughtfully.

"Two things," he said. "One: do you still love him?"

I shrugged and looked down at my hands.

"The person I love never existed," I said. "I invented them in my head."

He put a burningly hot hand under my chin and very softly brought my gaze back up to his. He was back to his normal self, and I hadn't a clue what he was thinking.

"Two," he said. "Will you go back to him?"

I rolled my eyes.

"Please," I said. "I'm soft-hearted and have terrible taste in men but I'm not actually stupid. I also quite like not being dead."

He let me go.

"That will do for now. My dear, I have to feed. We will talk another time."

He made as if to stand and I put a hand on his arm.

"Wait," I heard myself say, "you can drink my blood."

Where the hell had that come from? Even Benedict the inscrutable looked startled for a moment. Then he laughed.

"I see," he said. "Are we trying to draw a very broad line in the sand here?"

"We might be."

"Hmmm. And does it have the words 'Fuck you Oscar' inscribed beneath it, by any chance?"

"I guess," I admitted. "Do you mind?"

"Not at all," he said. "I just like to know where I stand. But this is all somewhat academic, isn't it? You must know that I can't drink your blood."

"No?"

"Let me revise that earlier comment. I can certainly hold you down and suck the stuff out of you while you scream and thrash and beg me to stop. But if you think that's my idea of a relaxing breakfast, you very much mistake the matter."

"Peter thought you could use your powers of attraction to make it work."

"My 'powers of attraction.' Dear Peter, he has such a lovely turn of phrase. Well, I can seduce you and drink your blood while we make love, certainly, but I very much doubt that was what you had in mind either."

Most certainly not. Benedict might be more scenic than I'd first thought, but he was still an arrogant, bloodthirsty tyrant who killed people when he was bored and played mind games so Machiavellian you never noticed they'd started until you lost. He was the last person in the world I planned to shag. I did, however, want my loathsome ex to know that the precious gift I'd been denying him for so long had gone to someone else... who happened to be his boss.

"Is that what it would take?" I asked carefully, looking into the flames of the fire rather than at his face.

"It would require some intimacy," he said.

He was right that I wanted some way of formalising the end of my relationship with Oscar. I couldn't think of anything more concrete than letting another vampire drink my blood. It would also be the biggest slap in the face for my ex that I could possibly imagine for me to select his boss, and I wasn't above a little petty revenge. But there was a limit to how far I would go for it, and that limit fell a long, long way short of sex with Benedict. Still…

"Could you seduce me just enough to drink my blood?" I asked.

"You are serious about this?"

"Yes."

"Very well."

He brought his lips towards mine, and I turned my face away.

"Ugh, don't kiss me!"

He burst out laughing.

"You are like the most expensive of courtesans—everything except a kiss. My dear, my lips will have to meet your neck at some point, you know. I wasn't planning on taking my breakfast through a straw. And if I was going to extract it with a hypodermic, we wouldn't have to go through this at all."

I squirmed awkwardly on the sofa.

"Oh, forget it," I said.

"No, I like a challenge. What are you willing to give me?"

I thought about it.

"I don't want to kiss you," I said eventually. "And I certainly don't want to take off my clothes."

He looked at me in some amusement; I was clad in jeans, boots and a long-sleeved cashmere winter jumper.

"I see," he said. "Meet me halfway and take off that top."

I peeled it off and dropped it on the floor. I felt more exposed than I was comfortable with in the little camisole I'd put on underneath.

"Happy?" I asked.

"Oh yes," he said. "You have no idea."

I don't know what I had expected, but for a while he just looked at me. Was he reading my mind, finding my weak spots?

"Do you even know what I am going to do?" he asked suddenly.

I shook my head.

"I have no idea."

He moved to sit on the rug in front of the fire and pulled me down next to him. He began to stroke my hair, running his fingers through it slowly.

"I am going to pull down the barriers between us," he said, "very gently and one by one, my own as well as yours." One arm circled my torso, his hand supporting my head as he lowered me down to the rug. "And when they are all gone, I will be able to give you all the pleasure that I feel. Do you understand?"

"No."

"You will."

It was a promise.

He didn't kiss me, and he didn't undress me. But then, he didn't need to. He had magic hands, and he knew it. His fingers traced little patterns in the soft sensitive skin where my hair met my temples. Just that was enough to make me gasp. They followed the line to the nape of my neck which I suddenly realised was an erogenous zone more vulnerable than I could have imagined. They danced across my shoulders and down my upper arms and played gently in the creases of my elbows, and my breath quickened. I could feel sweat on my upper lip and all he'd done was touch me.

And I felt it as he peeled down my resistances. It was intimate, as he had said, like having someone slide off your last piece of lingerie with their teeth, over and over again.

His fingers glided down my wrists and across my palms, exploring the sensitive gullies between my fingers. His touch was starting to burn with more than sheer heat. My last resistance was holding, a thin little paper wall that defied him. But it never really stood a chance. He brought one of my hands up to his mouth. He folded his hot lips over my fingertips, one by one, sucking them inside and letting the razor sharpness of his teeth graze the wet skin. He began to trace the lifeline of my palm with his tongue. I gazed at him, too paralysed with desire to protest as he undid the first few buttons of his own shirt. He pressed the moistened palm of my hand to the warm, muscled skin of his chest and the last barricade between us crumbled. I could feel his own desire flood into me. I felt his blood rise for me, a column of incandescent lust that burned so fiercely that I thought my hair would catch fire.

He brought his lips to my neck, and I turned my head so that the skin was stretched tight under his teeth.

"Stay with me," he said.

And he bit.

A wall of pleasure hit me like the tide and dragged me under. If there was pain, I couldn't feel it. If this was what vampires felt when they fed, it was worth dying for. Zealots wandered the desert and never found ecstasy like this. Skydivers would fall to their death and never feel this rush. My hair might not have caught fire, but every other part of my body was in flames. The sensation didn't peak and ebb, it just tore through me and carried me along, building into a white-hot world of molten bliss that I never wanted to leave.

I could hear my own voice through the haze of contentment. It was telling Benedict all the things I wanted him to do to me. The list was long. And explicit. Some of the items were fantasies I hadn't even shared with myself. For some he would need props. For a couple, he would have to phone a friend.

When I finally began to regain sentience, I realised I was lying on my back by the fire. Benedict was holding my wrists above my head in one hand. He had propped himself up with the other elbow, pinning me to the ground with the weight of his body. His lips were in my neck, but no longer really feeding. The sensation was not unlike being given a seriously intensive love bite by someone quite determined the whole geography class will know you made out last night. It was, however, about a million times more pleasurable and when he began to trace the line of my vein with his tongue, it nearly threw me straight back into the land of sobbing orgasms.

He eventually pulled his mouth away and buried his face in my hair. For a moment I felt his eyelashes on my cheek. I could still feel all his emotions mixed in with mine. I'd thought to find him feeling victorious or triumphant at having drunk my blood, but all I could sense was thick post-coital satisfaction and a very real delight at my response to him. Either that or he was a lot better at hiding his emotions than I was, which seemed more likely.

"I'm going to let you go now," he said.

I had no idea what he meant, but when he released my wrists and sat up, I gasped out loud.

"Oh my God."

I hadn't just removed his shirt—I'd almost torn it in half. It was ripped across the back so that on one side it hung open almost to his waist. And where I'd exposed his shoulder and chest, I'd given him the most impressive track of love bites I'd ever seen. Correction. They were real bites. With real tooth marks. I'd broken the skin in more than one place and blood was oozing out onto his skin. I licked my lips and tasted it again—that salty-sweet cognac taste I remembered.

"You are always unexpected," he said, trailing a finger in his own blood and then holding it to my lips.

It should have made me gag, but I was still too enmeshed with his own feelings and responses to find it repulsive. Instead, I licked off the blood and he traced the outline of my lips with his warm wet fingertip. That was all it took. My treacherous body tipped me straight back into climax, and he rather hastily caught my hands in his and held them against my chest as I rocked beneath him.

When I was done, he let me go again and lay on his side watching me. It bothered me that I could still feel his own responses mixed up in mine, but when I tried to sever the connection, I felt a sharp pain in my chest and Benedict locked his hands over mine again.

"Don't try to pull out too quickly," he said. "It will hurt. Let everything disentangle gently and your barriers will go back up on their own."

He was right. I forced myself to relax and gradually felt his emotions begin to fall away from mine. I'd never really appreciated the necromantic defences I erected against the undead, but now that I knew where to look, I could feel them re-establishing themselves. I lay back and let it happen.

Rather to my surprise, Benedict stroked my hair. It was quite the nicest thing I'd ever known him to do. It was, in fact, the only nice thing I'd ever known him do, so I just watched as he wound a fat orange ringlet around his fingers. He twined it with one of his own, making a coil of black and red. The sight of his long, elegant hands made me recall all the things I'd just asked him to do to me with them, and I felt myself blush.

He looked in the direction of my gaze and laughed, and I knew he'd guessed exactly what I was thinking.

"Quite so, my dear. I wish you meant a single one of the things you just said to me, but as you don't, I'm going to take another shower. If you change your mind, you are welcome to join me, and I will take the rest of the night off."

He stood up. He needed a shower. He was covered in smears of blood, and I thought most of it was his. He was also covered in a fair pattern of bloody fingerprints, too, and I rather thought those might be mine. When I saw how low they went, I closed my eyes and winced. He'd need to change his jeans as well. And, unless he went commando, his underwear, too.

"Is it always like that when you feed?" I asked.

"Good God, you have a very inflated idea of the calibre of my social life," he said brusquely. "If it was like that every time, I'd never leave the bedroom. Don't go anywhere."

I didn't have the energy anyway. I listened to the sound of water from the bathroom. I eventually found the willpower to take off the bloodstained camisole and put the cashmere jumper back on. I'd made it as far as the sofa by the time Benedict re-emerged from the bedroom.

He was wearing a clean version of exactly what he'd worn before. He was as unreadable as ever. The intimacy of the past hour might never have happened.

"I'll tell Aidan to take you home," he said shortly. "Tonight is complicated. I need to speak with you, but it can wait. Come through to the hall and find him when you're ready."

"Why was I in your room anyway?" I asked, hauling myself to my feet.

He shrugged.

"I didn't know where else to put you," he said. "Even I could see it would be a little insensitive to put you in Oscar's room."

I finally asked the question that mattered; I had to know before he left me.

"Benedict, where is Peter?"

He looked at me intently.

"My dear, I sent him with Oscar. It seemed for the best."

I sat down again. My feet wouldn't carry me. It hurt, but I could bear the loss of Oscar; I couldn't bear the loss of Peter. I put my face in my hands.

"He's gone and I never told him how I felt," I said.

"Did you know?"

"Not until now."

"None of us treated you well," he said. "Poor Toni."

"You warned me."

"Well, perhaps I should have tried harder. Goodbye, my dear."

And he left me to my own thoughts. They weren't very profound.

Chapter Eight

LIFE HAD TAUGHT me that there wasn't a lot of point in sitting around feeling sorry for yourself. It's a pastime that will earn you exactly zilch unless cramp or pins and needles are your thing. They weren't mine, so after splashing a bit more water around in the bathroom, I wandered out into the corridor. I could have sat by the fireside and cried my eyes out, but I planned to do that in my own house, close by my own drinks cabinet and my own box of tissues.

I also didn't want the vampire community to see me roaming around their halls with red swollen eyes and a tearstained face. They had a lot in common with a pack of rabid dogs from what I could tell. Best not to show weakness.

I had last visited the Assemblage some months before, but I vaguely remembered the layout. In the hallway of the rather modest stone mansion, a spiral staircase led down to the labyrinthian tunnels and caves beneath. A broad main passageway led through the Gallery. Half cavern, half ballroom, it was the most mesmerising space I had ever seen. Much of its appeal was tainted by it generally being full of vampires.

Benedict's rooms were at the end of a twisting corridor that also opened off the main passageway. I realised I had no idea whether he had meant me to look for Aidan in the Gallery or in the ground level hall of the main house. I was reluctant to wander into a room full of vampires when I could possibly avoid it, so I decided to look for Aidan upstairs first.

I was feeling astonishingly well for someone who had spent the last few days in a coma—one of the very few benefits of hanging around with vampires was their healing power, and I knew that I would have tremendous energy, not to mention amazing night vision—for days to come. Letting Benedict drink my blood had also burned off the uncomfortable froth of necromantic energy that would normally have sent me scurrying to the nearest graveyard. Disturbingly, I could still feel my bond with him, though it had faded to a whisper of its strength. For a moment I saw the cavern through his eyes, a flash of Grace's smile, the flicker of torches. It was uncanny and the connection couldn't snap too soon for my liking. Benedict was the last person I wanted to give free rein of my headspace. I shook my head and pushed the vision back and hastened on my way.

I had made it as far as the base of the spiral stairs when I heard footsteps coming down them towards me. I also felt a hugely powerful vampiric presence approaching that certainly wasn't Aidan. It wasn't anyone I'd ever encountered before, so I shrank into the shadows as best I could and hoped they wouldn't notice me.

It almost worked. He'd walked right past me before he stopped and jerked his head round. He hadn't heard or seen me, I was sure of that—he'd felt me. He stared at me like a hungry dog spotting an unguarded steak.

"My God," he said. "How does he do it? Where did he find you?"

He was a big man, maybe six foot, with short, auburn hair and a thin, hard mouth. He was dusting snow off a long, caped, black vicuna coat that probably cost more than my house. I pressed myself against the wall and glared at him. I didn't attempt to answer because—as per usual with vampires—I didn't have a clue what he was talking about.

"This time I will get it right," he said. "This time, I won't share you with my brother."

"Too bloody right," I responded, my tolerance for rhetorical vampire crap being very low. "I am not your sodding sharing platter, you undead freak. Now let me past."

But vampires are so insanely fast, and I almost didn't see him move as he threw himself onto me. A hand was clamped over my mouth with expert precision and try as I might, I couldn't get my teeth into it. I was tossed up into his arms, my face muffled in layers of coat, and I lost my bearings as he carried me swiftly along. I felt us descend more stairs and turn corners, but I knew from failing to find my way around before that the caverns beneath the Stone House were vast and complicated. I hadn't a clue where we were in moments. Then I felt him shift my weight in his arms as he opened a door, and I was thrust unceremoniously onto the floor.

I blinked and looked around me. The room was not unlike a small, plain version of the one that Oscar had occupied—a guest room, perhaps? The lower half of the stone walls had been panelled with dark oak and the upper halves brightened with square mirrors. Whitewashed vaulted ceiling panels threw back light from an iron candelabra. Two small fireplaces were burning away, with shiny candlesticks set over their mantelpieces, and it was just as warm as everywhere else. An elegant leather traveling pack reinforced my suspicion that my abductor was just passing through.

"Scream away," he said. "There's only me on this level so no one will hear you."

He stripped off his coat and looked round. One of the sofas was made in the French style, with wings held up by braided ropes. He tugged off the nearest rope and advanced on me. I swallowed. If he managed to tie my hands all would be lost.

I closed my eyes and reached out for him, but I knew instantly that there would be zero chance to fight him with my undead powers. He was ludicrously strong. As he had swept past me in the stairwell, I had felt his power billowing. Up close, it was fearsome. Tied up in silver chains with a couple of stakes sticking out of him I might stand a chance of banishing the man. Here and now? It wasn't going to happen.

And then I felt something else. It was slight but unmistakable: Benedict. I closed my eyes for just a moment, long enough to reach out to him and let him sense my fear and panic. Again, I had a flash of his sight. Someone was speaking to him, but he held out a hand, gesturing them to silence. Might he come? Could he get to me in time? All I needed to do was buy myself some time.

I opened my eyes again.

"Look," I blathered. "You really, really don't want to drink my blood, alright? I have horrible blood. All the vampires say so."

He frowned.

"What are you talking about?" He twirled the rope in his hands. "All blood tastes the same."

"Not mine," I said. "It's all the garlic. I really love snails. And garlic bread. Addicted to them. I have this horrible, manky, garlicky blood."

He threw his head back and laughed. His fangs were long and white. They looked extremely sharp, and I didn't think on this occasion that looks were deceiving.

"Nice try, little girl," he said, taking a step forward.

"And kimchi," I added frantically. "I've been munching it like candy since I was a child. Apparently, it's turned my blood sour. Who knew? Nasty, sour, garlicky blood."

He sneered. Fangs glittered in the candlelight.

"A slug!" I squeaked in desperation. "When I was two years old, apparently I ate a slug. My brother saw it. And I didn't just put it in my mouth and spit it out. Truly, I ate the whole thing. I mean…" I saw his eyebrows raise in consternation and rushed on. "I mean, they say you are what you eat, don't they? That means I'm literally part slug. You don't want to go around drinking slug blood, do you? Seriously. None of the other vampires would talk to you ever again. You'd be shunned! A pariah."

The vampire put his hand up to his face.

"By the living devil, you need to stop talking," he said. "I haven't had a headache since I was slain in battle eight hundred years ago, but I swear on all that's holy I can feel one building."

He reached out an arm. Icy fingers touched my face. The thought that he might bite me made my stomach churn, but I pushed it down. I could feel Benedict—a wash of passionate fury, a rush of air. He'd felt my call and I knew he was coming for me. I just needed to stall my attacker a little longer. I looked round the room hopelessly, but then my eyes fell on the shining candlesticks over the fireplaces. They were silver coloured and shiny. If they were real silver, they would be a mighty weapon against a vampire…

I flung myself past the vampire and towards the nearest fireplace. I was lucky that he had clearly expected me to flee towards the door, and I made it past him, but only just. He seized my arm an instant later, yanking me off my feet, but my fingertips had already closed around the shiny metal base of the candlestick. The candle itself flew wildly across the room as I fell, but I swung the heavy metal base upwards and caught him a glancing blow across his face.

There was a vile, hissing, scorching sound and he let out a howl of anguish and released me. Some sort of smoky ichor sprayed over my skin, and when I looked up at the vampire, it was to see a great black and red welt coursing down his face that looked both burnt and somehow rotten. It really wasn't a good look for him.

Before I could even get to my feet again, his hand struck me in the sternum, and I flew backwards. I tumbled to the floor by the fireplace, the candlestick flying out of my hands and smacking noisily to the floor somewhere. Winded, I pushed myself up on the heels of my hands, shook hair out of my face and glared at him. He was pacing to and fro; he was a man at the end of his tether. He looked hungry.

"I'm under the protection of Benedict Akil," I said, trying to stop my voice shaking. "You should let me go."

The vampire snorted in derision.

"Under his protection! He should have kept you under lock and key. When will they miss you?"

I shook my head. I had no idea. Was Aidan even expecting me? If I was wrong about Benedict, it might be dawn before anyone noticed Lavington Windsor wasn't where she wanted to be. Or ten minutes. Or never.

"Benedict is waiting for me," I hazarded desperately. "He'll come to find me."

If he believed me, I couldn't tell, but he stopped pacing.

"There's no time for anything else," he said. "I'll face the music when you're dead."

I rolled my eyes. Even with my imminent violent death seeming really quite likely at this juncture, the vampire's sheer undiluted machismo needled me.

"Seriously," I said. "Eight hundred years of eternal life and you can't come up with anything more original than that. *Hi, I'm a super strong vampire, and I'm going to kill you. See my amazing fangs and prepare to die screaming.* You know, even Batman and James Bond are evolving. I mean, I'm not suggesting you join the MeToo movement, but could you try something just slightly more nuanced? Supervillains are so 1980s. And, honestly, you don't have the looks for it. You need to have some kind of aura of mysterious power. A bit of a smoulder, maybe. Were you an accountant when you were alive?"

He looked pained.

"You literally never shut up, do you?" he said. "You'll be so agreeably quiet when you're dead."

And with that he hurled himself down next to me and—seizing me by the shoulders—pulled my neck up towards his mouth. There was a flash of fangs and then the hideous smell of scorched, suppurating flesh filled my nose and mouth. It was overwhelming and disgusting and, as he shifted my weight in his arms to bite into me, I threw up on him.

It wasn't quite as impressive as when I'd seen Bella's dead body in the morgue but Camilla had been generous with the sandwiches, so there was plenty to go around, so to speak. He swore and let me flop back to the floor. I managed to roll on to my front to stop myself choking.

"Damnation," he said. "You're as bad as the other one."

I didn't reply immediately—I was busy spitting bile onto the floor—and when I finally looked up it was to see that he had taken off his soiled shirt, exposing a broad, well-pelted chest. And his expression told me I'd definitely run out of time now; it was going to take a great deal more than slugs to save me. With a roar, he dropped to his knees and seized my shoulders again but, before he could bite, the door burst out of its frame with a thunderous crack.

It flew across the room into one of the mirrors, taking out half the candelabra on its trajectory. Shards of glass filled the air, and my skin was splattered with hot wax. The room was thrown into a spinning, flickering half-light. My near-death-induced burst of adrenaline was starting to ebb away, and I felt the room had caught fire and was gyrating around me.

Six-foot-four of Benedict filled the swirling dust of the battered doorframe. I'd never seen him so angry. I'd never seen *anyone* that angry. I could feel his power rolling off him in waves.

"Let her go," he said.

My captor reached down and grabbed the neck of the pretty cashmere jumper that Camilla had so thoughtfully left for me. The soft fabric tore almost in half as he hauled me to my feet and I let out a yelp of protest that he ignored. He held me against him, pressing my back into his bare chest. He had one hand wound in my hair, the other arm clamped across my shoulders and under my chin. I was horribly conscious of my exposed skin.

"I want her," he said. "Give her to me. I'll pay you. Who do you want? I'll give you anyone from my house."

"I said, let her go." It was a white-hot whisper of wrath. "Or I will stake you face-down to the floor, tear out your spine and remove your organs one by one through the gap."

"You can have my consort. I'll give you my sons."

"Did I stutter?"

My captor's grip slackened momentarily, and I leant down and sank my teeth into his wrist as hard as I could. He cursed and released me. I fled his grasp and ran across the room into Benedict's arms. He held me carefully for a moment, and I could feel his hands shaking with rage. Then he stripped off his dark red shirt and helped me into it, buttoning it carefully up almost to my neck. He swung me very easily into his arms and stepped away from the door. I realised that the corridor was full of vampires, and he had been blocking their view of my semi-clad state. I closed my eyes.

"I'll pay you." My auburn-haired kidnapper still hadn't given up. "Whatever you want, I'll pay."

Benedict snorted. It was a sound I hadn't thought I would ever be glad to hear, which only goes to show how wrong you can be.

"You will not touch her, and you will not speak to her," he said quietly. "You will not look at her. Do you hear me? You will not fucking think about her. She is mine and she is staying that way. If you cross me, I will kill you and raze your Assemblage to dust. Are we clear?"

"You couldn't take me on in a fair fight."

"You're in my territory now, Aneurin. There'll be no fair fight. The fairest fight I'll give you is to let you keep your own lips to scream through while I cut off all the other extremities. Aidan, take him to the lowest levels and chain him there. Then come up to my room and tell me how you messed up badly enough to let this happen."

"Yes, sir," I heard Aidan say miserably. "Of course."

I felt the earth dip away from me as it had once before. I felt too nauseous and shaky to care much. Some vampires can travel incredibly swiftly. I got the impression that Benedict could take someone with him. I opened my eyes when he sat me down on the edge of the marble sink bar in his bathroom and tugged off my boots.

He threw them to one side and then walked into the wet room where he turned on every jet that was going.

"Come," he said shortly.

I didn't. I just sat where I was feeling very sorry for myself. He looked at me in exasperation.

"What?" he said.

"I threw up in my hair," I said, tears starting to trickle down my face.

He sighed and took off his own boots. He picked me up again and dumped me on the floor of the wet room. Sitting down beside me, he watched as the hot water soaked us both to the skin, washing away blood, bits of exploded doorframe and other, less savoury, debris from my body. After about ten minutes, when we'd both been thoroughly steam cleaned, he leaned over to me and began to unbutton the shirt he'd dressed me in.

"What the bloody hell do you think you're doing?" I squeaked, shrinking back.

"I'm going to heal you," he said sharply. "Come here."

"Don't you dare undress me!"

"Oh, for God's sake."

He tugged me firmly into his grip. He slid one wet palm under the front of my shirt, and I felt the lovely golden flow of his healing wash over me. When it began to ebb, I jerked out of his hold and scooted away from him.

"Who in hell was that guy anyway?" I asked. "And what does he want with me?"

"His name is Aneurin Blackwood Bordel. He and his brother Isembard rule a somewhat warlike Assemblage in the north of Derbyshire. Yes, I know what you think, my dear, but mine is almost an ashram in comparison. He petitioned me a week or so ago for permission to send someone here. He is seeking a member of his personal coterie who disappeared under somewhat unfortunate circumstances. If I had known he would come himself, I would have taken care that the two of you didn't meet."

I shook my head.

"That's all very well, but why did he want to kill me?"

"He and his brother want their own necromancer. They are labouring under some misconceptions about what it will do for their powers."

"He said that he wouldn't share me with his brother this time."

"Hmmm. I am almost certain that they caught and drained a necromancer between them about six years ago, which would also explain how he came to sense you. I assume they now believe that sharing was the mistake."

"And was it?"

"By no means. If you want to enhance your powers the very last thing you want is a dead necromancer. They are remarkably little use."

He had a point. I couldn't raise myself from the dead...

"Is that why you saved my life?" I asked, narrowing my eyes. "You want me to help you enhance your powers?"

He laughed and stood up. He was soaked through, his hair a mess of wet black ringlets and his sodden jeans clinging to his legs. Once again, they were all he was wearing. I directed my gaze back to floor level. Three near-death experiences in one week should have been enough to slay my libido, but I didn't want to take any chances.

"Being with you is a constant wardrobe change," he said. "My dear, I want you for the sheer delight of it, and I mean to have you. I'll consider anything else a fringe benefit. Now, if you'll excuse me, I'll explore what can be salvaged of this fucking disaster of an evening; sadly, I don't think I get to kill him. I'll tell Camilla to find you something to wear. Again."

Camilla was one of the few people in the Assemblage I had time for. She was as human as I was, a sweet-natured girl with yards of pale blonde hair and blue eyes. I wasn't sure of her choice of life partner—she was in the coterie of a vampire called Grace who I didn't much care for—but Camilla was kindness itself.

She was taller than me, but apart from that we were much of a size. She took me up to her room in the attics of the old house and dug me out jeans that I turned up a couple of times and a fleece that would keep out the cold. I tugged my boots back on, grateful that they hadn't joined me in the shower. She also made me a ham sandwich, which by that time tasted as good as vampire blood.

"I've been feeding your cat, dearest," she said. "He's so fussy."

"Just leave it down long enough and he breaks," I said. "Really. He's just trying it on. He'll eat muesli when he's hungry enough."

"He likes poached salmon."

Did he now...? Well, he could go back to liking kibble and look back on the past week with misty affection.

"I'll bear that in mind," I said. "Is there another sandwich?"

After about half an hour, Aidan joined us. He looked terrible.

"I hate being in charge," he said, sitting on Camilla's bed. "Twenty-two years of crap and then after six months of peace with Oscar back at the helm, I'm back to square one. I'm not excusing him, Toni, just feeling inadequate."

"I don't understand anything," I said morosely.

"Oscar was always head honcho," Aidan said in glum tones. "Of anything to do with security, that is. When he was sent to Germany, I got lumbered with his role and I've been stuck with it ever since. No one in the bloody county was happier to see him come back than me."

I thought about what he'd said; it didn't gel with what Peter had told me.

"I thought he went to Heidelberg to take Peter to be cured by Doktor Lenz?" I said. "Isn't that what happened?"

Aidan shook his head.

"He certainly did that," he said. "But, Toni, I think that was just timing. Lenz was drowning under Eastern European vampire incursions and begged for help. Oscar went there under a very, very expensive secondment. Lenz is still paying Benedict through the teeth."

I cast my mind back to what Peter had said, that Oscar had taken him to Heidelberg and then stayed there to look after him when Peter's mother had died. In retrospect, it did sound an extremely unlikely tale. No matter how endearing Peter might have been as a child, I couldn't see Oscar as paternal. Aidan's story was far more convincing. Still, I also couldn't imagine Oscar bothering to disabuse an infatuated and hero-worshipping Peter of his misinterpretations. Or even being interested enough to notice them...

"You'd better take me home, Aidan," I said. "I have a cat to feed, and Camilla here has been spoiling him for a week."

I promised to return Camilla's clothes and hugged her goodnight. Aidan and I trudged through dirty snow that was halfway to becoming slush to a shiny four-by-four that sneered at the snow on the roads and mocked the sheet ice at the bottom of the Sandon Road.

Halfway home, he asked abruptly: "Does Aneurin think you're a necromancer?"

"Yes."

I could have denied it, but Aidan's job was to protect people—including me. I felt he was entitled to the information.

"And are you?"

"Yup. Do you think everyone knows?"

He shook his head.

"No, I arrived before the rest. I don't think they heard what was said."

I thought of something to ask him.

"Aidan, why would Aneurin think that a necromancer could give him power?"

"It's a natural assumption," he said in surprise. "It's common gossip. Benedict acquired most of his powers in the forty-three years or so he was bound to his consort. Before that, he was powerful but not extraordinary. I wasn't a vampire then, Toni, so I can't tell you much. I ascended in 1919—I'm one of the youngest vampires in the Assemblage."

He pulled the car up and put on the handbrake. I looked up and with a horrid shock, realised that he had driven me back to Lichley. The empty windows stared down at me, a house devoid of Oscar and denuded of Peter. I eyed it with dislike. Oscar's latest stupid car sat in the drive. I wondered if my bedroom window was still boarded up. I wondered if the lawn was still covered in glass. My love for Oscar was crystallising into hate in a much speedier fashion than I had anticipated. I still wished it would get a move on. Self-pity isn't an attractive emotion and I wanted to be done with it.

"I'm really sorry, Aidan. I had no idea you thought I would want to come here. Could you take me back to Colton?"

He looked surprised.

"Sure. I didn't realise you still owned that cottage. Didn't I remove a headless corpse from your lawn last summer?"

He spun the car round on the gravel and headed back through the main road. I watched the windows of my dream home recede behind me. Another thought occurred to me.

"Aidan, why is what Oscar did such a big deal? Why does anyone even care that he hurt me. Don't you vampires kill people all the time?"

"Not in my time," he replied with some surprise, "and certainly not in Staffordshire. Benedict makes the rules here, and about fifty years ago he outlawed the killing of innocent mortals. It's purely self-interest, you know; I think he foresaw the day we'd have to live more in the open. And killing a coterie member—yours or anyone else's—is a capital offence in the county unless they've betrayed the Assemblage."

"Like Diana?" I asked, remembering the dark-haired girl I'd met so briefly, who had died for selling secrets to rival vampires in return for her brother's life.

"Exactly like Diana," he said. "Poor little Diana. I miss her, Toni. I liked her. Listen, I'll come in with you, check everything is OK and safe."

I realised we had pulled up at the kerb outside my house. He followed me up to the porch where I dug out a key from under a pot.

"That's hardly safe," he said accusingly.

I shrugged.

"I don't have a lot of Monets in there right now," I said. "And if anyone wants to nick Winchester, I'll pay them."

He walked through the house—I had no idea what he was checking for, but I didn't really care either. When he was done, I bid him a weary goodbye. As he turned to go, a final thought occurred to me.

"Aidan, what happened about Hildred Rutherford? And the man who attacked me?"

"Oh, that. I forgot, you wouldn't know. She's dead, Toni. I went to the house on Ashbrow Lane straight after I spoke to Peter that night. Her coffin was lying in the yard full of dust. Someone had dragged it up from the icehouse. But I think she was killed before you were ever attacked at the arcade. Snow was covering the coffin, and it started falling late that afternoon, so I think she died just after you left."

Dead? I blinked but it was in surprise and not sadness. I wanted to be sorry at the news, but I couldn't be. Hildred had been a uniquely vile piece of work after her first death so I couldn't even pretend to be cast down by her second. Still, Benedict would probably find some way to blame me for it all.

"What about Melody and Kathy?"

"The house was empty. There wasn't so much as a teabag left behind. We haven't a clue who they really were or the guy. It turns out that the house was rented—they were only there for two weeks, and they never spoke to the neighbours. Melody Whitman gave a false name—there is no Melody Whitman—and she paid for everything in cash, lots of it. Listen, I need to head off. Benedict said to give you this."

It was a mobile number. I stuffed it into a pocket and hoped not to need it. If I had my way, when Aidan drove off down the road it would be the last time I ever saw one of the children of the night. I didn't like the games they played. I didn't understand the rules and I always seemed to be on the losing team.

Chapter Nine

I SAT AT my desk. It looked eerily tidy, especially for a Monday morning. For a while I couldn't work out where everything had gone. Finally, when all sensible options had been exhausted, I checked my filing cabinet. It was uncanny. Abbot, Armitage and Amerton had been filed under A. Benson and Beauvalet were under B. With a sense of dawning wonder, I checked C. Yup. Carmichael, Cadwallader and Cavendish. I was still shaking my head in disbelief when Bernie wandered over. He was wearing a nasty, beige tweed suit and a tie embellished with what looked like nipples. On closer inspection, they turned out to be nipples.

"Glad you're back," he said. "You're not still infectious, are you?"

He put a hand on my thigh. I dug my nails into it, and it vanished somewhere.

"Um, don't think so," I said vaguely, having no idea what excuse Camilla had given him for my extended absence. Had I been sick? And if so, with what? "Don't you stop being infectious when you show symptoms?"

Bernie shrugged vaguely and tugged a nostril hair.

"Thought that was 'flu, but you could be right," he said, leaving me to wonder if I was meant to be convalescing from Ebola. "Anyway, good to have you back. Your work experience student is working out really well."

"My what?"

"Paul," he said. "He's done everyone's filing and reinstalled the accounts software. Oh, and the coffee machine works since he took it apart. I've been paying him cash in hand, so I hope he doesn't need the work for course credits."

"He's meant to be studying," I snapped. "He has A levels to pass this summer."

"He does nothing but study," said Bernie. "I'm doing him a favour. He was hanging around like a spare limb."

"Where is he now, then?"

Bernie waved his arms vaguely, indicating that I was asking questions beyond his ken. I couldn't blame him—I didn't even remember telling Paul where I worked.

"He turns up after school," he said. "And I think Bethany's in love with him, so I don't want to do anything to break her concentration even further."

Our receptionist Bethany wasn't very tuned in at the best of times. She'd come to us straight from school with a glowing reference she'd clearly written herself. We'd let that slide as no one else had applied for the post. She disliked having to answer the phone when her nail varnish was drying. She couldn't spell, and her typing was of the type that made the term 'two-fingered' sound aspirational. God knows what banishing her new-found and possibly unrequited love from the office would do to her work ethic. Bernie had a point.

"I can't see her being Paul's type, to be honest," I said. "He's more the brainy sort. Kind of a geek."

Bernie gave me a look. It informed me that I was really stupid.

"Toni, she's blonde and she has breasts," he said. "No teenage boy is that picky."

Well, that told me.

"Anything else I should know about?"

"Could you sort out a replacement washing machine for Eleanor Johnson's place?" he said. "Paul says hers leaks."

I was realising that I had rather lumbered myself with Paul.

"Sure," I mumbled. "I'll go over to Mr Suki's later."

"Where did you find him, by the way?"

I stared at Bernie. I don't like telling lies but since the day Oscar walked into my pub six months ago, it had become my second career. I really couldn't bring myself to say that I'd met Paul because he was currently the chief suspect in a murder investigation and might be a weed dealer to boot. It wasn't a CV must-have. Unless, of course, Bernie had other hobbies I wasn't aware of. I almost hoped he did—all the ones I knew about were pretty distasteful.

"He goes to my old school," I said. "I'm mentoring him."

There. Almost accurate and nearly true.

It was no hardship to go and see Mr Sukshinder Singh, known to all and sundry as Mr Suki. He was a very gracious Sikh gentleman who sold white goods just off Gaolgate Street, a stone's throw from the prison. He'd built his store up from little more than a kiosk to an echoing warehouse. Behind one-way glass, an efficient little admin team processed orders and despatched engineers and fitters.

I always asked him meticulously about each member of his large and burgeoning family, and as a result I knew their particulars down to the last house move and adopted puppy. He had two daughters and a son. The two girls, one of whom had been in the year above me, had filled their father's heart with joy by becoming a doctor and a lawyer.

The son, Suki Junior, had shunned a conventional education. I remember Mr Suki throwing his hands in the air when my grandfather and I came in for a new freezer once.

"Why can't he just become a doctor? Or a lawyer? Or a doctor?" he'd wailed. "But he must go breaking his parents' hearts. When I was a boy, you didn't wander round 'finding your own path,' I tell you. You got qualified and made your mother happy."

Suki Junior had become a bond trader and then a hedge fund manager. He'd sold out for nearly eight figures two years ago. Mr Suki Senior didn't complain about career paths anymore.

Still—proof that money can't buy you happiness—I knew that Suki Junior hadn't had an easy life. He'd married a lovely Russian lady and adopted her two daughters about the time I graduated from college. Tragically, she died shortly afterwards in a boating accident. He hadn't married again, and I was also uneasily aware that Mr Suki had been eying me up as replacement daughter-in-law material for a while. I'd an inkling that he was trying to work out how childbearing my hips might be.

It's nice to be wanted, but I didn't think Suki Junior and I had a lot in common. He had a yacht. I had a second-hand cat. I let his dad sell me a washing machine and make me some tea.

"So, little Toni," Mr Suki said, placing a plate of chocolate digestives at my elbow, "how is your love life? Have you found a good man to marry yet?"

I looked at Mr Suki a little forlornly. He always asked me this question, and it was kindly meant. On the one hand, if I said yes, he would be happy for me; in his mind, a single woman was a loose end waiting to be tied in a bridal bow. On the other, if I said no, I was still available for Junior to snap up. I was a nice Staffordshire lass who would probably deter his son from succumbing to the bright lights of Birmingham. Or London. Or New York and Monaco.

But this time the question touched every nerve going. It was the first time anyone had asked about my attachment status since it had changed back to perilously single. Still, if it hadn't been Mr Suki, it would have been my best friend Claire. Or my brother. It was good to have a low-profile rehearsal.

"I'm as single as a single thing, Mr Suki," I said with feigned cheerfulness. "Who knows how I scare them all away? I used to think it was natural talent, but these days I've also had a lot of practice."

I tried to look nonchalant, but Mr Suki had been around the block. He probably built the block. He patted my arm paternally.

"You're a nice girl, little Toni," he said. "You know, my son Junior is a nice boy. And so lonely…"

Sure he was. And his yacht was staffed by eunuchs and all the champagne was flat. Still, as I said, it's nice to be wanted. Even by proxy.

"I'm sure he is, Mr Suki," I said. "You set it up. I'll put on a dress."

To be polite, I ate all the chocolate digestives before I left.

I got back to an office containing a receptionist who had decided that acid green nails were so last week and was redoing them in lime. It also sported a boss who was bored enough to upgrade his usual thigh grope in a breastward direction while I was making us both tea. He got a slap for his troubles but took it in good part.

"No one wants to buy property in this weather," he said, rubbing his reddening cheek. "We should take this month off each year. I pay you to sit here and email your girlfriends pictures of what you plan to wear on Friday night."

On a whim I rang my brother. Wills and I didn't live in each other's pockets, but we chatted on the phone often enough. He was an affectionate elder brother, and the passage of time had made the four-year age gap between us less of a divide.

To my surprise, he picked up on the second ring.

"Hey, Toni. You better?"

"I am, completely," I said hastily, making a mental note once again to ask Camilla what the hell she'd told everyone I was sick with. "Bright as a button."

"Come and meet Henry and me for lunch," he said. "It's my day off and we're just driving to the Fat Fox."

The Fat Fox was a pub that had accidentally hired a chef to cook bar snacks a couple of years back instead of the usual disinterested school leaver. Soon, the bemused landlord found his bar packed to the gunwales at mealtimes as locals thronged there to chow down on Freddy Omaha's raised game pie, venison Wellington and partridge goulash.

My brother and his boyfriend Henry Lake were already seated with a pint when I arrived. Henry's acting career—which had floundered for a while—was currently on the ascent after a supporting role in a swashbuckling blockbuster. Once or twice, breathless fans had asked for his autograph. I asked every time I met him just to watch the man blush. I liked them as a couple.

They both got up and hugged me when I arrived, and Henry ambled off to find me a drink. I sat down and leant my head against my brother's shoulder.

"Good to see you, bro," I said. "How did you even pull a day off in the middle of a murder investigation?"

"Oh, that," he sighed. "I'll tell you while Hen is at the bar, because he's sick of me moaning on about it. I don't have the case anymore, sis. CID took it because they think Bella may be the victim of a serial killer."

"What? Wills, this is Staffordshire. We don't have serial killers here. We have sheep."

"I told them, but they didn't listen, and it's my fault anyway, because what I said to Agnes in the morgue got the idea rolling. Remember—opened my fat mouth and suggested it was a serial killer? There was a girl in Dovedale; she was almost the same age as Bella, and another redhead. She was strangled and found at her school. It happened four months ago. They're looking for a link. We don't even have her body anymore—it's been taken to a lab somewhere to have more forensic tests done."

He took a long swig of his drink. I thought about Bella, and the coincidental timing of her death, her good or bad luck in arriving at the exact time that Mikey had popped to his car for an evening snack… While all the time Paul had been doing who knows what in the school grounds. Swotting for a chemistry test, if you believed him. Did I still believe him? I thought I did, but now I'd never be able to ask Bella if she'd known him. Of course, he swore they'd barely met, and I wanted that to be the truth…

"Don't serial killers plan stuff?" I said. "This was just sheer good luck—or bad luck, if you're Bella. No one could have planned to find a scatty redhead looking for her homework right there and then."

Henry chose that moment to return, bearing my very welcome pint of Badger, so Wills didn't answer. But I knew from his face that he agreed with me. I had a feeling I hadn't heard the last of Bella.

As we sat with our pints, Freddy Omaha came to take orders and stayed to flirt with me. I liked Freddy. I always had. He'd been a year below me at junior school, but hadn't followed me to the grammar. He'd left school at sixteen and become a mechanic, then a waiter and eventually a sous chef. He'd trained at a brasserie in Birmingham for a few years before his roots began to tug at him and he'd come back to the green grass of homely Staffordshire. I thought the flirting was automatic, but this lunchtime I responded with a little more enthusiasm than usual anyway.

Henry noticed even if Wills was oblivious. He cast me a thoughtful look.

"So, petal," he said, "how's tricks?"

"I make a living," I said. "Still got four limbs and two eyes."

"And your incredibly complicated love life?"

"Oh, Henry," I sighed, tears pricking behind my eyelids, "I think that just got catastrophically simpler."

He moved to put an arm round me, and I nestled into it. Henry was a big man; he gave quality, super-sized hugs. I'd been deliberately vague about the minutiae of my relationship—or even relationships—not least because I hadn't begun to work them out myself. At least now I wouldn't have to.

"No more Oscar, then?" he asked, without sounding unhappy about the prospect.

"Nope."

"No more Peter?"

Genuine concern that time. I sniffled.

"Oh, Hen, I don't think so. He's gone, and I don't know if he's coming back."

"Pet, I'm sorry. I liked him," he said, putting a second arm round me. "You want to talk about it?"

"You know, I'd like to talk about anything else."

I SWUNG BY the supermarket on my way home. I was going to have to get used to looking after myself again. I'd let Peter do it for far too many months. I bought the essentials of life—cat food, gin, tonic, lemons—and then frittered round getting those little treats that every jobbing necromancer needs in her kitchen. You know, four loaves of sliced white, two pounds of baked ham and an armful of half-price rotisserie chickens. And, because I hadn't seen Bredon for a while, a few punnets of strawberries and a pint of cream.

I drove home and packed my picnic basket. The sight of Peter's salt cellar made me a little tearful. I considered putting it at the back of a cupboard and pretending to forget about it until I actually did... but it was good at drawing fine lines. I popped it in the wicker hamper along with a bottle of London dry from the freezer and some vermouth. The snow was still eight inches deep—I would find out how Bredon felt about martinis.

It struck me as I walked up the hill that this was something I couldn't have managed a year ago. Carrying a full hamper in half a foot of snow as far as the church would have taken me all night. These days, I could almost scamper it. I couldn't pinpoint the exact change. Maybe it had begun when I had banished Livia and Claudio? It had definitely intensified since Benedict gave me blood. I wasn't going to recommend associating with vampires to my nearest and dearest, but there were fringe benefits. They didn't cancel out people trying to kill you all the time or sink their fangs into your neck on a recreational basis, but they were definitely there.

I reached the cemetery without breaking a sweat. As the weather cooled from summer into autumn, and finally into a damn inclement winter, I'd had to up my game on the picnic front. Bredon might not feel the cold, but I bloody well did. I'd started with breaking and entering. I'd selected the mausoleum of Juliana Lambert, beloved bride of Geoffrey, may she rest in peace. I'd partly chosen it because she wasn't there. Several times I'd tried to raise her, but I didn't even get an empty revenant. I doubted she'd ever been laid to rest here. Whatever the words carved in stone had to say, I thought they lied. There might be the ancient corpse of a dead bride interred here, but if so, her name wasn't Julia Lambert.

Very occasionally, I caught a hint of a presence, but it was strange somehow. I got a feeling of dislocation that was just different from any other grave I'd encountered before. I disliked not knowing what was going on, especially something unearthly involving the souls of the dead, so—with the maturity and good sense of a woman in charge of her life and determined to plan for her best future—I ignored it and pretended it didn't exist.

Inside the mausoleum was a chamber about nine foot square, with a slightly domed ceiling. Denuded of giant spiders and filled with rugs, cushions and candles, it made an agreeable venue for winter picnicking. There was also a tripod with a small, fixed telescope to aid the amateur astronomer; Bredon liked stars. I brushed away a week's worth of webs, lit every wick going, laid out the evening's feast and went to summon my dinner guest back from the dead.

I have to raise the dead. It's a compulsion—an addiction, if you like. I get restless and unhappy if I miss a night. Two would be unbearable. I would end up accidentally raising the Sunday roast and—believe me—that never makes for a relaxing meal. Summoning the bodies of animals is a bad idea full stop. They have no souls, so you don't need a name, but all you're raising is the empty body. And what you inevitably get alongside is hunger, rage and—if you are very unlucky—small demons. It's a pastime that's best avoided, so I spent my evenings wandering the graveyards of Staffordshire, honing my craft.

Once or twice a week, though, I treated myself. I raised Bredon for a night. He was the only zombie who remembered me, the only one of the hundreds—no, thousands—that I summoned who had any recollection of his undead existence. He was also completely lovely and had saved my life more than once. I thought of him as one of my dearest friends.

When I'd lit the last candle, laid out the final canapé and buried the gin in the snow, I walked to his grave through the white and silver Christmas scene. Crouching down, I pushed my cold hands through the snow to the stiff, frozen blades of grass buried beneath.

"Bredon," I whispered softly into the frosty air, my breath misting the night. "Bredon Havers, I summon you. Come to me."

Oscar always looked like a girl's romantic dream, while Benedict was the epitome of the bad boy your mother warned you against. But Bredon looked like a hero. Dark curly hair was set above big, laughing brown eyes and a smile that I found hard not to return. As always, he was wearing a rather lovely long coat embroidered with multi-coloured peacocks. His sword hung from an ornate belt. He could whirl it like a skipping rope; I could lift it given two hands and a strong motive.

He stepped out of the earth without a ripple. The snow around him lay smooth as milk.

"My dear Mistress Lavington," he said. "Dear heart, it snowed! I love England in the snow."

He took my hand and kissed it very elegantly. I let him finish—a little old-fashioned chivalry shouldn't be sniffed at—but when he was done, I stepped in and gave him a hug.

"Bredon," I said. "I've missed you."

"Beloved," he said again, "I also. But has much time passed?"

"A whole week," I said. "Come into the tomb, it's freezing."

We made our way down and he beamed at the spread I had prepared.

"My wonderful hostess," he said, "where should I sit?"

I laughed and pointed to his usual cushion. The stone casket—either empty or the resting place of the unknown, held a bottle of (cut-price) champagne and a pair of crystal saucers.

I was careful to maintain an air of casual contentment, but we both knew Bredon needed to eat right away. The undead awake in screaming hunger—if I didn't assuage it swiftly, our evening would rapidly become uncivilised. My grandfather would be shocked even to find me raising anyone without a circle of protection. I reckoned that Bredon and I had been friends long enough for me to break a few rules.

"Try these," I said, carefully offhand.

I presented him with a plate of sandwiches. It was a generous plate; on it lay the bastard offspring of two loaves of bread, a pound of ham and a block of cheddar. Bredon mainlined the whole lot in the time it took me to open the champagne and pour two glasses.

"So," he said, draining his glass, "how fares the world of the living? Your romance proceeds well?"

"Oh, Bredon," I sighed. "That was so the wrong question. It's a total disaster. I'm single and heartbroken. I thought he was the one, but he was totally the wrong one."

He took my hands in his and squeezed them affectionately.

"My very dear young lady, my heart is heavy for you," he said. "I know too well the pain of lost love."

"Tell me, Bredon. Maybe I'll stop feeling sorry for myself."

I poured him another saucer of champagne and added a teaspoon to my own glass while he disposed of a whole chicken. He arrayed himself on the cushions.

"So long ago," he mused. "I grew up close to here, as you know. My father's estate was small and run down. He was a gambler, and my grandfather before him. My mother had some dowry, but that was soon wasted. By the time I was a boy, the lands were all mortgaged and produced very little in rents. We lived in debt, always owing the servants wages, never paying the tradesmen on time.

"The Marlston estate that rang alongside ours—that was a very different story. Neat tenants' cottages, well-tilled earth, productive tracts of lush green that brought in revenue month after month.

"Squire Brewster held the estate. He'd bought it when the Marlstons fell into debt and fled abroad. He was a gentleman, if not a nobleman, and had just the one child, his daughter Patience. Ah, would that he had sired a dozen, and at least four boys. Then things might have been different. Patience and I grew up together as children. We climbed trees, pulled the feathers out of hens, chased the sheep and stole apples. No one else ever had my heart."

I looked at Bredon telling his story. His eyes told me he was elsewhere, in a summer meadow with his Patience. I pushed another roast chicken in his direction, and he devoured the whole thing, bones and all, remarkably neatly and without apparently noticing.

"Of course I asked for her hand," he continued, "but her father just laughed. He had one daughter, and she would have everything. He intended that his money would tug his descendants one rung further up the social ladder."

"That's horrible," I interrupted. "She was just a chess piece in some stupid game."

"Dear heart, that was the way of the world," he sighed. "I am older than you and, if I have acquired any wisdom in those extra years, I would say that we are all pawns in someone's game."

I narrowed my eyes at Bredon. Older? He looked younger each time I raised him. When he had first come to me, I'd pegged him as a man in his mid-forties, already a decade younger than he had been at his death. And as the months had passed, his appearance had altered. His hair was thicker and more lustrous, his skin less lined and his body both leaner and more muscular.

"What happened?" I asked. "Did he find some upper-class jerk for Patience to marry?"

"He did," Bredon sighed. "A widower, a baronet, with few morals and less charm. She married him and killed herself a year later. I decided that the next time I fell in love, no one would be able to deny me. I worked, I schemed, I traded, and I bartered. Within a decade I was one of the richest men in the county. And all for nothing. I never met another woman I cared for."

"Bredon, that's so sad," I exclaimed. "But what about your wife?"

"She was a gentle and lovely lady," he said. "A widow with four children already. She was gracious enough to let me give her the protection of my name and call her children my own. But the love that burns? That, I never felt again."

He fell silent. I decided that our picnic was taking on an altogether too sombre air.

"Gosh, Bredon," I said a little abruptly, "you open the strawberries while I mix our martinis. I need your advice."

We should really have had them before dinner, but Bredon predated the invention of the martini so I decided a little social solecism wouldn't offend him. I dug the gin bottle out of the snow.

I told him about poor murdered Bella, the complicated timings about when the gate had been open and shut, the secret way into the school that Paul had made, and the second murder that the police had decided pointed towards a single killer with a fondness for Titian-haired schoolgirls. I told him about summoning her in the morgue and totally failing to find out anything useful.

He thought for a while before asking: "Dear heart, have you heard of William of Ockham?"

"William the what-was-that?"

He laughed.

"No, then! He was a holy friar of St Francis, a learned man and a philosopher, many centuries before even I was born. He proposed an approach for explaining that which is unknown. In my day we spoke of it as lex parsimoniae, or even just Ockham's Razor. I am a poor excuse for a philosopher, but I understand the principle—that if you have several solutions and no other way to choose between them, then the simplest is the most likely. The one that requires the least invention and embellishment to bring it to pass…"

I understood. I had a problem to solve—who killed Bella?—but not enough information to be certain who had done it. Who would William the ancient Franciscan of Ockham have pointed an accusing finger at? Paul Mycroft, the student with the penchant for industrial wire cutters and recreational herbs? Spikey Mikey, the bad-tempered handyman, wandering the halls with his cleaning trolley? An unknown third person, sneaking through Paul's secret entrance to kill my poor doppelganger? Or the police's favoured perpetrator, a serial killer stalking the shires?

"Thank you, Bredon," I said. "I'll have to think about that."

"There is one more thing you could consider, Mistress Toni."

"There is?"

"Indeed. People kill for a very small number of reasons: fear, anger, jealousy, or personal gain."

"Or pleasure, if they're psychopaths," I interjected.

He nodded.

"You speak the truth, beloved. But it seems very few could apply to this death."

I wrinkled up my nose.

"She was a little girl, so it's unlikely that anyone who could kill her could also be afraid of her. And I don't see what could be gained by killing her, or how she could have made anyone that jealous."

He nodded again.

That left anger, then. I shook my head in defeat.

"I hear you, Bredon, but that makes no sense. Kids are annoying, but how on earth could she make someone furious enough to want to club her unconscious and then throttle her?"

He drained his martini with a flourish.

"As you say, dearest heart; it's hard to imagine, but perhaps anything else is even harder."

Chapter Ten

AT THE OFFICE the next morning, there was the usual flotsam and jetsam of a random Tuesday in January. A couple who had moved in the week before hadn't realised their house was on a public right of way. (Really? It was in the brochure, the deeds, the contract and on your solicitor's notes.) A potential viewer wanted to know the chances of getting planning permission to pebbledash the fourteenth-century stone walls of a Grade One Listed cottage. (Slim. Size zero to be specific.) Finally, I went round to Eleanor Johnson's house to supervise the installation of the new washing machine by Mr Suki's plumber, Barry.

Non-standard gauge pipework meant the work inevitably took far longer than planned, and I eventually turned on Eleanor's television and let my eyes glaze. By chance, the local channel was rerunning the documentary on Hildred Rutherford. I hadn't paid it a lot of attention when it was first broadcast. This time I watched it with different eyes. I hadn't liked the woman, but she had been murdered. Possibly minutes after I left her stupid coffin.

Hildred—A Good Witch for Our Times showed the vampire travelling round the north of England, staying with shell-shocked families preparing for the death of their terminally ill children and bringing the miracle of life into their homes. All the children she saved were girls, and most bore a striking physical resemblance to

Hildred as she must have looked when she was a child: freckled skin, long wavy hair and hazel eyes.

I disliked her just as much by the end of the rerun as I had the first time around. I was about to turn off the set when the anchor said something about staying tuned for part two after the news. I hadn't realised there was a sequel, so I wandered through to the kitchen and made myself some tea.

When I came back, a serious-faced newsman was warning of a possible serial killer. Two schoolgirls had died, he intoned grimly. CID was in overdrive to ensure there was no third victim.

They showed photographs of poor Bella when she had been alive, an adorable bundle of smiles and white teeth. Then they showed the previous victim, the thirteen-year-old from Dovedale... and I knew CID had made a stupid mistake.

There are any number of shades of red when it comes to hair. There's the dark Titian tone of a pre-Raphaelite mannequin. There's the fiery tangerine that God cursed me with. There's the pale blonde-come-carrot palette favoured by actresses and models. And there's the fresh-out-of-the-lab bottled kind, which comes in every hue from pustule purple vermillion to plutonium pink.

Minnie Cavendish was the latter. She was a striking Eurasian girl, with glowing bronze skin, chiselled cheekbones, and a head of shimmering flame that hung nearly to her waist. It looked as though it had started its life a sedate shade of raven black but she had coloured it with stripes of magenta, orange, scarlet, peach and saffron. If you had to tick a box for hair colour, you would have to pick red, but in every other way, she couldn't have been more different from Bella.

Some girls are young at twelve; others are old at thirteen. Bella had been a child, but Minnie was a young woman. She could easily have passed for seventeen. With some mascara and a fake ID card, she could have bought shandy at the bar. I was no expert on serial killers—unless Oscar, Grace and Benedict counted, which they probably did—but I just couldn't see a person who had been interested in Minnie having the slightest time for Bella or vice versa. Yes, on paper they were both redheads a year apart in age just a few miles apart. Yes, they had both been killed... But there, I was completely certain, the similarities ended. There was no serial killer. The police were barking up entirely the wrong tree.

I had a feeling that my brother had jumped to the same conclusions as I had. Thirty-one years with ginger hair meant he was used to the same typecasting. No wonder he had been annoyed when the case had been snatched out of his hands. My hunch had been right—I wasn't finished with Annabel Hornby, not by a long way.

As the news continued to do its best to oppress the proletariat—blizzards, tax increases, the declining population of hedgehogs, an MP who had been discovered in flagrante with his own dog—Barry popped his head around the door jamb.

"I need a pipe wrench," he said cheerfully and unhelpfully.

"Barry, if you're hoping I have one in my handbag, I took it out this morning," I said. "There wasn't room in between my fourteen lipsticks and my hair irons."

He laughed.

"No, I just meant I have to pop back to the office to get one," he said. "Are you OK to wait here a bit longer?"

I propped my feet up on the couch and waved the remote at him.

"It's a tough job, but I'm game," I said. "Take your time."

Part two of the Hildred Rutherford documentary was very different from the first. It was called *Hildred: A Wicked Witch for Our Times* and it was about all the families who had asked her for help—and who she had turned down because of her bizarre prejudices.

It was tear-jerking. If you hadn't disliked the wretched woman by the end of part one, you certainly did by the end of part two. The film crew had followed her around as she explained to increasingly despairing parents that she wouldn't heal their children because of their race, sex, religion, nationality, taste in clothes, hobbies or random sporting affiliations. She was vile and opinionated. It seemed just ludicrously ironic that the gift of healing had been bestowed on someone who was happy for most of the world to die in pain.

As the credits rolled past, instead of music, the documentary played the bitter words of bereaved parents. I almost switched it off too soon, but something stayed my hand. And then I heard it.

"I watched my daughter die," one father said, his voice breaking. "And all I could think was that just the tiniest touch of kindness could have saved her."

I heard myself gasp. I sat up on the sofa and stared at the screen. I had heard that voice before. It was the voice of the man who had very nearly wiped me off the face of the earth. It was the voice of Uncle Jasper, who had later claimed to be David Masters and then Jeremy Emerson.

I knew now why he had killed Hildred Rutherford. Given the same circumstances I would have been tempted to do so myself.

I stood up in such a rush that I knocked the empty teacup off the table. It smashed against the skirting board and pieces of china smattered down around my feet. I just looked at them, spread across the carpet, an edge of hand-painted rose petal on one, half a leaf on another, a sliver of stem; confusing nothings that, when put together, would make something you could understand...

I understood now.

Jasper must have had a daughter, a terrifyingly sick daughter, and he'd asked Hildred for her help. But—for whatever reason—the vampire had refused. Goodness knows, it wouldn't have had to be much of a reason. Listening to the woman's bile, maybe she hadn't liked his hairstyle... or his football team. Whatever, he'd plotted revenge. He'd come to that pitiful little rented house with the express aim of killing her. But how did Kathy and Melody come into it? Who were they and why had Melody been willing to help him commit such a desperate act? Had ill little Kathy been the bait to get Hildred there? It seemed likely.

Barry returned and finished installing, and I drove back to the office in a thoughtful mood. Jasper's motive in attacking me was presumably to stop me revealing his role in Hildred's death. But who to? And why had he thought I would be able to identify him? Had he known the moment he saw me that he was going to kill me?

Perhaps it wasn't himself that he wanted to protect... Who then? Melody? Or Kathy? And why? Or was it when I said that I had come from the Staffordshire Assemblage that he knew we would meet again? I had no idea.

I could use the phone number that Aidan had given me. Benedict probably had sufficient influence to find out who the documentary makers had interviewed and work out my attacker's identity. But I'd been planning to de-vampire my life. I didn't want to ask for help and get a whole load of grief as the bill. I also had a lot of sympathy with the man who had killed Hildred—it just didn't extend as far as letting him kill me, too.

But then, I'd given Uncle Jasper a damn good run for his money back in our brief fight to the death. I'd drawn first, second and third blood and totalled his sports car. Maybe he would give me a wide berth from now on. Maybe I could pretend I'd never met Kathy, never set eyes on ugly Mel, and never broken Jasper's face with a lump of rusty iron girder... And maybe tomorrow, Winchester would bring me a cup of tea in bed. I sighed and put Jasper, Melody, Kathy and Hildred bloody Rutherford from my mind. I wasn't going to go running to the nightwalkers for protection and that was that. If Jasper came after me a second time, I'd just have to kill him all by myself.

THE SUN HAD set long before I left the office, and I was feeling bad-tempered. My house would no longer contain Peter, and as a result it would instead be full of unwashed washing, encrusted crockery and absolutely nothing for dinner. I minded the domestic issues a lot less than I minded the loss of Peter. Nonetheless, the combination was more than enough to ruin my mood when I thought of going home to eat.

Paul had wandered in about half an hour before and had quietly filed Bernie's paperwork. He had then sat himself down on the client sofa and opened a textbook. I glanced over at Bethany. Yup, Bernie was right. While packing her bag, she was gazing at Paul with lambent adoration. When he glanced back at her, it morphed into a glare of snooty distain. When she had finished packing up, she breezed past him without so much as a backward glance. My squishy little heart bled for Paul; I didn't miss my teenage years.

"Come on, Paul," I said. "Pizza. I'm buying."

"Cool," he said, jumping to his feet and stuffing his book into a rucksack. "Where are we going?"

"Josepina's."

"Awesome," he said. "I love that place."

I loved the place, too. Josepina's House of Basil was a tiny takeaway tucked into the arcade by the prison. If you walked through the beaded curtain, which most people never thought to do, there were a couple of tables where Mama Josepina would dump down some red wine next to your pizza.

I found a parking space in an alleyway just a couple of minutes' walk from the pizzeria and we walked together. It struck me that he had a few questions to answer and it might be better to get them out of the way whilst we were on our own...

"So," I said as casually as I could, "how come you turned up at my office?"

He turned an astonished face to me.

"Toni, you vanished for a week! I was worried that Jasper guy had tracked you down and finished the job. I visited every estate agent in town. By the time I found your boss and he said you sick, I was ready to go to the police and risk them thinking I'd knocked off another redhead."

I blinked; he cared. The geeky teenager genuinely liked me! It made me reluctant to ask my next question—namely how he'd come to be sporting a black eye two days after Bella's death—especially as Paul was burbling about how welcoming Bethany had been, and how Bernie was paying him to help out and he really felt part of the team... Even as I dithered, my phone buzzed. It was a text from Claire.

It read:

Bored, bored, bored. Also, hungry.

I texted back.

Josepina's. Right now.

But it was an evening for small surprises, because before we made it to the front door, phone in hand mid-text, I walked smack bang into someone I'd been talking about just hours before. I didn't see him and crashed straight into his chest. It was the yacht-owning hedge fund millionaire, Suki Junior.

"Hey, it's Toni, isn't it?" he said, catching my arm to stop me falling off the kerb. "Dad was talking about you this morning."

"You need to watch out for your dad," I warned him. "He's a matchmaker at heart and he hates me being single. He's always telling me how lonely you are, pining away in your mansion with only your vintage wine collection, your private cinema and your Rolls Royce for company."

Fortunately, he took my teasing in good part.

"You have to love my dad," he said. "Either that or kill him. So, how are things, Toni? It's been—what?—a couple of years since I last saw you."

I shrugged vaguely; most people don't really mean it when they ask how you are.

"Just the same, to be honest. And you?"

"My life is amazing," he burst out unexpectedly. "I am just so happy! I can't tell you!"

I stared at him. He was beaming at me, beaming at Paul, beaming at a lady walking past with two Pekingese dogs tangling themselves up on long leashes. Yup, he meant it. He was one happy man.

"Um, great," I managed. "That's just great. Paul, this is Suki Junior."

"Call me Jay," he said. "Please. Everyone does."

"Everyone except your dad?" I teased.

"That's the one," he said good-naturedly, shaking hands with Paul.

Paul had been eyeing Jay while we had been chatting. The man was something of a local celebrity—local boy made good—and my knowing him had probably boosted my cool status further.

"We're just going for pizza," I said to Jay idly.

"Great," he said. "I love pizza."

Terrific. Now we were a party. We trooped into Josepina's. I hoped she could fit four of us.

She could, and by the time Claire joined us, the table was piled with crispy dough and the smell of grilled cheese filled the air. Jay had warned us that he was happy, and I'd rarely seen a man on such an emotional high. He talked almost without pause. Everything was wonderful: the snow, the pizza, the wine, the company.

When he paused for breath, I introduced Claire. She was my best friend from university who now worked as an events manager at the County Showground. She had clearly escaped from something posh and not particularly corporate and was wearing a tiny, pink, satin and snakeskin number with a bodice cut down almost to navel level at the front. Paul made a manful effort not to stare straight at her cleavage and failed.

Jay shook hands cheerfully, taking a break from telling us all how happy he was to welcome her, but only a brief one. Then he was back to eulogising on life and how sublime it was.

"Did you drug him?" Claire said when we fled to the loos.

I shook my head, touching up my lipstick in the mirror.

"That wasn't me," I said. "Whatever he took, I didn't sell it to him, and neither did Paul."

Claire dragged a brush through her hair. It wasn't necessary. Her hair was perfect.

"Yes, who is this delightful teenage geek of yours? I think you need to put him back where you found him—I'm not sure it's legal."

I snorted.

"Hardly! I seem to have accidentally hired him to fix our IT at the office and our receptionist has already claimed him. Anyway, according to Mr Suki, I'm meant to be dating Jay!"

"Ah, yes, our dashing and astonishingly single multimillionaire. I didn't know you knew him," she said. "I did a few events for his company before he sold out, but I've never spoken to him before."

I handed Claire my lipstick.

"I don't really know him," I said. "But Claire, I think he'd have been up for dinner with Genghis Khan tonight, or Hannibal Lector. The man's a walking definition of beatific."

Back at the table, we found our two escorts bonding.

"Really?" Jay was saying. "That's terrific. My daughter is starting there next term. Her sister is at boarding school, but she wanted to go to the grammar. She wants to be a doctor."

"If I get the grades, I'm going to Bristol to study medicine," said Paul. "The grammar's the right place, you know."

I was a rubbish mentor. I hadn't had a clue that Paul wanted to study medicine. He was even more of a Peter clone than I'd realised.

Jay, on the other hand, was the perfect impromptu host. He bought us all dinner, including wine and far too much homemade Italian ice cream. And then Sambuca.

He was curiously reticent about the cause of his good mood. I asked obliquely two or three times and then—curiosity overcoming good manners—quite directly several more. But Jay just shrugged and assured me it was nothing. Claire interrogated him at much greater length at which point he admitted there might be a cause—and then downright refused to tell us what it was.

Despite his evasiveness, we had an excellent time, and only left when Mama Josepina threw us out onto the street. Paul headed off back to an evening of ceramic ballerinas on the moped that the police had finally returned to him. Jay wandered off down the street—I thought he would stop a lot of random strangers and tell them what a wonderful evening it was. Claire and I walked back to her flat for coffee and gossip. I sprawled on the floor against her sofa and prepared myself for the third degree. It wasn't long in coming.

"Did you want to tell me why you are having dinner with the richest bachelor in Stafford instead of Peter?" she asked, handing me the sugar bowl. "He's nice, by the way."

I took the cup with a sigh.

"I don't know him that well and it wasn't a date and I didn't expect him to buy us all dinner," I said in a rush.

"To be honest, girlfriend, we lucked out there. If we'd bumped into him in the car showroom, he'd have bought us both a Ferrari by now. Why is he on cloud nine, do you know?"

"Not a clue. As I said, I don't know him well. His dad thinks I have childbearing hips."

She arranged herself on the carpet next to me.

"Nice avoiding of the subject—ten out of ten. Now, where were we?"

I wasn't going to lie to Claire. But I also didn't want to have an in-depth conversation about the Assemblage with anyone. I rather hoped I had shed it from my life forever when I watched Aidan drive away from my house.

"Claire, I don't know how to say this, but all of you were right, and I was wrong. You, Wills, Henry... you have all been telling me for months that Oscar was bad for me."

"Lav, darling, only because you looked so bloody miserable."

"Well, you were spot on. Oscar decided to prove the calibre of his affection by punching me in the face when we had a row."

I paused while Claire let fly a string of expletives.

"Yes, I agree. All of those. Anyway, his boss is furious and has sent him away somewhere. I have no idea where, and I wouldn't give a flying fuck except that he sent Peter with him and now I'm on my own."

"Crap," she said, putting an arm around me. "Crap, crap and crap. No Oscar and no Peter. Lav, darling, you date as many millionaires as you like."

"I don't want them," I said miserably, starting to sniffle. "The stupid thing is that I just want Peter back. Nothing works without him."

"The sewer is full of rats, Lav. Though I admit, Peter is a touch above the average rat. Might that happen, darling? Might you get him back?"

What to say? Oscar was the love of Peter's life. He'd already given up his world, his career and his adopted homeland for the man. Giving up me... that would be small fry by comparison.

"I don't think so, Claire. I think he's gone for good."

She shook her head in frustration.

"Better stay the night, darling. I have a bottle of vodka in the freezer."

"Thanks, but I won't. This week is tough enough without hangovers."

I LEFT HER soon after and drove on a whim up to Baswich cemetery. It was a little after midnight and the snow was still thick on the ground. Both of my parents and my grandfather were buried at the top of the hill, all three in the same grave. I didn't know what was drawing me there; perhaps seeing Jay, a man who'd lost the mother of his children, had drawn my mind back to my own family. Or perhaps, with Peter and Oscar gone and finding myself so alone again, I wanted to recall a time when I'd been surrounded by love. I wasn't sure but did it even matter? I'd never raised them, and I didn't plan to. I wanted to remember them as they had been when they were alive.

Not to say that there weren't questions I wanted to ask them. I wanted to ask my mother and father why they had ignored me as a child, left me at home with my grandfather and travelled the world without me. I wanted to ask my grandfather why he hated our necromantic powers so much that he'd tried to dissuade me from ever using them. I wanted to ask him if he'd known all about the Assemblage and—if so—why he hadn't told me about it.

But I wasn't going to disturb that family grave ("Ernest and Marchesa Windsor, united in true love, and their dear father and guide through life, Robert Windsor"). If I wanted answers to those questions, I would have to find them out another way. I walked through the snow in the place of the dead. It was quiet and dark and peaceful.

I left it that way.

Chapter Eleven

TUESDAY DAWNED BRIGHT and white. In the early hours of the morning, it had snowed again, adding a few frosty inches to the carpet that already blanketed the county. I rang my brother before I left for work.

"I'm going to raise Minnie Cavendish from the dead," I said without introduction. "Your colleagues have lost the plot."

"I told them that, sis," he said. "It was after I told them for the eleventh time that they took the case off me entirely. They live for serial killings and two schoolgirls a year apart with a box ticked saying they had the same colour hair was all it took. In fairness, they hadn't seen Bella's photo until afterwards by which time they'd impounded her body and all my files."

"Wills, I didn't realise," I said. "You tried your best, now let me give it a go. Where is she?"

"I hoped you'd ask, so I found out," he said. "Her body was released to her family a month ago. She's buried at the family church above Doveridge. But listen, Toni: it's about three miles further into the hills from Dovedale. You'll never make it in the Morris in this snow. I don't have an evening shift free for a week or so, but if you can wait until Friday, I'll have winter tyres put on the four-wheel drive and you can take that."

He was right. Dovedale is in the north of the county, bang on the border with Derbyshire. It's on the edge of the Peak District, a beautiful but precipitous range of hills that was made into a National Park. There wasn't much else to do with the place, to be honest. Half the sheep have vertigo. The rust-mobile wouldn't have made it further than the Ye Olde Gift Shoppe at Ashbourne.

I had a plan in place that gave me most of the week to kick my heels, but I had plenty to do. The crazy thing was that if it hadn't been for half the county trying to kill me and the other half commiserating with me about my newly pathetic single status, I would have been having a great week. January was typically my worst time when it came to commission payments, but not this year. I had been nursing the sale of a block of flats in Eccleshall for seven months and—out of the blue while I'd been unconscious at the Stone House—the contracts had finally been exchanged and all the signs were that the sale would be completed on the Thursday.

Not only that, but after an awkward hiatus when it came to my necromantic learning curve, my powers were blossoming. On Tuesday night, I'd finally managed to raise Sir Caspar de Beaumont from his four-hundred-and-twenty-year rest. I'd been trying for months. He was buried in a nice mausoleum at the back of St Chads and he'd been determinedly elusive to my call... No longer. He stood there in the snow with me, debating the charms of the English weather while eating late night kebab van chips with curry sauce.

I hated the thought of being grateful to Benedict for anything, but the awareness that he had given me of my barriers of protection had also given me a new-found control of them. They were two-way, as he had indicated, and I could soften aspects of them at will. The result was a more finely tuned mastery of my undead charges. For the rest of the week, I abandoned myself to sleep deprivation and awoke the older residents of Stafford's graveyards. They'd slept through my summoning before. Not anymore.

I was also far more aware of the nightwalkers around me. In the supermarket on the Wednesday evening, a vampire had passed behind me. She was young and weak, but I felt her without even turning round. I could pull out her name and her hair colour without so much as putting down the loaf of bread I was holding. And I felt her hunger—she hadn't fed and was waiting for the young man serving on till number four to finish his shift.

I reached out and explored a little further. She wasn't strong—with some blood and a following wind I could have taken her down without touching her—and she wasn't aware of me. She passed me in the bakery aisle by the warm jam doughnuts and never knew she'd spilled her secrets to me.

It was a breakthrough that I couldn't really have shared with anyone except Peter. In his absence, I celebrated with Winchester. He had a slice of chicken, and I had a glass of wine. Then the cat went to sleep and I had the rest of the bottle. Winchester wasn't a party cat.

Thursday dawned and by noon, even through the pangs and pains of my hangover, it became apparent that the sale of my block of flats really was going to be completed in the afternoon. I would have a commission cheque that would see me through until spring. By lucky coincidence, I was also having lunch with Claire and Helen. I sprang for a couple of bottles of champagne. By the third glass or so, the effects of the hair of the dog began to ease away my headache.

I'd been at school with Helen. She'd been a lot sportier than me and eventually became a swimming instructor at the local sports centre. At school she'd had long honey-coloured pigtails and baby blue eyes. These days, she cut her hair in a chic, short, urchin bob so that it dried quickly.

She'd got engaged to Bernie about a year before and was becoming increasingly stressed about the fact that a wedding date hadn't been beaten out of the man. I was uneasily aware that a beating would probably have done it, but I didn't like to say. Despite his many, many faults, I was fond of Bernie, but he wasn't boyfriend material. He certainly wasn't husband material. I thought she should cut and run for the hills, but I didn't say that either. There are things you have to find out all by yourself, and one of them is that your boyfriend is an arse. No one knew that better than me.

Helen fortified herself with a swig of champagne. She had the look of someone who had news to break. On the one had that was probably good—if we spent lunch talking about Helen, I could steer clear of talking about my sad, single status. On the other hand, if she was about to invite Claire and I to pick out bridesmaid dresses, I might just dissolve weeping into my champagne glass. I braced myself.

"So," said Helen, putting down her glass with much melodrama, "I have something to tell you."

We made noises of interested anticipation and I topped the three of us up. Helen leaned back in her chair with a martyred look.

"Bernie watches porn," she said.

Claire and I waited for the follow-through. After an uneasy silence, we realised there wasn't one.

"I see, sweetie," I said gently.

I didn't see. How could this possibly be news to her? Yes, Bernie watched porn. He watched quite a lot of it at work. I caught Claire's eye. Thinking about it, she organised a lot of local stag nights. She probably also knew whether he favoured glamorous grannies or big and busty.

"I caught him," Helen continued sadly. "He promised it was a one-off, but I don't know whether to believe him. Toni, what do you think?"

I stared at her in disbelief. Who did she think she was engaged to, Sir Galahad? Had I been this blinkered when I dated Oscar? I hated to believe so.

"Um," I said desperately. I began to blather. "Um, here's the thing, Helen. I don't think there's anything intrinsically wrong with it. I just don't like the premise. I mean, don't think that I spend my nights watching a lot of this stuff, but it all seems to be about surrender. You know, either the woman gets bullied or forced into something, but she ends up enjoying it after all. And I think that's just dumb. I mean, we're not talking about when your friends talk you into trying sushi for the first time. We are talking about having your free will taken away from you. No one wants that, surely?"

I had lost the plot, but I carried on anyway. I had stopped thinking about porn and Bernie a long time ago. I was just thinking of a blond-haired vampire who I had once loved like crazy telling me that he would make my decisions for me to ensure that he got what he wanted.

"I mean, at the end of the day, you aren't going to be grateful when someone forces you into a corner. You are just going to resent them for it. I want to pick my own corners."

Helen and Claire were both looking at me, Claire with gentle understanding and Helen in simple confusion. A nice, long, awkward silence broke out and hovered over the table.

"I hate making decisions," Helen said eventually. "I wouldn't mind Bernie making them."

CLAIRE AND I walked back to the office together having bid Helen goodbye; Helen wasn't sure she could face the offending Bernie yet.

"Lav, why is she even dating him?" Claire asked. "Does that man have any good features?"

I thought about the question.

"You know, Claire, he's actually really nice. I mean, apart from the wandering hands and the leching down your cleavage. He's kind, and I think if the chips were down, he wouldn't throw you to the lions to save his own skin. He was really remorseful when he got me into trouble once. I just don't think he makes a good boyfriend. He really loves Helen, but he'd still shag anything in a skirt or out of it."

She shrugged.

"Have you heard from Peter?" she asked.

I shook my head.

"Not a peep. But I didn't really expect to."

I opened the glass door and was showered in confetti as Bernie pulled a party popper over my head. I squeaked in excitement.

"They completed? Please tell me they completed."

"Uh huh," he said, hugging me. "Bankruptcy has been pushed out for another quarter."

I wasn't quite in a warm glow, but as Bernie and Bethany had also put a bottle of champagne on ice and Claire was kind enough to stay and share it, my afternoon went more than well. I watched the sun set through the murky office windows, tipping the snowy street into wintry darkness and was able to forget about my troubles for a while. Who knew, maybe they might be behind me?

They weren't. At around five, Claire and I went out to buy snacks. As the office door closed behind us, a black four-by-four with smoked windows pulled up at the curb. The driver's window slid down with a whirr and the vampire inside glared at me.

"Get in," said Grace.

I glared right back at her. I didn't know her well, but she'd never done anything to make me think well of her. She was Benedict's right hand and Camilla's girlfriend, but I'd always thought her a hard and unemotional person. Not tonight. Tears had run down her face and into the diamonds around her neck and her lips were swollen with crying.

"Absolutely no fucking way," I said very firmly.

I had given up on vampires, and not just for Lent. Anyway, anything that could make Grace cry would probably kill me. I would take a hard pass.

"Get in, or I will kill you and leave your corpse in the snow," she said.

I narrowed my eyes. I leaned into the car so that Claire wouldn't hear what I was saying.

"Grace, at least eight people who tried to kill me are dead, and seven of them were vampires. Do you really want to threaten me?"

She bit her lip.

"Just get in."

"Nope."

Claire leaned over. She had turned as white as the snow we stood in, but her voice was clear:

"Yah, just so we are on the same page, darling, if you threaten my friend, I will stake you through the heart with my own earrings if there is nothing else to hand."

Grace put her head in her hands. Tears leaked out.

"You have to help me," she said. "Maybe you can talk sense into him. He won't listen to me."

I edged away from the car.

"I don't want to know," I said. "None of you talk sense. Ever. I never understand what you are drivelling on about."

She looked at me piercingly. I'd seen that expression before. I'd seen it on the faces of all those parents that Hildred Rutherford had rejected who'd had to watch their own children die.

"If you can help me, I will be your friend," she said. "I will look out for you. I will take your part. I will protect you. For always."

I raised my hands in defeat. I didn't want her as my friend. It was her expression that persuaded me, not her promises.

"Fine," I said. "I'll come. But if I can't help you, don't blame me. Claire, I have to go. Don't worry—I'll be fine."

She started to protest but I shook my head and gave her a hug.

"Grace won't hurt me," I said. "She's all talk."

The first bit I hoped was true. The second was a total lie. I'd seen the vampire drenched in the blood of her enemies: she'd been having a simply marvellous time.

Grace opened the passenger door. I walked round and climbed in beside her. She was in her signature costume of a tiny black dress and towering stilettos.

"Thank you," she said. "Do you need me to compel your friend to forget this?"

I looked across at Claire and then back at Grace.

"No bloody way," I said. "You stay out of her head."

We drove in silence. I wasn't sure where we were going, but when we took the Rugeley Road out of town, I guessed we were heading back to the Stone House. It wasn't a place I'd intended to visit again in the next few decades, but I'd lost that fight back when I got in the car. Grace drove badly and crunched the gears. I didn't think she was behind the wheel often; if she spent more time in the driving seat, she would have worn lower heels.

She pulled up in the courtyard with a squeal of brakes.

"Come on," she said, shortly, stepping out of the car.

The snow had been carefully shovelled away by minions so that vampires in stupid shoes didn't have to walk through the drifts. I followed her into the house and down the spiral stairs.

"Where are we going?" I asked as she marched down into the torch-lit depths ahead of me.

"Benedict's rooms," she said shortly.

Damn. Just about the last place in the world I wanted to be. So much for getting vampires out of my life. They were like double-glazing salesmen: once they had your number, they were with you for all eternity. I trailed behind her as she headed up the winding passageway. This was becoming a distressingly frequent destination for me.

She didn't even knock. She just threw open the doors to left and right and stormed in. The rooms were as I remembered them. Benedict and Aidan were standing by the fire. Their stance suggested they were squabbling. Of course they were... what else would they be doing?

"No," said Benedict in his deep voice. "Absolutely not."

He turned round and saw me entering in Grace's wake. He blinked.

"Oh Christ, no," he said. "I've had enough emotional blackmail for one evening. Take her away."

Grace ran over to him, almost stumbling in her high heels. She caught his hand in a supplicating way.

"You won't listen to me," she said in pleading tones. "Listen to her."

Benedict brought his fingertips up to his temples.

"Grace, I have done nothing but listen to you for two days," he said. "We wrote these laws together. We set a path for our kind in the centuries ahead. Damn it, half of them were your idea. But now that they apply to you and yours you want to change them?"

"Yes!" She was crying again. "Yes, change your stupid laws. I don't care."

Benedict looked at me.

"Go on," he said in a weary voice. "Add your arguments. It's not like I'm going to be allowed to do anything else but listen to this melodrama until we're through."

I reluctantly walked over to where the three of them were standing by the fire. The room was deliciously warm. I couldn't afford to heat my little cottage to the same degree that Oscar had heated Lichley and for the past two weeks the boiler had started making a hideous groaning noise when I turned it on. Tonight was the first time I had been truly warm in days. I sat on one side of the club fender and let the heat of the flames ooze into my being.

"Don't look at me," I said. "I haven't a clue what's going on. I don't even know why I'm here. But that's par for the course, so you lot carry on."

Benedict burst out laughing.

"That's priceless, Grace. You've brought her here to plead your cause and you haven't even told her why. What makes you think she won't support me instead?"

"Precedent," I suggested sotto voce.

He looked amused.

"Well, at least Grace has brought some entertainment into this maudlin event. If she hasn't enlightened you, please do let me. Your so-charming ex-boyfriend has capped a truly awesome start to the year by killing a seventeen-year-old coterie member at the Assemblage I despatched him to."

The room span around me, and I reached to the wall for support. Just how stupid, how blind and how gullible had I been? Love had melted not only my heart but apparently my intuition, my common sense and all of my brain cells. I'd been dating a monster.

"Oh my God. What happened?"

Benedict shrugged a trifle grimly.

"As always, according to Oscar, it was just a mistake, and he wishes we would all stop making such a fuss about it. Sound familiar?"

I winced. So did Grace.

"Akil," she said beseechingly. "Don't make light of this, please."

"Make light of it? This is the second time in a month I have had to put up with this crap from Oscar. If he had transcended a week ago, Grace, I might let it go. But it's been, what? Three centuries? When will he learn self-control?"

"What happened?" I repeated, as much to break up their squabble as anything. "How did she die?"

"Oscar was feeding," said Benedict in tones of utter contempt, "and introducing the girl to the delights of vampire coitus and— how did he put it? Oh yes. He 'just got carried away.' Apparently, four pints was too many for her system to lose at once. Who could have guessed?"

I felt sick. I looked at Aidan, and he just looked away from me. I looked at Grace, but her eyes were fixed on Benedict.

"You made killing a coterie member a capital offence," I said, half to myself. "Peter told me."

Grace shook her head.

"She was just a mortal," she said. "Just a girl none of us have ever met. Why does she even matter?"

Benedict snorted.

"That's no way to bring Toni round to your cause," he said. "She's the one who believes in justice for the dead, remember? She wouldn't even let me give clemency to the Gambarinis."

"But this is Oscar," Grace said. "This is different."

"Why do you even care?" I asked.

She looked at me in mute appeal for a moment, and then crumpled. She sat down on one of the two sofas facing the fire. Aidan joined her and patted her hand distractedly, but she took it away and clasped both to her chest.

"He's mine," she said. "I made him. He is my scion."

She looked at the flames, but I could tell she was gazing into the past.

"He was so beautiful, Toni," she whispered. "He was a prize fighter, you know, not a gentleman. It was some dirty tavern with a ring, and there he was. Even as a mortal, he fought like a god. I knew then and there I would make him one of us. I stole him away and made him mine."

"I didn't know," I said lamely. "I had no idea."

"Benedict told me not to do it," she said. "Didn't you? Over and over again you told me not to. But I did it anyway."

Benedict looked at her. Something in his gaze was removed from his usual mockery, but I still found him very hard to read. He sat down on the other sofa and leaned back.

"Grace," he said. "This is all very heart rending. But how many times must this happen before even you lose patience? I told Oscar fifty years ago when I rewrote our laws that I wouldn't put up with his little mistakes any longer. Do you want me to cover up for him and carry on as though nothing has happened? My dear, I am done with it. When I agreed that he could return from Heidelberg, I said I was done with his games. But here we are again."

"Sir." It was Aidan, urgent and imploring. "Sir, I'll keep tabs on him. I'll put something in place. Please. I can manage this."

"No."

"I'll leave you," said Grace. "If you kill him, I'll leave you. I won't come back."

He turned a dark look on her.

"Don't threaten me, Grace. Don't blackmail me. It won't end well."

Tears were streaming down her face again.

"I didn't mean it. I'd never leave you. But don't do this."

Benedict stood up.

"Bring him in, Aidan," he said. "Let's get this over with."

Aidan left and I wished I could escape with him. I wanted to run for the door, but my legs had stopped working. I'd had to sit metres from this spot and watch Benedict rip Diana's throat out. I couldn't watch Oscar die.

Sure, I'd spent the past few days trying to convert my affection for Oscar into loathing. I'd done quite well—near death and getting dumped will do that for you—but I wasn't a vengeful person. I hadn't wished bad things on my ex. Certainly not terminally bad things.

And maybe at the back of my mind there was still a tiny kernel of doomed hope that all of this had to be a mistake, that Oscar was the perfect man I'd once believed him to be...

True, what I'd just heard revolted every cell in my body, but I wasn't some campaigner for capital punishment. On one hand, I was no pacifist, and I would defend myself in a crisis. But I'd also never believed that two wrongs somehow magically created a right. You just got two wrongs in a world that could use more hugs.

Grace looked at me. Around their cerulean irises, her eyes were red with weeping.

"Talk to him," she said. "Tell Akil he mustn't do this."

I looked at Benedict. He was pacing up and down next to his desk.

"Has Oscar done this kind of thing before?" I asked dully.

"Oh yes."

"Many times?"

"Yes."

I felt even sicker.

"You could have told me."

"My dear, I did try. Would you have believed me?"

I thought back. I'd been so in love, so carried away. Benedict's words of warning would have seemed like the scoldings of an old-fashioned parent, all dead set against the boy next door. No, I wouldn't have believed him.

"No, I suppose not. When was the last time?"

"Before he attacked you, you mean?"

"Yes."

He looked away from me at Grace. Her face was white and pinched. She answered for him.

"About three months ago. There was a girl here, a member of my coterie. They had become very involved without my realising it. She didn't die, but she was badly injured. Benedict healed her; he let it pass because she lived. Because I begged."

Three months ago. He'd been living at Lichley with Peter and me, but he'd managed somehow. There really was no limit to my stupidity. Was Grace mad to think I would plead Oscar's cause? I was fast approaching the point where I would offer to hold the stake ready.

I'd thought Oscar was selfish, but now I knew the truth. He was just a common or garden psychopath. He'd told me he loved me, but he only loved himself. I wondered who the girl was who had died. Did her family miss her? Did they even know the truth or did she just vanish one day, leaving them to wonder until their dying day what they had done wrong…?

I put my head in my hands.

"I'll give you your due, Benedict," I said through my clenched fingers. "You certainly had it in one when you told me not to listen to my heart."

"He has the emotional depth of grass," he said, "and the self-control of Atilla the Hun."

I heard the door go and Aidan walked in. Oscar followed behind him. Silver handcuffs held his arms pinioned behind him. He was wearing fawn-coloured chinos and a light, silk shirt in a similar shade. His hair was casually tousled. Handcuff or no handcuffs, he looked as elegant and unconcerned as ever. Scratch that—he looked absolutely delicious. He even looked pleased to see me.

"Toni," he said, his lovely smile lighting up his face. "My beautiful Toni. I've missed you."

Really? When had he found the bloody time?

Chapter Twelve

I GOT TO my feet as steadily as I could, which wasn't very. The room was starting to spin around me. I'd managed both to throw up and pass out on previous visits to the Assemblage and didn't fancy a repeat of either. Losing your dignity isn't as final as losing your virginity, but it is certainly less fun.

"I'll be right back," I said hopefully but unconvincingly.

I fled to the bathroom, filled the sink with cold water and plunged my hands in. I held them there for a minute while they drew the heat out of my body. Some people swore putting their head between their knees was the panacea. Cold water always worked for me.

"Do you want some ice?" Benedict's deep voice said at my shoulder, making me jump.

"Um, thanks. I would actually."

He was back moments later with an ice bucket and emptied the contents into the sink. I kept my hands in until the room stopped spinning and my nausea faded.

"Drink this," he said.

He was holding out a cut glass of honey-coloured liquid. I necked half of it—it was the same cognac that Peter had brought me so many months ago. It did the trick, and I dried my hands and turned to face my bête noir.

"I won't watch Oscar die," I said.

"I won't make you," he said. "Come."

I followed him back through. The scene was unchanged: Grace white and shellshocked, Aidan deflated and miserable, Oscar apparently completely unbothered. I curled up in a corner of an unoccupied sofa.

"Right," said Benedict. "Where were we?"

He installed himself in a green velvet club chair with wooden arms and looked over at Aidan, who made a rather helpless gesture.

"Sir, please find another way. I'll make it work. You make the rules and I enforce them, and I'm fine with that—but find some wiggle room this time."

"No. Grace?"

She looked at him rather hopelessly.

"I've said it all," she said. "I'll do anything. Find another way."

"No. Oscar?"

Oscar knelt very elegantly at Benedict's feet. He had the air of someone off to watch cricket.

"You'll do what you want," he said easily. "You always do. I'm not begging for my life."

"Fair enough," said Benedict and stood up. "Right."

"What about me?" I interrupted. "I got dragged all the way here. Doesn't my opinion count?"

He looked at me in surprise.

"Probably not, but feel free," he said.

I looked at Oscar. He smiled slightly. He was as beautiful as ever. I waited for my heartstrings to feel a tug. They just didn't. But then, I wasn't even seeing him anymore. I was seeing Peter. Peter, who bandaged my bruises and stroked my hair in the dark, who made cold nights warm and bad times good. He would never be mine, but I couldn't bear what he would think of me if he knew I'd had the chance to save Oscar for him and hadn't done it. If Oscar had been teetering on a cliff, right then and there, I would happily have given him a shove... if not for Peter. I couldn't do it.

I looked up at Benedict and shrugged.

"Find another way," I said.

"What?"

"You make all the sodding rules. So bend them."

"Christ all-bloody-mighty," he said. "Dracula would never have made it out of Transylvania if he'd been lumbered with you lot. And what are you going to bribe me with, Miss Windsor? Last time I checked your balance, you didn't have a lot left to offer."

I stared at him in revulsion. Was he really going to ask me that? When I'd sworn fealty to him in the autumn, I'd held only two things back. I'd said I wouldn't have sex with him, and I wouldn't give him my blood… and then I'd given him my blood. Just great. I had exactly one thing left to offer, and he knew it. I wished I'd let Grace just go home in tears. Then Oscar would have got what he deserved, and I wouldn't have had to give a damn.

I looked Benedict straight in the eyes.

"Fine," I said. "You can have whatever you want."

He didn't even blink.

"Aidan, take Oscar back downstairs," he said, leaning back in his chair. "When I find the energy to care, I will work out what to do with him. Grace—sod off before I change my mind."

I watched them leave and tried not to hyperventilate. I wanted more ice, but it wasn't going to help. I necked the rest of the cognac, but a glass wasn't nearly enough. At that point I had nothing else to lose, so I lost my temper.

"You're a hive of wasps, the whole lot of you," I said bitterly. "What do you want me to do, lie back and think of England? Or if Oscar is done with those handcuffs, you could loop them round the bedpost for me. When I had my colours done, they told me to wear gold, not silver, but I guess you won't be worrying about the accessorising. You're a piece of work."

Whatever I'd said, it was the wrong thing. He moved with that terrifying vampire speed that always shocked me and I found myself yanked to my feet and pressed up close to him. He curled my hair into a knot at the nape of my neck with one hand and slowly twisted it to tilt my face up to his.

"Some of my kind think we should leave killing behind us," he said, so quietly that if it hadn't been for his fury I would have wondered if he was even talking to me. "But they're wrong. To feel the blood of your defeated enemy dry on your skin... there is much sweetness in that. How have they forgotten the joy of hunting down your foe across the dark of the night and crushing him beneath you? Did they ever really know how sweet that feels?"

He twisted his hand a little tighter and pressed me even closer to him. I had completely forgotten how to breathe.

"But rape, my dear... to hold down a woman's soft, struggling limbs while she pleads for her freedom, to force your flesh into hers and feel it tear around you like ripe fruit while she screams her pain into your mouth..." His mouth twisted. "My dear, there is no sweetness in that."

He let me go so suddenly that I stumbled to my knees. I was too confused for some moments to do anything other than stare up at him. I tried to speak, but nothing came out. He held out a hand. I ignored it.

"Get up," he said, his voice back to its usual unreadable timbre. "I'll take you home."

"I hate you and I wouldn't go to the end of the street with you," I said. "I'd rather walk home in the snow."

Damn it, I never knew when to stop.

"You wear me down," he said unexpectedly. "Get out."

"I don't—" I began.

"Out."

I clambered to my feet and walked to the door. I wanted to turn round and say something—what, I wasn't sure—but I couldn't because by then tears were rolling down my cheeks and I couldn't let him see them. The emotion of the evening had simply proven too much. I fumbled the catch twice before pulling one of the doors towards me and escaping into the dim, torch-lit length of the corridor.

I wasn't alone. Grace was waiting for me. She looked so happy I could have thumped her. She came over and put her hands on my shoulders and kissed my forehead in a very formal way. Maybe it meant something in the book of undead etiquette, but I didn't know, and I certainly didn't care. It also brought into stark relief the fact that she was eight inches taller than me in her shoes, two dress sizes smaller and wearing enough diamonds to buy my house. She also hadn't spent the day battling off a hangover. All in all, she wasn't growing on me, which was a great shame as she had apparently decided we were now sisters and was wiping away my tears with her fingertips.

"I won't forget," she said. "I'll never forget."

"I'm not sure I will either," I said morosely. "I can't remember a worse evening. Grace, could you drive me home please? Benedict and I kind of agreed I would freeze to death in a snowdrift, but it sounds like a lot of effort and I'm hungry."

She looked confused.

"Don't you want to see Oscar?" she said. "I can arrange it."

I looked at her. She was remarkably pretty by anyone's standards; even amongst the vampires she stood out. She had vivid blue, almond-shaped eyes and thick, black lashes longer than mine. Her ebony hair was straight and shimmery, and put me in mind of a shampoo advert. In the looks department, she had it all. I was no longer sure about the brains... but then she was biased.

"Grace," I said carefully, "Oscar tried to kill me, remember? I'm not hopelessly in love with him anymore. I honestly wish he was dead, but I'm sick of people getting killed."

It wasn't the whole truth, but we weren't sisters, so it was as close as she was getting.

"I'll take you home then," she said. "I'm sorry, I didn't think."

She leant forward. I thought she intended to kiss my forehead again, but instead she cupped my face very gently with her hands and kissed me on the lips. And there wasn't anything even slightly sisterly about it.

I didn't push her away instantly because it was so unexpected. I didn't push her away later because it was so unexpectedly nice. No man was ever going to kiss me with lips that soft and surround me with hair scented with almond oil. When she finally finished and drew her mouth away from mine, I stepped out of the circle of her embrace with a reluctance that surprised me.

"Grace," I said carefully, "that's not what I had in mind when I asked you to take me home."

The moment might have been awkward but she didn't seem offended or cast down; I guessed that vampires had large enough egos to cope with the occasional rebuff.

"You don't like girls?" she asked.

Exactly one and a half minutes earlier, I might have answered that question differently. Now the answer was less clear.

"It's not that, Grace," I said, surprising myself. "But I don't plan to run headfirst into anything else while my heart's still so bruised."

Not to mention that it would add a substantial level of complication to afternoon teas with Camilla.

"I understand," she said. And presumably to show me that there were no hard feelings, she kissed me again. It lasted slightly longer the second time and might have lasted longer still except that the door opened behind us, and Benedict stepped into the corridor and caught us mid smooch. He looked from me to Grace and back again.

"Good God, you don't waste time," he said and stalked off down the corridor.

Grace tossed her head. She seemed to have gotten over her earlier tears and hysterics and regained her usual poise.

"Dog in the manger," she said, idly stroking my hair. "If he doesn't want you for himself, why is he glaring at me?"

"Um, about that," I said awkwardly. "He might have made overtures."

"Did you turn him down?" she asked with surprise. "He's not having a good year, is he...? Never mind, it's a very salutatory lesson for him and one I very much doubt he appreciated."

"He certainly didn't seem to," I admitted. "Not at all."

We walked together to the car, and I found myself liking Grace much more than I had previously. She was far more straightforward than I had expected a person who looked—and dressed—like a glamour model would turn out to be. You could easily imagine someone who looked like such a siren playing more mind games—but in an Assemblage with Oscar and Benedict around, you probably sickened of mind games pretty quickly.

She and I also had an uneasy bond—we both knew what it was like to love Oscar with all of our stupid hearts when, really, our heads must have been screaming at us to wake up and see him for the prize jerk he really was.

I was also starting to understand some of Camilla's affection for her. I didn't want her as my girlfriend, but I was beginning to appreciate the idea having her on my side. She was honest and direct, she seemed to keep the bargains she had made, and she was no stranger to true love and loyalty. They were good traits, though not being a vampire was also starting to look like an excellent trait to me; I could learn from my mistakes.

When we got to the car, she unlocked it and glowered down at her insane heels.

"Damn it, do you want to drive?" she said.

I installed myself in the driver's seat and started the engine.

"Why do you always wear such crazy shoes?" I asked, pulling onto the drive.

It was a question worth asking—seven-inch, diamante, platform stilettos and a sensible four-wheel-drive car. Fortunately, she didn't seem to mind being asked.

"I get sick of all the men looming over me," she said. "Without heels I'm not that much taller than you are, you know. Benedict is six four, even Oscar's nearly six foot... I can't tell you what a happy decade it was for me when the Venetians invented chopines. Oh, and Toni, I like pretty things; God knows I never had any when I was alive."

"I can't walk in them," I admitted, "but I wouldn't mind adding a few inches every now and then."

"A few centuries of practice and it's child's play," she assured me, "and as a vampire, my balance is much better."

I headed down towards the river and drove across the bridge. The cold snap was showing no signs of breaking, and the trees along the bank were still fluffy with snow. I was happy not to be hitch-hiking.

"Grace, why would Oscar want to make me a vampire?" I asked suddenly. "I've been wondering for days. Peter said that once I was a nightwalker, Oscar and I wouldn't be in love anymore. So why would he even bother?"

"Oh, Toni, our urge to create is very strong," she said. "Stronger even than in mortals, I sometimes think. It robs us of logic and reason in much the same way. And the truth is, every single one of us believes our love will be the one that survives, that will transcend death."

"You think that's what Oscar thought?"

She nodded.

"I'm quite certain of it. And just to keep illogical hope from dying, it occasionally happens. Peter probably didn't know, but there are a very few vampires and their scions who've retained their passion for one another. Just a handful, but it isn't entirely a myth."

"Do you regret it? Not just you, but generally…"

"No. In general, the affection we feel for our children, our scions, is much as you mortals feel, unconditional and often undeserved."

"Even when they turn out to be serial killers?"

She laughed a touch bitterly.

"Even then. But Toni, we're a damn bloodthirsty bunch, you know. If you go back far enough, I'm pretty sure none of us has a clean sheet. That's why the Heidelberg Accord gave a free pardon for crimes against mortals committed more than seventy years ago. Without that amnesty, we'd all be on the hook for something. And we kill each other like it's going out of fashion. At the end of the day, we're vampires. We crave blood and sex. And power."

"Do you only make scions out of people you love?"

"Left to ourselves, yes. But I think that's one of the things that singles out our leaders, people like Benedict, who can rule an Assemblage. He can make dispassionate choices. Like Aidan."

"He made Aidan, too?" I asked in some surprise; I was learning a lot in one evening.

"Aidan was a soldier, and a brilliant one, but he was horribly injured at the end of the war. Benedict sought him out and approached him in some dismal little military hospital. He was rotting. He didn't have long to live... Benedict offered to free him from pain and give him immortality. Not many people would turn that down."

We had reached the car park where I left the Morris that morning. I pulled up to the kerb but left the engine running.

"Grace, what happened to Aneurin?" I asked.

"Oh, him. Benedict let him go; he was furious, but he said he didn't want open war. He made Aneurin take an oath not to enter the county again, though, and he demanded reparations for you; they're still negotiating a figure."

"Good," I said. "I need a new boiler. Why was he here in the first place?"

Grace shrugged.

"I wasn't paying much attention, but he sent a message to Benedict several days before saying that he was pursuing a member of his coterie who was either in some trouble or determined to create some. He said the man was in Staffordshire. He wanted permission to come and look for him. We all assumed he would send one of his Assemblage—it's odd that he came himself."

"I certainly wish he hadn't. Think your shoes can cope with the drive back?"

"They'll manage," she said. "Somehow."

I opened the door and stepped onto the pavement. Grace slammed the passenger door shut and walked round. She looked at me thoughtfully. Then, putting her hands up to the back of her neck, she unhooked the collar of diamonds she was wearing. Before I realised what she had planned, she had draped them round my neck and closed the clasp.

"I want you to have these," she said. "Benedict gave them to me when I became his scion."

"You can't give me these," I gasped.

"No one has ever done anything that selfless for me," she said simply. "You came to help me, even though you didn't want to and even after I had threatened you. And you made Benedict change his mind when you believed Oscar deserved to die. I see that now. Take them."

They were cold round my neck. If they'd come off the neck of a mortal, they would have been warm. In the smoked window of the car, I could see them glitter.

"Fine," I said. "I'd like them."

I thought she might kiss me again, but she just got into the driver's seat and looked up at me with a tight smile.

"They look good on you," she said.

I watched the headlights recede. Oscar would have Peter and I would have diamonds. And Benedict could have whatever he wanted. It was a crap trade.

Chapter Thirteen

DOVEDALE IS RECKONED the most beautiful spot in the Peak District. Thousands come on sunny, summer afternoons to walk through the ancient ash woods and gawp at the crazy rock formations that tower over them. In the winter, the place is deserted and some of the steeper walks can be dangerous. The side roads are narrow and precipitous. I certainly didn't want to drive up in the dark, so I took Friday afternoon off and picked up the four-wheel drive from Will and Henry's house at lunchtime. I left them the rust-mobile in its stead, though I didn't think either of them would drive it. It wasn't nearly cool enough for Wills, with its asymmetric pattern of rust spots and only three hub caps, and I doubted Henry would even fit.

It was a good trade for a long, icy journey. Even in the snow, the car ate up the road, and I'd forgotten just how much more pleasant driving could be in a car with power steering and functional heating. I stopped at a tiny supermarket in Ashbourne for zombie snacks and, at the in-house café, I filled a thermos with coffee. I also filled the tank to bursting. It would be dark once I finished my tasks. If I ended up sleeping in the car, I wanted the heating to last the night. I'd packed a rug, too; I think ahead.

The drive would have taken me just under two hours in the summer. In the snow, I thought maybe three. I was a touch ambitious, and the sun was just thinking about setting when I pulled my car up to the church lychgate and turned off the engine. The air was biting as I got out; I was deeply grateful for fur-lined boots, leather gloves, thick canvas jeans and about eleven jumpers under my coat. Once again, I regretted not buying a new hat to replace the one I'd given Kathy and tied my silk scarf a little more firmly around my neck.

The Church of the Holy Trinity and St Etheldreda stood about half a mile outside the little village of Doveridge. It was on the east side of the Dove, meaning it sat just inside Derbyshire rather than Staffordshire. When it was built, there was another village here, which I think in the Domesday Book was called Ilam Ridge. Now there was just the church. A neat little cemetery housed a mix of old and new graves. It was a jobbing necromancer's delight.

There were enough footprints and car tracks in the snow to hint at a regular Sunday service, but I doubted there would be other visitors and certainly not on a Friday night as the sun was setting. It wasn't hard to find Minnie's grave—they don't bury many people any more at these tiny little churches—and I just looked for the only one with fresh flowers poking out of the snow. But to my surprise, there were two, set right next to each other.

'Minnie, our loving angel,' the leftmost tombstone read. There were some dates, far too close together, and a quote from a book I'd never heard of, all carved so recently that the edges of the letters were still sharp. Frost-bitten, dead bouquets were piled around.

I leaned over to read the engravings on the second fresh grave. 'Daniel Hereward, beloved son. Gone too soon.'

The dates told me that Daniel had been seventeen when he died about three weeks ago. I looked at my phone for signal—there was enough for a text or two.

I typed:

Hey Wills. Who the hell was Daniel Hereward?

I sat on Minnie's gravestone and, as I waited, the sun set. I felt the dead stir beneath the snow. I felt the power of the earth creep into me. After a few minutes my brother replied.

Minnie's boyfriend. He killed himself the day after her funeral.

So many lives ruined. But I was glad Wills had warned me.

You can't raise suicides. Well, you can, but there is nothing there, just an empty shell. And it's not a clever move to raise the dead when they have no souls left, take it from me.

I took my salt cellar and drew a rough circle around Minnie's grave. The salt ate through the snow, leaving a white canyon trail around the lumpy piles of dead flowers. I took out my current perfume atomiser and sprayed along the line. The ethanol in the perfume acted like a perfect de-icer and widened and deepened the track until grassy tips were poking through. I balanced a few paper plates of food on the snow just inside my circle of protection. Minnie had lucked out—she had a twenty-four pack of own-brand sausage rolls that had ended up on the half-price shelf and some nearly out-of-date and heavily discounted mince pies. There was a tin of chocolate biscuits if she turned out to be chatty. Then I perched back on my heels and reached for her.

Her presence was so slight I could barely sense it. Minnie hadn't spent many years on this earth, and she was shedding the place without regrets.

"Minnie Cavendish, I summon you," I whispered into the dark air.

My words turned into frost and drifted unheeded to icy darkness. Minnie was resting, and she wasn't heeding my call. I needed blood.

I scrabbled around in my handbag and at the bottom found the little gold knife I needed. It had belonged to my great-great-grandfather Ignatius, the infamous necromancer in our family. He'd summoned the dead from their graves and demons from Hell. He'd also clearly been of a practical bent: the knife allowed you to score lines across your skin about a quarter of an inch deep and no deeper. Since I'd started using it, my left wrist had become a tapestry of little scars. Looking down, I realised that Benedict's healing had erased them. Once again, my freckled skin was as unblemished as a baby's. I shook my head and prepared to ruin it.

"Minnie Cavendish, I summon you from your rest."

I drew the knife across my wrist and let the drops fall onto the snow. I pressed my hand into the icy softness and felt the blood sucked into the earth.

"Come to me. Come to me tonight."

No, not enough. I took the little knife a second time and criss-crossed the first cut, playing noughts and crosses on my own skin. I pushed my hand back into the cold mix of soil, rotting petals and melting slush that was by then the surface of Minnie's grave. I would bet money she'd been just this hard to prise out of bed for school.

"Come along now, young lady," I said. "Get your lazy arse out of this grave or there's going to be trouble."

And finally, she came. I doubted it was the threats, but who could say? I didn't have a textbook for my hobby. I wouldn't say I made it up as I went along but, being honest, I was winging it a lot of the time.

Minnie looked much as she had in the photograph I'd seen on the afternoon news: pretty but not beautiful with crazy highlights in her hair and more makeup than any girl that age could need. She was dressed in jeans and a t-shirt emblazoned with badgers in Stetsons. I don't miss being a teenager, but Minnie looked like fun.

Correction: she looked like she'd been fun when she was alive. Right now, she was hungry and elsewhere. She blinked and looked at the snow. She didn't seem much interested in anything. She stood in the mess of her own grave and looked around idly like someone waiting in line for a doughnut they no longer wanted. There wasn't a lot of Minnie left. If I'd come a week later, there might have been nothing at all.

"Hello, Minnie," I said, a little breathless. "Here you are."

She didn't answer, just looked at me blankly. I held out a plate of sausage rolls.

"Eat these, Minnie, I know you're hungry."

She ate them one after the other like chocolate drops. The summoned dead are an all-you-can-eat buffet's worst nightmare. She swallowed half a dozen in the time it took me to clear my throat and remember why I'd raised her.

"Tell me about your death, Minnie. How did you die?"

She took a pause from mainlining flaky pastry to answer.

"Danny strangled me," she said blandly. "He was such a creep."

"Daniel?"

She nodded.

"I just wanted to hang with my friends," she said, spraying me with fragments of sausage roll. "Or spend time in my room listening to music now and then. But he wouldn't leave me alone. Every night. Texting me thirty times a day. He bought me a stupid ring. We were meant to be going to the cinema and I just couldn't be bothered. I told him to save me a seat and then I walked to the school playground and sat on the swings. It was so nice being on my own, not being smothered. Then he rang me to say the film was starting and I told him to bugger off and find a new girlfriend. Ten minutes later he was there. He said if he couldn't have me no one could. And he put his hands round my neck and killed me. What a monumental jerk."

I stared at her in horror. The worst part? Those were exactly the words Oscar had said when he'd nearly killed me.

"I'm sorry, Minnie," I said. "I'm so sorry you had to go through that again for me."

She didn't react. Like many of the revenants I called, she generally only responded when I asked questions or gave commands.

"Are those mince pies for me?" she asked.

I let her go. I didn't feel victorious, and I didn't feel vindicated. There was certainly no serial killer, because Daniel had been dead and buried while Bella was still alive. But I was no closer to knowing who had killed Bella, and for Minnie's family, and certainly Daniel's, what I had uncovered was much worse. Right now, Minnie's parents wanted a stranger brought to justice, but Minnie hadn't been killed by a stranger. She'd met her untimely end at the hands of a boyfriend they thought had loved her enough to be buried at her side. And Daniel's family thought their son had died of grief—alas, like Lady Macbeth, it was guilt that had dragged him under.

"Crap," I said.

I sat on Minnie's tombstone and ate one of the mince pies. They were a little stale and not spicy enough for me. I sipped a little coffee from my thermos. It was still hot but, sitting up there on the hill in the cold and the dark, it wasn't enough to warm my heart. Half the country seemed to want to kill me. No one wanted to date me. And all my special powers had done for me tonight was reinforce just how dark the underbelly of life could be. And nasty. Killing your girlfriend because you couldn't get your own way... Maybe I should give up on men and just get few more cats?

"I could be a mad cat lady," I assured Minnie's grave confidently. "Or at least a generally quite annoyed cat lady."

I looked across at Daniel's grave. They say grief makes you irrational. I took out the salt cellar and the perfume again. And then I took out Ignatius' little knife. Maybe I was just feeling nihilistic, but I pushed the warning signs at the back of my head away and drew a very, very thick circle of protection. And I reached into the ground and pulled up the empty vessel that had once been Daniel Hereward.

I could see why she'd liked him at first. He looked like a boyband singer, with floppy, dark hair and chiselled cheekbones. But his brown eyes were blank and empty. He stood there looking at me. He was wearing school uniform, and his tie was askew. I just sat and watched him right back. After a while the hunger got to him, and he began to roar and wail. I just sat. Eventually he was sprawled on top of his own grave, growling at me and foaming a little at the mouth. I waited. And then it happened.

His body convulsed as though a bolt of lightning had struck it full on. There was even a whiff of magma in the air, a burned coal-dust aroma, the scent of ancient fires and firmament. I thought I could see his skin steaming slightly. Zombies are hot to the touch, but demons... what can I say? Don't shake hands.

Daniel's body twitched and flailed a little as its occupant accustomed itself to its new dwelling. Then he turned to me and attempted a smile. It wasn't a great smile, but then demons don't really understand emotions, so he was never ever going to get it quite right.

"Toni," he said, spraying a little spit as he tested out his new mouth.

"Toni, my favourite, my little girl. My angel. Beautiful Lavington. So fair… Did you miss me?"

He spat out a mouthful of blood on to the snow. He was already burning through Daniel's body like the Sunday roast. But that would be tuppence to what he'd do to my body if he got out of the circle. Do not mess with demons, unless you really, really want to die slowly in searing pain with the smell of your roasting flesh filling your nostrils. Scratch that. From what I knew of my visitor, come the end you wouldn't have a nostril left to sniff with.

"Hello, Azazel," I said tonelessly. "I greet you."

The less you say, the less chance you'll tie yourself in knots. Don't ask questions without a written contract. Don't say thank you. Don't say please. Honestly, just don't speak with demons, especially Azazel. What had I been thinking?

You see, demons know everything. They know everything you've ever done, even when you were on your own in a dark room. History to them is an open book with a damn good index. The only thing they don't know is what you think, and they have no understanding of human emotions. It's like trying to understand colour when they only see in black and white. Which is why they sometimes seem to offer the craziest bribes to get what they want. They don't really understand why a child wants chocolate, but Paris wanted the love of Helen of Troy. They vaguely understand that mortals want money and power, but not why, and they have no comprehension of affection, honour or loyalty. Thank God.

"Toni, sweetest child," he said, his voice sounding more like his own as he grew accustomed to Daniel's lips; gravelly and oily all at the same time, compelling and resonant, never really human, though, as if a lizard had learned to talk. I'd forgotten how much it made my skin crawl. "You've come to me for help. Your own dear Azazel. I can see you suffer. I will give you happiness."

Azazel would give me a hole in the head if he could, but I still just sat on Minnie's grave and watched the performance.

"Bring it on," I said.

"Darling child, what is it you've come to me for? Ah, your beloved.

You want him back. You need me to reignite Oscar Guillaume's love for you."

Oscar Guillaume? What the fucking fuck? But he hadn't finished.

"I will bring him back to you. He will come to you on his knees begging you to forgive him. For a thousand years he will declaim his love for you. I will give you passion that transcends death."

Of course that was what I wanted. The full-on affection of a cold-blooded killer who would be more controlling than Daniel Hereward. For a freaking millennium. No, thank you very much, Azazel. I shook my head.

"No? My lonely Lavington, I should have guessed. Your German lover, your sweet man with his kind words and his gentle touch. I will bring you Peter Hilliard. He will forget his past loves and his past loyalties. He will want only you, only to serve you and make you happy. He will nurture you and adore you."

Good old Azazel. He didn't have a clue, did he...? Why would I want to change Peter into something else, when he was just perfect as he was? And what sort of monster would I be if I thought it was alright to take away his choices and replace them with my own? Azazel could see I wasn't buying. He hurried on.

"Ah, I see. She has given you diamonds and promises, but you don't want to share. I will take away her coterie and then she will have only you. Only you for eternity. I can do it, little Lavington. Let me help you. You know I love you. I only want to heal your pain."

He was on a roll. What next? Nothing, apparently. He was licking his lips. I rather thought they were starting to melt.

"Come on, Azazel, you aren't on form tonight," I said drily. "You haven't offered me Benedict's devoted love yet. Or maybe even you know that's not realistic."

His eyes glittered. He thought he had me.

"Ah, you don't want the knight or the bishop or even the queen, do you, my lovely, lovely child? You want the king, and I will give you what you want. A love that burns hotter than the fires of Hell and brighter than the halls of Heaven. I will make him raise you up until the whole of the night is beneath your wings. I will give you desire that will make the moon seem like the sun and fulfilment that turns the night into brightest day."

I was sick of his lies and his promises, but he'd actually solved my problem without me even realising I had one: there was absolutely no way he could bribe me with something to make me happy because I didn't have a clue myself what it would take. And if I didn't know what I wanted, then I was damn well not going to mooch round the place feeling sorry for myself because I didn't have it.

"Goodbye, Azazel," I said, and I took out the little golden knife again. "It's time for you to go."

He screamed. He pleaded. He offered me eternal youth, wealth beyond my wildest dreams and the death of my enemies. He was really stretching at that point because he offered me those every single time and they hadn't worked yet. I looked at the smoking form in front of me; Daniel's eyes were starting to disintegrate, and his face was losing form. If I didn't get rid of Azazel soon, Daniel's body would turn to ash and the demon would be free anyway. Not a good idea.

"Azazel, child of God and protégé of Lucifer, I banish you," I began, pressing bloody palms into the snow.

"No, no, no!" he wailed. "Not yet. I have to show God what I did. I never meant for this to happen. I only meant to make them happy."

"Azazel, scion of Heaven and denizen of Hell, I banish you."

The circle was a blaze of gold. I was doing it right.

"If I could tell him, just once, he would understand," he shrieked. "It was a kindness!"

Daniel's body was starting to smoke and char. I had to hurry.

"Azazel, as God spurned you, so do I. Begone to the darkness from which you came, you lying piece of hellspawn."

The last phrase was one of my own, but I liked it. It gave a little bit of oomph to the original mantra.

"No! Please no," he howled a final time, but even as Daniel's lips began to glow like coals, the tendrils of the earth pulled Azazel down, through Sheol and beyond. All that was left was a crumbling empty corpse and a smell of embers. I banished poor old Daniel next and then drank a little more coffee. I warmed a few mince pies in the smouldering circle Azazel had left behind. They tasted a little better hot; not a lot, mind—you need more brandy and a few more cloves.

Chapter Fourteen

ONE THING WAS for certain. I was never going to need to join a gym. Banishing demons was hard work. Every single limb felt as though it had individually run a marathon with zero help from its peers and my head was spinning. Half a flask of coffee and some stale mince pies weren't going to leave me fit for an icy midnight trip back to town. I had a lot of familiarity with sleep deprivation, and I knew my limits.

I was quite prepared to sleep in the car, but I decided to explore comfier options first. The elderly lock on the church door was no match for my picks. Waving my torch around, I found a tray of prayer candles marked at fifty pence a pop. I thrust a twenty-pound note into the collection box and lit as many of them as I could be bothered. The church was as cold as the churchyard, but in the tiny priest's room, there was a little gas fire. I turned it up to max, curled up under a pile of surplices, chasubles and other sacred vestments, and hoped God would look past any minor sacrilege on my part.

I woke at dawn and breakfasted on the last mince pie and some cold coffee, after which I went out to clear up the mess I'd made the night before. Raising the dead doesn't usually leave much refuse behind but, in the snow, it was perfectly clear that something arcane had been going on. I used the shovel from my car to clear the graves entirely of snow and put the somewhat charred flowers in the bin by the lychgate. Finally, I climbed over the cemetery wall to the adjacent field and cut berry-laden winter holly boughs and made two wreaths to sit at the foot of each gravestone. I knew from experience that graves this recent would be visited frequently. I didn't want grieving relatives to find an unloved mess awaiting them.

Heading back into the church, I lit a few more candles, because after a chat with Azazel, my soul still felt kind of grubby. Finally, I cleared the priest's room of all evidence of my night's illicit stay. I was about to leave when—to my horror—the room's owner himself came in. He didn't look surprised to see me, but then, he must have seen my car and noticed the church doors were open.

"Hello, sister," he said quietly.

I stopped in my tracks. He was not a tall man; still taller than me but I had him pegged at about five six. He had fair, sandy hair and a Celtic complexion. He was wearing dark woollen trousers and a thick winter coat, but it was open enough that at the neck I could see his dog collar. I'd spent seven years at the Roman Catholic grammar; I rather thought I was in a lot of trouble.

"Father," I stammered apologetically. "Nothing is damaged. It was really cold. I left some money. I haven't taken anything."

"I saw that, sister," he said. "The alms box was empty when I locked up last night. Did you tidy up the graves, too?"

"Yes, that was me. I'm sorry—"

He interrupted me.

"They look very nice, and now I won't have to do it myself. The families will be here tomorrow for a ceremony, and it was one of my tasks for today. Would you like something hot to drink before you go?"

I nodded. I was surprised. I'd met a lot of priests when I was a schoolgirl. They'd tended to be hard men, good at handing out judgement—and detention. But here was a man who lived up in the hills with his parishioners, not down in the town with the raff and scaff of urban life. Perhaps that made a difference.

"God, you know, I would. I have some biscuits in my car."

"Then bring them to the feast. I am Father Luke Emmanuel, by the way."

His car was a fourteen-year-old hatchback in need of a re-spray. His hot drink was black coffee poured out of a thermos not unlike my own. I was still a bit too embarrassed to talk with him when he broke the ice:

"Did you know them, Danny and Minnie?"

Ah. I didn't like lying. Lying to a man of God had to be worse. I picked a careful path.

"I didn't, but my brother is investigating the other girl who was killed. The one in Rugeley. She went to my school."

"I understand; you feel an affinity."

"Maybe. I am Toni, by the way."

I gulped some coffee. He took a biscuit politely from the packet.

"Do you believe in God, Toni?"

I had to laugh.

"Father Luke, I've met the Devil. I'd be in a very bad place if I didn't believe God was out there to challenge him."

He looked at me in interest.

"I've never met the Devil, my sister. For which much thanks. There are vampires in these hills, they say, and I've not met them either. Are they the seeds of Satan?"

I thought about how to answer him. Yes and no, and no and yes?

"Father, you know what, two nights ago, I met a vampire. I won't go all out and tell you she was a good person. But she knew all about love and loyalty. I've met a lot of people I'd throw off a cliff first."

He looked thoughtful this time.

"Thank you, Toni. That's something I didn't know."

I thought about Daniel and Minnie, and how much worse things would be for their families once they knew the truth. If the police continued to look for a serial killer, they'd get absolutely nowhere in a month of Sundays. I could change that.

"Father, can I ask you something in return? Is it ever OK to lie to people about something important? You know, withhold things that really matter just because the truth would hurt much more…"

He nodded, certain of his ground this time around.

"I can answer that question with no room for doubt, my sister. Come with me."

He took me up the aisle to the lectern. A big, leather-bound book was open on the desktop, embossed in gold and with fat, tasselled cords to mark the pages. He turned them with confidence and opened a page for me.

"Read," he said gently, indicating a line.

I read it out loud.

"OK, here we go: 'Number eight: thou shalt not bear false witness against thy neighbour.' Father Luke, I know this from school. We usually just say that you mustn't tell lies."

"Child, people often seek guidance in moments of confusion. I feel I am singularly fortunate in that regard. When the path is unclear ahead of me, I have a guidebook to help me chart the way. You asked and here the answer is clear. The truth is precious. People are entitled to the truth. Who are we to decide if it will make them happy or not? I myself would prefer a hard truth to a happy web of lies."

"Of course, now you put it like that, it's obvious. It's just…"

And I suddenly saw. I saw what I hadn't been able to see the previous night when Azazel had been looking for my weak spot. I saw what could make me happy and it had always been there.

"Father, I have to zoom. I don't want to sound overly gushing or anything, but what you just said has really helped me."

I hugged him and he looked a little taken aback.

"It's what I'm here for, sister."

"Um, yes, but this has really cleared things up. I know where I'm going now. Good luck with the vampires—avoid them if you can, because they're bad news."

And I got in my brother's car and set off down the hill in the pallid January sun.

I'd been wondering, when I asked the priest about honesty, if I could contemplate concealing the truth about Daniel killing poor Minnie. And he'd convinced me that I couldn't. I might have got there myself in time; I'd got there a lot quicker with Father Luke's help.

But he'd taught me a bigger lesson. The other thing I'd realised was that, whether or not I would have believed it at first, my life would have taken a very different turn if I'd known the truth about Oscar. And so would Peter's. If we'd known what an out-and-out wanker Oscar was, we'd have made different decisions. We'd needed the truth, and we hadn't had it.

And in that moment, standing by the pulpit with Father Luke, I understood that I'd held Peter up to a less exacting glass than myself, and that was just stupid. I would never, ever have stayed with Oscar after I found out what he'd done, even if he hadn't hurt me personally. I would have broken my heart with both hands and a mallet, but I would have left him. And so would Peter.

As I drove down the road, I realised that it would actually have taken much, much less to drive Peter away. Yes, he'd lived with vampires for his whole life, but violence sickened him, and far more than it did me. He would have wanted the Gambarinis punished, for example—I knew that. But he would never have arranged to have them vigorously ripped limb from limb by a horde of hungry zombies while he watched from the side of the cemetery.

So, one of two things held true: either he didn't yet know the truth about Oscar, or—like me—he had already cut and run and was alone. Thinking about it, I had to wonder if he would have wanted to stay with Oscar at all after what had happened to me, let alone the latest tragic victim. Either way, I had to speak with him. Father Luke had given me the green light to fight for what I really wanted. And it turned out to be Peter.

I pulled in at the same supermarket in Ashbourne where I had filled my coffee flask the previous afternoon. Father Luke's advice had nourished my soul, rather than my stomach, and black coffee and chocolate biscuits will only get you so far on an icy winter's day and it was past lunchtime already. At the empty in-house café,

I ordered two rounds of bacon butties and a white coffee with extra sugar. I had to pull a shelf stacker off the dairy aisle to serve me, after stripping him of his headphones, but I needed sustenance. I picked one of the two tables just under the insufficient electric heater.

As my late breakfast was assembled for me, I took off half a dozen layers and then sat with my head whirling. Did Peter know what Oscar had done? If so, where the hell was he, and why hadn't he called me? Scratch that—why hadn't he called me full stop? I'd been unconscious and at death's door when he'd left. Had he talked to other people for an update on my health? I couldn't believe he didn't care. In the confusion that my rejection and loneliness had created for me, I supposed I had pictured him somewhere far, far away, curled up in domestic bliss with Oscar. But we hadn't managed domestic bliss with Oscar with the two of us working nearly full time on it. I'd been stupid—I hadn't thought things through. I hadn't really thought at all, just focused on feeling sorry for myself.

And though I didn't know where Benedict had sent Peter and Oscar, I didn't think it was far. It was close enough that when Oscar had fucked things up again, he'd been sent back to Stafford. So Peter wasn't on a desert island somewhere, but because I was wallowing in self-pity, I simply hadn't asked.

My coffee and bacon sandwiches arrived. After the first round, I rang my brother. I had to get it out of the way before I could think about more important things. He sounded sleepy, and I remembered he was working nights.

"Sorry, bro, but this is important. I raised Minnie last night."

"You did? That's great. Hang on." I heard the sound of someone vigorously rubbing their face in an attempt to find consciousness. "OK. Hit me with it, sis."

"No serial killer. No conspiracy. No connection with Bella. Her boyfriend strangled her on the swings for not being devoted enough."

There was a long silence. For a while I couldn't decide if my brother had fallen back to sleep or not. Then he said slowly:

"But he had an alibi."

"He lied."

"He was in the cinema, Toni. He was watching a film when she died."

"Nope."

"Crap."

"Yup."

"Are you sure? I mean, really sure?"

I shook my head. My brother couldn't see it, but I couldn't help myself.

"What can I say, Wills? Yes, I am totally one hundred per cent sure. The dead don't lie, and certainly not to me."

I couldn't see him either, but I knew when he replied that he was nodding.

"OK, Toni. I believe you. Leave it with me."

I could tell he was about to end the call, and I rushed in:

"Wills, they have to know, don't they? I mean, Minnie and Daniel's families. The truth has to come out?"

God might have told Father Luke directly, but I wanted to be really sure of my ground. My brother didn't hesitate.

"Of course, Toni. There's no other way. If you don't have the truth, you can't have justice. Never think that."

That done and out of the way, I sat looking at my phone. Could I just tell Peter that—if he didn't know it already—I really loved him? Was it that simple? After months in a tunnel, there was a light at the end. Yes, I really did think it was that simple.

I typed,

Peter, please come back. I want to spend the rest of my life with you.

I didn't press send. I just sat the phone on the table in front of me and read the words over and over. I thought they were the right ones. I drained my coffee. Did I want another? It hadn't been very nice. As I debated my beverage options, another customer hauled the poor old shelf stacker away from the milk and cheese racks and into the café. A muffled, lisping voice ordered white tea. No, I decided, no more coffee. I heard the shelf stacker wander back to his task, the strains of Iron Maiden leaking out from behind his headphones. I heard the tea drinker putting his tray down behind me, on the only other table that was near the pitiful heater. Then I made my fatal mistake; I turned round and looked at him.

No wonder he was struggling to speak. Where they'd wired his jaw back together, they'd made a lovely mess. He also had two black eyes and a broken nose on display. Oh, and about forty stitches. I hadn't thought Jasper good-looking when I met him the first time; no one would think so now. His shock when he saw me was palpable. He absolutely reeled.

"You little bitch," he slurred. "No one will save you this time."

I did my best. I screamed and made a break for it. But I doubted my screams would penetrate our shelf stacker's heavy metal, and Jasper was a lot quicker than me—as well as between me and the exit. He seized a handful of my hair as I tried to run past him and I went over in a heap, sending his table flying and showering us both in tea. I heard my phone smash on the floor somewhere.

"You twat," I yelled, trying to get to my feet. "You broke my phone again! I just bought that! And I had a *really* important text to send."

"You need to shut up now," I heard his slurred voice say.

Then something whacked me on the back of my head. I vaguely thought it was my chair, but that was my last thought for a while.

I CAME ROUND to find myself squashed into a small, dark place. A freezing cold, dark space. There was a feeling of motion and the sound of an engine and an agonising pain in the back of my head. I rather thought I'd been gagged with my own silk scarf and my hands were cuffed behind me. I groped around, finding something that felt like Wellington boots and maybe a shovel. I realised in a rush of panic that I was probably in the boot of Wills' car. I felt around for my handbag, but found only a can of de-icer and what felt like a road atlas, a smooth paper cover with a wire, spiral-bound spine.

Could you open a boot from the inside? No one ever seemed to in films. They waited to be killed or rescued. I couldn't get my cuffed hands high enough to find out anyway. I knew I could pick handcuffs—I'd done it once before when Oscar and I were chained up in a cellar—but I needed picks. I needed some springy wire or metal... I moved my hands back to the road atlas and began to tease out some of the wire spine.

It kept me occupied and stopped me from panicking. I managed to gradually pull out about three inches and, by bending it to and fro at the same point, to snap it off. In the pitch dark, that might be all I would manage, but I straightened it out as much as I could and carefully bent it in half. It was the nastiest lock pick I had ever tried to work with, but at least I had one. The other problem, though, was that the boot of the car was getting gradually colder, and so were my fingers. I kept going, but before I had really worked out if I was making progress, the car jerked to a halt and the engine was turned off. I folded the bent wire into the palm of my hand and hoped for better luck in a warmer climate.

The boot opened moments later. I tried to pretend I was still out cold, but Jasper grabbed a handful of my hair and yanked, and I cried out without meaning to.

"I thought you'd be awake by now," he lisped through his swollen, stitched lips. "Pleased with your handiwork?"

He gave a horrible parody of a grin with his reconstructed face, revealing that about four of his teeth were missing on one side. I didn't say anything. To agree would have been provocative, and to disagree would have been worse. I'd just had a lecture from God on telling lies, and the way things were going... well, let's just say I thought I could do with the Almighty on my side quite imminently. Oh, and more to the point, I'd been gagged with my own scarf. I assumed it had been a rhetorical question.

He manhandled me out of the boot, and somehow in the process my gag finally came off. I looked around—Wills' car was just feet away, a still-attached tow rope showing how he'd joined the cars together. We were outside a tiny stone cottage, with no neighbours anywhere in sight that I could see, and judging from the geography around us, we weren't a million miles from the church in which I had spent the night. We were certainly somewhere up in the Peaks above Dovedale. Were we in Staffordshire or Derbyshire? He shoved me ahead of him towards the front door. I considered making a break for it, but in the snow and with my hands tied behind me, I didn't think it would achieve much more than to win me a face full of ice and gravel.

The door was unlocked—who would bother to lock it out here in the middle of nowhere?—and he pushed it open and elbowed me into a small room, a kitchen-cum-living room that took up the whole of the ground floor. It was almost completely bare. There was a single sofa. In the kitchen area I caught sight of an old electric kettle. Open wooden stairs led out of sight. Still, compared to the car, it was welcomingly warm.

"Up," he said, digging me in the small of my back and directing me to the staircase.

I made my way up. A low-ceilinged bedroom was sparsely furnished, with just an iron-framed bed draped in white and a chest of drawers. An open door revealed a tiny bathroom. Jasper unlocked one cuff—fortunately not the one round the hand in which I'd palmed my makeshift lockpick—and looped it around a bar of the headboard before refastening it round my wrist. I struggled ineffectively. I was still dizzy and nauseous from being lamped on the head and climbing up the stairs hadn't helped.

Jasper looked down at me, chained to the bed with my arms pinioned above my head and my hair spread across the white covers.

"You're very pretty," he said suddenly.

I looked up at him in horror and he laughed a little bitterly.

"Yes, that's what I meant, and I probably would," he said. "But with all the painkillers I'm on, the closest I'll get to an erection is if I take the train to Paris and visit the Champ de Mars."

I rolled my eyes at him.

"Where did you even get the cuffs?" I asked.

I was keen to change the subject but he just grinned again, or rather, leered at me again through the mess that I'd made of his mouth.

"There's a sex shop next door to the supermarket," he said. "They had them in silver, black or marabou."

Thankfully, before the conversation could deteriorate any further, I heard the door open again downstairs and a woman's voice called up to us. She sounded out of breath.

"Jasper, are you here? I came as soon as I got your message. I bought all the tools you said. They cost a fortune."

It was Melody. I recognised her voice instantly. Jasper headed down the stairs. I heard them leave the cottage, and I was left on my own.

I shuffled back on the bed until the cufflinks were draped more loosely around the headboard, and then I set to. In the light, and without the worry of being discovered trying to free myself, it was easy. Within minutes, I had unlocked one of the cuffs and was working on the second when I heard the front door go. I slipped the cuff back around my wrist without locking it and tried to drape myself in roughly the same position I had been in. I was just in time. Moments later I heard Jasper's step on the stairs, and he reappeared.

"How are you going to kill me?" I asked conversationally through the pounding in the back of my skull.

He shrugged.

"I've nixed the brakes on your car," he said. "Melody brought me the tools to do it. There are plenty of hairpin bends around here. In the snow, no one will be too surprised. There's a nice hundred-foot drop on the switchback road just below Thorpe Cloud. I worked it out on the drive. I'll wait until it's dark."

"You're as bad as her," I said.

"Who?"

"Hildred."

He literally growled with rage.

"I'm not like her! Nothing like that evil, fucking witch. She decided my Jenny could die. Just like that, because of my affiliations. Nothing I said would move her."

"And you've decided I have to die, just like that. Just to make sure you don't pay the price for your stupid revenge plot."

He laughed again.

"Me, oh no. I won't get my life back. I don't know what I'd do with it now anyway. But I can't have this come back on Mel and Kathy, I told you. People dismiss Mel, because she's not a looker. But she's kind. We met her at the children's ward in Stoke Hospital. She had Kathy on her hands, but she still made time for me and for Jenny. Always. She understood what I had to do—she wasn't keen on it, but she understood. I won't have her carry the can for this."

The woman herself called up the stairs again.

"Jasper, I have to go. Call me when you can."

"Wait," he said. "I'll see you off."

He headed down the stairs again and I heard them talking. I slid my hand out of the unlocked cuff and scurried to the window. It was locked. I watched as Mel got into a little yellow car and drove away. The sky was darkening around the cottage. I must have been out cold in the boot of the car for a long time before I came round. It would be night soon.

"Sod this," I muttered. "There must be something."

I searched the chest of drawers, but it didn't contain so much as a sock. The tiny bathroom contained a packet of aspirin and a loo roll. The window here was open, but it was so minute that Winchester would have struggled to squeeze through, let alone me. I heard Jasper at the foot of the stairs and flung myself onto the bed yet again, hooking the cuffs back around to fake my continued imprisonment.

He climbed up the stairs to the foot of the bed and looked at me thoughtfully. The sun was setting and the light fading. He turned on the bedroom light.

"You were a right pain," he said. "But I'll give you this, you're a fighter. I'll make sure it doesn't hurt."

"What about my father?" I asked suddenly.

"What?"

"Do you think he will miss his daughter?"

It was a stupid question. My father would never have noticed if anyone had wiped me off the face of the earth. He'd always struggled to remember my name. No, that was wrong. He'd never bother to struggle because it wasn't important enough. But Jasper didn't know that…

"Don't give me that. It's not the same."

"Your only complaint about Hildred is that she shouldn't have got to choose who lived and who died. So why the bloody hell do you get to choose?"

He shook his head, but he did look conflicted. Maybe I was making progress. Suddenly, below us, the front door was flung open with such force that we both heard it bang back against the inside wall.

"Mel?" said Jasper in some confusion. "Mel, is that you?"

He looked down the stairs out of my line of sight, and his face paled in shock as he saw what I couldn't. His mouth fell open, as far as the stitches would let it, and it stayed there. He didn't attempt to speak. What was it Homer said? 'My doom is come upon me.' I'd seen terror before. I was seeing it again.

"Oh, Jasper, you've led me such a fine dance," a voice said from the front room. "Did you think I wouldn't find you? Why would you ever think that?"

I was nearly as shocked as Jasper because I knew that voice, too. It was the voice of the man who had tried to drink my blood in the Assemblage, the vampire chief who had sworn to kill me just a week ago and then promised Benedict Akil anything he wanted to let him keep me.

It was Aneurin Blackwood Bordel.

Chapter Fifteen

JASPER STRAIGHTENED HIS spine—the man was no coward, I had to give him that.

"Ani," he said, "I don't know. I guess I should be surprised it took you so long."

Aneurin gave a rather mocking laugh. He had a voice that filled the cottage. He must have been standing just at the foot of the stairs or I would have seen him. I shrank back on the bed. He was distracted right now but in the Assemblage he'd been able to sense me even from metres away, sense me and come to kill me... Had my situation just got better or worse?

"I found you four days ago," he said. "But, owing to unfortunate circumstances, I couldn't come near you until you left Staffordshire today and crossed the border back into Derbyshire. Do you have any idea what your little revenge spree is going to cost me? I already can't pay that Persian bastard Benedict Akil the reparations I owe him. And now he has asked that your slaughter of a vampire in his territory be added to the tally. I'll be fortunate to come out of this with a shirt to my back."

"I'm not sorry," said Jasper, in the voice of a man who didn't care a lot about anything anymore. He walked down the stairs and out of my sight. "No one could have been more loyal to you than I have until all this. But you wouldn't help me either. I gave you everything, my whole life, and this is the only thing I've ever asked in return, to help my little Jenny."

I could hear Aneurin striding about the floor now; he hadn't struck me as someone who did a lot of standing still.

"I tried to help," he protested.

"No, you didn't. Isembard told you it didn't matter, and you just did what he said. Well, I did what I did, and I can't be sorry. I watched Hildred's ashes rise up to the sky just like Jenny's and I can't regret that."

"And was your revenge sweet?" asked Aneurin. "Worth the price?"

"There was nothing sweet about it," said Jasper blankly, "but it was all I was going to get."

"That's certainly true," said Aneurin. "But I've always found it quite delectable. It will make the loss of your company more bearable. I will miss you, Jasper."

Jasper laughed, but it was bitter laughter.

"You'll get over it quick enough," he said. "Can I ask you a favour, Ani, being as we have come to the end of the road?"

"You can always ask," said Aneurin carelessly. "You might even get what you want. Unless, of course, you want to live."

"There's a girl upstairs. She can identify the woman who helped me. I was going to kill her—maybe you could just impel her to forget…"

"Is she from the Staffordshire Assemblage?" asked Aneurin. "If so, I might be able to trade her in for some good will."

"I think she belongs to Benedict personally."

"Christ. Thank God I found you before you ran my bill up even higher. Yes, I'll do that for you. Come now, let's be done with this."

I winced. I had some idea what was going to happen, and I was happy not to have to watch. I had to listen though. The noises weren't nice. It struck me that at least Jasper was dying happily. Or was that worse, that a vampire could make your own body betray you in that way? Jasper would feel all the pleasure of Aneurin's feeding as the life was drained from his body. Me, when Aneurin came up the stairs and found me, I'd probably get the same death. It would just hurt more.

Well, there was no way out of here bar the stairs. I didn't fancy greeting Aneurin lying on my back all trussed up like I was ready to be his second course, so I unpicked the second cuff from my wrist and chucked the pair on the floor. It was a mystery to me why people thought they were a good idea to spice things up in bed. Suppose I thought of something really excellent to do with my hands halfway through the proceedings? All parties would get short-changed.

I stopped my musing and tried to turn my mind to more urgent things. Aneurin would at least arrive very well fed. Could I persuade him not to kill me? He wanted a necromancer to give him power and I hadn't a clue how to do that. But neither did he. Could I drag things out long enough to change the odds, give myself a chance to escape? It had worked the last time…

He bounded up the steps two at a time with an easy stride, but he was shocked enough when he saw me that he nearly fell back down them again. His face when he recognised me was a picture—he was absolutely flabbergasted. I decided to rush in while he was still thrown.

"Well," I said, looking up at him from the bed, and trying not to remember that the last time I'd seen him he'd ripped half my clothes off and tried to kill me, "you've saved my life today. I think the slate between us is clean."

He was dressed with some elegance in well-tailored, grey wool trousers and a wine-red shirt. He'd done well to choose dark colours, because the whole lot was splattered with fresh blood. Around his chest it appeared to have dripped in a waterfall. There was a meaty, iron smell drifting from his clothes and up the stairs. I forced down nausea—throwing up wouldn't make this miserable little cottage smell one iota better.

His short, auburn hair was slightly disarrayed, and the thin, hard mouth I'd disliked the first time I met him was somewhat obscured by a froth of blood. He was a messy feeder. He strode up and down in front of me, and I could feel the wash of his power billowing out, the same dark force that had disconcerted me so much the first time I'd encountered him.

"You," he said finally. "What are you doing here?"

His voice was still angry but now he was intrigued, too.

"Trying to leave," I said hopefully.

"If I'd known he'd brought me such a prize, I might have been less harsh with Jasper."

"I doubt that," I said.

He looked at me quizzically. I realised he was someone who wasn't used to having people answer him back or be snarky in his general direction. I didn't think he'd risen from the grave with an intact sense of humour. Then he shrugged.

"Benedict's a fool to let you out of his sight," he said, and he threw me on to the bed.

Unlike Jasper, Aneurin wasn't on painkillers. He'd nearly killed me once already. He'd only stopped last time because we'd been interrupted. No one was going to interrupt us this evening. I put my hands over my eyes to think but nothing came, nothing at all.

I looked up at him to find him hesitating. Did he need to gloat, to crow, to revel in his victory? Did he want me to add the frisson of putting up a fight? I had a feeling that he was simply sated after his encounter with Jasper. I tried not to hyperventilate as he moved to loom over me. He caught my forearms in his hands and pinned them much as Jasper had with the cuffs.

He looked down at me. His face was flushed, and his narrow, blood-smeared mouth parted in anticipation. His eyes were the palest of electric blue, and I doubted there'd been the slightest touch of kindness in them even when he'd been alive. What had Grace said—vampires craved blood and sex? Oh yes, and power... I swallowed the pint or so of saliva that seemed to have filled my mouth. Could I use that against him?

"I know more about you now," he said, putting a hand to my neck and grasping the fabric of my top. "You're the great-great-granddaughter of Ignatius Windsor. Benedict stole you from the General, and now he's banished your lover to keep you for himself."

I stared at him. You give someone a handful of facts, and it's amazing the interpretation they will put on them. But even as I stared at him, I decided there was no point in disabusing him of his crazy ideas. They might be exactly what I needed.

"Yes," I said softly, my mind working overtime. "He stole my lover away from me. Now he wants me for himself. Don't hurt me—I'm no good to you dead and you know it really. If you help me to kill him and win Oscar back, I'll make you the most powerful vampire who ever walked under the stars. I'll give you all the powers you have ever dreamed of."

He gazed at me, and his hand dropped away from my throat. People say it's easy to believe something you want to believe. I was selling him a lie he'd want to buy into. Would he bite? He didn't seem to be able to summon up the energy to kill me.

"You'd say anything," he said slowly. "Anything to save your life."

Pretty much, but maybe I'd already said it. I'd piqued his interest. If he hadn't already been gorged from his slaughter of Jasper, I doubted I'd have got this far, but he was. The electric anticipation that characterised Oscar when he craved blood was missing. I doubted even warlike Aneurin got to murder and drain mortals all that often.

He pulled back from me and moved to stand at the foot of the bed. I closed my eyes for a moment in relief, but just for the tiniest instance. No time for this, Toni. I got to my feet and walked shakily round the bed to him. I stood as close as I dared and looked up so that he would see how little and helpless I was next to his mighty self.

"I'll show you," I said. "You'll be amazed."

He looked at me speculatively.

"Tonight?"

"Right now. We'll start now."

Start what, though? Aneurin knew exactly what I was. How the hell was I going to pull this off? If he wasn't allowed to enter Staffordshire, I wouldn't get the chance to pull the same trick I'd worked on the Gambarinis and just bury him under the sheer weight of zombies. Then I knew: if I could get him back to Minnie

Cavendish's grave, I might just live through the night.

I walked down the stairs ahead of him and, after a moment's hesitation, he followed. I had him. And, as I looked back, I saw that he had left the cuffs on the floor. Things were looking up. He was right that I would say anything to save my life. It wasn't my favourite approach, but this time I couldn't think of another one. I was going to lie my way out of this. All the way to the bank.

When I'd been in the front room before, I'd thought it plain and sparsely furnished. It's amazing the difference a semi-decapitated corpse and two or three pints of blood will make. Jasper's body lay sprawled in the middle of the floor, his throat ripped open so deeply that I could see his spine. I'd seen drained bodies before, but never as fresh as this. His skin had a white, deflated, wrinkled look to it, throwing the green and purple bruises I'd given him into even starker relief.

Blood had sprayed across the walls and even the ceiling in arcs and pooled on the floor where it was still oozing sluggishly out of Jasper's throat. The meaty smell was overwhelming, the tang of flesh so strong in my sinuses I tossed my head to try and shake it out.

I didn't stay in the room. I wanted the remains of the pitiful half-breakfast I'd managed to eat that day to stay in my stomach. I hurried out into the clean night air, with Aneurin at my heels.

I found my bag on the passenger seat of Wills' car, contents intact. No phone, alas, but all the usual accoutrements a jobbing necromancer needs. I looked speculatively at Aneurin—was he the type who'd need candles and chants to convince him? No. He would be a results man.

"We'll take your car," I said, gesturing at the big-wheeled beast he appeared to have arrived in. "Jasper has buggered up the brakes in mine. We need a corpse to raise to begin your transformation and there's a nice fresh grave up at St Etheldreda's."

He got in and started the engine. He looked at me suspiciously. I hoped the fact that I hadn't attempted to ask him to let me go might assuage his suspicions, and it seemed to be so.

"What do you want?" he asked in his caustic voice. "You tell me your schemes, little necromancer."

I ticked my fingers as though going through a wish list.

"I want Benedict Akil dead. Then Oscar can come back to me. We can kill two birds with one stone if you like—maybe he can work for you. I will help you to boost your powers. It takes time. You know it took Benedict more than forty years."

Had it? Who knew? I didn't, but I sure as hell knew that Aneurin Blackwood Bordel didn't either. I looked at him. I was going for excited, eyes glowing and heart full of hope for love reunited.

"You won't be sorry you saved me," I said. "Not one bit."

He drove competently. The snow on the roads had compacted rather than melted while I'd been unconscious in the boot of a car or chained to a bed, and I was glad for the car's big, ridged wheels. I knew that if my plan worked, I would be driving back this way on my own. Of course, if it backfired, I'd be dead or worse…

"Was it you?" he asked after a couple of miles. "Was it you who told Benedict that Jasper killed Hildred?"

"I don't know how he knew," I admitted. "I told him that there was someone called Jasper there. And then she was killed a few hours later."

"The name would have been enough," he said. "I had already asked him for permission to come to the county to look for Jasper. I didn't work out for a long time why he had come. I'd helped him get in touch with Hildred."

"I can't imagine that helped his cause with her," I said. "I gather she didn't like other vampires."

"She was fond enough of that damned German philanthropist," he growled. "All of them coo over Lenz like he's Superman. It makes me sick. Jasper never told me what happened. I only found out his little girl was dead a few days after he'd left. I assumed he'd taken her with him."

"Jenny," I said. "Her name was Jenny."

He shrugged.

"She was just a mortal," he said. "She didn't matter. I could have told him that."

I looked across at my undead chauffeur. He wasn't good at people, and he wasn't learning. I put a warm hand on his arm. Benedict had told me how alluring warm human flesh felt to vampires, how attractive our body heat was. Well, I would use the hand I'd been dealt.

"I will matter to you," I said.

He parked at the little church, just by the lychgate as I had. The two graves I had cleaned up just that morning were starkly black against the blanket of snow that smothered everything around them. I thought about what I wanted to do and how tired I was. I'd had little sleep the previous night, and almost nothing to eat all day. I'd been clubbed unconscious and nearly frozen to death. I was as weak as a kitten and there was actually no way I could pull this off in my current state. I turned to Aneurin and put my hand on his arm again; I kept it there much longer than necessary. I needed to distract him as much as possible. I didn't want him calling all my crazy lies into question.

Peter had told me that all vampires have certain core powers: strength and speed, the ability to heal to some degree and the means to compel mortals to their will... Well, I needed strength and I needed to heal. I turned to Aneurin.

"I need to drink your blood," I said.

He blinked.

"You never said that. I thought I would drink yours."

I looked confused; well, I tried to. I hoped it was working.

"I'm sorry, Aneurin. I forgot you don't know how this works yet. My blood has no power in it yet. I need your strength for the task ahead, and then you will drink the power from me."

He rolled up a shirt sleeve and brought his wrist to his mouth. There was a flash of fang and then he held out his arm to me.

The blood was horribly black in the dim light from the car interior. My stomach churned. I was lying naked in the snow with Oscar. 'Just drink it,' I heard his voice in my mind. 'Why do you do this?'

I looked up at Aneurin in panic. He just looked a little curious about my hesitation. I had to do this. I'd failed to do it for five months with a man I loved and trusted. Now I had to do it with a man I thoroughly disliked who had tried to kill me last time we'd met.

I closed my eyes. There were the perfect curves of Benedict's chest, him dipping his fingertips in his own blood for me... "You are always unexpected," he'd said. I closed my lips around Aneurin's wrist and drank.

It was nearly as unpleasant as I'd imagined. It didn't actually taste that bad—it was like a salty liqueur, fiery and uncanny—but it was thick and cloying and given the weather it was also ice cold. I could feel Aneurin's wrist flex under my mouth as I sucked. I swallowed, suppressing the urge to gag. I drank until I was choking. I felt the pain in my head recede and my strength build. The shakiness in my legs had gone. Yes, I could fight the undead now. I would take Aneurin down with the energy in his own stupid vampire blood.

"You didn't enjoy that," he said suddenly, surprise in his voice. "And you didn't want me to feed on you either. I remember the old man screamed, too. He felt no pleasure."

I looked up at him in confusion. Who was he talking about? Why did he think I would know? I pushed my concerns down and concentrated on the task at hand. I could see a little better in the darkness now. I didn't think it would last, but it would last the night. Vampires can see like cats at night. Usually, the only thing I had that was catlike was a fondness for salmon.

"No," I said. "I'm a necromancer, Aneurin. Vampire powers don't work on me in the same way. Come on now. The grave up there is only three weeks old."

"Why didn't you use Jasper's body?" he asked suddenly.

I was grateful that I had my back to him. Why indeed... how about because I was making this crap up as I was going along?

"You drained him," I said as though it was obvious. "If you wanted to use his body, you should have strangled him or something."

With the sun down, the January night air was icy and I was pining for my coat and my many layers of jumpers. Were they still at the supermarket café? I rubbed my hands up and down my arms as I led Aneurin to Danny's grave.

It was as I had left it that morning, cleaned of snow and with the holly wreath set in place. I had a feeling it was about to get messed up again. I re-read the inscription: 'Daniel Hereward, beloved son. Gone too soon.' And about to be recalled again rather sooner than expected...

"I saw a necromancer raise the dead, a couple of hundred years ago," said Aneurin suddenly. "He raised a shuffling parody of a man. I couldn't see why our kind had always been so afraid of you."

I began to inscribe my circle of protection. I didn't bother with the salt cellar—I couldn't risk a perimeter that fragile. I just poured a thick line onto the grass straight from the bag of table salt.

"Well," I said, "I'm afraid my denizen of the undead tonight is likely to be much the same. So don't be too disappointed."

Against his better judgement, I could tell, he was intrigued. He watched as I moistened the line. I didn't worry about saving any perfume. I just yanked the lid off the atomiser and poured out a scented stream, soaking the roughly circular arc of salt.

"How does it work?" he asked.

I took out Ignatius' little knife and reluctantly scored some more lines in my wrists; they were starting to look like patchwork. I let the blood drip along the circumferences of my circle of protection. I'd already had more than enough of blood for one evening, which was a shame as I thought the majority of it was yet to come.

"I'll raise him, you'll tear out his heart and together we will draw out his essence," I said, feeling I was getting nearly as good at making up paranormal bollocks as Uri Geller. "Then, when you drink my blood, you will receive all the powers he would have possessed as a vampire."

"Is that how Benedict did it? I always wondered. Marchesa said she didn't know."

He was talking to himself, but I gave him a sideways glance. Had he said what I thought he'd said? I wanted to question him further, but I didn't dare risk him losing confidence in me.

There was no time like the present.

"Daniel Hereward, I summon you," I said clearly. "Come to me."

He came, stepping effortlessly through the soil to stand in the circle. He looked just as he had the previous night when I had first called him from his rest: a pretty, empty, hungry vessel who'd thrown away his life. Aneurin made as if to step into the circle and I put my hand on his arm to restrain him.

"Wait," I said. "Let him exhaust himself first."

I kept my hand on his arm, willing my mortal warmth to distract him. The first time we'd been together he'd half stripped and nearly murdered me. The second time, he'd been a hair's breadth from doing the same whilst raping me. But I needed him to believe me just a little longer, just another minute. I stroked his arm lightly as though we were friends filled with anticipation. Rather late in the day, I was starting to get an inkling that most vampires were very, very bad at understanding certain human emotions; just like Azazel, they found many of our motivations hard to fathom. Aneurin wasn't calling my apparent admiration of him into question, even after everything he'd done. He clearly felt it was his due.

We watched as poor old Daniel's body went through the previous night's Oscar-winning performance of wailing and flailing. I hoped his shambling incompetence would reassure Aneurin. I didn't need my wannabe dark master getting cold feet at this stage. Because I didn't think we'd have to wait long for Azazel. I rather thought he'd be waiting in the wings.

"Get ready," I said when we got to the foaming-at-the-mouth finale.

And then there it was… the convulsion of the body, the hint of smoky mist, the faintest whiff of brimstone. I nodded at Aneurin, and he stepped without a care in the world into the circle of protection.

I didn't watch. I tried not to listen, but it didn't help much. Azazel claimed he only wanted to work his way back into Heaven. Well, he had a funny way of showing it. You don't need to keep your eyes centre stage to tell when a desperate vampire is being flayed, eviscerated and torn limb from limb. The sound effects and the body parts crossing your peripheral vision will keep you well informed. I felt Aneurin's blood spray across my face in clammy waves. Some droplets were warm, others already cooked into little globules. I saw an arm, maybe a leg. Was that a spleen or a gall bladder? Anyway, definitely an organ bouncing across the cemetery, but there my biology ran out.

I waited until the screams stopped and a greasy cloud of charred vampire dust showered down on me. Fragments stuck to the blood like Halloween sequins. I looked up at Azazel. He was red and sticky, as though he had been dipped in gore, his nails and his teeth snagged with tissue.

"I saved you, little Lavington, dear sweet Lavington. You are in my debt," he crowed. "You owe me."

"Crap to that," I said. "You want to save up pennies for Heaven? Well, I brought you a gift—an evil vampire you could slay to boost your tally with God. You owe me, you conniving little shit."

We glared at each other across the lake of gore and when he finally dropped his eyes, I knew we had at least reached a stalemate. He was still trying to distract me for long enough to break out of Daniel's body, but I knew I hadn't sold my soul. I sliced four more gouges across my left wrist with my great-great-grandfather's knife, and then across my right. I crouched in the snow, pressing my palms into the ground.

"Azazel, child of God and protégé of Lucifer, I banish you."

"Wait!" he shrieked. "I will tell you how your parents died. You can finally have your revenge."

He would, too, but only if the truth would ruin my life.

"Azazel, scion of Heaven and denizen of Hell, I banish you."

"Not yet!" he countered. "I will tell you what Benedict Akil wants. You can ruin all his plans and bring down the Children of Diometes."

You know what, I could probably do that by accident in between breakfast and lunch. I was anathema to my own plans; no one else's stood a chance. A nice bright flame caught on the second circle. Aneurin's blood was working a treat.

"Azazel, as God spurned you, so do I. Begone to the darkness from which you came."

"Peter will leave you," he said. "I can tell you how to make him stay."

I stared at him. For a moment he had me, the one thing I might have bargained for... but before I could react, he was gone, his presence only evidenced by the scent of burning rock and the carnage of his tussle with Aneurin. I stood stock-still in silence for a moment, filled with relief because if he'd endured a moment longer, I might have buckled. Then I took a deep breath and sent Daniel after him.

I sat on my heels in the graveyard, all alone, with only thoughts that were making me uncomfortable to keep me company. I sat there long enough to start to shiver. Then I helped myself to Aneurin's car and drove home. His nice vicuna coat was flung across the back seat, and it kept me warm for the drive. I rather thought he must have had it cleaned—last time I saw it, it had been splattered with my blood. Hell, maybe he'd had two... I phoned the breakdown company and asked them to pick up Wills' car the next day. Finally, I took the world's longest, hottest bath—complete with bubbles, music and a glass of wine—bandaged up my wrists and went to bed.

Chapter Sixteen

SUNDAY MORNING DAWNED cold and windy. Somewhere across the border in Derbyshire, Father Luke was comforting grieving relatives. Somewhere closer to home, my brother would be wondering where his car was and when I was bringing it back. Not a million miles away, a woman who called herself Melody was probably watching the news to read about my tragic death on icy Peak roads. But in the little stone cottage of Lavington Windsor, peace reigned. I lay in bed until noon with Winchester and a crappy romance novel that Camilla had lent to me. I made brief forays to the kitchen for coffee and toast. At some point I knew I needed to get up, get dressed and buy another new phone, but I put the moment off until the sun was high in the sky.

Everything I had worn the previous day was splattered with blood. Some was dried to a nasty brown. Other bits looked scorched and cooked. Several of the stains were unpleasantly three-dimensional. All were dusted with the final remains of one Aneurin Blackwood Bordel. Peter would have probably soaked them in some secret mixture of lemon juice and baking soda or some crap like that. I threw them in the bin. I hesitated over my lovely fur-lined boots, but they'd got the brunt of Azazel's impersonation of an industrial shredder. I was close to tearful as I threw them in the wheelie bin along with my handbag.

I revised my shopping list to include new winter boots and also resolved to finally replace the woolly hat I'd given to Kathy.

Thinking about Kathy set me off though. I'd been avoiding thinking about my previous night's adventures, but once my mind had turned that way, I couldn't stop. Benedict had told me that Aneurin had come to the Stone House seeking a member of his personal coterie who had gone AWOL. Aneurin must have told Benedict the man's name... Then Peter and I had told Aidan what I'd discovered at Melody's house—in particular, a man called Uncle Jasper—and Hildred had been found murdered shortly afterwards. At that point, Benedict must have worked out that Jasper was responsible because he'd demanded reparations from Aneurin for Jasper's crimes.

That was all very well. I finally knew who Jasper was, the missing member of Aneurin's coterie and the man Aneurin had come to Staffordshire to find. I also knew why Jasper had killed Hildred— for refusing to save his daughter Jenny—but I still hadn't a damn clue why he wanted to kill me. He'd told Aneurin I could identify Melody, but I couldn't. I didn't have a clue who the damn woman was... or Kathy, for that matter.

I was angry with Benedict for not telling me what he'd found out. I didn't know how much of a difference it would have made, if any, but I'd been kept in the dark and I hated that. I added it to the tally of things I hated about him, which wasn't getting any shorter. I had a strong feeling I ought to tell him about Aneurin—at the very least that the dead vampire's car was parked outside my door. But a sense of vengeance trumped actual sense. Benedict sodding Akil hadn't confided in me, so he could damn well live in ignorance.

I dragged on some clothes, cleaned and re-dressed my throbbing wrists, and staggered downstairs for more coffee. A white, hand-delivered envelope was sitting on the mat in the hallway at the bottom of the stairs. I couldn't recall if it had been lying there the previous night when I'd hauled my blood-stained self home.

I took it into the kitchen and postponed opening it until I was sat at the table with a steaming mug. It was addressed in an overly neat, round hand to one Ms Lavington Windsor; Ts were crossed, Is were dotted. I opened it with reluctance.

It was from one Marjorie Bessant, Head of Pastoral Services at Rugeley Grammar. I'd never heard of her. I'd certainly never met her but, long before I'd finished her missive, I knew I didn't want to. She informed me that it had come to her attention that I was mentoring one Paul Mycroft. She felt it incumbent on her to let me know that she thought this was an entirely bad idea. She explained that I was far too young to take on a case as challenging as that of Paul's given his troubled background; she didn't divulge her own age. She hinted at the many evil things his past had contained, as though he'd previously been convicted of at least a double murder rather than selling the occasional joint or pill under the desk in double Maths. She went on to elaborate that I didn't have the right qualifications to be doing whatever it was she thought I was doing; I wasn't informed of her qualifications. Finally, she asked very archly if I was aware how many days of school my charge had missed. I was forced to assume this was a genuine question, as she didn't go on to tell me the total.

I sighed. Then I crumpled up her letter and threw it into the bin. I added another task to the list queuing up to ruin my quiet Sunday morning, namely to find young master Paul and give him a complete bollocking.

I also decided that as I no longer owned a winter coat, warm boots or gloves that were fit to wear, that particular item could wait until I'd gone shopping. My car was at Wills and Henry's house, their car was probably on the back of a pickup truck, and while Aneurin's car was parked outside my house, I was quite certain I wasn't insured to drive it. I sighed and called a taxi to take me to Lichley.

I'd noticed Oscar's car was still sitting outside my former love nest when Aidan had tried to drop me off there a week ago. I was certainly insured to drive the thing, and there was nothing else at hand. It had a long German name and leather seats and when you pressed a button the roof kindly retracted into the boot and squashed anything you'd put in there. It wasn't my cup of tea, but the heating worked. Of course, I would have to sell my soul to Azazel in order to fill up the tank if it was empty, but I could tool it around town for a couple of days until I was able to give my brother back his own car and reclaim the rust-mobile.

I let myself into the hall and wandered round disconsolately for half an hour. The place appeared immaculate, and I guessed that some kind of housekeeping service had been arranged. The window in my former bedroom had been repaired, and the ruined bedding replaced. The dirty washing in the washing basket had been laundered and put away. For a moment my heart leapt into my throat at the thought that Peter might be in residence but, in the kitchen, I found the fridge empty. Had Peter been anywhere near the place, it would have been stuffed to the gunwales with healthy green things and two litres of skimmed milk.

Oscar's car keys were where I'd expected them, hanging on a hook beside the coat rack. I took them and unlocked the car. I opened the boot, and—given that the weather meant I wasn't going to have to worry about the dumb retracting roof—I filled it with some of the clothes and bits and pieces that I was vaguely bothered about. I hadn't felt up to doing it before, clearing out my possessions. I still didn't have much enthusiasm, but it felt like a start. I was moving on from Oscar. I was starting by nicking his car.

After two hours of retail therapy, I felt less despondent. One entirely successful trip into Stafford had yielded new fur-lined boots even softer than their predecessors, as well as many nice warm things that I probably didn't need but felt my recent commission success could stretch to. I acquired yet another mobile phone and even bought a replacement woollen hat for the one I'd given to Kathy. Finally, I splashed out on a soft, emerald-green, beaded cashmere top, a coordinating leather mini-skirt and matching high-heeled boots that came up just over my knees. I didn't need them either, but what the hell—they would look nice with Grace's diamonds.

Reinforced by my gratuitous spending spree, I drove to Eleanor Johnson's gnome-ridden dwelling and rang the doorbell. Paul answered after a couple of rings. He didn't look displeased to see me, but I was very quickly eclipsed by the sight of Oscar's car parked in the driveway.

"That," he said in tones of awe, "is the coolest car ever."

I looked at the car. Was it cool? It was cherry coloured and sported a lot of chrome. It was flat and sleek and a right pain to get in and out of. It was loud, it guzzled petrol and it had the storage capacity of one of my smaller handbags. Much like the rust-mobile, it was way too small to shag in. But cool? Clearly it was cool.

"It's my ex-boyfriend's," I said vaguely. "Mine's elsewhere."

Paul squinted at me. He came from a tough background and the first time we'd ever spoken it was after he'd seen me fighting for my life. I had a feeling he hero-worshipped me just a tiny bit.

"Does he know you've taken it?" he asked.

"Nope."

"Will he mind?"

"Who cares? I needed a car. And maybe. But he's an arse. Is there any tea?"

We trooped in past the ceramic ballerinas and into the kitchen. I put the kettle on. The delights of living in a house free of status dogs and crystal meth pipes hadn't yet worn thin on Paul, and Eleanor's place was immaculate. The drawing room was rather littered with textbooks and sheets of paper, and the kitchen stacked very neatly with packets of instant noodles, but otherwise you wouldn't have guessed a teenager was in residence.

Paul made us both a mug of tea and I took mine to the sofa. He joined me rather warily. I think he knew what was coming. I took a deep breath.

"So," I said. "Are you acquainted with some interfering bint rejoicing in the name of Marjorie Bessant?"

"Bossy Bessant? I should think so. I spend half my time at the school trying to avoid her. I was on her register the day I started at the grammar and even though I've spent more than six years without a bloody detention she's always on my case. The whole thing with poor little Bella is like Christmas to her. Bossy'll be gutted if they ever manage to show I wasn't the murderer."

I hadn't been all that surprised that Marjorie had found out I'd passed myself off as Paul's mentor. Rugeley was a small town, the grammar was a small school, and everyone knew everyone. Someone would tell someone until eventually someone told Marjorie. Probably Bernie had told Helen who'd told her Mum who'd told the entire bridge club... But there are consequences to all things. A lie made to cover my arse was coming back to bite my arse. It was bang on target.

"Well, if it's any consolation, I don't like her either," I admitted. "But Paul, she wrote to me and said you've skipped a lot of school. Just so we're clear, I've no intention of talking with that cow behind your back, so her note is in the bin and it's staying there; I won't be answering it. But this is your A level year. You have to get into university. What the bloody hell is going on?"

He looked at me mulishly. I glared back. We didn't know each other that well, and I didn't have any right to take him to task. I was hoping the favours I'd done him and his slight awe of me would act in my favour. After a few moments, he dropped his gaze and looked into his mug.

"What do you think?" he said. "I tried. But they all stare at me like I am Freddy fricking Kruger. Either I killed Bella, or I made it possible for her killer to get away with it. Either way, the entire school hates me more than Hitler. My moped got trashed the day I got it back and I don't dare take my phone through the gates. It would last, like, four minutes. I can't put a book down without the pages getting ripped out. The teachers pretend they don't notice because they all feel the same. Toni, I am not going to school because I don't want my fucking jaw broken in the lunch break, alright."

My heart went out to Paul; I'd been a bit of an outcast at school, but he was a walking talking epitome of the word pariah. We needed to find out who'd really killed Bella, and we needed to do it soon before Paul fell behind any further and ballsed up his exams. I sat with my head in my hands for a minute.

I needed advice. Wills was already out of ideas, and it wasn't casual girlfriend conversation that I could take to Claire. And my

Peter wasn't around anymore for me to pick his brains. There were a lot more questions I wanted to ask Bella, now I knew more and had time to mull things over, but CID had taken her body away so I no longer had that option. And so far, in everything that had happened, Bredon had been the only person who'd made the slightest helpful suggestion—that someone had slaughtered her in anger. Fine. I would go back to Bredon and ask him for advice.

I looked over at Paul. The mulish look had settled in, and I couldn't really blame him. It wasn't fair to even try to force him back to school under the conditions he'd just described.

"OK," I said. "I give in. Try to study here for now. We'll have to sort this out ourselves and find out who really killed Bella. I'll pick you up just after dark. I have a friend who gives good advice. We can ask him how to go about clearing your name."

Paul looked startled.

"You really think your friend could help us?" he asked. "Is he a rozzer?"

I laughed.

"Hardly. But he has got me out of a hole before. Paul, I'll come when it's dark. Wear lots of warm clothes."

I left him looking a little happier and hoped I hadn't raised any false hopes. It seemed likely that Bella's killer would eventually be identified but, at this rate, not until Paul's academic career had been ruined. I would do my best.

I had some Sunday left to kill and a swanky car to drive round in, so I decided to do something I had been putting off for a while. I decided to find a new graveyard. Baswich Cemetery was the largest for miles, but it was way too central. I'd abandoned it as a regular haunt because it became clear I would get caught out sooner or later. And more to the point, all the graves were new. I wouldn't stretch myself raising the dead from a rest of just a decade or two. You don't get to be a virtuoso by playing chopsticks. I wanted to summon those who'd mouldered in their tombs for time immemorial not just since Tuesday last. Also, it wasn't a short drive. Baswich was out.

All the churches in the centre of Rugeley were out, too. The town was too busy at night. I would get caught in the act there just as quickly. So where? I hadn't visited it, but I was vaguely aware that there was a ruined church past Blithbury, St Virgil's. Ruined meant old, so it might just fit the bill. It was only ten minutes' drive, and it was in the middle of nowhere. It would be deserted at night.

I had to laugh when I got there. It would have been outrageously Gothic even before the belfry fell in and all the buttresses along the north side decided to take a nap against the supporting wall. Now it looked like the corniest film set ever, just waiting for the likes of Bredon, Benedict and Grace to come and strike a pose at full moon, charmingly accessorised by a few bats and a Sisters of Mercy soundtrack.

My hopes weren't raised high, though. True, there was a modest but suitably mouldering collection of tombs and gravestones clustered around. That was the plus. The minus was an enormous yellow digger that appeared to be scooping them up one by one and loading them on to a flatbed truck. It didn't look like there would be any point in my popping back after dark to see who would answer my call.

I watched for a while. Whoever was operating the machine knew what they were doing. After a few minutes I waved to him, and he turned off the engine and climbed down. I pegged him in his late sixties, short white hair under a cap, dusty cords topped by a fluorescent orange windproof jacket. He was wearing steel-toed workman's boots, ideal when you are hefting around things that weigh as much as a piano. He had rather twinkly brown eyes and not many teeth.

"Alright there, miss," he said cheerfully. "I'm sure I should tell you to wear a hard hat."

He held out a rather grubby paw, which I shook.

"I will if you like," I said. "Though I'm not sure it would help if you did drop a gravestone on my head."

He seemed amused.

"Probably not, young miss, and we might not be able to get it down over all those curls. Were you after me for something? I am Harold Shaw, by the way."

"Oh, and I'm Toni. Pleased to meet you, Harold. Not really, I came to look at the church, but you seem to be taking it away stone by stone."

"I am just doing graves, me. The construction company will be doing the rest."

"I'm lost... rest of what?"

Harold was happy to sit on one of the remaining gravestones and tell me everything, including his life story and the names of all his grandchildren. But broadly, the church had been sold to property developers. The building was coming down, and eight little modern villas were going up in its place and across the site of the graveyard. However, the bishop of the diocese had insisted the graves be moved to consecrated ground for the sale to go through. Harold was moving them one by one to Baswich where they were being re-erected in a little plot at the top of the hill.

I nodded idly. St Virgil's was out then. A thought struck me.

"Harold, you aren't moving the bodies, the actual graves. You're just taking the stones that mark them."

He seemed amused.

"Well, miss, I mean Toni, these are old."

"I know that. They're all covered in moss."

"No, really old, miss. The very youngest was put underground nearly two hundred and fifty years ago; most of these here corpsicles were buried more than four hundred years gone. There's nothing else to take away now bar the stones. If I dug all day, the most I would find is a coffin nail. If they were fifty years old, even seventy, well, maybe there would be some point. But look at this ground, it's wet and loamy. Nothing buried here would last."

No? You learn something new every day. I had also learned that I wouldn't be raising the inhabitants of St Virgil's graveyard anytime soon. Something that Harold had said had struck a chord somewhere at the back of my mind, but I couldn't pinpoint it.

I bid him a very cheery good afternoon. I hadn't found a new cemetery, but Staffordshire looked pretty arrayed around me in the snow and people appeared to have stopped trying to kill me. Admittedly, that might be because they were all dead... I pushed such negative thoughts aside and drove home.

I picked Paul up at sunset. He didn't ask questions, which I appreciated, not least because it struck me as a rare characteristic in a teenager. We drove in a companionable silence almost all the way to Colton Hill. But when I parked at the old church, his curiosity overcame him.

"Why are we meeting your friend at a graveyard?" he asked.

It was a reasonable question. It didn't have a reasonable answer that I was prepared to give him. I wanted him to explain his story to Bredon himself, in case I'd somehow missed something, but I also didn't want him to know that Bredon was, to put in bluntly, extremely dead.

"It's complicated," I settled on.

He shrugged.

"Don't tell me then," he said in wounded tones.

"Fine, I won't then."

"Fine."

"Fine."

The silence became less companionable as I got out of the car and pulled a few extra layers on. I rather thought Paul was glaring at me, but it was too dark to tell.

"Would you bring the picnic basket from the boot and follow me in a couple of minutes?" I asked. "I'll be in one of the mausoleums. You'll find it by the light."

He nodded curtly, and I walked briskly to Bredon's grave.

"Bredon Havers, come to me, I summon you," I whispered.

Each time I raised him, he came to me more easily. It had been six months or so since we first met, and it felt increasingly as though he was waiting for my call. That night he stepped through the snowy ground as if it was merely mist. He stood in the moonlit winter whiteness in his peacock-embroidered coat, his hand already on his sword. He relaxed when he saw me.

"Beloved," he said, taking my hand and kissing it. "But you have brought a friend."

I turned round in shock. At my elbow stood Paul Mycroft, staring white-faced at the revenant I'd called back from the dead. He'd been a lot quicker with the picnic basket than I'd expected.

"Oh my God, you're some kind of necromancer," he said, before adding wistfully, "That's so cool."

Chapter Seventeen

"Um," I said helpfully.

I searched for the right thing to say; nothing came. I worked hard to keep my necromancy secret. Vampires might have decided to come out of the coffin and reveal themselves to the world but I was quite happy for my powers to remain a secret. Inwardly cursing my carelessness, I just looked from Paul to Bredon and back again. Fortunately, nothing floored Bredon. Certainly nothing would make him forget his manners.

"Dear heart," he said to me coaxingly, "will you introduce me to your friend?"

Thankfully my own upbringing kicked in at that point.

"Of course," I said. "Paul, this is my good friend Bredon Havers. He is a resident here and will be joining us for dinner. Bredon, this is Paul Mycroft. He saved my life a week ago, and now he needs our help. Or rather yours, because I'm all out of ideas."

Bredon took Paul's hand with great courtesy.

"Sir," he said, "I am more than delighted to make your acquaintance. And more grateful than you can imagine for your services to Mistress Lavington. How do you do?"

Paul looked a little panicked, but manfully shook Bredon's large hand.

"Yeah, OK," he ventured, before hazarding: "Pleased to meet

you, too?"

"Indeed," said Bredon. "Are you also a resident of this place?"

He gestured to the tombs around us, and I realised with a little pang that—apart from the people he'd killed for me—Bredon had encountered only me in all the months I'd known him. The only time he'd briefly bumped into anyone else, they'd been other zombies I'd drafted in to help us in general slaughtering activities. And the vampires I'd needed him to kill. Now he was asking, as politely as he knew how, if Paul was also dead…

Paul misunderstood the question, but managed to answer it anyway.

"I live down the hill," he said. "In Rugeley."

"Almost a local, then," said Bredon. "You must tell me how it has changed since my day."

With his gentle manners he began to draw Paul out as I rather frantically dusted out the mausoleum of someone who wasn't Julia Lambert, tucked the tripod and telescope out of the way, and laid out dinner. I hadn't been sure what Paul would eat apart from pizza and full English; in my day, teenagers shunned anything that resembled a vegetable and considered salad to be garnish, so I'd added half the deli counter to the usual spread I put out for Bredon.

"Guys," I called. "Come eat. Don't wait."

I'd misjudged Paul. He ate everything. His appetite couldn't quite match a zombie's—he didn't eat the bones as well as the chicken—but even I was impressed. And the two seemed to be getting on; I supposed that in Bredon's day, someone Paul's age would have been considered an adult. Certainly, Bredon didn't talk down to him at all. Long before we had even reached the strawberries and cream, the two were laughing together, Paul blossoming somewhat under the attention.

I waited until they both seemed replete before broaching the subject of our visit to Bredon.

"So," I said. "Bredon, you remember that girl who died? The one at the school."

"I do, beloved. Do you still seek her killer?"

"Yup. Everyone thinks it was Paul, but it wasn't, so we need to find out who really did it."

And we went through it all again. The gates, the cameras, the secret illicit entrance, the caretaker, the floor cleaner, the polisher, the bicycles and the rain. I had a feeling it all came back to the rain... in England, it so often does, but I couldn't see how.

Bredon sat with his chin in his hands. Finally, he looked up at Paul.

"Your secret entrance," he said. "Did anyone else ever know of it? Is it possible that there was a mystery third person there that night? Ockham's Razor says not, but what do you think?"

Paul shook his head.

"No," he said. "I don't want to put a noose round my neck, but no way. I was in the next morning, remember? I would have noticed if anyone else had come though. Honestly, I would. It was like my secret place—I took care not to leave tracks, and no one else had."

"Did you tell the police that?" I interrupted.

"Toni, they didn't listen to a word I said. Eventually I just stopped talking."

Bredon nodded.

"Then here is the problem, young man. If he killed your poor Bella, this caretaker's actions are incomprehensible. If he had no knowledge of your secret entrance, then he proved himself a killer. The school was locked, and even had it not been, your magic cameras show who came and went. And there was no one."

He was right. If Spikey Mikey had killed Bella, it made no sense that he had locked up the school and gone home. Unless he knew about the secret entrance... but Paul said he didn't. We were going round in circles.

I looked at Paul. He hadn't done it. That was the only thing I was sure of. I didn't have a shred of evidence to prove it. I was trusting my gut and that... Well, historically that hadn't always turned out well for me.

"Then that's not what happened," I said. "Let's work out where we're wrong. What do we know for sure?"

But that was the problem. If Paul was innocent, something else that we thought we knew had to be wrong.

At six-thirty, Spikey Mikey had unlocked the gates and let himself into the school. He claimed he'd locked them behind him, and the cameras agreed. He said that he had cleaned the downstairs floor of the main school block until eight when he had breezed out to have a snack in the car—leaving the gates and the school open to visitors. But there was a camera, and it only showed one visitor—Bella.

Mikey had returned from his break, finished up his work and headed home. He said he'd never gone upstairs and never seen Bella, that he had discovered her body on the Saturday when he'd come back to finish his cleaning job.

And there was the problem with his testimony. If it hadn't been for Paul's secret gate, Mikey would have been charged with murder within hours. Because without the secret gate, he was the only person who could have killed Bella. He'd given a testimony that would have sent him down for life. But Paul was adamant no one had found his secret entrance. Mikey was telling a story that totally incriminated himself—and so was Paul. If either of them had killed Bella, it made no sense.

We were missing something. I didn't know what. I gave up and rang my brother. My companions went back to inhaling food while eavesdropping on one side of the conversation.

"Hey there, sis," Wills said in gloriously cheerful tones. "Love you."

"Ah, you're in the pub."

"No more nights for a month. Celebration time. Coming to join me?"

"Tempting, but no. How are things? Did you make any progress with Daniel and Minnie?"

"A bit. He went to the cinema, just as he said. He bought one ticket and saved a seat next to him. There wasn't assigned seating, so he just kept telling people there was someone sitting there. But eventually the cinema was full, and the usher told him to give up the seat he was saving. Apparently, he had a bit of a barney with the girl who wanted to sit there, so the usher remembers him. And Toni, the usher remembers him leaving the cinema because he took the time to apologise for being a tosser earlier."

"But he could have left the film and come back?"

"Yes, he could. But who would remember that in the dark?"

I thought about that.

"Wills, there is one person who would certainly have noticed— the girl he wouldn't give Minnie's seat up to. She would have been resentful and aware of him—she would certainly remember if he wasn't in his chair for lots of the film."

My brother thought for a moment.

"You are right—you always are. Now all I have to do is find her."

"Shouldn't be hard, bro—she was the last person to buy a ticket. If she paid with a card, you have her."

I cut through his effusive thanks.

"Listen, back to Bella. There's something wrong with the statements—both Paul and Mikey are incriminating themselves. It makes no sense. If Mikey didn't know about Paul's entrance, he proved himself a killer because the cameras show no one else came through the main gates. If Paul was the killer, why did he come back the next day when the place would be crawling with cops and he'd be caught for sure and have to tell you how he got in? What am I missing? Are there any details that you didn't tell me?"

"Of course there are," he said, and I heard him pause to swig at a pint. "But none that seemed to matter. What do you want to know?"

"Why did Mikey take his break at eight?"

"That's easy. He cleans the floors with the shampooing machine, but it leaves them damp. So, he takes a break, has a snack, comes back and they are dry. Then he can run the polisher round and finish the job."

Damn. That made total sense.

"Come on, Wills, help me out here. He must have done something else odd that night."

"Well, he did, but it didn't matter, so I didn't mention it. He forgot to lock up when he went home."

"What?"

"He said he felt a bit queer—his words—and forgot to lock up when he left. The school and the gates were open overnight."

"And you didn't think this was relevant?"

"It wasn't, because no one came through the gates. I've gone through the camera tapes, remember... Only two people came through the gates after the school closed—Bella and Mikey. And only one of them left. So, yes, it was odd that he didn't lock up, but it didn't make any difference."

But it did. I was certain of that, I just couldn't see why.

"You still haven't arrested anyone though..."

"It's not my case anymore remember? And the boys at CID are still chasing down imaginary serial killers and have ruled out both Mikey and Paul because they both have an alibi for Minnie Cavendish's murder."

"But you still suspect Paul," I said warily.

My brother sighed.

"I mean, of course I do," he said. "Right now I suspect everybody because the entire county could have sneaked in through that secret entrance and done the deed but, yes, he's top of my list. Why?"

I shrugged, even though I knew he couldn't see me.

"He seemed like a nice guy," I said.

"Yeah, you thought your ex Kit was an absolute poppet, remember? Before he jacked Henry's car and pawned your washing machine."

I hastily bid Wills a happy evening in the pub, sent my love to Henry and ended the call. Around me, our evening picnic was continuing. Bredon was most of the way through the final chicken. Paul, in true teenager style, had finished the sausage rolls.

"Well," he said through a mouthful of pastry. "Any joy?"

I shook my head.

"No, but I don't think we're missing anything anymore. I think we just haven't seen the light. Paul, there's something really simple going on and we have managed not to notice."

"Then we need to do a reconstruction of the crime," he said. "You can be our token redhead. We'll try not to get you killed."

I laughed and then stopped. He was completely right. We'd tried everything else.

"Yup, that's what we'll do," I said. "On Friday, when Mikey's cleaning the floors. We'll find out why he killed Bella."

Paul stared at me in shock. Bredon, meanwhile, began on the strawberries, so I poured lemonade into a glass and helped myself to one.

"Really," Paul said. "I meant it as a joke."

I nodded.

"I know, but you're right. I said we're missing something. When we go back to the scene of the crime and walk through everything, we'll work out what. We just need to make sure that Spikey Mikey doesn't catch us in the act. Or the police. Or anyone else... On Friday, we'll go back to the scene of the crime and catch a killer."

I hesitated to dismiss Bredon. I hadn't seen much of him recently, and he and Paul seemed to be getting on well. So, instead, I opened another bottle of wine, dragged a case of crisps out from the back seat of the car, and left them to it. I lay back against the cushions and idly watched them chatting. Bredon was enjoying male company and Paul was enjoying conversation with an adult who spoke to him as an equal. Eventually, some casual reference revealed a shared interest in astronomy, and they took the telescope out into the churchyard. Later I heard some whooping and what might be the sounds of a snowball fight. I let my eyes close and dozed.

"Toni!" Paul was shaking me. "Toni, wake up. It's nearly dawn and Bredon says you need to send him back."

"Oh my God, yes, right now." I leapt to my feet, grabbing on to Paul for balance. "Where is he?"

"Right outside, but is it really urgent?"

I didn't answer, just rushed out of the mausoleum into the cold night air, skidding on the icy wet ground and nearly tumbling arse over elbow. I found Bredon standing in the snow. He looked a little concerned, as well he might. The sun wasn't over the horizon, but there was a hint of silver in the sky.

"I am here, dear heart," he said. "I was reluctant to disturb your rest, but the hour grows late."

I stood on tiptoes to kiss him.

"Wake me next time, silly," I said. "And a damn sight sooner. Bredon Havers, I release you. Return to the earth from which you came. Right now."

We had seconds to spare. I watched him step gracefully back into the ground, rather more easily than I could get into my bath. The snowy surface swallowed him up and he was gone.

"That is awesome," said Paul at my shoulder. "Can you teach me to do that?"

"No," I snapped. "And why didn't you wake me sooner?"

He looked wounded.

"You didn't tell me to," he said, quite reasonably. "Why are you upset?"

"Because Bredon nearly died!" I yelled at him, tears pricking behind my eyes. "He nearly died because I fell asleep."

There was a silence. Paul broke it.

"Toni, he's already dead. What are you worried about?"

"You don't understand; vampires and zombies, when they're killed, they can't come back. The soul separates from the body and there is nothing there. I raised some of the corpses in this graveyard to fight off some vampires last year, and they got totalled and now I can't raise them anymore. When I was young, I made that mistake, too—raising the dead too close to dawn. They rotted away, and the next night, I couldn't call them. You've seen how sweet Bredon is—I would never have forgiven myself."

To my surprise, Paul burst out laughing.

"Your life is insane," he said. "I thought I had problems. I'm suspected of murder and about to flunk school, but at least I've never had to worry that somebody dead might stay that way."

"Oh, you're right, I suppose," I said. "But there's no textbook for what I do and what I should do. And Bredon's become one of my best friends."

I drove Paul home and then myself. I took a brief shower and dressed for work. Coming back downstairs, I discovered that the post had blessed me with another essay from Bossy Bessant. This time she had upped her ammunition and was hinting at a conviction for something appalling that sounded like at least a double homicide, and which I dismissed as the ravings of a despotic paper pusher. Really, the woman needed some yoga, a stout mug of herbal tea and a jolly good shag and not necessarily in that order. I binned her oeuvre along with an advert for a luxury timeshare apartment in Malaga built on the site of an old leper colony and a leaflet offering cut-price penis extensions in Belarus. The edge of the envelope caught on the rim of the bin, though. As I moved to push it inside I remembered, with some irritation that I had forgotten, yet again, to ask Paul how he had acquired his black eye... I mentally rolled my eyes and put the coffee machine on.

Making myself coffee, I pondered what I said to Paul about working out my powers. I had to make up the rules as I went along. The only person who might have helped guide me had been my grandfather and he was dead. And truth be told, he'd never seemed to care for his abilities. He never wanted to raise the sleeping dead from their rest.

Or there was my great-great-grandfather Ignatius, but he was dead, too. It struck me that I didn't know where Ignatius was buried. Not that I would have summoned him—I had an aversion to raising my own family—but wandering by the family graves at Baswich the other night had brought the omission to the surface. Why wasn't he buried with his wife and children? They were all in the little Catholic church at Eccleshall, but not Ignatius.

I remembered the photograph of Benedict and Ignatius that I'd unearthed from the family album. Might the vampire know where my great-great-grandfather was buried? If I saw him, I would ask him, I decided. I didn't plan to see him, though; that was another sleeping dog best left to lie undisturbed.

I could also ask him where Peter was. The thought left me maudlin and lonely, and without thinking I rang my brother Wills.

He sounded hungover and sleepy.

"Go 'way, sis," he moaned. "My head hurts and the sun won't stop shining."

"I don't care," I said. "I'm miserable and alone and you're in bed with Henry the Hot and it's not fair. Wills, why didn't our parents like me? I was an OK kid. I never got arrested. I worked hard."

There was a long, hard silence.

"Toni, we've had this conversation a million times. I don't know. The important thing is that you still have me, and I do love you. OK?"

"Wills, they could never even remember my name. And it's not an easy one to forget. Having given me a name that sucked this badly, how come they couldn't even remember it?"

Of course I'd been jealous. Wills got a bicycle and a games console; they would drive out to watch him play football. I got a who-the-hell-is-she look every now and then if I was lucky. They didn't seem like bad people; they just acted like I didn't exist most of the time. I remember they would phone from their various trips and chat to my grandfather. When they finished, they would speak with my brother. Never me. If I answered the phone, they would politely ask if Granddad or Wills was around.

"She never even brushed my hair, Wills. Not once that I can remember."

"Toni, it's early. I feel like death. It's my day off and I want a lie in. I love you, but please piss off now. Henry, take the phone."

There was some scuffling and Henry's kind voice came on.

"Let him be, pet. He's green around the gills and he threw up on his shoes. You want me to come round?"

"Hen, I'm OK. Really. I was just feeling sorry for myself. I'll catch you later in the week. Hugs."

I ended the call.

I needed to stop feeling sorry for myself. Paul had said I had problems, but the fact of the matter was that I'd been excruciatingly lucky in recent days. Three people had already tried to kill me. Now two of them were dead. Strictly speaking, Oscar was dead, too, but, in the manner of vampires, he just wouldn't stop walking around being an arse.

And I'd managed not to end up indebted to Azazel, something I was supremely grateful for. The direct influence demons can have on this earth is modest. Yes, they can inhabit an empty dead body, or even possess a live one, but not for long. Organic flesh isn't strong enough, and they burn through it in minutes. Their strength is in words, in manipulation, in lies... They know everything except your thoughts, and they will use what they know to screw you over royally. They promise you knowledge, but the price is always too high, and they try always to offer wisdom that will ruin your life, not bless it. I'd got off lightly. I was steering clear of Azazel, too, from now on.

They say the road to Hell is paved with good intentions. Azazel could take me there by a very direct route, but I was pretty sure the ground would only be paved with blood, death and misery. And I could conjure up plenty of that all by myself. Azazel could stick it; he was on his own.

chapter Eighteen

I'D CHOSEN AN odd venue for it, but I'd actually had a good night's sleep curled up on a bunch of cushions in a graveyard crypt. I felt refreshed and full of verve. After some more coffee, I drove to work in Oscar's car. It wasn't growing on me, so my first job was to ring the garage. They'd mended the brakes on Wills' beastie and were happy to drop it off at his house that afternoon. For a few shekels more, they agreed to pick up mine and bring it back to the cottage.

That sorted, I made coffee for Bernie and another mug for myself. The man had picked up a bag of doughnuts, so we breakfasted on those and had our usual moan about how late our inept receptionist Bethany was. It wouldn't progress beyond a moan. We'd been burning through receptionists at a shocking pace until she'd arrived—I blamed Bernie's wandering hands—but she had stuck with us for six months and was pleasant company. She wasn't much as a receptionist but then we didn't need much. She could stay.

"What's on the roster for today then, boss?" I asked after my second doughnut. "Because I hate to ruin your mood, but my diary has a nice blank middle-of-January look to it all week."

He heaved a sigh, but he was too full of coffee and doughnut to put much genuine angst behind it.

"And yet I am still paying you. You know, Toni, would you go over to Mr Suki's? I'm waiting for all the white goods for that cottage over in Cheswardine, and they didn't come in this morning. He's not usually late with anything and he didn't ring either. Half of them are integrated units, and now the fitter's twiddling his thumbs."

He couldn't have given me a more welcome task. Mr Suki would make me tea and try to set me up on a date. No one would try to kill me, and I would be spared waiting on the pavement for wannabe homebuyers who'd looked out of the window at the snow that morning and returned to their eiderdowns. I drove to the shop and parked Oscar's wank-mobile as unobtrusively as possible; I didn't want people thinking it was mine.

Mr Suki greeted me as courteously as ever, but he looked harassed, and sleep deprived. The shop was a mess. It was also full of dissatisfied customers wagging receipts and complaining loudly. He waved his hands at the scene of chaos around us.

"Little Toni," he said apologetically. "I am so sorry. Nothing is right this morning. Is it possible for you to wait?"

"Of course, Mr Suki," I said hastily. "But what happened. And can I help?"

He waved his hands again. He was a great hand waver.

"My office manager has vanished," he said forlornly. "She took a phone call on Saturday in the middle of the deliveries, got up from her desk and never came back. I can't even get on to the computer. I don't know how to link the dockets with the receipts or work out who is waiting for deliveries. There is a lady who fills in for her sometimes, but I rang, and she is on a cruise for six weeks in the Bahamas."

I took it in my stride.

"No problem, Mr Suki. I work with the world's least cooperative computer system. Lead me to it and if I can't do it on my own, I know a man who can."

It wasn't as though I had anything else to do with my time. I also wasn't going to get Bernie's white goods any other way. Mr Suki kept me liberally supplied with tea and gossip and, with his help, it took me just an hour to unite the grumbling customers with their deliveries. Mystery disappearing office manager had stapled all her passwords to the notice board. Her lack of interest in security meant that after another hour, Mr Suki was able to wave off a van full of washing machines. What I couldn't do was work out how to put on new orders—for that I would need Paul.

"Mr Suki, I have a very nice young man who could come in for a couple of hours a day until you get someone to replace your manager," I said, starting on my third chocolate digestive and my fourth cup of tea after abandoning a fifth attempt to get the system to order a new batch of toasters. "Or until she turns up. He's saving up to go to university. He wants to study medicine like your granddaughter. Jay has met him, now that I think of it."

"My little Toni, I would be most grateful," Mr Suki intoned. "Any friend of yours would be agreeable. May I bring you another cup of tea?"

"Not unless it's accompanied by a bonus extra bladder, no thank you," I said without thinking and he looked a little startled. I saw his frown of confusion and rapidly added, "That's very kind of you, Mr Suki, but I'm good for tea. I do hope you find your office manager."

"Indeed. She is a good friend of my family, and I am most concerned. I sent one of the delivery boys to her house, but there was no answer. I worry that something has happened to her, poor Melody."

"What?"

He looked a little taken aback at the volume of my question.

"I said that I am worried something has happened to Melody," he said.

As he spoke, he moved my handbag to one side and gestured at a photograph in a cheerful china frame. My bag had concealed it the whole time I'd been working. It was Melody, alright. Her badly dyed blonde locks looked just as bad on celluloid as they had in person. She was holding the hand of a plump, pretty little girl with waist-length hair the colour of butter. The girl was wearing denim dungarees and smiling broadly. On closer examination,

I realised it was Kathy, a little younger and before she had been so sick that she'd needed Hildred Rutherford's blood to heal her.

I would have recognised Melody anywhere; she was a very distinctive-looking woman. And she'd known that. She must have seen me dozens of times—I came into this shop a couple of times a month—and it was the most uncanny of coincidences that I'd never noticed her myself. Either she must have been behind the mirrored glass of the office or on another part of the shop floor each and every time I'd visited. She must have guessed that her luck would never hold.

If I'd thought about it at all, I would have assumed that—like Jasper—she wasn't local. If I'd set up an elaborate plan to kill a vampire, I wouldn't have done it on my home turf. But perhaps she hadn't dared to make sick little Kathy travel too far.

She'd met Jasper at Stoke Hospital, that much was clear. His daughter Jenny had been ill; so had Kathy. They'd formed a bond—two adults mad with worry over two sick little girls. Jasper had said that Melody had been kind to him. So, when Jenny died, they must have hatched a plot. Hildred would be approached to heal Kathy, and once the girl was well, the vampire would die. And they'd done it. The problem was me—I'd walked into their little venge-fest and told them I'd come from Benedict's Assemblage. So then I had to die, too. I'd briefly escaped but then handed myself on a plate to Jasper when I stopped for bacon sandwiches at the supermarket café. And once again, Melody had been roped in to help with murder.

On Saturday, she'd had a call from Jasper. He'd given her a list of the tools he wanted in order to sabotage my car, and she rushed out to oblige him. But she'd left us shortly before the sun set on Saturday afternoon. And Aneurin was dead not long after that, so why hadn't she turned up for work this morning? Why was she still missing on Monday, two days later?

I mulled it over in my mind. She wouldn't have come into work on the Sunday. This was Staffordshire. No one worked on a Sunday. So, it was perfectly possible that she'd been fine until last night. But now? My hopes for Melody weren't high; this was a woman who'd messed with vampires and got on their wrong side. And now she'd vanished. My money said she was already dead.

I murmured a few soothing platitudes to poor Mr Suki and promised to speak with Paul. I was too distracted with my own thoughts to do more, so I drove back to the office and spent a quiet afternoon dodging Bernie's caresses.

I pulled out some old receipts from Mr Suki's shop. They were all signed by his office manager, one Melody White. She'd had the sense to give a false surname when she'd hired the ugly little house in Ashbrow Lane, but she'd kept her own first name. A first name that was so unusual in central England that it would be quite enough to give her away, certainly to anyone clever and determined and with good resources at his disposal... I had a feeling I knew exactly what had happened to Melody. And if I was right, Mr Suki was going to need a new office manager because he was never seeing this one again. I texted Paul and we arranged for him to present himself at the shop when he had time.

By three Bethany was bored and Bernie and I were sick of each other's company. We closed up the office and went our separate ways. I drove back to my house in Oscar's car and was pleased to see that my own had been delivered by the garage. It was parked on the road next to Aneurin's. I was going to have to do something about my growing fleet at some point.

On the one hand I was happy to get off early. On the other, I had nothing to do and no one to do it with. I fried a pork chop to share with Winchester. That left me an entire evening free to do sod all, so I attempted to cheer myself up by trying on my new green leather boots with the mini-skirt and frivolous top I had bought to go with them. I had just decided that they agreeably bridged the gap between sexy and slutty when the doorbell rang. I assumed it would be Wills and opened the door without thinking. It wasn't. It was Aidan.

"Nope," I said.

I shut the door in his face, and he was so surprised that he let me. I didn't dislike him, but he was a vampire. I didn't do vampires anymore.

"Toni," he called through the letterbox. "Toni, please open the door."

"Aidan, go away. I've given up vampires for Lent, OK?"

"It's not Lent until spring."

"Well, I need the practice so I've started early."

I heard him try the handle and swear.

"Toni, Benedict sent me," he said miserably. "I can't go back alone. Please don't make me come and get you."

"Oh, crap."

I didn't want my front door tastefully rearranged into two pieces and I didn't want to be dragged anywhere in an undignified manner. Or at all. I picked up my handbag and my new coat and joined Aidan outside on the porch. Snowflakes were half-heartedly falling through the air.

"I'm not happy about this," I said and walked past him to the rust-mobile.

"We can go in my car," he protested.

"You can walk for all I care," I said. "But I'm going in mine because I want to be able to make a quick getaway."

Aidan trailed after me and got grudgingly into the passenger seat. I'd assumed he would follow in his car. Perhaps he was worried I'd climb out of the window of mine halfway down the Bishton Road and give him the slip. I turned on the headlights and pulled the car away from the kerb.

"Why are you driving this pile of rust when you have Oscar's car and…" He broke off. "And dear God, you have Aneurin's car. Toni, what the hell is going on?"

"I'm not driving Oscar's because it says 'I am a wanky tosspot' and I'm not driving Aneurin's because I am not insured to," I said unhelpfully. "And if you can play your cards close to your chest, so can I. Happy?"

He didn't say anything for a while. I drove down through the village and navigated the bridge at the bottom, which was more challenging than usual due to the icy road conditions and the presence of two teenagers leaning over it. One of them appeared to be vomiting into the river. I remembered that Monday night was the youth club disco. I really didn't miss my teenage years.

"What do you think I'm not telling you that I should have?" asked Aidan eventually.

"How about that you lot worked out who Jasper was?" I snapped back. "How about that you also worked out who Melody was? Oh yes, and how about that one of you killed her over the weekend?"

"Oh. That."

He didn't attempt to deny it; I'd been right. We drove in silence for the entirety of the journey. Only when I had pulled into the courtyard of the Stone House and turned off the engine did he attempt to speak again.

"Toni, I don't have the authority to share that kind of information with you."

I looked at him. He looked stressed. He always looked stressed. The man needed a massage or something. Or a quiet evening in watching crap TV. I should lend him Winchester for a week or so. The cat's one virtue was its ability to relax.

"I didn't say I was blaming you, Aidan," I said, a little more kindly. "But then you can hardly blame me for not confiding in you. I know my way from here."

I left the keys and my coat in the car and stalked into the house. The hall was empty, and I made my way down the spiral stairs and along the winding corridor to Benedict's rooms without interruption. Somehow, despite my best efforts, I kept ending up here. I didn't have Grace's courage, so I knocked on the door. To my surprise, it was Grace who opened it.

"Here's the lady herself," she said warmly, stepping back to let me in. "We were just talking about you. Only nice things, of course. At least"—and at this point she shot Benedict a grin—"at least on my part."

I looked across the room. He was sprawled elegantly on one of the sofas by the fire. I rather thought he'd been outside. His hair was damp, and he was wearing heavy leather boots a great deal more suited to walking in the snow than mine. A dark coat that gave Aneurin's a run for its money had been tossed onto a chair.

I was suddenly angry with him all over again. Angry with him for not telling me about Jasper, for not telling me about Melody, for killing her and leaving me in the dark. Angry with him for ordering me over here like I was some minion. And angrier still that he was lounging at his ease exuding arrogant confidence while I hadn't a clue what he wanted. He raised an eyebrow at my expression of wrath.

"God, it's getting worse," he drawled. "You're furious with me before you've got through the door this time. Don't you finding it exhausting constantly bearing a grudge?"

"That is not how it is, and you know it," I snapped. "And if you've dragged me out here just to wind me up then I'm going straight back home."

Grace looked from Benedict to me and then back. She seemed amused.

"And I think I'll be off," she said. "The air is crackling so much it will ruin my blow-dry. Don't kill her, Akil. You'll only be sorry afterwards."

She breezed out and shut the door quietly, leaving me standing on the spot glaring at Benedict. He didn't wither under my gaze. As per usual, I couldn't even gauge his mood, but he said in appeasing tones:

"My dear, this is unnecessary. Sit down and try to stop hating me for a moment."

"Why must you always torment me?"

"Because you make it irresistible."

"You can't have everything your own way all the time, you know. And you can't just kill everyone who gets in your way."

I found myself pacing up and down, but he merely laughed out loud.

"You are always telling me what I can't do. Usually just after I've done it. And you're a fine one to talk about killing people who get in the way. You wiped out the entire Gambarini clan single-handedly behind my back because I wouldn't do it for you. The main difference between the two of us is that I don't rip the heads off. Even my appetite for decapitated corpses was growing a little jaded last summer."

"Oh, shut up."

He looked at me for a few moments and then to my surprise held out a hand.

"My dear, we can do better than this," he said. "Can we not have peace between us for a little while?"

I looked at his hand, and then with some reluctance took it. He had huge hands; they made mine look like a child's. I felt the heat from his palm warm my own, which was still chilled from the drive. He ran his fingers over the scabs on my wrist, my war wounds from banishing demons I should have steered clear of. They weren't healing well.

"You should take more care," he said quietly.

He held out his other hand. The fight went out of me then. I sat down next to him and let him take both of my hands in his. I closed my eyes as the soft golden wash of his healing flowed through me. I hadn't realised how much my wrists had been throbbing until they stopped.

He didn't let go of my hands immediately, just held them in his warm grip. I found myself feeling conflicted. I didn't like him, but when I'd given him my blood, I'd been perilously intimate with him. He'd let me feel ecstasy coursing through his body. He'd held me in his arms while I cried out his name and told him my innermost desires. I'd done it for revenge, but the motive wasn't what mattered anymore. It's hard to hate someone you've shared that much pleasure with. And though I doubted his motives, he had saved my life and Peter's. I couldn't hate him. But peace?

"Thank you," I said. "But no, Benedict. I don't think we can have peace between us. I don't think you do either."

He let go of my hands.

"How about just for tonight then, Miss Windsor? This evening is going to be hard enough for you."

I didn't like the sound of that one bit. I cast him a rather fearful look.

"Really?"

"Lay your enmity for me aside for a night."

"I can do that, I suppose," I said warily. "What do you have to tell me? Have you sold me to Isembard after all?"

"Not yet. Let me make you a drink."

I sat back and watched him. He knew all my weak spots, including my fondness for a Classic, in my opinion the only cocktail worth making. And there's much enjoyment to be had in watching a good-looking man strip the foil off a bottle of champagne and force out the cork. He mixed me my drink with easy competence, then sat down next to me and placed it in my hand. I drank to our brittle truce.

"Have you ever drunk champagne?" I asked suddenly. "I mean, when you were alive."

He shook his head.

"My dear, it wasn't around in my day. I've never had the pleasure."

I frowned.

"What did you drink then, in your day?"

He lay back against the sofa.

"Hmmmm. There's a question. And not one I've been asked before. Dirty water, if you must know. Sometimes boiled with leaves. I don't miss it."

I laughed, but only lightly. He had told me that I was about to have a very bad time. I wasn't one for procrastinating. I wanted it over with.

"I don't suppose I would either," I said. "Well, this is as good a time as ever. Go on—lay it on. Ruin my evening for me before I start to enjoy it or something."

He nodded but was silent for a while. I realised with surprise that he was reluctant to say whatever it was he'd summoned me here for. Finally, he spoke.

"My dear, Peter has contacted me," he said in his deep voice. "He has left Oscar. And he is anxious to return to Heidelberg. He is taking a plane back to Germany tomorrow."

Chapter Nineteen

WITH THAT UNCANNY vampire speed, he caught my glass as I dropped it. I suppose he had expected it, but his movements were so fast I almost didn't realise what had happened. He'd done it so smoothly that not a drop spilled. I put my hands over my eyes for a few moments. Azazel had been right all along—he'd told me Peter would leave me.

"I see," I said with as much composure as I could manage. I didn't see, of course...

Benedict handed me back my glass, which I drained.

"He wishes to say goodbye to you," he said. "I was high-handed enough to say that I would arrange it. He will be here in an hour or so."

I looked into the fire. I'd lost Oscar, and I was coping with that. All things considered I'd come out of the affair lightly. My heart had been relatively briefly broken. It's surprising how quickly love dies when you find out your ex is a psychopathic arsehole. I wasn't going to cope with losing Peter nearly so easily. He'd made himself a very warm place in my heart without me even realising it.

Benedict was speaking and I realised I'd completely missed what he was saying.

"I'm sorry," I said vaguely. "I tuned out for a moment."

"I noticed. I said, I'm taking you to meet someone."

He got to his feet and headed for the door. I scurried reluctantly after him.

"Slow down," I said. "And I don't want to see anyone."

Benedict didn't slow down, and apparently wasn't listening either.

"He's an old friend of mine," he continued, "and before you say it, my dear, I do have one or two."

"I told you, I don't want to do this," I protested.

"That's a shame. He's come a long way just to meet you."

He led me down a couple of flights of stairs and round a confusing maze of corridors. I had to scurry to keep up with him and I had no idea where I was. He eventually stopped outside an arched door that look exactly like all the other ones we'd passed and raised his hand to knock.

"Wait," I said hastily. "Before you do that, tell me this. Why didn't Peter call me himself? Why ask you?"

"My dear, Peter blames himself for what happened to you. He is eaten up with guilt. He cannot imagine why you would ever think of forgiving him."

I waved my hands in the air in a goodly impression of Mr Suki.

"That's senseless. Why would he think anything so stupid?"

"He left you with Oscar while he wandered down to the gate with Aidan. He now believes that it was unforgivable of him to have left you in danger. There is something else I don't think he is telling me, but I am hardly his confidante. They apparently had a conversation that now distresses him. Now, if you'll forgive me…"

And he raised his hand again and rapped sharply on the door.

"Ja," said a light male voice.

Benedict opened the door and ushered me into a room very similar to the one Aneurin had dragged me to. On a large sofa, a man was sitting with his back to us, warming his hands at the fire. Correction: a vampire. I could feel him from where I stood.

"Look what I've brought you," Benedict said to him.

The vampire stood up and came towards me. I'd seen his face a thousand times, but never expected to meet him in person. I was probably standing in a room with the most famous person in Europe. It was the hero of Germany, the man so beloved that everyone called him by his first name. It was Herr Doktor Lenz Lange.

He stepped forward and very civilly shook my hand. He was not particularly imposing physically, being only a few inches taller than me, with white hair and a scholarly face. He was only the second vampire I'd ever known who looked old. Before his second death, farmer Hugh Bonner had the appearance of an old man. Lenz looked to be in his early seventies, skeletally thin with lined and bone-white skin. He had very pale electric blue eyes, the unearthly blue of the undead. Without those, he would have looked like a kindly old grandfather. But the eyes gave him away. They saw everything. This was no kindly old man. I'd felt his power from across the room.

"I have much pleasure to meet you," he said, in slightly broken English. "Herr Akil, my old friend, another red-headed necromancer? You are in the danger of becoming predictable in your old age."

"Alas, she's not mine," Benedict replied. "She doesn't like me. It must be my warm and easy-going nature. Toni, I am going to leave you. Lenz has a tale of lost love to tell you that is likely to make you long for something light-hearted and upbeat like *Romeo and Juliet* or *Oedipus Rex* and I am not sure I can stomach it a second time."

"I thought *Oedipus Rex* was just raunchy, not a tragedy," I said, distracted. "Doesn't he kill his father and marry his mother?"

"You're forgetting your classics, my dear. Then the land is cursed with plague, half the kingdom dies and when he finds out what he's done Oedipus tears out his eyes and wanders off blindly into the desert to starve. Euripides at his most jolly. I'll send someone to find you when Peter arrives."

And he was gone. I turned back to my mysterious visitor.

"Have you really come to England just to see me?" I asked.

"Ja, young lady. I am afraid we are, how do you say, at odds. You see, I would like my Peter back."

I stared at him.

"Well, apparently that's going to happen," I said, "so why don't you pop off back to Heidelberg and let me be miserable in peace?"

He didn't answer me immediately. Instead, he sat down again on the fat sofa and patted the seat next to him invitingly.

"Come here where it's warm, fräulein," he said. "Let me look at you."

I sat down grudgingly. He had a lot of charm somehow. I should have guessed as much—he couldn't have compelled every single journalist in Europe otherwise. He held me in his rather piercing gaze for a while.

"Ja, I see," he said. "Warm, kind, clever, gentle... opposite to Oscar in every way. My poor Peter. I should have looked after him better."

"Does he know you are here?" I interrupted. "Or that you're talking with me?"

The white-haired vampire shook his head.

"He wouldn't thank me for the interference," he said. "No, young lady. My concern is that when Peter sees you again, he will change his mind. Half an hour in your company, and he will be tearing up that nice plane ticket and utilising his dual citizenship to stay with you."

"Well, Doktor Lange, I'll be honest: I would give a limb to have Peter stay here with me. Maybe two. I'll certainly be trying to persuade him, I can promise you that."

He nodded.

"Ja, but it would be better for him, you see, to come back. Much better."

I didn't agree but I wasn't going to argue. I just sat there thinking stubborn thoughts. After a while, Lenz spoke again.

"Let me tell you a tale, fräulein," he said. "It starts twenty-five years ago..."

Oscar had met Peter's mother in the street in Stafford. It was that random. They'd passed in the night, and he'd thought her pretty. She was a doctor, a single mother walking home from a late shift to look after her little boy. In that moment, her life had been changed forever. Within months, Oscar had made her his consort. She was in love with her magnetic vampire boyfriend... Then inevitably he began to pressure her to transition, to become a vampire. Like me—

and like Peter—she'd refused.

Benedict, watchful of Oscar's temper, had seen the way the tide had turned and tried to persuade her to leave him—she'd taken that about as well as I had. But then two things had happened. Firstly, little Peter, by then six, had fallen ill with leukaemia. And from distant Heidelberg, Lenz had asked Benedict for help. The doctor was under huge pressure. Many Assemblages disagreed with Europe's plans to use him as the poster child for their coming out party. Benedict had offered Lenz his greatest military asset. He'd offered his warrior, Oscar the General.

I found the tale interesting for another reason at that point. Lenz's exposure, and the discovery of the undead living in our midst, had in theory come about entirely by accident. A bright-eyed journalist had investigated the clinic and weaselled out Lenz's secrets. Now the doctor was implying that the exposé was completely fake, that more than a quarter of a century ago the nightwalkers had been planning Lenz's unveiling. They'd set the whole thing up, ensuring the world's first out-and-proud vampire was an entirely heroic and worthy man, full of love for the most vulnerable members of society, laying his own wishes aside to save dying children. Had the journalist been fed information? Had he simply been ambushed in a dark alley and compelled to pen his tales?

Lenz continued with his story. Peter's mother had been made an offer by Benedict: Oscar would take her sick son to a mystery German vampire who would cure him. Benedict's intention was that Peter would come back without Oscar. The short-fused vampire would remain in Heidelberg until all thoughts of romance had ebbed. Which they would have done, I had no doubt. Oscar was impulsive and passionate, but I now knew that fidelity or loyalty were not traits that troubled him. Out of sight was out of mind...

"But then Peter's mother was killed in a traffic accident," I interrupted.

Lenz looked troubled.

"Nein, fräulein. She threw herself off one of your motorway bridges and was crushed under the wheels of an articulated vehicle."

"A lorry?"

"Ja. Not so very accidental. I think her son's sickness and Oscar's violence had worn her down. We acted too late."

Once Peter was cured, Lenz had kept him. Indeed, he'd adopted six-year-old Peter and never returned him to England. Little Peter was clever, stubborn, defiant and charming, exactly the child to capture gruff old Lenz's heart. As a schoolboy, he had announced his intention of becoming a doctor. After graduating, he took on increasing responsibility.

"I struggle to run my little clinic now without him," said Lenz forlornly.

"It's just a job," I argued. "He could practice here."

"No, no, what we do is a calling, a vocation. And my Peter is a sensitive soul. Recovery rates in our hospital are one hundred per cent. I wonder what they measure in a rural children's cancer ward—less than fifty? Do you think our gentle Peter would be able to cope with watching most of his patients die?"

I'd been a fool to stay and listen. Lenz had every journalist in Europe in the palm of his hand. I would end up thinking it was my idea if I wasn't careful. I got up and moved away to sit on the rug by the fire, letting the warmth of the flames seep into me.

"Don't think you will win me over," I said. "I can make Peter happy. And you should have prevented this—you should never have let Oscar near him."

Lenz thought he had been so clever. Whenever Oscar's interest landed on a young nurse or a charming junior doctor, they would be transferred to another hospital. It wasn't something you'd catch on to—unless perhaps you were as bright as a button, and you lived in the clinic.

"Peter never told me about their relationship," explained Lenz. "He concealed it for more than a decade so that I wouldn't split them up."

"Ten years! Doctor Lange, Peter is only twenty-nine."

Lenz waved his hands. He was a hand waver just like me.

"Ja, I know, I know."

Lenz had found out quite by accident last spring but, when challenged, Peter was unabashed. He loved Oscar, he was quite certain Oscar loved him, too. Yes, Oscar was pressuring him increasingly to transcend, sometimes getting angry... Lenz had panicked. He had asked Benedict to summon Oscar back. Heidelberg no longer needed protection—Germany's military might protected Lenz in the wake of his exposure and grateful parents held candlelit vigils at the clinic door. The General could go back to England.

And go he had. But the evening following Oscar's departure, when Lenz awoke, Peter was gone, too. He'd bought a plane ticket and joined Oscar in London and there was not a thing the German vampire could do about it. And when Oscar had finally returned to Staffordshire, Peter had travelled with him. He had thrown over his only family, his career and his adopted homeland for Oscar. He'd given up everything that mattered to him for love... of bloody Oscar.

"You think it would be best for Peter to return to Germany and his friends," I said, and Lenz nodded his head vigorously.

"Young lady, he has adored Oscar for so much of his life and been in love with him for more than half of it. Now that is over, and his heart is most wounded. Yes, you would be kind to him, I see that. But in Heidelberg he is valued; he has many friends, a career and a home that is very familiar to him. Me, his father. Here, everything is a reminder of his perceived failures and poor choices. And, thanks to your generosity of spirit, he will have to face Oscar sooner rather than later. I am not sure if he could cope."

"Oh, bollocks, you are right. How can you be right about this? It's not fair!"

I started to cry, and he handed me a large white handkerchief and patted my shoulder. When I was done, I got to my feet.

"I won't tell him we spoke," I said. "I'll go now, or I might start crying again."

To my surprise he embraced me and kissed my forehead.

"Thank you," he said. "Besten dank."

I GOT LOST twice on my way up to the Gallery.

None of what Lenz had told me came as a huge surprise. I also now understood Peter's reticence in telling me himself... it hardly put Oscar in a good light.

I was distracted from my rather nihilistic thoughts by the sound of music. Somewhere up on one of the balconies what sounded like a string quartet was playing something rhythmic and lilting. Below, on the raised central area of the Gallery, chairs and side tables had been cleared away and people were dancing. It wasn't the sort of dancing I'd ever done. There was a lot of silk rustling, nifty footwork and elegant turning around clasped hands. I crept past and sat myself against one of the pillars to watch.

For whatever reason, my status at the Assemblage had always seemed fairly high, and several people—vampire and mortal— kindly asked me to dance. I declined politely. After a few minutes Grace wandered in and caught sight of me. She slithered down very neatly to join me against my pillar. I was surprisingly happy to see her.

"Not dancing?" she murmured.

"Grace, I have two left feet on the dance floor. I can barely manage the conga."

She glanced across at the string quartet and then shot me a rather lovely smile.

"I can see if they know it," she said, "but the rest of the dance floor might object."

"Thanks, I'm fine here."

"And you escaped from Benedict un-throttled... quite an achievement given the way you were going for it when I left."

"We worked things out," I said, noncommittally. I gestured across at the elegantly gyrating company. "What's the occasion here?"

Grace pointed over at a tall, laughing girl, twirling around in a long gold dress. Perfectly coiffured chestnut locks had been arranged in a style that put me in mind of old black and white films. Nineteen-forties? Maybe older... She was wearing very scarlet lipstick. I reached out for her with my senses... definitely a vampire. An old, powerful vampire.

"Sophy has come back to us," Grace said. "She has been in France for nearly a century working off reparations and is very happy to be back. So, we are having a little celebration."

I heard footsteps and looked around to see Aidan heading our way. Grace smiled up at him easily.

"Have you come to ask Toni to dance?" she asked. "She won't dance with me."

"Don't do it, Aidan," I said. "When I get on the dance floor you will discover my body to be composed entirely of elbows. It's not a pretty sight."

He shook his head and didn't say anything. I remembered our altercation of earlier and scrambled to my feet. I gave him a little hug.

"I'm sorry I was a total cow, Aidan," I said. "Please don't be cross with me."

He gave me an awkward half smile.

"I promise not to," he said. "But I've come looking for you. Peter is waiting for you in Benedict's rooms."

"Let's go then," I said, hoping I sounded calmer than I felt.

He trailed after me as I walked back the way I had come. A thought occurred to me.

"Aidan," I said. "What about Kathy? What about the girl who was staying with Melody at the house? The girl that Hildred was healing... What happened to her?"

"We don't even know who she was," he said. "Melody lived on her own. She has no children and no other family that we could trace. She certainly doesn't have a daughter called Kathy."

"Oh. Well, that's good at least."

I was relieved to know that the little girl who had been so brave as her hair fell out and her breath drained away wouldn't be left an orphan. But who on earth was she? I wanted to know—but probably not badly enough to start digging into the acquaintances of a woman who'd been kidnapped, murdered and then 'disappeared' by vampires… I didn't want to end up carrying the can for Benedict's poor impulse control.

Benedict was coming out of his room as we approached it, and I glared up at him.

"Still cross with me?" he said.

"Yes. You knew what he would ask me."

He shrugged.

"He's persuasive," he said. "I take it he convinced you?"

"Yes," I said shortly. "How much time do I have?"

"I expect you to put Peter on a plane at Birmingham International tomorrow at five," he said.

"Fine, I'll do that."

"Good. Then we are in agreement."

"No," I said, and he raised his eyebrows. "We're not in agreement—there's no peace between us."

He shook his head in apparent disbelief.

"How does he do it? The man should be prime minister…"

"Who?" I interrupted. "What do you mean?"

"Peter blames himself. You blame me. Grace blames everyone else. It's really remarkable. Why can't you all just blame Oscar and be done with it?"

And he opened the dark wooden door quietly and let me into his room. Inside, a figure was perched on the near side of the club fender by the fire.

It was Peter.

He didn't look in good form. He was wearing a shirt that I rather thought was Aidan's and it didn't suit him. His face had a tired and haunted look, and I got the distinct impression that whatever Benedict and he had talked about hadn't made for an agreeable conversation. He turned and looked at me and I waited for him to run up and catch me in his arms, but he didn't. He looked away, back into the fire, and just sat there biting his lip.

I sought for a way to break the silence but couldn't. In the end, it was Benedict who came to my rescue.

"As promised, I have brought Miss Windsor to you. In other news, I will have your books couriered over to Heidelberg. And now, if you both will forgive me, I would like my room back."

I didn't look at him. I looked at Peter. He didn't look back at me. Instead he got to his feet with some hesitancy, picked up a bulky carryall and his doctor's bag, and joined us at the door. His hair, which I had always thought too short, had grown out a little. I wanted to tell him that it suited him but he didn't seem interested in me or my opinions. Instead he held out a hand to Benedict.

"Thank you," he said. "I appreciate what you said. I'll be on my way."

We walked down the corridor together without speaking and then up the spiral stairs that led to the hall. He didn't touch me. I couldn't believe what was happening. I could barely remember a time when we hadn't walked hand in hand. Now there were a million miles of restraint between us.

Peter opened the door to the courtyard for me with distant courtesy and I looked up at him as I passed through. His expression was bleak and for a moment I held out my hand, but he merely closed the door behind us.

"Where are you parked?" he asked quietly.

I led the way.

"It's not locked," I said, climbing into the driver's seat. "Where am I taking you?"

He fastened the seatbelt carefully; it seemed to take his full attention.

"Grace has booked me a room for the night at the Swan," he said. "If that's not too far."

I needed tissues. I twisted around and leaned over into the back seat where I found a squashed half box under my coat and blew my nose vigorously.

"Don't you want to come home with me?" I asked, trying not sniffle.

Peter didn't answer for a moment. Then he shook his head.

"It's better this way," he said.

"Fine," I snapped and started the engine.

I took the car down onto the main road and indicated left towards Stafford instead of right towards Colton. Bugger it, if Peter was going to be the world's biggest pain in the arse, so be it. If all he was going to do was sit there and exude resentment and misery, I couldn't exactly stop him.

"Fine," I said again for emphasis, and then in case he hadn't heard me the first two times: "Fine, fine, fine."

"Toni, I..."

"Shut up," I said. "Shut the fuck up if you have nothing nice to say."

Chapter Twenty

Breaking my heart seemed to have turned into everyone's favourite pastime; I hadn't expected Peter to chip in with so much gusto, but then he'd never done anything by halves. I somehow managed to put the car into third gear instead of first and stall it pulling out. I swore, restarted the engine and turned onto the road. I made it almost half a mile before all the tears welling up in my eyes made it impossible to see the road ahead and I pulled in with a curse to the nearest layby.

"You bloody drive," I said. "I can't see where I'm going."

I got out and slammed the door and stood in eight inches of snow in my new high-heeled boots. Peter walked round to me, but I turned away so that he couldn't see the tears that had made their way down to my chin by that point.

"Liebling," he said softly. "Don't do this."

I kept my back to him.

"Get in the car," I snapped.

He tried to put his arms around me, but I shouldered him aside and nearly fell flat on my face in the snowy verge. His second attempt was better, and he levered me into his embrace and turned me round until he could pull my face in against his chest and stroke my hair.

"Hush," he said. "Don't cry. Not over me."

He kissed my hair as he pressed me against him, soft, comforting little kisses with lips a thousand times warmer than Oscar's. I raised my face so that the next one fell onto my lips. And the next one. And the next. And all the ones after that. The gaps between them became shorter and the kisses became longer until we were finally locked in one of those unending smooches where you have to stop before one of you runs out of oxygen but neither of you wants to break first...

Eventually one of us broke, I wasn't sure which. Peter looked down at me in absolute shock. Whatever he'd expected, it wasn't this.

"Please tell me this is going to happen," he said in a voice raw with lust.

"Oh, it's going to happen," I assured him, pressing my body along the length of his and reaching a hand up to pull his mouth back to mine. "It's going to happen even if I have to tie you up." Mindful of the vagaries of English grammar I added, "Or tie you down."

"That won't be necessary," he said, sliding cashmere off my shoulder so that he could put his warm hands there instead, and then his mouth. "Though either would be fine if that's what you want." He slid his tongue back up my neck to my ear and explored the area thoroughly and rather moistly. "Or both."

He kissed me until my knees were so weak with desire that we had to lean against the car to carry on. I pushed him away and looked up at him.

"Peter, I love you, but I am freezing my tits off out here."

"Ah."

He led me around to the passenger side and opened the door. I slid into the car, which—in the manner of very vintage vehicles with minimal heating—was fractionally warmer than the January night air. He closed the door and then climbed into the other side.

"Where were we?" he said.

"You'd got to about here," I said helpfully, putting both his hands on my waist and then pulling his face back down to my neck. "Or maybe a little further."

He just kissed me for a while, exploring first my lips and then the soft contours of my mouth with his tongue. I was forced to concede that he was a very good kisser. While I don't mean that I had expected him to be rubbish or anything, the truth was that Peter never came across as much of a player... Then again, a vampire Assemblage was hardly a monastery.

But then his mouth began to move south and his hands north, and I realised that his talents didn't stop at kissing. He slid his hands under the soft fabric of my top and used his teeth to tug it out of the way at the top. Then he used his teeth gently a little lower down.

"Oh my God, that's nice," I whispered.

"You're nice," he responded, moving one hand from my chest and sliding it down to the hem of my skirt and then up again in between my thighs, pushing them apart and heading higher. "You are beautiful, and warm, and sexy and..." His hand reached a significant point in its journey, namely the lace edge of my thong, "...and very soft."

I doubted that was mutual, and responded by tugging his shirt—or Aidan's, or whoever's it was—out of the waistband of his jeans and sliding my hands onto his lower back. It was firm and infinitely strokable. I let my hands explore the curves further down and felt his muscles ripple under my touch. There wasn't much room in the car, but there was a clear reluctance on both our parts to bother with any relocating. Peter rather suddenly moved both of his hands to my thighs.

"Lift," he said shortly, and I raised my hips so that he could push the leather of my mini-skirt up to my waist and tug down the fabric of my thong. He pulled it first off one boot and then the other and tossed it somewhere into the back of the car.

"Am I ever going to see that again?"

"Maybe not," he said, sliding his hand back between my thighs, "but you won't be needing it imminently."

He went back to kissing me in the general cleavage area,

some parts more persistently than others. Below my waist, his fingertips began to explore. He was seeking for the perfect spot and when I let my head fall back with a gasp, he knew he'd found it. He drove me so easily into climax that it caught me by surprise and then he kept me there until I was gasping for breath. I tried to say something, but syllables were way too complicated, so all that came out was a little cry. I was strung as tightly as the top string of a violin.

When I had the energy, I caught his shoulders and pulled his mouth back to mine and we had a rather gloriously confused time because he was trying to lick the saltiness of me off his own fingers while I was trying to kiss him. It's an occupation the word lascivious was coined for, and infinitely arousing, but probably not one I'd recommend trying in a car. When we'd finished, he pulled back and looked at me in a speculative manner. I couldn't blame him. My skirt was around my waist, my top had almost joined it and my knickers were Christ-knows-where. I was wearing nothing from the hipbones down but leather boots.

I broke in hastily, before he could launch himself at me again:

"Peter, I've had this car since I graduated. The heating's never worked in those six years, so I doubt it's going to spontaneously kick in tonight. And even if it did, believe me: you cannot have sex in this car. I've tried. It's too small. Truly."

He laughed and put the engine back into gear. To my relief he executed a neat U-turn in the road and headed off in the direction of Colton. I attempted to organise my clothing into a slightly less slutty format, which was close to impossible given which ones were now missing entirely.

"If the weather was any warmer, liebling, I'd be happy to prove you wrong," he said, taking his hand off the clutch to slide across my thigh. "But I think we might head for warmer climes."

I didn't answer him. I was terrified not only of breaking the mood but also of what I might say. "Don't leave me," was close to the top. "Stay with me forever, not just for tonight," was also high up on the list. He'd stopped being icy and distant from me but for how long? Were we about to have goodbye sex? I'd never had goodbye sex, and I didn't want to. I wanted to have hello sex, welcome-to-the-rest-of-your-life sex... I pushed the thoughts aside and reached across to undo the buttons at the top of his jeans.

He moved his own hand off my thigh and pressed my fingers hard against his crotch. I could feel the length of him; he was about as aroused as a man could get. He pressed my hand down a little harder and I felt his flesh jump beneath my touch. I moved to try for more intimate contact, but he stopped me.

"Which hedge did you want me to crash into, liebling?" he said in a slightly unsteady voice.

"The one at the corner of the Bishton turning," I suggested.

"Ja, well, if you do that again, you'll probably get what you want," he said.

I laughed and withdrew my hand.

"I think I'm going to get what I want shortly," I conceded. "I can wait a little longer."

He parked at the kerb outside my cottage. I was vaguely aware that Aneurin's car had gone. I rather thought Aidan might be responsible for that. I didn't have time to dwell, though, because Peter came round to the passenger door and helped me out. Another half-inch of snow had made the path and steps to my porch somewhat perilous for a girl in high-heeled boots with smooth leather soles. As a result, the journey left me clinging to him and giggling and by the time we got to the front door, things were a little heated between us again.

I took too long searching for the front door key; by the time I eventually located it at the bottom of my handbag, Peter had lost patience and I found myself pushed against the door by the weight of his body, being very thoroughly kissed again. I felt him shift his weight so that he could kiss his way down my neck, and then again so that he could move lower. He eased up the soft fabric of my top so that he could kiss his way across the skin of my stomach and run his tongue around the waistband of my skirt.

Then he was on his knees and had rucked my skirt up so that he could kiss his way down the line of one hip and then...

Oh my God. He was about to go down on me, in the snow, in my own porch, in full sight of anyone who happened to be walking past. I knew I should stop him, but I just couldn't bring myself to. It was my all-time, number-one favourite leisure activity and I couldn't remember the last time it happened. Instead of stopping him, I dropped my handbag and keys on the ground, moved both hands behind me onto the doorframe, and just held on.

Peter knew exactly what he was doing. Heat flooded my body, and I closed my eyes. I can't dignify the sound I made by calling it anything else but a squeak. I took one hand off the doorframe to hold it across my own mouth because I was in danger of raising the neighbourhood. The other one I needed just to stop myself collapsing into the snow.

I vaguely hoped in the back of my mind that Miss Heliotrope from next door wouldn't choose that evening to take her foul little pug Waffle for a walk past my house. I would have been mightily embarrassed if the teenagers on the other side had picked that exact moment to have a lamb karai, two peshwari naans and some sag aloo delivered to their door. Thankfully, neither of these events transpired before Peter peeled himself off me, retrieved my keys and handbag from the ground, and let us both into the house.

He dropped my handbag on the floor, picked me up in his arms and carried me up the stairs. He dropped me on the bed and stripped off his shirt. I put on the sidelight so that I could admire the muscles on his shoulders in the soft illumination.

"You should have made love to me the first time you dropped me on this bed," I said, looking up at him.

He removed his shoes and socks and joined me on the eiderdown. He stripped off my rather mangled cashmere top and fought with the catch of my bra.

"I planned to," he said, "but you fell asleep."

The bra gave up its fight and he tugged it off and hurled it somewhere into the chaos of my bedroom. He cupped my breasts in his hands and buried his face in my cleavage.

"Well," I said to the top of his head, "I won't do that this time."

He pulled back from me and unzipped my skirt. I lay back and raised my hips so that he could slide it down to my knees, then I sat back up and lifted my legs so that he could pull it off the rest of the way over my boots.

"Nein," he said. "You won't be getting any sleep tonight. I brought something to keep you awake."

There was an agreeable little tussle at this point because I decided to undo the remaining buttons of his jeans just as he had exactly the same idea. It turned out that what would have been easy with two hands was nigh on impossible with four, but marvellous fun nonetheless.

"Is that what you brought?" I asked, as I gave up the battle and he stripped off the last of his clothes.

"Yes," he said a little breathlessly. "I think it will do the trick."

He pushed me back onto the pillows and pressed himself against me. I'd realised in the car that he was well endowed, but I was just realising now that I'd underestimated quite how well...

"Good God, Peter. Where have you been hiding this?" I said.

I'd seen it before—just not in that mood. I reached down to lock my hands around him, to stroke smooth, hard flesh and trace my fingers over the tight skin.

"In the usual place," he said, clearly flattered at my response. "You'd have been welcome to it any time."

He drew back to wrap his hands around mine and press my fingers in a touch harder. He thrust a little inside my grasp and I heard his breath falter.

"Well," I said, "I hate to burst your bubble, but we don't grow them this size in England. It must be a German thing. Maybe it's the beer. I don't have anywhere this is going to fit."

He took his hands off mine and moved his body lower. I slid my fingers around the back of his hips, ready to pull him inside me.

"You and your appalling English education system," he said,

angling his hips. "I'll show you where it goes. I think you'll find it a perfect fit."

He leaned on one elbow to stop himself from crushing me and used his other hand to gather my hips off the bed and angle things exactly as he wanted them. When he finally began to move inside me, the friction was blissful. There was nothing tentative about Peter's lovemaking. There was, however, plenty of duration. There was also a lot of technique that rather brought home how sexually experienced I wasn't.

Oscar had been an enthusiastic if uncomplicated lover. He made up for any lack of sophistication with sheer staying power. He didn't need to get everything right first time because he could just keep going... Peter got everything right first time and he knew it. He hadn't just studied medicine; he'd put a lot of practice into his sexual proclivities, and he was clearly a first class student with a lot of coursework behind him. He finally came in a delicious wet heat that filled me to overflowing and had me grabbing at the mattress again.

I lay for a while in a little puddle of stunned pleasure. People surprised me all the time and I never got used to it. Peter had joked about me tying him down, but I had his measure now. I was pretty sure that if I asked him to strap me to the bedposts for round two, he'd not only be delighted to oblige, but would know exactly how to improvise the shackles with a bunch of silk scarves, not to mention precisely which knots to use. If there were manuals for this, he'd read them all. Hell, he'd probably written some of them.

"We have to move," he said, breaking into my reverie.

"We do? I'm very happy here," I said, indicating my general happiness with the situation by biting his earlobe.

"Not very far," he said, angling his neck to give me better purchase, "but you are still wearing your boots, and the heels are sharp, and that bloody cat is licking my foot."

We lost the boots and agreed that Winchester was definitely poaching on my turf. Peter lay on his back, and I wrapped as much of myself around him as I could and laid my head on his chest.

"So," I said, "now that I have you here and you can't escape, can you please explain why you think I should be cross with you?"

"Oh, that," he said, a little forlornly. "I do need to explain. Gott, where to begin? I was frustrated, Toni my treasure, by your complete rejection of my advances. I'd promised you I wouldn't mind, so I was stuck. I had just assumed that in time you would warm to me. But you didn't."

"I did, actually, as you can see," I interrupted, stroking a hand down his broad chest, an action I'd been yearning to take for months but had resisted. "I just didn't know what to do about it."

"You seemed immune to every lure. And I'd fallen for you the first moment I saw you. You were dripping wet, perched on the side of the bath wearing a towel about the size of a doily. You were delicious and so fierce. I wanted to have you then and there against the side of the shower—just so we're clear I'll be doing that shortly—but you didn't really notice me. You were full of thoughts of Oscar, and you stayed that way."

He turned his face away and I realised that whatever he had to tell me, he wasn't going to be able to look me in the eyes while he said it.

"I shouldn't have done it," he said, "I know I shouldn't, but Aidan and I got on well. He's about the only vampire in the Assemblage I had time for except Oscar. So I told him about you, that you wouldn't let me touch you. He laughed and said I should just wait until you were in a good mood and pounce on you. But I didn't want to use some kind of subterfuge—Toni, I just wanted you to want me. So, that night when I told him about Hildred and what had happened to you, he asked me how my grand seduction was going... Toni, while Oscar was nearly killing you, I was standing by the bloody gate talking with Aidan about the best way to get into your knickers! And I knew Oscar was in a tetchy mood, but instead of making sure you were alright, I hung around the gate gossiping about getting my end away with you. Now do you know why I hate myself?"

I didn't laugh—it was too tragic to laugh—but I found myself in the awkward position of being grateful to Benedict again.

"You're blaming the wrong person," I said. "Peter, my darling Peter, you weren't behaving like Gandhi, but it wasn't you who smashed my skull in because I said no. I know you've been his biggest fan, but you need to let Oscar carry the can for this one. You can't make this your fault. Now for goodness' sake, shag me again before this conversation gets miserable, because I'm in a really good mood right now and I want to stay that way."

Chapter Twenty-One

BY LUNCHTIME, I had made it as far as the kitchen table in my dressing gown. I hadn't had much sleep. I wasn't sure Peter had had any. I'd taken two showers. The first, not a solo effort, had left me flat out on the tiled bathroom floor, covered with soapsuds, with Peter sprawled next to me, leaning against the shower wall.

"If I had the energy, I would do that to you again," he said. "About six times. But I don't."

"Once was enough for now," I replied, gazing at the ceiling. A tube of shower gel was pressing into my spine. "We should pause for now. I think we broke something."

"Are you OK?"

"I was thinking of the shower door."

"Oh yes, that."

I took a second shower when Peter went out for croissants. As a recreational activity, the first one couldn't have been bettered. As an exercise in personal hygiene, it left a little to be desired.

I had gone as far as putting on a pot of coffee and calling in sick to work when Peter returned bearing a paper bag full of pastry. He dumped it on the kitchen table and came over to me. He was wearing his own clothes at last—there'd been enough of them left lying around my cottage—and he looked a damn sight better than he had the previous evening. I wasn't sure what I looked like.

Thoroughly boinked and covered in third-degree love bites would have been my guess, but there was no mirror in the kitchen.

Peter seemed to think I looked fine. He knelt down by the chair and put his head in my lap.

"I have a bad feeling about this," I said. "Please just have breakfast with me before you break my heart."

He looked up at me. Yup, he was going to break my heart.

"I booked a car to take me to the airport," he said. "It will be here at two o'clock."

I drank some of my coffee while I worked out how to respond. It didn't really work, so eventually I just said:

"I would have driven you."

"If you were with me, I don't know if I could get on the plane."

"Peter," I said, stroking his hair, "I won't help you out on that front. I don't want you to get on the plane. I don't want you to go anywhere."

"Toni, you are so special to me," he said, "you are the reason the sun still shines for me in the morning. But I want my life back. I'd like you to be in it, but I want to go home. I should never have left."

"You don't like it here?"

"Here, in this cottage, yes. Anywhere else in England, no. I am sick of people getting killed. I am sick of people trying to kill me."

"I think they've stopped doing that, you know."

He got up off the floor and sat next to me at the table.

"I have been miserable since the day I left Germany," he said. "All that passion and no contentment. All that guilt at deserting my post... And Oscar never cared for me the way I loved him. He never asked me to come, you know; it was all my own idea. You are the only thing that has made me happy. I don't even like England."

I looked at him and, in that moment, I knew that I could change his mind. I could persuade him to delay, one day at a time. It wouldn't even be that hard... and if I hadn't talked to Dr Lenz Lange the previous night, I would have done it. But the wretched vampire had been right. Why should Peter have to give up everything to make me happy?

So instead, I said teasingly, "What don't you like about England? What's not to like? It's perfect."

He took my jesting tone and went with it.

"I can't stand those stupid glass bottles the milk comes in with the silver tops that the birds peck through," he said. "I have to get away from them. And all those TV programmes with people obsessing about antiques. They're unhealthy."

A lump rose in my throat but I swallowed it down.

"Fine," I said. "I respect that. I'm being dumped because you don't like English milk bottles or our obsession with antiques. Entirely reasonable. Now come back to bed."

I didn't cry when he left me. I didn't beg him to stay. I felt like doing both, but I kept a little pride. About an ounce or so. Enough to soak a hanky or two when I heard the door close.

AFTER HE HAD gone, the house felt empty. It was far from empty; I was a bit of a hoarder as well as messy. If there was a scale, from monk to fire hazard, I didn't come in at the ascetic end of it. But it felt empty, so I drove into work, somewhat amused to find that—in the heat of the moment—Peter had left his doctor's bag in my car. Ah well; if I ever wanted recreational strength painkillers, I had a least a year's supply, not to mention a lot of sterile gauze. I stomped into the office and assured a bemused Bernie that my mystery migraine had eased off enough for me to be functional.

"What needs sorting out?" I asked him, slumping at my desk and putting my head down. "Please tell me there's nothing."

"Not a lot," Bernie said cheerfully. "Except your house-sitter Paul needs to find somewhere else to squat. Eleanor Johnson's family decided they like her nearly as much as you do so she'll be on a plane back from Sydney at the weekend. And talking of Paul, Mr Suki phoned. I thought he was about to cry with happiness. Your protégé has apparently worked out how to order toasters or something. I got lost somewhere."

"Oh, arse, Bernie. What am I going to do with Paul? He can't go home, and I can't let him down."

Bernie shrugged.

"He seems young to be living on his own," he said. "Even at university he'd get a lot of support. And he'd be in shared accommodation. As an interim solution, I can see why you went for it, but it was never ideal long term. Are those love bites?"

"Maybe."

"Never knew they caused migraines…"

"Shut your face. Bernie, can I take tomorrow off, too?"

"Sure, there's no work on and you never take any time off. Are you OK?"

I looked across at my boss. He had wandering hands and a questionable attitude to women. But what I'd said to Claire was also true—he was kind and a good friend to me.

"Despite those love bites, I'm single and miserable," I said. "The object of my affections has buggered off and my house looks like a tip. The two aren't unrelated and together they're making me feel sorry for myself."

Bernie reached over and patted my hand. He didn't even aim for my breast.

"Toni," he said, "I can't get your man back for you, whoever he was, but you could tidy your house. If you want, I will send one of the cleaning services we use for rentals round. You might have to throw away half of your belongings so that they can see the floor, but we could do it."

"Thanks," I muttered. "I'll think about it."

In fact, when the next morning dawned, as cold and snowy as the previous few, I realised I could kill two birds with one stone. I phoned not the cleaning company, but their storage arm and asked them to drop off a dozen empty tea chests that morning and pick them up in the afternoon. Then in a spirit of hope, I phoned Henry Lake. There was a short list, but he was at the top.

My brother's boyfriend answered on the third ring.

"Hey, petal," he said. "You ringing to rescue me from humping bags of rock salt?"

Henry's dad ran a small builders' merchant in the hills above Cannock, and Henry would help out in between acting jobs. The fact that he was up there suggested work was thin. It seemed a shame. I thought the world needed to see more of Henry.

"If you want to swap it for humping tea chests."

"Indoor work with free coffee? It's cold enough out here to freeze the balls off a brass monkey."

"Yup. And doughnuts."

"Give me half an hour."

He turned up bearing pizza and blinked at the array of tea chests lined up by my porch.

"Pet, how busy have you been?" he said, wrapping me up in a toasted-cheese-scented hug. "We can get a lot of dead bodies into these. Probably two apiece."

"Not today, Josephine," I said. "Today we're clearing out my spare room."

Henry whistled under his breath. It was a sexy noise. I bet he'd learned it at stage school.

"In one day?" he said. "We'd better mainline this pizza and get started then, because I didn't bring a JCB."

The cottage had two bedrooms. Until his death, my grandfather had occupied the main one and my parents the little spare room. My brother and I had shared the loft when we were young. After my parents started travelling, I had stayed up there and he had taken their little room. When he'd moved into police accommodation, I couldn't be bothered to shift all my things downstairs. I'd been on the verge of heading to university, and it had all seemed far too much trouble. Inevitably, we all started using the smaller room as somewhere to put things that didn't go anywhere else, and it had begun to fill up with stuff. It was only after my parents and Gramps had died that I'd moved from the loft into the main bedroom.

The spare room—as a result—had been a dumping ground for a decade. And I rarely made it up to the attic that had once been my personal space. Scrambling up the ladder had seemed cool when I was a kid or even a teenager. These days, I accepted that the spiders had mastery over that space. I would challenge them when I needed my own recording studio. Or somewhere to hide bodies that wouldn't fit into tea chests.

"Hen, it's about time," I told him. "I don't even know what's in there. Damn it, we might well find the odd corpse, for all I know. There's a load of boxes from my family... there are even a couple of crates that belong to my ex, Kit Maybury."

"I remember him. Hot blond. Bad boy."

"Totally. He's still in jail. Anyway, I need that room and I'm sick of it being the repository of miserable memories. So, I'm going to dump the whole lot into storage and go through it another day when I can be arsed. If that day ever comes. Game?"

"Petal, I'm game," he said. "Let's finish this extra spicy and get going. It's a whole heap better than lugging sacks around on the top of the hill in this wind."

We packed up Kit's bits and pieces, including a set of free weights that had been adorning my bedroom floor for two years. That was easy. Boxes of clothes that I vaguely recognised as my parents' and grandfather's were more emotional. We went through the pockets and then Henry drove the whole lot down to the Red Cross shop in Rugeley, along with the contents of an entire bookshelf of archaeology books.

After that we were on a roll and I ruthlessly binned damaged and dated furniture, ugly vases and strange mementoes of my parents' travels, including the skeleton of a small sheep in a glass case, a box of Christmas baubles made out of plaited straw that crumbled to dust when I touched them and four jars of pickled shark meat from Iceland.

By mid-afternoon, we had reduced the room to a bed—yes, there'd been a bed in there all along—a bookcase, a desk, and two rather lovely wooden chests that I thought could hold a lamp or maybe store jumpers. For now, I'd filled one with every piece of paper we'd come across. I could read them at my leisure. The second was locked. That wasn't a problem for me, and I assured Henry I could pick it open later.

After the storage company had taken the chests away, we toasted our victory with a cold beer in the kitchen.

"So," said Henry, after downing about half of his in a single swig, "has this whirl of activity been prompted by any significant event?"

I took a deep breath.

"Peter has gone back to Heidelberg," I said all in a rush. "He said he loved me and would like to be with me, but that he wanted his life back. And then he left."

Henry put down his glass and took mine off me. He pulled me into a big, warm hug.

"I'm sorry," he said. "I know you didn't want him to leave. Might he come back?"

"I don't know," I sniffled. "Maybe. Maybe not."

"If he doesn't…" Henry trailed off for a moment. "Pet, if you love someone, you make things happen. How do you feel about learning German? I've heard Heidelberg's a lovely city."

I shook my head.

"I offered," I admitted. "I said I'd go with him, but he said that he lives in the hospital and works ninety hours a week and I'd be on my own."

Henry let go of me and finished his beer.

"Give him some time," he said. "If he doesn't come back to you, then I guess he doesn't really love you. And at least you'll know."

And with that I had to be content. I waved him off and wandered upstairs to pick the lock on the second chest. It was old and rusty. I squirted olive oil in until the barrel eased up and then worked the mechanism open. I lifted the chest lid, which fitted with almost hermetic tightness, and a nasty herby, manky smell drifted out. The contents completely bewildered me.

It was filled with dozens upon dozens of those tiny self-seal bags that gamers use for counters and amateur jewellers store beads in. But these were filled with what I could only describe as stuff… dried things, powdered things, grated things and uncannily whole things. There was a container of what looked like miniscule skeletons, another packed with dark leaves, one filled with shrivelled berries—

they were berries, right? I mean, they looked like teensy eyeballs, but surely they were berries? Each bag was carefully labelled. In Latin. I never took Latin. I slammed the chest shut and lit a candle until that stale, unpleasant smell had been driven away.

Fine, no jumpers in there. It could have a lamp on it.

I drove over to Eleanor Johnson's next, but Paul wasn't there, so in a spirit of hope, I headed to Mr Suki's. Not only was Paul there, apparently done with hardware sales for the day and leafing through a textbook, but so was Jay, bouncing round the shop smiling at random customers. He seemed quite delighted to see me and rushed over to be buoyant in my general direction.

"Toni," he exclaimed. "Thanks so much for helping my dad out. How can I ever thank you?"

I blinked at him. All I'd done was hack into Mr Suki's computer system so that Bernie got the washing machine he was waiting for. But if Jay wanted to be grateful…

"You could take us all out for pizza again on Saturday," I said without missing a beat. "Josepina's at eight."

If I'd been cheeky, he didn't mind. He took out his expensive phone and carefully inserted the appointment. Then he bounded off to be enthusiastic at someone else and I went to find Paul.

"Can I borrow you for an hour?" I said. "I need to ask you something."

He stuffed a receipt for a freestanding double freezer in a page and closed the book.

"Sure," he said. "Is it bad news?"

"Yes," I said carefully, "and maybe no. You can tell me after."

I drove him to my little cottage and showed him the spare room. It was plain and had once been painted white. The white had faded to cream. It was pretty bare, but I'd stuck the heating on when I left, and it was at least toasty warm. Winchester had already installed himself on the bed.

"Eleanor Johnson's coming back this weekend," I said. "You have to move out. I thought you could stay here."

He was silent for a minute.

"Move in with you?" he eventually asked.

"Yup."

"In your home?"

"Si."

"Wow. Are you sure?"

I waved my hands.

"Listen, Paul, I don't like living alone. I never did. But I'm a necromancer—I go out almost every night to raise the dead. It's hard for me to have a housemate. It was tough when Claire stayed here, constantly having to pretend I had insomnia. But you already know. I think it will be fine. Just for Christ's sake be tidier than me or we'll both die of cholera. Oh, and let's try and keep it from my brother 'til we've proved you're innocent, OK?"

He hugged me. The geeky teenager actually hugged me.

"I'll be a good housemate," he said. "I'm pretty tidy."

We shook hands. I noticed in that moment that the bruising on his face had completely healed up.

"I meant to ask you how you got that black eye," I said.

He stiffened and pulled his hand away.

"Don't," he said. "Let's just say I walked into a door, shall we?"

I gave him a glare.

"Just like that?"

He hunched into his shoulders a touch.

"Well, maybe I ran into a door, OK?"

I shrugged. I just asked him to move in with me; it was a little late to start distrusting him.

"Let's go and get your stuff," I said.

There wasn't much—some clothes, a computer, a games console, too many books... Oh yes, and a drum kit. A full drum kit, complete with hi-hat. I rather wished I had known about that before. Some things you find out about too late. But I was used to that. At least he wasn't some kind of serial killer like the last guy I'd moved in with. I thought we'd muddle through.

Chapter Twenty-Two

THE WEEK WENT past quietly. It was appealingly vampire free. I met Bredon twice, both times with Paul, and bought the pair of them a vintage copy of Carl Sagan's *Cosmos* and a camera to work with the telescope. In my spare time, I continued my trawl of the county's cemeteries, though without success. The perfect graveyard was evading me, but I would track it down.

On Thursday the newspapers held a sad little story. Police had found a gaping hole in the alibi of one Daniel Hereward, the boyfriend of Minnie Cavendish. They had tracked down the girl who had sat next to him in the cinema. She said he'd stayed for maybe five minutes and then crept off. He'd returned moments before the credits rolled.

Once they knew what they were looking for, camera footage from a neighbouring pub showed him sneaking off in the direction of the park and then back again. There was a photograph of poor Daniel's mother with her hands over her face. I felt nauseous just reading it. But Father Luke Emmanuel had been right and so had my brother. People have a right to the truth.

Friday dawned a little warmer than expected. I rather thought that the snow, still blanketing the county, wouldn't last another night. The sky was full of clouds, but they had a nasty wet look to them, not the clean shimmer of snow. We were in for a good soaking.

A crime reconstruction had seemed an obvious course of action, but now that the time was approaching, I wondered whether it was the best of ideas for a diminutive redhead to return to the murder scene of a diminutive redhead with all the original players waiting in the wings… What the hell, it was too late to back out now. Paul needed to go back to school. A couple of weeks might not matter when you were learning the basic arithmetic and the wives of Henry the Eighth but much more would be a disaster to an aspiring medic in his final year of school.

That said, he was proving to be an unobtrusive housemate. He ate vast quantities of food, but my hobbies meant that I was used to overstocking my kitchen. He did the washing up and played the drums only when I was out. If he had other, less savoury teenage habits, he took them elsewhere. And I ignored a third hand-delivered note from Bossy Bessant, hinting with increasing fervour at his heinous and desperately criminal past. This one suggested that Paul's fiendish past was in fact so bad that I should fear for my very existence. It drivelled on about the lives he'd ruined with his callous regard for his fellow beings. It suggested a judge who should have known better had extended unearned lenience to a child so depraved that hanging should have been brought back solely for his benefit. I tore it into little strips and dropped them one by one into the bin. I wasn't Paul's legal guardian—he was eighteen, after all—and I was doing everything in my powers to get the boy back into school as it was. She could go and eat a lemon as far as I was concerned.

At five I came home from the office with fish and chips, which Paul and I inhaled with too much vinegar and an excess of salt. We put on all the warm clothes we possessed and gathered a couple of torches and I put on Grace's diamonds for luck. I'd decided that I didn't want my car too close to the school, so we parked one street away and walked the rest.

It was about five-thirty when we arrived, and the pitch-black sky had finally started raining, turning the snow that had blanketed the county for weeks into slush around our ankles. That made our reconstruction even more appropriate—it had been tanking it down the night that Bella had died. Mikey had arrived at about six-thirty and unlocked the gates. I wanted to be ready and in place when he turned up this time around.

"What's your plan?" asked Paul. "It just occurred to me that now we know about the cameras, well, we don't want to be seen on them, do we?"

I looked at him in sudden curiosity.

"Didn't you know about the cameras?" I asked. "Didn't the students know at all? Would Bella have known?"

He shook his head.

"I had no idea, and if anyone had known it would have been me," he replied with great certainty. "There's no way Bella would have realised she was being filmed when she went into the school."

The cameras had been concealed to stop people vandalising them. None of the students knew they were there. It was an interesting snippet, just like Mikey failing to lock the school up when he left, but it didn't help me. I had a feeling that I couldn't see the wood for the trees.

"I don't know what this all means, but we will work it out tonight," I said firmly. "Come Monday, I want you back at school. Now, I need to be inside the grounds when Mikey gets here, so let's hurry. We will only get one chance at this, I think."

He looked at me warily.

"I thought you would pick the locks," he said. "If we can't use the gates because of the cameras, how are we getting in?"

"Paul," I said firmly, "I don't expect you to tell me all your secrets. We haven't known each other that long. But you wouldn't have brought professional tools and cut yourself a gate in the fence that must have taken more than a couple of hours unless you knew this was a good place to come out of hours. I reckon you'd been sneaking in for months. You just decided to make it easier for yourself. So tonight, we will go in the route you used to use. Now lead the way."

His expression had changed to one of grudging respect.

"Does anyone get one over you?" he asked.

I thought of Oscar convincing me to move in with him the third time we'd ever met. I thought of the Italian boyfriend at university bonking me on Fridays and Claire on Saturdays and inventing constellations to seduce us to. I thought of Benedict drinking my blood, then putting on a new shirt and telling his staff to drive me home.

"Not twice," I said firmly.

He led me around the back of the school grounds; it was even darker here, away from the streetlights that illuminated the front of the school, and I took out my phone to light the way. Paul seemed to know the route without any light at all, and I followed his slightly gangling form, his shadow long-limbed and distorted in the beam of light from my screen.

We pushed through some scraggy bushes and overhanging trees to where he had cut his secret entrance though the wire fence. He'd chosen his hidden route well. Nothing overlooked us where we stood beneath the canopy of the trees and there would be no passers-by to catch us. The panel that had been cut open had been replaced, but a few traces of crime scene tape still dangled from nearby wires. Paul led me deeper into the undergrowth until we were pushing our way through the side of an evergreen tree that abutted the wire fence. Past the tree another blocked our escape, but in between the tall trunk of an oak rose up parallel to the fence. It hung over a patch of stony scrubland, which I rather thought must be hidden behind the bushes at the far end of the tennis court.

"There," he said, pointing up. "I would climb up to that branch that hangs over the fence and drop down."

I looked at his route. It was do-able. Just. Then...

"How did you get back out?" I asked. "Did you levitate?"

He laughed.

"I'd bring a rope," he said. "I learned ropes in the gym. It's one of the few sporty things I'm good at."

The branch must have been twelve feet up. I couldn't possibly climb a rope that high. I was going to have enough trouble climbing the tree… but we'd come this far.

"Fine," I lied. "Me, too. I've got a tow rope in the car."

He put a hand on the trunk but at that moment my phone rang, and the ring tone proclaimed it to be my brother. I frowned.

"Paul, I'd better take this," I said. "Just in case it's important."

He nodded and I connected, putting Wills on speaker.

"Hey," I said. "If you want any corpses raising, you'll have to wait until tomorrow—unless the vending machines in the morgue have suddenly started dispensing chicken and chips, in which case I'm your girl."

"Hmm," he said. He didn't sound very happy. "A little bird told me that Paul Mycroft has been coming by your office. I need you to stay away from him."

I looked across at Paul and raised my eyebrows.

"Maybe your little bird should cheep about something else," I said. "Or maybe come into the office, buy a house and boost my commission payments."

My brother grunted.

"Look, sis, just for a change, could you take my advice, please? Steer clear of Mycroft. He's dangerous and I've just issued a warrant for his arrest because it's my case again and the little toerag has gone missing."

Even in the tepid light of my phone I saw the colour drain from Paul's face.

"Wills…" I interrupted, but he was in full flow.

"Toni, we might not be far off with the serial killer thing, after all. A CID mate tipped me off that Mycroft has a juvi record that's been sealed because he was underage. In a murder investigation, I can demand access to it. It will be on my desk tomorrow, but my mate gave me a heads-up: two kids died—a fifteen-year-old girl and her boyfriend."

I shook my head involuntarily, but Wills couldn't see it and he just carried on.

"Maybe we were right all along: maybe she knew what Mycroft was dealing and blackmailed him."

Bredon and I had dismissed fear as a motive; Wills was saying we'd been wrong, that Paul had killed Bella to protect himself from a worse fate…

I looked into Paul's eyes. He hadn't moved. He was just watching me. He was close enough that he could have reached out a hand and snatched the phone away, but he didn't. I bit my lip.

"So, if you see him again, sis, just dial 999 and run, OK? Promise?"

A sensible woman would have blurted out who she was with. She would have asked her policeman brother to despatch the emergency services to come to her rescue and then fled into the darkness. Instead I just closed my eyes for a heartbeat and then opened them again. I'd never been a sensible woman.

"Yeah," I whispered. "Sure thing. Will do."

He ended the call, and I looked down at the phone in my hand. It wasn't too late. I didn't even have to dial the police; I could just press the emergency button and hold it down. But I didn't; I hesitated just too long and Paul reached out his hand.

Chapter Twenty-Three

HE DIDN'T TAKE the phone though. He just gripped my wrist and held on to it as though he was drowning. On impulse I reached out my other hand too and he took it in a fervid grasp.

I shook my head. I didn't know what I was trying to say—that I knew he wouldn't hurt me whatever had transpired before, that I wouldn't turn on him because we were friends, that I knew it was all a mistake... All of those or something else? I struggled to find words.

"Paul," I began, but he interrupted me. His voice was hollow and far away.

"I had a twin sister," he said. "We weren't all that alike, but she was amazing. So much fun. She was more like my brothers in one way, though—she did a lot of drugs. One day, she was doing a line of charlie with her shitty boyfriend and her heart stopped. Just like that. Turned out her boyfriend had cut it with Ecsital and she had a seizure; she had a dodgy valve in one ventricle and we never knew."

"Paul," I tried again, but he waved me to silence.

"At her funeral I got drunk," he said. "A fifteen-year-old boy horribly drunk, so naturally I went and accosted her boyfriend. He was twice my size and would probably have absolutely minced me, but I managed to break a window at the crematorium and push over some other poor family's flower arrangements before I gave him a lucky shove and he fell under a hearse, OK? Your brother is right; I killed him, but the judge thought the circumstances were extenuating enough that he gave me probation and a pass if I kept my slate clean. Toni, I know you all think I'm the school's provider of jollies, but I never was. I've kept my slate clean."

I shook my head.

"I believe you," I said. "Truly. I always knew you wouldn't have hurt Bella. I never doubted you—you must know that. But Paul, this makes it all the more urgent that we clear your name quickly. If you think it's bad at the grammar school when people think you killed a little schoolgirl, you don't want to know what happens when you're remanded in custody! Kid killers are lucky to emerge with all their own limbs still attached."

He grinned reluctantly.

"Well, I'm sure I'd meet all my cousins there so it would be quite the family reunion. But you're right—I'd like to avoid it."

He looked past me at the security lights of the school, just visible through the leaves. It was an irony that we were breaking into a place I'd spent my entire teenage years wishing to leave. It was also an irony that I was trying to break into it with the one person that everyone in the world except me seemed to think was the killer. But there you go; the whole world was in the wrong and I was in the right. It wouldn't be the first time.

"I have this recurring dream that I'm in school but it's dark and something horrible is chasing me," he said. "You?"

"I'm naked in music class and I don't know how to play the flute," I said. "I hope it's not prophetic."

He shrugged.

"Time to find out," he said. "You go and get the rope from the car."

And he put a hand on one branch of the tree and began to effortlessly pull himself up. He shinned up the trunk with depressing ease and shimmied out along the branch. I thought he was showing off, but even so, he wasn't breaking a sweat.

"It's not so hard," he said aiming for casual. "You just…"

The branch broke with a deafening crack. Paul tumbled to the ground with a little yelp that turned into a shriek of pain when he landed on one knee. I heard it break from where I was standing. It wasn't a nice noise.

"Oh my God, are you alright?" I called, the utter pointlessness of my question only occurring to me after the words had left my mouth. "I mean, um, how are you?"

Paul rolled over and gave a little whimper. Thankfully, the trees had kept the area clear of the weather, or he would have been lying in about four inches of snowy slush.

"I broke my leg," he hissed through his teeth. "Maybe both of them. Christ, this hurts."

He rolled a little more. I thought quickly. Peter had left his doctor's bag in the car, and I hadn't got around to moving it. There was a rug, too, and the rope...

"Wait," I called. "I promise I'm coming back. Hold on."

I sprinted to the car, taking care not to turn my own ankle in the rapidly melting snow. The rain had gathered pace and by the time I got to the rust-mobile, my hair was wet through despite my hat. I grabbed Peter's bag, the tow rope and the rug, and made my way back to Paul's secret entrance without losing my way. I tied the rug round my waist with the rope, looped my own handbag around my neck along with the other bag from the car, and went up the tree like a squirrel. Adrenaline gives you wings.

The branch had broken off a fair way over the school grounds. Paul had been unlucky—if he'd stayed closer to the trunk, he would probably have been fine. I tied the rope in place, well back from the break and where the branch looked stronger, and then, mentally crossing my fingers, dangled from the farthest point and let go. I landed safely a couple of feet from my guide. Up close I could see he'd broken his watch when he landed. And his phone.

"Right," I said, "first things first. Take two of these."

I shook two pink tablets out of the hospital bag and held a bottle of water to Paul's mouth while he forced them down.

"What are they?" he asked, his voice fraught and pain ridden.

"Morphine," I said, pushing him back down. "You really will feel better in about two minutes."

I took off my coat and one of my jumpers. Rolling the jumper up, I used it as a cushion under his neck and then draped my coat and the rug over him.

"Do you know first aid, too?" he asked hopefully.

"Nope," I said, taking out my phone. "We dumped that one on Bethany. Damn it, Paul, this is a disaster."

I didn't want to call an ambulance. My brother would find out that I'd broken into a crime scene with one of the chief suspects moments after he'd told me to avoid him. That was bad. Worse was how guilty it would make Paul look. Mikey had an excuse to be around—it was his job—but Paul? He was already the chief suspect and should never have been on the grounds in the first place.

And even if I managed somehow to get him out unspotted, two broken legs were quite enough to ruin his last year of school. They would scupper his chances of making it to university and put paid to his plans not to join the family business of spreading drug-induced misery through the county's lower echelons.

I put my head in my hands. I couldn't see another way. There was only one person who could get me out of this, and I really didn't want to owe him any more favours. I scrabbled through my bag until I found the piece of paper that Aidan had given to me. With reluctant fingers I dialled the mobile number on it.

"Damn," I said as I heard the ring. "Damn, damn and damn."

To my surprise, Benedict answered it himself.

"What a lovely surprise," he said with deceptive sweetness. "Did you miss me?"

His words completely threw me.

"No, I mean yes, I mean… oh, stop it," I blathered. "Look, I am sorry about what I said. I'll eat as much humble pie as you like. But I really need your help and it has to be you. My friend has broken his legs and the police mustn't find us here. It's a disaster and it's all my fault."

He laughed.

"My poor little tiger," he said softly. "I'll come, of course. Can it wait?"

"What? I mean, thank you, and yes, for a little. Why?"

"I have Isembard here," he said. "Isembard Blackwood Bordel. He is seeking his brother."

"Ha!" I said, adding before I could bite off my own tongue: "Tell him to take a dustpan and brush."

There was a pause. If there had been a wall, I would have banged my head against it. There wasn't.

"I wondered when you planned to tell me about that," he said. "Where are you?"

"At Havers Grammar in Rugeley," I said. "Somewhere behind the tennis court."

"Give me two hours," he said, and ended the call.

I looked at the phone. How did I get myself into these messes? I was never ever going to be free of the bloody vampires. I had thought my last contact with them had just flown off to Heidelberg, taking my heart with him. Now it looked like I was as much in their net as ever.

"Who'zat?" asked Paul, sounding woozy. "Is he dead, too? Zombie coming to rescue me…"

"Not quite," I said. "Well, sort of. Paul, everything will be alright. The man I just spoke to will come and get us out of this."

There was no reply. Some people react more than others to drugs. Paul was fast asleep. I looked at him. He looked cosy and safe… We had just the one chance to pull this off. Maybe I still could.

"You wait here," I said, even though I knew he couldn't hear me. "I'll leave you my phone. I'm going to go and do what we planned. Now stay warm."

And I loped off into the rain and the melting snow.

I had a suspicion lurking in the back of my mind that it wasn't the best idea I'd ever had, to go and continue our reconstruction all on my own. But one of my failings was that I never listened to that bit of my brain. I'd always been better at remembering song lyrics than keeping out of trouble. I could still remember my school song, and I hadn't sung it since the day I headed out from my last exam close to a decade ago. There was Sister Mary Hallahorn, who'd blessed the name of the Lord, Sister Mary Gillaham, who'd praised the Lord, and Sister Mary Markus, who'd preached the word of the Lord... Yup, every verse still taking up lobes of my brain that could have been put to a better purpose.

Paul and I had wasted time. It was nearly six-thirty by the time I made it to the front of the school, and I could see Spikey Mikey unlocking the gates. I stayed in the shadows—there were plenty— fairly confident that any noises I made would be muffled by the rain.

As per his testimony, he walked through the gates without a backwards glance and, locking them again behind him, headed to the main doors. I moved as close as I dared and watched him as he let himself in to the hallway and began turning on lights. The building came to life, windows emitting a cheery glow and revealing rooms full of chairs, art projects and the general clutter and confusion of English education. One illuminated pane revealed a room full of defunct whiteboards, old computer monitors and what looked like a box full of dead Bunsen burners...

Hang on. A light in my brain went on. He'd walked through *without a backwards glance.* I knew what I was like when I walked past the security cameras in a shop, sucking my tummy in and swinging my hips. It was automatic if you were one of those people who cared about their appearance, the sort of person who would trim their beards into a Spikey van Dyke...

I punched the air.

I knew now why Spikey Mikey had left the gates unlocked when he'd left for the night. I knew why he thought he'd get away with everything. He simply didn't know about the security cameras. By leaving the school open, he thought the police wouldn't have a clue who'd come and gone, or when. He thought he'd covered his back. He could "find" Bella's body on Saturday morning, report it like a Boy Scout and get off scot-free... because absolutely anyone in the town could have come in and killed her.

Only Paul's opening in the hedge had saved him. If it hadn't been for that, Mikey would be sampling spam and mash in the lockup with the rest of Stafford's finest. As it was, he was roaming the school cleaning the floors... Not for long, I swore. Tonight was going to be his last night on the job.

I watched him through the windows as he made his way around the ground floor with the cleaning machine. It took a long time, and I was soaked to the bone and frozen through long before he was finished. He obviously had a clear route that he followed, never going over the same area twice as he removed the dust and dirt of hundreds of pairs of designer trainers from the tiles.

Both floors were essentially constructed around a central ring of corridor. The ground floor had become much larger, as newer classrooms were thrown up around it on an ad hoc basis and linked by inconvenient passages, but he could still follow a roughly circular route.

His last port of call was the cloakroom with the lift. He was in there for a long while and when I finally caught sight of him again, it was at an upper window. Of course... he'd taken the floor shampooer up in the lift to do the top floor the next morning.

He hadn't mentioned it in his testimony, though. In fact, he said he'd not been up to the top floor at all the night Bella died. In my mind his story was starting to look full of very small holes. Ockham's Razor had said it was Spikey Mikey all along. Good old William of Ockham.

I stood in the darkness when he stepped out of the school doors to take his break. Once again, he left the school doors unlocked but—with the twenty-twenty vision of hindsight—this time he locked the gates.

I stepped out of the rain and into the school hall.

It was exactly what Bella had done on a Friday night just a few short weeks ago. What had happened next? Had she gone straight upstairs to fetch her things? I walked slowly across the hall, imagining her thoughts and paused next to the snack machine, unchanged since my own days here and still dispensing chocolate and crisps.

She would never have been in the school at night before, never come here on her own in the dark... Would she have wandered? Explored? Mikey had put lights on here and there to light his way, but not that many. The place was eerie enough to me, fifteen years older than little Bella. No, I thought she would have hurried on her errand, hoping to re-join her friends if she was fast enough.

I walked past the vending machine to the stairs. She would have come up here, made her way to the top floor... I followed the dead girl's path upwards, my footsteps hideously loud in my ears. At the tops of the stairs, Mikey's trolley stood next to the floor shampooer, ready to clean this floor of the school tomorrow morning. Bella must have walked past them, too.

There were almost no lights on up here. Mikey had switched on just enough to make his way back after bringing the floor cleaner up in the lift. I walked to Bella's classroom, dimly illuminated by a fluorescent tube halfway up the stairs that shed a little light into the corridor outside. A single desk was brand new, a sharp contrast to its carved and graffitied neighbours. The school had wisely removed Bella's. Had they disposed of it? Stored it for the police?

I walked over and lifted the lid. Inside it was empty of schoolbooks, but her classmates had filled it with stickers and cards and dried flowers, a hundred messages of love... I shut it with a lump in my throat. Murder never ruins just one life.

I left the classroom and walked back to the stairwell. She'd made it this far and then... I looked down the stairs and in that moment realised that almost every single bit of Spikey Mikey's statement had been a lie. He said he'd no idea that Bella had come in and made her way up to the upper storey while he'd been eating his sarnies in the car. But that had to be a pile of crap. Because when he got back from his snack he would have walked into the hall and seen exactly what I was looking at... a clear track of wet, muddy footprints leading straight across his immaculate hall floor and up the stairs, petering out just a couple of steps from the top.

I was so shocked that I just stood there looking at them. It was easy to have missed... the police hadn't thought of it and neither had I. It was only by coming here and walking a mile in Bella's shoes—Bella's dirty, wet shoes—that I'd found the biggest flaw in Mikey's tale. It had been pouring with rain when Bella arrived, she'd been playing football in the park... her shoes would have been a million times grubbier than mine. There was no way on earth he could have walked into this hall and not known that someone had come in. And there would have been a single track. He would have known the intruder was still up there.

I put my face in my hands. He'd killed her, and then he'd callously scrubbed away her footprints with the clean machine so he could claim he never knew she'd come in. And then he'd left the gates open to give himself an alibi. I'd been scared of him as a schoolgirl for no reason I could put my finger on. Now, as an adult, I was utterly terrified and with good reason.

I stood so long that I was still in place when Mikey walked back through the doors. He absolutely started when he saw my footprints and then gaped up at me, standing in the half light at the top of the stairs. He must have had a horrible moment of déjà vu when he saw the thin illumination shining through my red hair because he paled and gave a little cry.

"A ghost!" he called out loud in a thin voice. "Are you a ghost?"

Chapter Twenty-Four

I'D NOT SEEN him for nine years, but he hadn't changed much. His sandy hair was a touch more grizzled, but the pointy, over-trimmed beard that had earned him his nickname was still in place. He was muscly for a tall man, but then he spent his life on his feet. No desk job for Mikey. The permanently grumpy expression that his pale brown eyes usually held had been temporarily replaced by fear. I didn't think that would last. I took a step backwards. Mikey had never been known for his sweet nature.

"How could you do it?" I asked without thinking. "A twelve-year-old girl. What were you even thinking?"

He began to walk up the stairs. In his hand he was clutching the handle to the floor polisher.

"I just hit you," he said. "I always did it. You'd all yelp and run away but you'd always be back."

What?

"Oh my God," I whispered. "You didn't even mean to do it."

It was the new floor polisher. The handle of the old one had been a stick of plastic two feet long. Yes, if we annoyed him, he'd dish out a whack with it and we'd scurry on our way. But he'd had a new floor polisher. This one was a stainless-steel machine that must have weighed as much as my car. Its handle was more like a baseball bat made of lead. He hefted it in his hands as he drew closer to me.

"I saw you," he said, almost as though talking to herself. "You were looking at the Dominican window."

I turned around and looked. I could see what had caught Bella's eye. Streetlights shone through the glass, illuminating the figures of the saint in a way you never saw in the day. Underneath, glazed letters spelled out the motto of the Dominican order, with curlicues picked out in gold, amber and yellow: 'Laudare, Benedicere, Prædicare.' I still had no idea what the words meant. We'd sung them in the school song every day for the seven years I'd spent at this place. They hadn't helped me then and I couldn't see them helping me tonight. Mikey's fear was fading; he looked angry again.

He was drawing closer, and put one hand on the cleaning trolley to push it out of his way. There was a distinctive squeaking noise of elderly wheels on tiles…

"That's what she heard," I whispered, almost to myself. "She heard a noise before you hit her. It was your sodding trolley, you murdering jerk."

"You fell," he said, almost at my side. "There was so much blood. I knew I'd be in trouble. But even when I'd throttled you nothing seemed better. Everything was still such a mess. I was so angry with you."

What had Wills said? That she'd been strangled after being struck with a blunt object… the metal handle of the new cleaning machine looked pretty blunt. And pretty damn close for comfort… I looked up at him. He was an angry man who'd been angry for so long that it had burned him up like straw. He'd been a seething mass of fury, hating us for getting his school dirty, for not appreciating him, for just existing. He'd lashed out at us all the time, but we'd never reported it. But then he'd lashed out at Bella, probably without thinking with his brand new, much heavier machine… And when he'd seen her bleeding out on the floor, instead of dialling 999, he'd put his hands around her neck and finished the job.

He finished her off in cold blood and, having wiped her off the face of this earth, he'd then wiped away her final footprints and gone about his evening.

"Get away from me," I said. "You could have just called an ambulance when you saw she was injured. Instead, you wrung her neck and then left her lying in the corridor like a lump of meat and just cleaned away the evidence around her to save your miserable skin."

He was staring at me, the last hint of horror bleeding away into rage.

"You're not her," he said. "What's your game, you redheaded witch?"

He raised his hand. The spell that had glued me to the spot broke and I turned in terror and fled along the pitch-black corridor.

I'd dreamed all the school dreams psychoanalysts go on about— you're in class but you aren't wearing all your clothes, or you haven't got your books, or you can't remember your name, you're wandering around the halls, but no one can see you... Take it from me, not one bears comparison with being chased around in the dark by a murderous caretaker trying to bludgeon your brains out with the handle of a floor polisher.

I didn't want to flee into the blackness, but he was blocking my path to the better lit end of the corridor. I thought I knew my way, but it was close to a decade since I'd been here, and never in the dark. Before I'd gone fifty yards, I was disorientated and confused. Drinking Aneurin's blood had helped my night vision, but not enough.

For a few moments, I was utterly lost, then with relief I recognised the storage cupboard to the art room. No one had added a lock, so I whisked myself inside and pulled the door most of the way shut.

It smelt of damp paint and wet clay. I leaned back against a pile of easels and caught my breath. I could hear my trouser hems dripping on the floor. Out in the corridor, Mikey was fumbling for light switches. That was good—and bad. I'd be able to find my way if I could see it but, given enough light, he could probably find me first by the wet trail I was leaving behind.

Arnold Plankman had once removed my bra in this cupboard, an experience I rated much better than the current one. For a start,

I hadn't been soaking wet and freezing cold, or in danger of being clubbed to death. It had been midsummer, and Arnold had been happy to share his coat. I'd been pleased with the encounter until Arnold inscribed the details in black marker pen on the door of the home economics lab. I still felt he'd been oversharing.

I watched Mikey through the crack of the hinge until he came right up to the cupboard, reaching for a light switch just inches away... and then I kicked the door open with my foot as hard as I could straight into him.

I felt it smack into the side of his face. He gave a yell and flailed backwards, arms spinning. I heard the handle of the floor polisher whang into a wall somewhere and roll away with a clanking sound. Mikey still blocked my path back to the stairs, though, so I legged it further into the darkness. I had gained just a few seconds start on him. Lights started going on behind me. Could I make it round the loop of corridor and back to the stairs ahead of him?

I careered around the corner; I knew I was out of sight for a moment and stopped to re-orientate myself. I realised that Mikey was no longer following me. His footsteps had fallen silent. He probably planned to wait back at the stairs and head me off. I shook my head. He couldn't be in all places at once. I would try the lift. He'd come up in it just minutes before, so the lower doors should be shut.

With silence now my priority I tiptoed around the corridor. A little light was drifting in from the streets outside and my eyes had adjusted sufficiently for me to make my way without tripping. I opened the stiff door into the storage room that housed the lift. It was much darker, and I reached my destination largely by feeling my way through mounds of defunct equipment and broken desks. The lift was still open wide. I crept in, pulled across the slatted outer door and then the inner one. The slats cut out most of the remaining light but there were only two buttons—up and down. The lift was so old that there wasn't even a basic alarm bell. I pressed the lower button, and the lift motors came to life.

I'd never been in the school when it was empty. Every single time I'd made an illicit journey in this ancient elevator, I'd been surrounded by four hundred of my peers yelling their way through a lunch break. I'd never realised just how damn loud the lift was. It creaked and shrieked its way down like a politician defending an expenses claim. There was no way that Spikey Mikey wouldn't hear me.

My memory had also failed to remember just how slow the wretched contraption was. We descended inch by painful inch, lurching down to ground level at the most scenic of paces. My cat could move faster than this, and Winchester's preferred vehicle was a warm lap. I realised in horror that unless Spikey Mikey's legs had spontaneously fallen off, along with both of his ears, he would know exactly what I was doing and he would probably be able to get to the lift's downstairs doors long before I did. Frantic, I pressed the button for the upper storey, but the vintage mechanics clearly predated multitasking. We could return to the upper floor once we had visited the ground level, and not before.

"Fuck," I muttered as the grinding of gears lowered us infinitesimally lower. "Fuck, fuck, fuckity fuck."

At the base of the door, banded light began to creep in, a broken line of yellow that grew as the bottom of the lift emerged into the room below. It morphed into triangles and diamonds which—as the lift finally deposited me at ground level—revealed a fragmented image of Spikey Mikey standing waiting for me, panting but prepared.

I jabbed the up button a few more times to no avail. Mikey was too quick. He seized the outer door by the handle and flung it open, the diamonds closing to slits as the grid of the door squeezed itself against the wall like garden trellis. He made to open the inner door, but I held on to the inside handle. There was a locking clip that I held pressed in and he found himself yanking at the door without result.

I heard him curse under his breath. Then—letting go of the little outer handle—he fitted his hands into the diamonds of the door slats and yanked. I waited until he had put his full strength into it and then released the inner lock. The door slammed open and the metal diamonds slammed shut on his fingers, crushing them in a steely grip.

He gave a great howl of pain, both his hands temporarily trapped in the vice of the door slats. I went past him like a greyhound after a bunny and galloped through the cloakroom. I skittered into the main corridor and pelted towards the main school doors. I put both hands onto the leftmost panel and pushed.

Mikey had locked them.

"I don't sodding well believe this," I muttered. "This is the second time in a month I've been locked in by a homicidal maniac. Not even James Bond has to put up with this much crap."

I beat futilely at the doors. They had no plans to open. I looked down the corridor. Mikey was fifty yards away, blood dripping from his hands. He didn't look happy. I'd seen happier people at the Stafford morgue. On the slabs. I'd wanted to reconstruct the murder scene of a hapless redhead. If I didn't think of a way out of this soon, I was going to get a reconstruction of all the wrong bits.

I fled down the corridor in the other direction, hearing Mikey hard on my heels. I was running round in circles now, and I'd run right out of ideas. The last time I'd been pelting down this corridor had been nine years ago. I'd set the fire alarm off to try and get out of high-jump trials...

Fire alarm... fire doors. That was it. The dark, dead-end corridors that came off the central ring into the likes of the Gillaham and the Fountain Block weren't really dead ends. Each of the classrooms had a fire door. Spikey Mikey couldn't lock those. I spun off into the next one I came to, vaguely registering that it was the Cemetery Block where in my day they taught gymnastics.

They still did. I pushed open the door and stepped into the darkness, completely forgetting the three little steps that led down to the gym floor. I tumbled down them in a flurry, landing in a heap on the hard linoleum floor and smacking my head straight into the beam of a wooden pommel horse.

I saw stars. I didn't need to be an astrologist to know they were telling me I was in trouble. As I struggled to clear my head and scramble to my feet, I heard Mikey open the door behind me. He put on the lights and, blinking in the brightness, I could see the fire door I'd been aiming for. It was just twenty feet away across the other side of the gym. I'd made it as far as my knees when a shove between my shoulder blades drove me onto my face. I heard my forehead crack into the floor and my front teeth sliced into my upper lip.

There were more stars. They said I was in more trouble. I tasted blood, and—for a change—it was my own.

"You're all disrespectful," I heard him hiss. "I keep this place running, but do any of you care?"

He was manhandling me. I realised he was tying my hands behind my back with one of the skipping ropes. I tried to tug free, but I was still gasping with pain and hadn't yet worked out how to move my limbs properly.

"You don't have to do this," I whispered. "I didn't come here to hurt you."

He began to drag me across the floor... where was he taking me? With a sinking feeling I realised we were heading for the weights rack. I could see the stack of kettle bells. They went up to thirty-six kilos, ideal for crushing small skulls.

"You came here to trap me," he spat back. "I know."

Well, he was right about that, but it didn't seem prudent to say so. I could see little but his feet as he tugged me along. They were clad in workman's boots with steel toes. Who had I seen recently who wore those? Oh yes, that nice man at the graveyard, Harold Shaw. The one who told me that if you move really old graves, you just take the headstones and leave the corpses where they are...

I looked down at the floor of the gym, or the Cemetery Block as we all called it. The founding nuns had been buried there. Their graves had been moved to Baswich decades ago, but I knew now that if Harold was right, the bit that mattered still lay under the floor. Necromancy might not be an exact science, and worms and grubs might well have left nothing to excite a pathologist, but I was certain that, if only I knew their names, I could make any remaining souls answer my call.

The stack of weights was fifteen feet away, then twelve, then ten... I mentally slapped myself in the face. Of course I knew their names. They were in the bloody school song. I had sung it five times a week for seven years.

I reached out with my necromantic senses. Sister Mary Hallahorn? Nothing there. She'd long since departed. Sister Mary Gillaham? Not a sign. She was praising the name of the Lord elsewhere. But Sister Mary Markus... Oh, she was there.

"Sister Mary Markus," I whispered. "Come to me this night."

Mikey stopped pulling me along the floor for a moment.

"What was that?" he said.

I didn't answer. I could feel the nun's presence, but she resisted me. I spat a mouthful of blood onto the floor and rested my cheek in it. I felt the powers of the earth sear into me.

"Sister Mary Markus," I said with more confidence, and I felt her buckle. "Come to me! I summon you."

And she came. She was tiny, a diminutive figure, clad all in white with a black wimple. Around her lined face, the odd silver wisp of hair was creeping out. She looked disturbingly holy, and I felt the tiniest bit guilty at disturbing her rest.

Guilt clearly wasn't what Spikey Mikey felt when he saw her step easily out of the stained linoleum of the gym floor and look around her, blinking like an owl. He let me go and emitted a high-pitched wail of terror. He seemed frozen to the spot.

I spat out a little more blood and rolled on to my back. I raised my head and looked at the scene in front of me. There was Spikey Mikey, clutching a thirty-six-kilogram kettle bell and gawping. He seemed welded to the spot, though I knew that couldn't last. There was tiny Sister Mary Markus, gazing up at him dispassionately. And there was me, trussed up like the Christmas goose. I could see only one way out of this, and I didn't like it. To prove my point, the little dead nun turned to look at me.

"I'm hungry," she said in a gentle English voice.

Yes, I didn't have long to dither about my options.

"Kill him," I said to her. "Kill him now."

She shook her head a little.

"I preach the truth," she said.

I shrugged. I was a Catholic, too. We could both play at that game.

"This is self-defence and you, Mother All-Too-Superior, are my weapon," I said, as much to myself as her. "God will cut us a little slack for this one. Now get a move on, sister, and wring his wretched neck."

She glowered at me, but I was the necromancer and I was in charge. Mikey still seemed spellbound, so she simply reached up and caught him around the throat with both hands. She squeezed for a moment, apparently effortlessly, and there was a sharp crunch. His head flopped slightly to one side, and he lolled in her grasp for a few brief seconds. Then she released her hands and he dropped limply to the floor beside me. The kettlebell smacked into the ground with a determined thunk and rolled onto its side.

I lay still for a minute or so while I rallied my resources. Mikey's face was just inches from mine, and it wasn't an agreeable sight. His open eyes were bulging slightly and one was bloodshot. His tongue protruded from his mouth. A line of drool ran from his lips. I closed my eyes. I felt I could sleep for a week. The voice of Sister Mary Markus jolted me out of my stupor.

"I hunger," she said sternly.

I dismissed her hastily and hoped we didn't meet again. I was sure she would remember exactly what I'd done. I'd be sent off to say fifty Our Fathers and twenty-five Glory Be's as recompense and I didn't fancy that.

I worked my hands free of Mikey's knots. It took a while, and by the time I was done I was very sick of lying next to his cooling carcass. I had, however, worked out a plan of action. I was going to denude the tuck machine of zombie-friendly snacks and raise Spikey Mikey from his eternal rest. Then Mikey would obligingly write his confessional suicide note before hanging himself from the stairwell. It was a flawless plan. What could possibly go wrong? I gathered a pile of skipping ropes together...

I ran my tongue over my shredded bleeding lip. There was a bruise the size of an egg forming on my forehead and a larger one somewhere under my hair. I had rope burns on my wrists and I'd grazed both my knees when I fell down the stairs. I was a mess.

"I need better hobbies," I said out loud. "Macramé. Tennis. Trainspotting. Baking. Anything. Michael Spectre, get your dead arse into gear. It's time for you to kill yourself."

Chapter Twenty-Five

PLANS NEVER WORK the way you think they will. It's always the little things that catch you out. Like the snack machine was out of order, so I had to get Mikey to kick the glass door in. Or that Mikey the zombie couldn't actually remember how to write, so I had to drag his hand around to produce the world's worst scribbled murder confession and suicide note. I hoped the coroner would attribute the bad handwriting to the mess that the lift door had made of Mikey's fingers. I had also forgotten about the muddy footprints I'd been leaving, and had to mop those up, too. I didn't want to give the impression Mikey had been receiving visitors.

And then there was the whole noose thing. Mikey stood patiently next to me while I totally failed to tie the final skipping rope into a neck-snapping loop. I'd seen them on pirate films, and they didn't look that hard, but the fact was that the most complicated knot I knew how to tie was the one that fastened lace-up shoes.

After far too many minutes, I had something that looked about right. I looped it over Mikey's head and stood back for a moment.

"It's very you," I assured him. "Now, you're going to climb over the railing here, I'm going to banish you and your empty corpse will drop like a rock to dangle grimly over the stairwell. Got it?"

Benedict's voice behind me made me jump; I had no idea how he had got in or even found me.

"Perfect," he said. "I'm sorely tempted to let you go ahead."

"What do you mean?" I said, turning round. "What have I done wrong?"

He blinked when he saw my face.

"Good God," he said. "Can't you keep out of trouble for a couple of hours? I'd have come sooner if I realised you had a death wish."

He held out a hand autocratically. It must have stopped raining because there wasn't so much as a raindrop on the man. He was as perfectly dressed as always, sporting very dark blue jeans and an exquisitely cut white shirt. I always struggled to gauge his mood, but I put him down as particularly pleased with himself that evening.

"I have to sort this out," I protested.

"First things first," he said. "Come."

I didn't really mind. He caught me gently by my shoulders and pushed the power of his healing into me. It felt delicious as the pain in my head ebbed and the stinging in my fat, swollen lip receded.

I gave a sigh of relief, which quickly morphed into a squeak of protest when he took advantage of my unguarded state to lean down and lick the blood off my lips.

"Stop that," I said. "I have to hang Mikey."

"I hardly dare ask why he is waiting patiently at the top of the stairs with a rope round his neck," Benedict said blandly, letting me go.

"He's faking his own suicide," I said.

"Hmmm. You know, my dear, your rope is too thin, the drop is too long and that knot is too loose. It will rip his head clean off. Now I know that's a speciality of yours—indeed, I've almost missed it—but it's probably not the effect you were aiming for tonight."

"Rats. Are you sure?"

"Oh yes."

I sighed.

"Can you tie it?"

"I can."

I watched as Benedict shortened and retied my noose using a double thickness of rope. It took him about twenty-five seconds.

He flipped it casually round Mikey's neck and stood back to admire his handiwork.

"I'm hungry again," said Mikey forlornly.

"Tough," I said. "You already ate all the crisps, remember? I told you to pace yourself."

I turned round to find Benedict standing frozen to the spot and staring at Mikey as though the zombie had just sprouted wings or begun to tap dance. Yes, I had actually jolted the imperturbable one out of his serenity.

"How did you do that?" he asked.

There was an unaccustomed tension in his deep voice that startled me.

"Do what?" I asked in confusion. "I just raised him. I'm a necromancer, remember?"

He shook his head.

"He spoke."

I shrugged.

"All my zombies speak," I said. "Shouldn't they?"

Benedict walked round Mikey, still standing patiently with a rope round his neck.

"By no means," he said. "Necromancers use the power of the day to raise the bodies of the dead. But to animate their spirits..." He looked at me curiously. "My dear, that's witchcraft."

He put a hand on Mikey's arm and closed his dark blue eyes for a moment. When he opened them again, he looked at me rather impenetrably.

"I see," he said. "You're pulling the power straight out of the earth. I had no idea you were a witch, though it's hardly surprising. Well, you can send him on his way now."

I shrugged, not really sure what to make of the things he'd said.

"Climb over the railing, Mikey," I said. When he had, I intoned: "Michael Spectre, I release you to your rest. Return to the earth from which I called you."

His corpse went limp and sagged. It slumped off the edge of the balcony and dropped into the stairwell. There was a nasty crack and then a long length of dead Mikey was dangling by its neck, feet just inches above the floor, rotating unpleasantly in the fluorescent light.

"Ugh," I said. "Well, I'm done here. Seriously, I'm more than done. Will you come and heal Paul for me? I left him asleep under the hedge."

We walked down the stairs together. I realised the main doors were unlocked and swinging open. I cast a curious look at my companion, but he ignored it. Outside the rain had stopped and the snow, which had blanketed the county for so many weeks, had been washed away. They say school days are the best days of your life; this had been very nearly the last day of mine.

"I've done that," Benedict said casually, "and I sent him home. Isn't he a little young for you?"

"Oh, for God's sake," I said. "And that was very high-handed of you. I need to go home and check he's alright."

"Oh no, you don't," he said. "You can come back with me and make the rest of my evening more bearable. I just spent two hours listening to Isembard moaning on. It was enough to make me doubt the merits of eternal life."

"That's hardly my fault," I protested.

He moved to me quite suddenly and put his arms around me.

"I spent half of it arguing over your reparations and the other swearing blind I didn't know where Ani had gone, so yes, it's your fault," he said. "Hold on."

I felt the earth dip and swirl and closed my eyes in panic. When things stopped spinning around me, I looked around to find we were standing in a side street next to Benedict's car. He unlocked it and opened the passenger door.

"Get in," he said briefly.

"I don't want to go with you at all," I complained. "I'm soaking wet and freezing cold. My shoes are soggy, and my hair is starting to frizz. And I'm tired. Can't I just go home?"

He stood by the door. He didn't say anything more. I got in.

"You're very ungrateful," he said, folding himself in the driver's side.

"It's just you," I retorted. "You make it very hard to be grateful by being so annoying all the time."

I thought he was amused but it was hard to be sure. I glared at him across the car, but he kept his eyes on the road, leaving me to direct my enmity at his profile. He was, as always, annoyingly handsome, and the flicker of the streetlights caught his high cheekbones and the full curves of his lips as we sped through the village. I caught my mind wandering to his other attractions and hastily dragged it back. I reminded myself that the man was also annoyingly annoying, not to mention a psychopath, and turned my own attention to the road.

Benedict had never driven me anywhere before. He drove with deceptive smoothness, but at about four times the speed limit. He made Peter look like a chauffeur. When we left the village he floored the accelerator and ignored all road signs, corners, red lights and small, unwary mammals. We reached the Stone House in half the time it would have taken me. The car stopped in a wash of spray as he turned into the courtyard using the handbrake and a flick of the wheel.

I was still catching my breath when he opened the door for me. I glared up at him.

"I'm still soaked through," I said, hauling myself out of the car.

"You can borrow something off Grace or Camilla," he said. "Or you can scamper around in my bedspread again if you like. I'd prefer that. It's a good colour on you and it's almost entirely transparent."

I swept past him with a toss of my hair and went to find Camilla. She was sprawled on her bed, reading a novel. She leapt to her feet and gave me a very welcoming hug.

"Dearest, Benedict said he was going to pick you up, not drown you! What happened?"

I sat moistly on the end of her eiderdown.

"I got caught in the rain," I said. "Do you have something I could wear?"

She began to scrabble through a drawer.

"I have the perfect dress," she said, tossing piles of chiffon out of the way. "I ordered it for Grace, but it's the wrong shape.

It will look lovely on someone curvy like you."

It was made of black, laser-cut suede and not very much of that. I had to agree that it looked a million dollars, even with bare feet. I felt it deserved better hair than I was sporting, though, so I hung my head upside down and waved Camilla's hairdryer at it for ten minutes.

"Yes?" I asked her when I was done.

"Absolutely yes," she said. "Two glasses of champagne and you'll be human again."

We walked down to the gallery together.

"I heard Peter had gone," she said, squeezing my hand. "I'm so sorry."

I bit my lip.

"Camilla, I wanted him to stay so badly," I admitted. "But he'd had such a rotten time of it. I kind of understand his decision."

"I don't, you know," she said. "I think if you love someone, you find a way to be together."

Was she right? Had I let Benedict—and even Oscar—mislead me? Should I have begged harder, maybe told Peter the truth about Lenz and his schemes or even just bought a one-way ticket to Germany? I shook my head. What was done was done.

I heard music from the gallery. It sounded familiar and I wondered if I would find Sophy's string quartet playing again. When we entered, though, the room was almost entirely empty. The music was coming from a portable stereo sitting on a chair, and the lady herself was twirling around the dance floor with Aidan. His footwork wasn't up to the job, and they were laughing as she tried to show him how to make some complicated turn. They waved cheerfully enough at us as we entered. I didn't like the Assemblage, but I didn't hate it as much as I once had. Being made welcome will do that to you.

Sophy and Aidan were the only dancers. Perhaps she'd hoped for more company. I thought it was going to take her a while to convert the Assemblage into a more sociable institution, but I wished her luck. The place could do with being more friendly. A lot more friendly.

"Grace is up in one of the upper balconies," said Camilla. "I'll show you."

I hadn't explored the Gallery much—I still thought it was one of the loveliest spaces I'd ever seen, but it was always rather overfull of vampires for my taste. The front section, carved and ornamented in an art nouveau style, gave way to a more natural cavern, laced with the walkways and galleries that gave it its name. In the flickering light of the braziers that illuminated it, you could see stone and metal stairs spiralling into the upper levels, forming a three-dimensional maze that I would have needed a map to navigate.

Camilla seemed to know her way well, though. Behind one of the broader pillars, a small bar area was concealed. She secured us a couple of glasses and a bottle of champagne from a bucket of ice, and led me up a tiny, spiral stair. We found Grace in an elegant little space not unlike a theatre box but without any kind of barrier or railing at the edge. It looked over the raised area where Sophy and Aidan were failing to make their turn for the fifteenth time. Grace was sprawled on a mound of rugs and cushions watching the dancers below.

"Welcome ladies," she said. "Sophy is making another attempt to teach Aidan the cotillion. I fear she is doomed. Ah, Toni, you are wearing my diamonds. They look very lovely with that dress."

I smiled a little shyly.

"I can hardly bring myself to take them off," I admitted. "I have to tell you, they look just fine with my pyjamas."

She laughed and patted the cushions next to her. Camilla and I made ourselves comfortable.

"What's Sophy like?" I asked.

"She's very quiet still," Grace said. "She didn't enjoy her time in France. Benedict never wanted to send her away, but she didn't give him a lot of choice."

"What on earth did she do?"

Grace shrugged.

"Pretty much everything she shouldn't. She was embroiled in a dispute with another vampire. He killed her consort, and she then killed him."

"That sounds like vampire justice to me."

"It would have been, but first she chained him with silver and killed all seven members of his coterie in front of him," said Grace. "And all of their families."

Ah. I looked down at pretty Sophy. Tonight's dress was pewter silk embroidered with rose buds. She looked like a debutante. She looked like butter wouldn't melt in her mouth. I thought of Kit Maybury's knicker-dropping smile. I thought of Oscar's seductively divine good looks. I thought of Benedict on the night we'd ended up in his shower together; he'd been naked from the waist up and soaking wet...

I shook my head. Yes, looks could be deceiving. It was something to remember.

Before I could totally banish the thought of a wet, half-naked Benedict from my mind, the man himself loped up the stairs to join us. His earlier good mood seemed undented as he flung himself down next to me and raised his eyebrows at my miniscule, leather dress.

"I see you found something to wear," he said. "I approve. I have handkerchiefs larger than that. With fewer holes."

I had to laugh.

"Naturally I wanted your bedspread, but Camilla thought this was better."

"I have something that will go with it," he said, digging a hand in his pocket. "Catch."

There was a hint of sparkle as he tossed something in the air. I grabbed frantically and just managed to stop it falling straight over the edge and into the dancers below. It was a gold and diamond cuff, two inches wide and set with stones the size of peas.

"What in heaven's name is this?" I gasped.

I clasped it around my wrist in case he decided he'd given me the wrong thing.

"Your reparations," he said. "Isembard made such a fuss. It's an heirloom and he didn't want to give it up."

"Well, he can't have it back," I said hastily.

Grace looked amused.

"It's a massive case of one-upmanship, that's what it is," she said.

"Dear Grace," Benedict said softly. "It's also a hint. She looks lovely in diamonds, but she's mine. Keep your hands off my necromancer."

Grace just laughed out loud, but I sat up in protest.

"I'm not yours," I remonstrated. "Not in a million years."

Benedict leant against the pillows. Despite his protestations, I thought he'd had a splendid evening making Isembard Blackwood Bordel miserable.

"Oh no," he said easily. "Don't take that tone with me or I'll call Isembard back and see what he'll trade me for you. I haven't bankrupted the man yet."

I looked at him with resignation. I had no idea what he wanted, particularly what he wanted with me. But in a mood this good, he was hard to loathe with my usual intensity. Grace and Camilla had bored of our banter, and were calling down to Sophy and Aidan, giving the poor man unhelpful suggestions on his footwork.

It reminded me a little of the night Oscar had nearly killed me, when he'd been sparring in the cellar at Lichley with Aidan, and Peter had been teasing them. Somehow, this evening was more pleasant even though the only person in the room I really liked was Camilla.

Benedict looked at me suddenly and smiled. It seemed a very genuine smile, and not one that I'd seen before. Typical of the man, he had a beautiful smile.

"I'll charge a very high price for you," he said.

There was laughter in his deep voice.

"You're confusing," I said without thinking. "Sometimes I almost like you. Then you do something that confounds me like killing Melody."

He looked at me in silence for a moment. Then:

"You're angry that I killed Melody?"

"Was it really necessary? How involved was she anyway?"

He put a hand under my chin and looked at me thoughtfully.

"Hmmm. Let me see... On Saturday night, Aidan finally tracked her down through the payment she made for Hildred's coffin. I visited her house and compelled her to tell me the truth. All of it, including that she'd left you handcuffed to a bed with Jasper that afternoon and that he'd killed you at dusk. She rather thought he would have enjoyed himself first. I chased her through the dark and killed her very slowly. I let her get away a few times and then caught her again… I haven't done that for a while. My hair was wet with her blood."

I swallowed. I tried to turn my face away, but he wouldn't let me.

"I drove to your house, but you weren't there. Your milk hadn't been taken in and that orange cat of yours was frantic. I took in the bottles and fed him… did you notice?"

I shook my head, hypnotised.

"And then you appeared," he continued. "You drove up in Aneurin's car. You were covered in his blood and the ashes of his passing. You let yourself in and made a couple of casual phone calls. You ran a bath… I couldn't quite believe my eyes. You'd gorged yourself on his blood—which he wouldn't have given lightly—and then you'd slaughtered him. You helped yourself to his car, you even took his coat, and then you drove home for a little night music and a glass of wine. It was quite glorious."

He let me go, and the spell was broken.

"Are you complimenting me on my bloodthirstiness?" I asked grimly. "It's not something I'm proud of."

"Not at all," he said. "It's your sheer nerve that impresses me. Particularly the way you left his car there like a trophy for me. I had it dumped in Ashbourne, if you're interested."

I swallowed the rest of my glass of champagne.

"Not really. I preferred it when you were giving me diamonds and complimenting me on my dress."

He showed me his teeth.

"My dear, it wasn't the dress I admired so much as its minimal coverage."

I brazenly put my chin up at him.

"Oscar always said he could smell my blood through my skin like caramel," I said.

He snorted with laughter.

"Oscar was a French peasant who never tasted it and still can't spell it," he retorted.

His words reminded me of what Azazel had said.

"French…" I blurted out without thinking. "Oscar Guillaume."

He blinked and raised his voice.

"Grace, did Oscar ever tell you his real name?" he asked.

I turned to look at her, but she shook her head.

"No, he never would. Why?"

"Nothing," Benedict said, turning back to me. "So, who told you? Oscar certainly didn't and I never knew it."

I looked down at my hands. Then I glanced across at Camilla and Grace—they were still teasing Aidan, not listening to the two of us.

"Azazel," I whispered. "Azazel told me."

He took my hands in a light but urgent grip.

"Toni, stay away from him," he said, very softly. "Never summon him. Don't try to bargain with him. It never ends well."

I nodded.

"That's what my grandfather said," I agreed.

He snorted again.

"He was a massive hypocrite," he said. "He bargained with Azazel exactly twice. The first timed backfired totally and the second cost him his life."

I stared at him.

"How do you know all this?" I asked. "I didn't think you'd ever met my grandfather."

"Well, we certainly weren't friends, my dear, but I've known your family for five generations."

"You knew my great-great-grandfather Ignatius," I said carefully. "I was aware of that."

"I knew him?" he said, a little incredulously. "Is that what you thought?"

I was confused.

"Am I wrong?" I asked.

He stood up and held down a hand and I let him pull me to my feet.

"You're not a gossip, are you?" he said. "Almost anyone in this Assemblage could have told you."

He gestured to the stairs, and I preceded him down.

"Told me what?" I asked. "And where are we going?"

"Not far," he said.

He led me a little further into the depths of the gallery. Through a low arch, a small reading room had been papered in red flock. Club chairs were scattered around, and several beautifully framed old photographs hung on the wall. One stood out. It was almost exactly the same shot of Benedict and Ignatius that I had at home, but not quite. Was it taken a few seconds later? The two men stood fractionally closer to each other, their expressions just that bit less guarded.

"Oh my God," I said. "Lenz said you had a thing for red-headed necromancers. Peter said your consort was a necromancer. I never guessed it was Ignatius."

I stared at him. He met my gaze gently.

"I know what you're thinking, little tiger, and no," he said. "You aren't like him, not at all. Come now, I'll take you home."

I laughed, a little embarrassed. The last time he'd offered I'd thrown it back in his face. This time I nodded.

"Thank you," I said. "I'm flagging. I can pick my car up from Rugeley tomorrow."

We walked through the gallery, the smoky, winter aroma of the braziers scenting the air. Benedict walked slowly enough that I didn't have to scurry to keep up with him.

"Benedict," I said suddenly, "Azazel always claims he was once an angel and was thrown into Hell for giving a gift to a mortal man. He says he just wants to explain it all to God so that he can return to Heaven. Is he lying?"

Benedict laughed a little bitterly.

"There's a grain of truth in what he says, my dear. But I know what he did, and take it from me: he is never getting back into Heaven."

There was a finality in his voice; I didn't think there was any point in asking more.

Afterwards, I remembered putting on my damp boots and walking to Benedict's car. I could even remember him opening the door to let me in. But that was the last part of the evening I could recall. I woke up in my own cottage in my own bed when the cat began to demand breakfast. I was still clad in Camilla's leather dress, along with more diamonds than most supermodels ever get to wear. But I was alone. The world had turned, and a chapter of my life had ended.

Chapter Twenty-Six

I'D MEANT TO do about a thousand things before going to sleep. I'd not done a single one of them. Instead, I'd drunk champagne with Camilla and made the huge tactical error of flirting with Benedict. I had a feeling I'd pay for that. Probably in blood, a prospect I was somewhat ambivalent about after the previous occasion. It had been enjoyable if massively confusing.

I crawled out of bed, with very little inclination to do so, scrambled into some clothes and made my way to the kitchen. I dialled my brother's number and then stuck the phone under my chin while I began the essential morning tasks of feeding the cat, making coffee and toasting toast.

"Hey," he said, sounding sleepy. "How's tricks, sis?"

"Yeah, um, good. Listen, Wills, this is super important. You need to think of an errand right now that's going to take you casually past the grammar school. Then you can idly notice that Mikey's car is parked outside, and the school doors are open when he promised to keep them shut. What you do next is up to you, but hurry."

"Have you been up to your old tricks again?"

"Maybe, but he tried to kill me—and he very nearly managed it— so I didn't have a lot of choice. But he wrote a very nice confession before I left him. Can you arrange for the county's least competent and most sleep-deprived pathologist to do the post mortem?

Because I might have broken his neck twice by accident."

I heard him sigh.

"It won't even be hard," he said. "That nice locum we borrowed from Wolverhampton has just worked thirty-two hours straight sorting through the Lithuanian tour bus that hit the central reservation at junction fourteen. If I insist she goes straight on to this before she goes home, I doubt she'll be able to tell if he died of bubonic plague."

"That should work," I said. "I did my best, but it won't hold up to quality forensics."

By the time Paul wandered sleepily into the kitchen, I had the radio on, a pot of coffee bubbling and a fine mound of toast. He helped himself as the newsreader informed us of the local titbits of the day. Melting snow had flooded an aquarium store in Stone; the proprietor was touring the town with a net, fishing liberated shubunkins and clownfish out of the gutter. Daniel Hereward's grave was being relocated to an unmarked spot in an unnamed graveyard after being vandalised. Police were seeking a missing person, one Melody White, who had vanished a week ago...

"So," said Paul, after four entire slices of toast had vanished. "I was pretty woozy last night, but I don't think I dreamt up the completely terrifying vampire who mended both my legs and then told me to bugger off."

"Sadly, he's completely real," I replied, "and I hope you remembered to say thank you, because I think that I forgot."

He inhaled another slice.

"I said it all," he said. "Thank you. I'm not worthy. Please don't kill me. You name it... He could hardly shut me up."

"Well, don't worry," I said, always full of hope, "we won't be seeing him again. In other news, you can go back to school tomorrow. Spikey Mikey has confessed to killing Bella."

"That's brilliant!" he exclaimed. "What happened?"

I looked at Paul. He was eighteen years old. In the past few weeks, he'd been arrested, suspected of murder, had to move out of his horrid home and then broken both his legs and had to lie under a hedge for two hours in the rain... I didn't think he needed a lot more piled on his plate.

"It's a bit tragic, actually," I said. "He hung himself after writing a confession. I called the police, but I didn't want to do it until you were safely out of the way."

He nodded, chastened.

"I'm sorry you had to find that on your own," he said, reaching across the table and giving my hand a brief squeeze. "Really. I should have been there with you."

"Um, thanks," I said. "Listen, Jay is taking us all out for pizza again tonight. I wondered if you wanted to ask Bethany."

He was quiet for a moment and then shook his head.

"Nah," he said. "She's a bit crazy. She blows hot and cold all the time. When I don't pay her any attention, she's all over me, and when I do, she turns into the ice maiden. It does my head in."

I couldn't agree with him more. Playing hard to get had never been one of my party tricks. I was always too keen to be got.

"Fair enough," I said. "I prefer people who are just themselves. I hope you don't want to practice your drums today, because I plan to go back to bed and stay there until pizza time."

If he played them, they didn't wake me. He could have thrown them down the stairs and I'd have turned over with a yawn. Frankly, the final trumpet at the end of days wouldn't have stood a chance. I got up in enough time to wash my hair and put on the black dress that Camilla had given me. And I wore my diamonds—everyone would think they were paste, after all. Paul whistled when he saw what I was wearing.

"You're prettier than Bethany," he said. "I've decided blondes are overrated."

"You'd change your mind again if you saw her wearing anything this short," I said. "Get changed if you're going to. I've booked us a cab so that I can drink way too much tonight."

We arrived at Josepina's a little early, but Claire was ahead of us. She was on her second glass of Chianti, regaling Josepina with a hilarious tale of the stag party she'd had to call the police to the previous evening. After an awkward incident with a chocolate fountain, a sticky but entirely naked groom and best man had been siphoned into a squad car at midnight. The coppers had borrowed a rug. Claire didn't want it back.

When Josepina took Paul through to the kitchen to learn how to spin dough, Claire poured a glass for me.

"Bottoms up," she said as we raised our drinks. "How's tricks, Lav, darling?"

"Well, let's see, where to start…" I mused, sipping at my wine. "I might just have finally got round to playing doctors and nurses."

"OMG, you shagged Peter. That's delicious. Tell all: how was he?"

There was a question…

"Exhausting," I said without hesitation. "We hit the duvet at about seven, and he left at two the next day. I think he only took a break for breakfast, and it wasn't much more than a re-fuelling stop. We shagged in every room in my house including the porch."

Claire drained her wine and poured us both another.

"Tell me more before Paul comes back," she said lazily. "More."

"Um, experienced," I said. "He's very, very experienced."

"Sweetie, that was unexpected," she said. "Cite examples."

No one else had ever gone down on me in my own front porch until I was calling his name loudly enough to wake the neighbours. No one else had ever lathered me up with enough soap suds to bring my coefficient of friction down to zero and then pleasured me up against the shower door until the reinforced glass gave way. No one else had ever… I shook my head and decided not to share specifics. It turned out that Peter was not a man with any inhibitions.

"Put it this way: tucked away among all those medical textbooks, I am now sure that he must have a well-thumbed copy of the *Karma Sutra*," I said. "The extended edition. And I would guess that each page is annotated in biro, ranking the position in terms of orgasms achieved and calories burned, along with a list of his favourite variations. I couldn't walk the next day and I now think I might be double-jointed."

She laughed, and we would have said more, but at that moment, Jay walked into the restaurant. He was holding a little girl by the hand. I did a double take. It was Kathy, and she was wearing my hat, the one I had given to her at Melody White's kitchen table.

"Kathy," I exclaimed without thinking, and she ran across the room and hugged me. "Oh, my goodness."

Jay didn't seem surprised. He probably thought I'd run into Kathy a thousand times at Mr Suki's shop...

"Hey," he said easily. "I hope it's OK that I brought Ekaterina. She wanted to meet Paul, and I didn't want to leave her alone tonight."

"No, not at all," I said. "It's more than fine. Kathy, I'm so glad you still like the hat! How's the hair?"

"Better," she said with a grin, removing the beanie to reveal a wispy golden fuzz... "Still too cold in this weather though."

Josepina scooped her up to join Paul in making pizza bases, and Jay poured himself a glass of wine.

"I would have left her with Mum and Dad, but she's been really upset about her godmother going missing," he explained. "Melody, you know, Dad's office manager. She's vanished without a trace."

I drained my wine in a single gulp. My sympathy for Melody had vanished the previous night when I found out she'd deliberately left me to be raped and murdered so she wouldn't get herself into trouble.

"Shocking," I said. "Poor you."

"I owe her so much," he continued. "I thought this vampire healing thing was an Internet scam. I wouldn't have anything to do with it. But Melody ignored me. When the hospital said there was nothing more they could do, she told me she was taking Kathy to Paris. Instead, she took her to this Hildred woman and now Kathy's cured. I've put up a reward, you know. I really want to find her."

Good luck to him. I had no idea what the vampires had done with Melody's body, but I doubted it was going to surface in an identifiable form, if at all. From what I could remember of the village she lived in, it backed onto a pig farm. I might be avoiding local sausages for a couple of weeks.

"We should order some food, you know," I said to distract him. "What toppings does Kathy like?"

We didn't make it a late night. Kathy needed an early bed and neither Claire nor I felt like intimate gossip with Paul in tow. Jay good-naturedly gave everyone a lift back to their various domiciles, expressing hopes that we could do it again very soon... I didn't deter him. He seemed a nice addition to my friend group, and he was very good at paying for dinner.

As I unlocked the door to my little home, Paul blurted out:

"We should have taken Bredon, you know."

I stared at him.

"Are you mad?" I asked. "What if something had gone wrong?"

He shrugged.

"You can't just do things that are sure to turn out right," he said. "You'd never go outside if you followed that one through. And how's he going to make new friends if he only ever sees you and me?"

Paul's words shocked me. I'd been treating Bredon as though I owned him, and you don't get to own people, even dead ones.

"You're right," I said. "We'll take him next time. God knows, it's the one place in the county he'll never go hungry. Listen, Paul, before we turn in, I need something from your room. Make us some tea, would you, while I get it."

Witchcraft. I'd never heard of witchcraft before last night, except as a children's tale. But there were vampires, so why not witches? I took the lamp off the strange chest that Henry and I had uncovered. I opened it and the same odd smell drifted out and into the room.

Paul came in behind me with tea as I was rifling through the packets.

"What's that?" he asked.

"It's a chest that belonged to someone in my family," I said. "I want to work out who."

He knelt next to me.

"Cool," he said, stroking the lock. "Well, it's not very old."

"Really? How do you know? It looks old to me."

He pointed to the metal of the keyhole.

"It's machine-made," he said. "And Korean. Trust me, my dad fenced a lot of antiques. It's no more than thirty years old."

Not my grandfather's after all then. Close to the bottom, the polythene bags gave way to old envelopes that had been recycled as herb packets. The address was for the house we were standing in and the name on each one was the same: Marchesa Windsor, my mother.

I slammed the lid shut with a bang. If I hadn't wanted the answer, I shouldn't have looked for it. No wonder Benedict had said it wasn't surprising that I was a witch. My mother had been one.

"Forget it, Paul," I said. "It doesn't matter. Let's drink this tea and feed the cat. He's been complaining about his feeding hours. According to him, there should be twenty-four of them. Then I'm ready to sleep for a week. Oh, and you never did tell me how you got that black eye."

He looked surprised.

"I did! I told you I ran into a door."

I blinked.

"You were serious?"

"Well…" He looked shifty. "When your brother came round to question my Mum, his partner might have noticed the two stolen cars, eight pilfered motorbikes and four thousand sheets of finest Albanian Ebenezer my brother Eddie had been stockpiling round at the house. And given that he was only out on bail, that didn't go down well. He decided to blame me and, as I was legging it to the door, I tripped over my own drum kit and lamped myself in the face on the door jamb. Eddie nearly wet himself laughing; he was still sniggering when your brother cuffed him and dragged him out to the car. It wasn't my finest moment."

"Ah."

All my worrying had been for nothing. Was that better than

when I never worried about things at all and then they crept up on me and tried to kill me? I wasn't sure.

We sat together in my little kitchen. In the space of a month, I'd lost two boyfriends and gained a lodger. Four people had tried to kill me, but they were all dead and I was alive. I'd given my blood to a vampire and my love to Peter and in return I'd got diamonds and a broken heart. It was still a lousy trade, but the diamonds were pretty.

I also had more questions than answers. How had Azazel's wiles killed my grandfather when he had died in a train crash with my parents? And what was the bargain that had backfired so badly? Why had no one ever told me that my mother was a witch? More importantly, how come Aneurin had known her name? The priest had told me the truth always mattered, and I believed him. But right now... Right now, I was afraid to find out.

To be continued...

Acknowledgements

MY MUM WAS a great reader. Every spare moment that she possessed was spent with her nose in a book. She devoured classic and modern literature, historical romance, whodunits, coming-of-age fantasy, horror, science fiction... seriously, if it had a spine and some pages, she was up for it. Or down for it. Probably both.

She rarely re-read books and, when she was finished with one, she would idly pop it into one of the tea chests that filled our shed; I remember them as being stuffed with endless paper dreams— and a lot of silverfish. I would dig through and find Stephen King cheek by jowl with John Fowles and Robertson Davies, Ursula K. le Guin tucked up next to Dashiell Hammett, and endless Michael Moorcock pulp fiction paperbacks stacked up—all out of order— alongside banks of Georgette Heyer.

This taught me A Few Important Things, in particular that it was OK to read all the time, indiscriminately and without purpose, and that no genre was better than any other. Thank heavens for my mother; she also made excellent potato salad.

She told me that, when I was very young, I was determined to be a chef. I don't know that I showed any particular aptitude for cooking and I am also the clumsiest person ever to walk the earth, so she didn't encourage that youthful ambition. At university, however, I announced that I had found my vocation and that I would henceforth be a novelist. This came as a surprise to everyone.

I certainly had no experience or talent at writing. I had given up all the arts at the earliest possible age, focusing instead on maths and science which blended better with the sickly and somewhat confused creature I had evolved into: half goth, half geek, all elbows, obsessed with computers, The Sisters of Mercy, vampires and my black cat William. Still, my mother—ever the optimist— told me to go for it and that she couldn't wait to read them.

So, what happened next? I'm not sure. I did become a writer, almost immediately, but there were always bills to pay and more reliable ways of writing to pay them than trying to write the next bestseller. I penned textbooks. I worked as a financial journalist, writing for *Bloomberg*, the *FT* and the *Sunday Times*. I ghost wrote a self-help book for a gazillionaire hedge-fund manager. (It was crap, but I got paid.) Yes yes, I was always going to write those novels for my mother to read but there was never quite the time. I had to write a speech for someone to make at an awards ceremony, I had to write about pollution in Boston harbour, I had to write about great land hunting in the Central African Republic... And then my mother died.

I was so close. I was already writing the Lavington Windsor Mysteries; I just hadn't finished one yet. I had finally knuckled down with my keyboard and begun spinning Toni's adventures, her misadventures, her mishaps and her misdemeanours. I wasn't so many chapters away from Actually Finishing An Actual Book... I was, nonetheless, irredeemably and irrevocably Just Too Late. That taught me Another Important Thing. Don't wait to follow your dreams. Go out there, with the biggest butterfly net you can make with your life, and hunt them down. Don't let them get away.

Oh, and spend some time with your mother. For all that's precious, at least prise that potato salad recipe out of her before it's too late for that too.

My humble and heartfelt thanks to Hugo, Jess, Shelagh, Al and Dave for their patient reading. Huge hugs to Gem for the wonderful artwork and to David for the constant support. And of course, my dear love to Esther, the original Lavington, for the inspiration.

About the Author

Alice James was born in Staffordshire, where she grew up reading novels and spending a lot of time with sheep. She was lucky enough to have a mother who was addicted to science fiction and a father who was fond of long country walks, so she grew up with her head in the stars and her feet on the ground. After studying maths at university and training to be a Cobol programmer(!), she began writing novels to get the weird people in her head to go somewhere else. She now lives in Oxfordshire with a fine selection of cats, fulfilling her teenage gothic fantasies by moving into a converted chapel with an ancient spiral staircase—and gravestones in the garden. Her go-to comfort dish is a big plate of dumplings, her number one cocktail is a Manhattan and her favourite polygon is a triangle, though she has a soft spot for concave rhomboids.

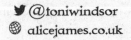

🐦 @toniwindsor
🌐 alicejames.co.uk

FIND US ONLINE!

www.rebellionpublishing.com

/solarisbooks   /solarisbks   /solarisbooks

SIGN UP TO OUR NEWSLETTER!

rebellionpublishing.com/newsletter

YOUR REVIEWS MATTER!

Enjoy this book? Got something to say?

Leave a review on Amazon, GoodReads or with your
favourite bookseller and let the world know!